PRAISE

"In Rachel Miranda's brilliant and beautiful debut novel, family love is the strongest power in the universe. *Broken Chocolate* is both a suspenseful medical drama and a marvel of empathy and insight."
BRIAN MORTON, AUTHOR OF *STARTING OUT IN THE EVENING*, WINNER OF THE PUSHCART PRIZE AND GUGGENHEIM FELLOWSHIP

"Rachel Miranda's *Broken Chocolate* is about a traumatic brain injury, but it is, more fundamentally, about faith and family, about the fissures and fractures brought about by tragedy and, along with them, the resilience and love. It's a resonant, compelling debut."
JOSHUA HENKIN, AUTHOR OF *MORNINGSIDE HEIGHTS*, WINNER OF THE EDWARD LEWIS WALLANT PRIZE FOR JEWISH FICTION AND A FINALIST FOR THE NATIONAL JEWISH BOOK AWARD

"Rachel Miranda's debut novel illuminates how easy it is to lose our bearings after sudden and inexplicable loss. The Sandor family will stick with me—their struggles, and even more so, their powerful ways of leaning against each other, taking turns holding each other up. This story enlarges our understanding of grief and recovery, moving adeptly through big themes and small moments. *Broken Chocolate* is as poignant as it is uplifting."
DENTON LOVING, AUTHOR OF *FELLER* AND *TAMP*, WINNER OF THE TENNESSEE BOOK PRIZE FOR POETRY

"Fifteen-year-old Zoey lies in a coma, and the Sandor family wants just one thing: for everything to go back to the way it was. Rachel Miranda guides us through their harrowing journey with compassion, precision, and suspense. *Broken Chocolate* tells a fundamental truth about life's liminal spaces: they never promise fairy tale endings, but if we're willing to stay present, they often brim with wonders all the same."

JUNE GERVAIS, AUTHOR OF *JOBS FOR GIRLS WITH ARTISTIC FLAIR*

"Rachel Miranda's debut novel, *Broken Chocolate*, transports us into the rich world of the Sandor family in the wake of a devastating accident. With a keen eye for detail and poignant storytelling, Miranda invites us to root for these characters as they fail, falter, and chart a new path forward. We witness their quiet, everyday struggles and cheer them on as they find their way back to each other. This book reminds us of the magic of embracing our lives and our loved ones as they are, not as we wish they would be."

EMILY MOHN-SLATE, AUTHOR OF *THE FALLS*,
WINNER OF THE NEW AMERICAN POETRY PRIZE

ABOUT THE AUTHOR

Rachel Miranda emigrated from Switzerland to America at the age of eight and now lives in the greater New York area. She is the author of *The World at Our Table: A Euro-American Cookbook of Family Favorites*, and writes a Substack series called *Air Hunger*. She is a freelance editor specializing in translated literature and scholarly works, and managing editor of Plamen Press. She earned a Master of Fine Arts in Writing and Literature from Bennington Writing Seminars and continues to savor every chance to play with the English language. *Broken Chocolate* is her debut novel.

rachelmiranda.com

BROKEN CHOCOLATE

RACHEL MIRANDA

Broken Chocolate

Print Edition
ISBN: 978-3-98832-218-0
Published by Vine Leaves Press 2026

Cover design by Jessica Bell
Interior design by Amie McCracken
Author photo by Ahna Tessler Photography

"I want to do something splendid before I go into my castle, something heroic or wonderful that won't be forgotten after I'm dead. I don't know what, but I'm on the watch for it, and mean to astonish you all someday."

Louisa May Alcott, *Little Women*, 1867

For all the TBI patients and caregivers I've had the privilege to meet, who have reimagined their lives with grace, courage, and humor.

For my lung donor, who gave me back my life.

For my generous, analytical, loving, unruly, gorgeous family: Without you, there would be no meaningful life for me to reimagine.

JUNE 21, 2005
DAY 0

It is beyond cold where she is, like waiting at the bus stop in deep winter, when the frigid air creaks and groans. She is in an igloo, the walls round and smooth and gleaming white; they give off a glacial burn. She sits on the floor and reaches her arms out to touch the sides. She starts to shiver, there is ice shining in her hair and snow falling all around her, she is a snow angel. The world grows quiet. She is drowsy. She lies down and spreads her wings, the snow becomes a blanket she wraps around herself until she is warm. She sleeps.

Zev opens his eyes. The room is dark. His phone is ringing. He can see the outline of the fireplace, and Zoey's cello in its stand by the piano. He must've fallen asleep in the living room when he got home from his last exam. He fumbles for his flip phone that has slipped out of his pocket into the sofa cushions.

"Hey, Mom, wassup?"

"Zev? Oh, honey. Were you sleeping?" she squeaks.

"Um, I guess so. Why do you sound so weird?"

"Well …"

He hears a hissing on the line, and it takes a minute to realize Mom is pushing a huge breath out through her teeth. "There's been—Zoey's had an accident."

She still sounds Mickey Mouse-ish, and Zev wonders if he's actually awake. He struggles to clear the fog from his brain.

"What? What do you mean? What kind of accident?"

"She was running sprints this morning in the park, and, well, they think … they think her heart was affected by the heat … and …"

Mom keeps talking, but what she says makes no sense, and her voice is high, he realizes, because she's trying not to cry. He hears her words as if from underwater. *Heart stopped … head hit a rock … ambulance … unresponsive.*

"Wait, I don't get it. *What* happened? You're saying it's her heart?"

"Well, it was," says Mom. "At this point, it's more about the head injury."

He's almost sure now that he's still sleeping, and this is some sort of god-awful nightmare that his own burned-out brain has conjured from one of Dad's stories about his patients. But just in case, he says, "*I* can get her to wake up. When are you coming home to get me?"

"Oh, honey. If only you could … but it's best if you sit tight for now. Peter Becker's got her on a cutting-edge treatment, and she's heavily sedated. And anyway, you have to be sixteen to visit the ICU—"

"But that's only a couple of weeks from now! And Zoey needs me. Can't Dad sneak me in?"

"I don't think so, Zev."

That makes even less sense, since he and his three siblings have basically grown up in that hospital, where Dad is king. For sure, a dream.

"Nana's there at the house with Lottie … and Ethan's my next call, if I can reach him," Mom adds, her voice going squeaky again.

Zev mumbles something suitably exit-like and hangs up.

Flashes of a different sort of dream flow into the silence—his twin sister in an igloo? At least it's a vivid image, something he can hold onto.

He switches on a light, finds one of his drawing pads splayed on the hall table—he leaves them scattered around the house like half-eaten sandwiches, as Dad points out all too often—and digs a stub of pencil out of his jeans. He sketches the scene before it fades from his mind, shades in the igloo walls with broad strokes, makes lighter lines for the falling snow, and uses the thinnest edge of the tip to draw Zoey sleeping inside, a snow angel in an ice cave. When he's done, he stares at the picture for a minute, jots the date on the bottom out of habit, closes the sketchbook, and takes it with him up to bed, shoving it deep under the mattress. He falls instantly back to sleep.

•

When he wakes again, the sunlight is making a trapezoid on his bed. The air around him is weirdly empty. He lies there for a minute, gazing at the crack in the plaster that bifurcates as it crosses his ceiling at a forty-five-degree angle.

Bifurcate (verb) [bi.fur.kayt]: divide into two branches; go in different directions; go separate ways, break up, pull apart. Synonyms: diverge, divide, cleave, crack.

He recites the definition to himself, a habit he has cultivated as an antidote for social anxiety. He loves that word, *bifurcate*, which came from Mom; together they delight in finding words with multiple levels of meaning. Dad might be the one with a dozen years of graduate school, but Mom knows *all* the SAT words, and Zev has been stockpiling them for ages. Only now is he finally old enough to need them for the SATs.

It was Mom's idea for him to recite definitions in his head to keep the hulking beast of social anxiety under control. He thought she was nuts until he actually did it. Who knew? Well, Mom did, of course. And as a bonus, he's got this enormous vocabulary. But there's a painful irony in having all those words at your disposal and being afraid to use them in person. Whenever he's face to face with anyone outside this house, he's braced for his body's betrayal, the sweaty palms and creeping flush, the awful knot in his gut. Most times, those beautiful words fly right out the window.

The window … Zev turns his head on the pillow and stares out. He's always slow to wake up, but this is different. He is adrift, like on a raft in the middle of the ocean.

He searches his mind for points of reference. One: It must be afternoon because the sunbeam's coming into his room at a certain angle in relation to that crack on the ceiling.

Two: It's bizarrely quiet. Where is everyone? Zoey is probably spending the afternoon running sprints at East Rock Park while he sleeps off his trig final. Not his best event, even with his twin's perfect notes to prep him.

Zev sits up and stares at the opposite wall, which tilts slightly—or is it his painting that's gone crooked? He's only recently hung the still life of fresh fruits piled on the kitchen island—one of his best efforts yet, and a secret homage to Mom's cooking.

Three: Last night was their end-of-school family dinner, the one Mom's been making every year for as long as he can remember. She has few house rules, but one of them is that unless you're dying of the plague or two continents away, you never miss a birthday breakfast or an end-of-school dinner. Shabbat dinners are a little more lax, but not by much. Not even Dad gets a pass, never mind his schedule at the hospital. So, the six of them gather at their slab of a kitchen table like some sort of TV family. Dad tells a story about one of his terrifying patients whose brain was ruined in a freak accident and who is now learning to speak after five years of silence; Lottie chatters about her latest playground drama, untroubled at being relegated to caboose status by the simple fact of her birth; Ethan asks a million clinical questions so he can try again to claim his rightful place as the first-born and inheritor of Dad's legacy—though everyone knows Zoey has won it, just by being Zoey. Dad is fooling no one by pretending he doesn't have a favorite. But Zoey doesn't lord it over Ethan—or any of them. She's got too much class for that. Instead, she teases Zev about his ridiculous appetite and the exclamations of ecstasy he mumbles out around giant mouthfuls, the uncharacteristic flow of words coming from him unbidden, as if he's speaking in tongues or something.

He and Mom hover at the peripheries of this circus. Zev is, as always, content to catch Zoey's updraft. Being invisible is his super-power. And Mom is like a curly blonde hummingbird, moving efficiently and quickly, but somehow never losing her Zen-master calm.

It is in the kitchen that Mom is the greatest master of all. He can still taste that sweet, creamy butternut squash lasagna, the tangy salad with goat cheese and candied walnuts and those little slivers of orange she segments one at a time, by hand, to get only the sweetest morsels without the bitter part. And then, there's that perfect mocha thing for dessert that she makes year after year at his request, always managing to outdo his memory of it from the year before.

Zoey has never gotten all that excited about Mom's culinary sleight of hand. She says food is a fuel delivery system to keep her churning at the top of her game—really, Zev thinks, at the top of every game his twin chooses to play. But Zoey can't touch Mom's skills in the kitchen, and nobody else in the world even comes close.

Zev doesn't mind sharing when people come over for dinner, though he has not been thrilled to hear that his mother's apricot tarts can now be bought at the Kol Tov Bakery.

Even the way her food looks on the plate, with its vivid complementary colors, is like a rare work of art, a living Cezanne.

Complementary (adjective) [kom.ple.men.ta.ree]: forming a satisfactory or balanced whole; interdependent. Synonyms: paired, balancing, harmonizing, corresponding.

Why is his brain spitting out definitions here, in the safety of his room? Maybe because he feels so creepily disconnected. He must've crashed hard after dinner. He has been desperate for summer to come, for time to work on his own art projects, time to waste in the sun on the lifeguard stand, time away from the exhausting social scene that is high school. Sitting around the table with everyone at dinner would've drained the last drops of life from his introvert battery.

Wait a minute. How could *Ethan* have been at dinner last night? It's been eighteen months since he pulled that bit of big-brother fuckery and joined the Marines. He's been in Afghanistan for all of 2005.

That means last night's end-of-school dinner *never happened*. His mind must've done a mash-up of all the other dinners. Or is this another dream? But he's not the one who remembers his dreams; that's Zoey's territory.

Zoey.

Something happened to her.

There was that surreal phone call from Mom at the hospital, but he's so sure he dreamed that … Wait. It's the dinner that wasn't real; the phone call *was*. Is *unresponsive* the same as *unconscious*? The thought of Zoey unconscious is impossible. She's always so—so present. But when Zev feels around inside himself, it's as if some vital thread has unspooled and he has lost sight of the other end of it for the first time in his life.

Adrift.

Zev's heart thuds crazily as last night's phone call slowly reassembles itself. He scrambles out of bed and dives into his clothes before his brain even registers that he's vertical. Did Mom actually say Zoey had a heart attack? That makes no sense. No, it was something about a head injury. Unless maybe he's making that part up? He's heard enough of Dad's horror stories over the years that it wouldn't surprise him. Memory plays tricks all the time.

He needs to talk to Mom. Right. Now. He tries her cell phone, but she doesn't answer, and neither does Dad. Not that he ever does, when he's with patients.

Zev paces his room. He remembers Mom saying something about Peter Becker and a "cutting-edge treatment." Zev knows this doctor from Dad's holiday parties. Halo of white hair like Einstein, and Dad has an Einstein-y nickname for him, too. *The Brain Trust.*

Zev is sure Mom wasn't giving him the whole story. If Zoey's heavily sedated and already unconscious, it *must* be a brain injury. That much he knows from Dad's endless anecdotes: *When in doubt, the best medicine is sleep*, he'd say, shaking his head at the freakish unpredictability of his patients' scrambled but *remarkably elastic* brains.

What could've happened to Zoey at the park, of all places? And where does the heart thing come in? The more he thinks about it, the less it makes sense.

Ethan would be able to explain, with his years as a volunteer EMT and now, as a military medic in a war zone. Zev wishes he had a number to try, but these days his brother is decidedly out of reach. Why couldn't he have gone off to a nice liberal arts college like everyone else's brother? Until now, Zev has felt nothing but a sort of terrified admiration for Ethan, taking on these missions to hell with his unflagging, demented morale. He has always been such an *oldest*, a stand-up guy, someone everybody could count on. Except now, when Zev needs him here, he's off fighting the Taliban instead.

Zev plunges down the staircase and into the kitchen. There's got to be *someone* who can give him an update. But the house is totally quiet. He stares out the rear window and sees Lottie in the backyard with Nana.

Shit.

The rest of the conversation with Mom falls into place. If she has called Nana in for reinforcements, things must be bad.

He pushes open the screen door and tumbles outside, words jumping out of his mouth with no forethought. "Nana, what the fuck's going on?"

Right away, the blush creeps up his neck and onto his face. Even with relatives, it never fails. And he *never* swears in front of his super-formal professor-grandmother. His brain is apparently still checked out.

Lottie looks up at him from the flagstones, eyes huge, her Barbie dolls and their fluorescent paraphernalia strewn about like they've been hit by a hurricane.

"Zev! *Language!* We're having a Barbie picnic. Wanna join?"

Zev shakes his head. "Not now, peanut," he mumbles.

Nana pats the garden chair next to hers. "Zev, sit down. You look half asleep still, though it's beyond me how you can sleep for sixteen hours at a stretch."

The air is hot and sticky. Zev doesn't want to sit down, but he slumps into the chair anyway and Nana pats his arm sympathetically.

His stomach ratchets into a tighter knot. Since when is Nana ever *sympathetic*?

"Whatever's going on, tell me, Nana! I'm not a little kid."

He can feel his face going a deeper red as he realizes how unhinged he sounds.

His grandmother looks at him over her half-moon glasses and he squirms under her gaze. "No, I don't suppose you are. According to your mother's latest report, Zoey is in the Intensive Care Unit and, I am sorry to say, still unresponsive."

That word again. His stomach lurches at the way she says it, though he has known this is what she would say. "But it's been over twenty-four hours already. Is she, like, in a *coma*?"

He glances at Lottie to see if she's following the conversation. Lottie doesn't look up, but her hands, which have been busy trying to wrestle a strip of neon fabric onto one of her dolls, go still. Nana takes no notice; she's the only adult he knows who isn't obsessed with keeping important information out of the hands of children. It's one of her best features.

"Yes, Zev. Apparently, she is in a coma."

Her grave tone gives him the creeps, and he paradoxically wishes she would sugarcoat things a little for once. But her academic—almost surgical—demeanor is her trademark; she treats every interaction like she's lecturing about human evolution.

"And what're we supposed to do now, sit here and wait?"

"No, in point of fact, your parents have asked me to bring you both to the hospital for some medical tests."

More weirdness. Why would he and Lottie need tests? Probably another one of Dad's endless "preventive measures." He's like a one-man early warning system with five targets to protect.

"Your mother tells me it's a precaution, to rule out any familial risk of cardiac vulnerability."

That combination of words doesn't sound at all appealing. He knows that *cardiac* equals *heart.*

Vulnerability (noun) [vuhl.ner.uh.bil.uh.tee]: the quality or state of being exposed to attack or harm, either physically or emotionally. Synonyms: susceptibility, weakness, exposure.

Lottie has perked up at the prospect of going to the hospital, where the Sandor kids have celebrity status.

"If we're going to Daddy's work, then we get to see Zoey. Right, Nana?"

She jumps to her feet and gathers up her mess.

"No, Charlotte, only children over sixteen are admitted to the Intensive Care Unit."

Lottie's small back stiffens, her arms full of bright pink bundles. Even their grandmother knows she hates being called by her full name, ever since reading *Charlotte's Web*. It makes her too sad, she says. But that's Nana: She doesn't do nicknames.

"This applies to you as well, Zev."

"I know, I know. Mom was only too quick to remind me."

There is an angry pulse in his forehead. The sun is magnetically attracted to his thick black hair, and an itchy sweat is creeping over his scalp. He lurches to his feet, knocking over a wrought iron chair, which makes a tremendous clatter on the patio stones.

"This is crazy! It's not like she broke her leg. She's in a *coma*!" he hears himself shouting. "Besides, it's only two weeks till our sixteenth birthday, and what's the point of Dad being a doctor if he can't even— I'm going in there, and no one can stop me."

He doesn't dare look at Nana, who has stood up to right the fallen chair, unfazed by his outburst.

"Young man, the ICU is no place—"

"I don't care!" he yells. "I can't just … sit there taking tests and— and doing nothing!"

He stomps into the house and bangs the back door shut. Inside it's much cooler, but he's still pouring sweat. His mind is jumpy with fear. What's *wrong* with him? And what about Zoey's heart? And why would *his* heart need to be tested? And where is Dad during all of this, anyway?

He can't believe how he yelled at Nana. There will be fallout. He paces the floor, impatient to leave though he's freaked about going. Still, once he gets there, he'll find a way to make them understand:

Zoey needs him. Maybe they haven't thought of that, since it's always been the other way around.

Nana comes inside with Lottie and says stiffly that she'll need a few minutes to freshen up. Zev keeps his eyes averted as he says he's taking the keys to Mom's minivan so he can turn it on and cool it off. He sits in the driver's seat without adjusting it, his legs folding nearly up to his chin, and awkwardly starts the ignition, thinking, *Only two more weeks until we can get our learner's permits.* The countdown has been going on for, like, two years.

But then: *What if Zoey isn't better?*

Impossible. She has to be.

He clambers out of the car, turns to go back into the house, and runs right into Mikayla, who has appeared behind him without a sound.

"Oh! Shit. Sorry, didn't see you there," Zev mumbles. Mikayla always walks like a cat.

She takes a step back but holds on to his arm as if to steady herself. Her hand feels like a little starfish, soothing and cool. Even though Mikayla is practically furniture around here, living next door as she has for most of his life, the flush creeps up his neck and sets his face on fire. It would be nice if he could ease up a bit on the self-immolation, wouldn't it? She's only been Zoey's best friend for ten years.

Zev is about to continue on his way indoors when Mikayla lets out a hiccup that trails off in a sob. She mutters something incomprehensible, throws her arms around him, buries her face in his chest, and bawls.

Zev freezes. Her head is bent over so he can see where her neck meets the cap of her black hair. The scent of it surrounds him, redolent of the honeysuckle he and Zoey used to pick at East Rock Park on their long summer rambles. His arms come up automatically, and he rubs Mikayla's back until her bird-wing shoulders stop shaking. His mouth is dry and pasty.

Redolent (adj.) [red.l.uhnt]: fragrant, having a pleasant odor; suggestive; reminiscent. Synonyms: ambrosial, balmy, evocative.

The act of calming her down comforts him, too; they're breathing in perfect synchronicity. A preternatural quiet descends on them in the early summer air. When Mikayla pulls out of the hug, she does not entirely let go. She tips her head and looks up at him, teardrops clinging to her dark lashes.

She shakes her head. "Zoey," she whispers, her lip trembling.

Zev nods and his face somehow shapes itself into a smile. She is *so small*—he wants to shield her from … well, from everything. She looks like she's about to say something else when the front door opens and Nana and Lottie come out, startling them both as if they've been alone in some private space.

Mikayla shakes her head again. *See you later*, she mouths, and walks over to her driveway without looking back.

Zev is dazed for the entire twelve-minute car ride to Yale New Haven Hospital, replaying the scene in his mind. What happened back there? Everything feels different. He only catches up with his body when he's standing at the information desk watching Nana try to sort out where to go and what to do. Zev could've told her whatever she needed to know, but she's not asking. The hospital is one of the few places where his grandmother has no power to intimidate, which of course makes her even more imperious than usual.

"I am Dr. Hinda Czeslaw, and these children belong to my son-in-law, Dr. Samuel Sandor. How might I alert him to their arrival without creating a disturbance in the Intensive Care Unit?"

Her hands tremble a little, but her back is ramrod straight. Zev feels for her. It hadn't occurred to him before that she must be upset about Zoey, too.

"Yes, I know these kids," says the nurse.

Zev is sure that's true, though he doesn't recognize her at all. Because of Dad's status as a demigod and his annual holiday parties, everybody around here knows them.

"They're in ICU3. If you take the kids to the family waiting room, I'll go tell Dr. and Mrs. Sandor you're here."

"Thank you, miss. Come, children." Nana marches down the hall ahead of them, squinting at signs as she goes, and Zev and Lottie exchange nervous smiles—surely they know the way better than she does. But Zev shakes his head, and Lottie nods her understanding and puts her sweaty little hand in his. Poor kid. If he's this scared, he can't even imagine how she's feeling. He squeezes her hand, glad for the human contact.

Zev is relieved to find the waiting room vacant except for one diminutive elderly couple huddled in a corner, their dark heads bent close as they murmur in some ancient language. He blushes and averts his eyes. He has no desire to witness another family's pain; his own will be bad enough. What if Mom cries? There's already a tight ache in his own throat.

Mom comes in and sees them standing clustered there. Her eyes are bloodshot, and her hair is wild, her skin so pale it's as if her freckles have faded overnight. She leans down and hugs Lottie, inhaling deeply and exhaling a small sound of pleasure, something she does when she's been away from them for a bit. Usually, Zoey is there to catch Zev's eye and they share a secret smile. But this time, when Mom stands up to hug him, he's mortified to feel tears squeezing out of the corners of his eyes. He dashes them away with his forearm as he pulls out of the hug, hoping she didn't see.

Mom turns to Nana. "Hello, Mother," she says.

Nana doesn't put a hand on Mom.

"Hello, Olivia. You look a fright."

Mom says nothing. And honestly, what could she say to that?

Zev tries to imagine what it must've been like to grow up with Nana for a mother, but his mind can't stretch that far. His own mother is kind to everyone, even the toll collector on the Mass Pike. Nana isn't exactly mean; she's more like marble—cold and hard—though she warms up when Zoey is around. One time, when Zev asked her for the secret to Nana's affection, Zoey shrugged and said, "Nana's all about knowing what you want and going after it. I think we just understand each other."

"I believe I will go to her while you sort out the other children," says Nana now, disappearing down the hall.

"So, I know you two must have a lot of questions—" Mom says.

"Just one. When can I see her?" Zev blurts.

His mouth stays a little open though he's not talking anymore. He is surprised at how confident he has managed to sound. Like Zoey would, if the roles were reversed.

Mom raises her eyebrows. "I was *going* to say that Dr. Wang is waiting for you in the Cardiac Lab, so let's walk and talk. I know testing sounds kind of strange and scary, but honestly, they're humoring Dad and me because of what happened to Zoey."

"But what *did* happen?" Lottie asks.

Mom looks down at Lottie, obviously calculating how much she can say. Eight years old is old enough to hear some things, but not necessarily to understand all of them.

"Zoey had a problem with her ... with her heartbeat while she was running sprints at the park, and she blacked out. Maybe it was the heat ... We don't really know," Mom says, sounding wounded. "But when she fell, she hit her head on a rock, and *that's* the injury that's giving her trouble now."

Zev tries to translate this latest spate of parent-speak into truth. A freak accident—that's what Dad would call it. As director of Traumatic Brain Injury at Yale New Haven Hospital, he's seen the results of a thousand freak accidents. The bizarre convergence almost short-circuits Zev's own brain completely. Dad is supposed to be some kind of TBI rehab genius. But what's the point of being a superhero if you can't even rescue your own kid?

"Her heart is working fine now," Mom is saying. "But Dr. Wang wants to do some tests to rule out the chance that either of you could ever have a similar problem. He'll put you through a series of scans and exercises while he measures your heart rate to make sure everything works the way it's supposed to. Which I'm sure it will."

Zev knows there's nothing wrong with his heart that can be measured on a machine. But they must be pretty worried, rushing them into testing like this.

Lottie leans her head against Mom's hand. "What about Ethan?" she asks in a small voice. "How will *he* get tested?"

"We'll take care of him, don't you worry."

Mom opens a door marked *Cardiac Lab*. "Lottie, you come with me. Zev, you're in here, and when you're done, you come right back to the waiting room. Dad will want to see you. Okay?"

Zev nods but keeps his head down. He knows he'll never convince his parents to let him see Zoey. But already this time apart from her has made him feel smaller—and he can hardly afford to be less of himself than he was before.

For the next two hours, Zev relies on his coronary arteries to do their job, while his brain is otherwise occupied figuring out how to infiltrate the ICU. This is the kind of defiant scheme Zoey would've dragged him into, and the idea of trying to pull it off without her sends his pulse galloping.

"Zev, can you take some nice, slow breaths for me?" says his tester, sounding like she's trying to keep the concern out of her voice.

So he breathes, innnnnnn, ouuuuuuut, innnnnnn, ouuuuuuut, and pictures his blood flowing through his veins, willing it to slow down, telling it to take its time. This is a trick Ethan has taught him, for surviving in a trench.

Next, he recites silently: **Infiltrate** (noun) [in.fil.trayt]: enter an organization in order to spy on it; enter enemy territory secretly; permeate fluid through another substance. Synonyms: access, insinuate, penetrate, intrude.

"Nice! That looks great," says the tester, calm again. Sandor family magic to the rescue.

He turns his attention back to his plans, running through all the variables and contingencies while they've got him running on the treadmill.

When they're done, he walks back to the waiting room in a disembodied fever. Mom is not there, and Dad is deep in conversation with Dr. Wang, the heart guy, while Lottie leans into him. Dad has put a hand on her head and pulled her into a leg-hug while he talks.

He is usually at his most animated at work, joking with the nurses and conferring enthusiastically with his colleagues—but now Dad looks like a ghost, his face gray and expressionless. It's as if Zoey's coma is contagious. A nurse comes in and tells him something. She still calls him Dr. Sandor even though he's not the doctor here—he's the parent.

Or at least, he should be. Shouldn't he?

Zev hangs back, watching to make sure Dad hasn't noticed him there. Not hard: He's extra good at being invisible to Dad.

Without a word, Zev goes around the corner and slips through the double doors marked *Critical Care*. No one will question him if he acts like he belongs—that's what Zoey would say. He strides down the hall as if his guts aren't melting with fear, watching the signs: *ICU1. ICU2. ICU3.*

He enters the small sterile square of space and gazes around, his artist's eyes seeking warmth, color, life. But there isn't any here. There is only stainless-steel machinery with its toneless *bleep, bleep, bleep*. Zoey looks freaky and artificial, with tubes running in and out of every part of her.

Fear is screeching in Zev's head, but Zoey is impossibly silent. He reaches inside himself, looking for the thread that has always bound him to his twin, but he can't find it. Trembling, he sits down and picks up her hand, which feels papery and cold and looks tiny lying there, inert. *Unresponsive.* Now he gets it. He tries to warm her, but he's afraid to rub too hard. What are the rules?

He leans in and whispers in her ear: "I'm here, Zo. It's okay. You can wake up now."

He waits, expectant. He's been so sure she would wake up as soon as she heard his voice that now he's all out of ideas.

Besides the winking, beeping monitors, not a single thing stirs in the room, but something dark is shifting inside him, moving closer, trying to take over. He squeezes her hand harder.

"Zoey, wake up! What's going on? Come on. This is … crazy."

Nothing.

"I need you. Please. Wake. Up."

In the face of her silence, the darkness in his chest blooms, a terrible void, a hemorrhage of nothing. The pain spreads into his arms and legs, icy and malevolent. Breathing is out of the question. If he moves at all, he will shatter into a billion shards. An eternity passes while he sits there, paralyzed. Dark spots float around in the air.

At some point, his lizard brain takes over. He gasps in a breath. He realizes his hands are still clamped onto hers, leaving small marks on her wrist that are already turning purple. He drops her hand, sucking in huge, shaky gulps of air.

He runs.

Zev rejoins his family in the waiting room, but he's not really there. He has left something behind with Zoey, some elemental part of himself that he can't spare. Maybe the monstrous pain inside him is a sort of supernatural branding, a wound to match hers in place of the thread that used to bind them together.

He can't see how they will come out of this in one piece.

DAY 2

Sam wondered if Ethan had grown since he'd been deployed. It wasn't impossible, at nineteen. Their eldest was now easily as tall as him—and looked even taller in his uniform and cap emblazoned with the crest of the United States Marines. It was astonishing that Ethan had been able to get emergency leave so quickly, Sam thought: He'd imagined the Marines as an entirely inflexible organization, but within twelve hours of receiving Liv's call about Zoey, Ethan had called from a satellite phone on a transport helicopter to say he was on his way home from Kabul. When Liv saw him standing in the doorway of ICU3, she gave a strangled cry and held him for a long time. She met Sam's glance over their son's bowed shoulder, and her amber eyes—a color Sam had never seen on another living human except their twins—were incandescent with relief.

"Oh, Ethan! I can't believe you're actually here!"

"Where else would I be, Mom? I had to come home. That's what Compassionate Leave is for," Ethan said in his serious way, disentangling himself from his mother. "My CO gave me forty-eight hours and said I can probably get another couple of days next month, depending. He was so great about it." He turned to Sam with tentative eyes. "Hey, Dad."

"Hey yourself, E," said Sam. "You look good, son."

He gave Ethan the briefest of hugs, and a hearty pat on the shoulder. Liv stepped in again and leaned against Ethan, rubbing his back with one hand as if to console him for Sam's inadequate greeting.

Sam knew Ethan might misinterpret his signals and think he was still angry at him for enlisting, but he was willing to risk it. If he held on to the boy for too long, he was sure he would break down, and that mustn't happen.

He had been feeling disoriented ever since Zoey was brought in, and it was worse now, with Ethan standing here in front of him. He was unable to shake the sense that the universe had slid sideways into some impossible alternate space.

"This whole thing makes no sense," Ethan said in a pained voice, as if Sam's thoughts were audible.

Sam had done his best to keep his clinical filters in place for the last two days, but now he looked at Zoey through Ethan's eyes: her mouth pulled into a one-sided sneer by the breathing tube, her lips already cracked from chapping, her skin a strange, pasty color, and one side of her face overlaid by a cumulus cloud of purple bruises beginning to fade to yellow. Her long hair was tangled and greasy against the sheet, and her body looked small and vulnerable, flanked by a cohort of top-heavy IV poles and draped in layers of bleached hospital blankets to keep her shivering under control during the hypothermia they had induced to minimize brain swelling.

The ICU nurse came in and saw them clustered around the end of the bed. "Don't mind me, folks. Dr. Sandor." She nodded to him. "Only I need to hang a new bag."

Sam smiled absently at her, the lilting Caribbean accent a momentary balm. "Of course. Whatever you need to do."

What was her name again? Something related to fruit. Cherry? Tangerine? No ... *Clementine*, that was it. She had been with the hospital a long time, and she was excellent.

"Dad, isn't there something more we can do?"

By *we*, Sam knew Ethan meant *him*.

Clementine looked up and smiled at Ethan's words. Was she smiling because of his son's naive faith in him, or because she already knew the answer to the question?

"I'm afraid not, son. Right now, we just have to wait."

Liv leaned against Sam, as if she was consoling him now, too. She knew it was impossible, what he was trying to do—that he was teetering between two intolerable worlds. How did she do that? How did she comfort everyone around her, even in the midst of her own crisis?

Ethan asked him to review why Zoey needed to be sedated while she was already in a coma, and Sam explained about mild induced hypothermia, or MIH, as they called it.

"Think of it as an allover ice pack to reduce inflammation in her brain."

"But why isn't she shivering like crazy?"

Sam pointed to the bag Clementine had hung.

"Pancuronium bromide. It subdues the natural shiver reflex while she's in MIH," he explained, leaning over and absently smoothing Zoey's tangled hair.

"Are there any risks, any downsides to the MIH that we don't know about?"

"As far as we know, there's little risk to Zoey, and there's a good likelihood it will improve her long-term neurological outcome as well as her short-term chances for survival."

"Jesus, Dad." Ethan was silent for a moment.

Maybe Sam shouldn't have retreated quite so far into clinical mode. Ethan might be a Marine medic, but he was Zoey's brother first.

"And there's no inside angle you could be working, something the rest of them might've missed?"

Sam could hear the subtext: *Why can't you fix it, Dad?* A hard kernel of resentment lodged itself in his windpipe. He could feel Liv looking at him, too, waiting to see what he would say—as if she didn't know that there was nothing at all to do but wait. As if he wasn't already breaking every ethics rule by involving himself with Zoey's clinical care in the first place.

He sat down on the rigid orange plastic chair. The room looked different from this angle than from the end of the bed where the charts hung. How could he make his family understand? All the dinnertime stories he had told them over the years about his patients who had prevailed against insurmountable odds were predicated on the existence of a window of opportunity. And this window had not opened for Zoey yet. Who knew whether it ever would?

•

When people came through the doors of Sam's wing, they had already lost whatever they were going to lose: short-term memory, coherent speech, use of their legs, range of motion in the fingers of their right hand. With as much tenderness and humor as his role permitted, Sam would pinpoint the minuscule functions each patient needed to perform in order to begin the long journey toward recovery. In the most severely injured person, this might mean an entire team focused on coaxing a single finger to move the joystick of an electric wheelchair. Anything to grant the patient a glimpse of freedom.

Sam thought of himself as a cartographer of post-catastrophic landscapes, plotting a course to a better future for each patient. Over the last twenty years, he had amassed a rare combination of skills, an admixture of other specialties that included psychiatry, neurology, orthopedics, and hope. He had remarked to Liv once that he would be at a loss if, God forbid, one of their own children ever sustained a brain injury, since there were no other specialists in the area who did what he did. His patients and their families told him he had a true gift. But sometimes the new patients didn't know why they were there.

"I'm a specialist in rehabilitation medicine, a *physiatrist*," he would explain. But they and their loved ones shrugged to indicate how inconsequential his title was. They only wanted to know if he could *fix it*.

People often asked Sam whether he didn't find this work terribly depressing, and he would explain that, in fact, his clinic was an optimistic place, provided one was willing to be realistically hopeful. The true work could not begin until people stopped insisting that life had to return to the way it was before. Often, the patients weren't even aware of what they had lost, and it was their caregivers who suffered the greater sorrow. Given enough time, though, Sam was usually able to persuade them to set sensible goals, to arrive at a new concept of meaningful work by using the map he helped each of them draw.

But who would be the guide when the mapmaker lost his way? That was the question plaguing Sam as he and Liv stood in the ICU with Ethan.

Clementine stuck her head in the door again. "Excuse me, Dr. Sandor," she said in her musical Trinidadian accent. "I have Zoey down for a position change right about now. But if you're visiting, it can surely wait?"

"Right. Position change. That's fine. I'll do it myself. Thanks."

The nurse made a startled sound, nodded, and closed the door.

Liv put a hand on his arm. "Is this something Ethan or I can help with?"

"No, I've got it," he said, and moved to shift Zoey from her back to her side. He pushed his arms under her deadweight, grasped the sheet and tugged upward, hard enough to roll her forward but not so hard as to dislodge her many clinical appendages. Even so, all the monitors began to beep and ring and buzz at once.

Liv jumped, started forward, stopped.

Without a word, Sam leaned over and hugged Zoey into place, putting a wedge behind her back so her position was secure. He reached out and reset the machines, those dispassionate reporters of Zoey's vital signs, telling them that, despite the recent unexplained aberration, her heart was now pumping blood through her body at a regular rate.

A position change wasn't rocket science, but it would have taken much longer to explain to Liv or Ethan than to do himself. What he hadn't counted on was the physical closeness that such a maneuver required, the way his hands came into repeated contact with Zoey's too-cool skin, the way his insides shrank at the floppiness of her arms.

Those forty-five seconds had erased every shred of his composure. Grief washed through him like saline, and for a moment, Sam lost his bearings.

He had been preparing for this sort of disaster ever since Ethan enlisted. Liv would say that he had spent his entire fatherhood preparing for it, and he couldn't deny that the sudden loss of his own parents when he was seventeen had permanently colored his view of things. But he had always told himself he was doing a fair job of keeping a lid on his irrational fears.

It was so unusual for the kids in their hypereducated, privileged circle of friends to entertain the idea of military service that Liv and Sam had been dismissive of Ethan's interest at first, and when they realized he was serious about joining the Marines after high school, Sam had launched an aggressive campaign of dissuasion that immediately degenerated into a fight.

"Why would you even consider such a thing?" he'd yelled, after catching sight of the glossy recruitment package Ethan had left lying on the kitchen counter.

"Why don't you ever *listen*?" Ethan had yelled back.

Liv stayed out of it. She abhorred conflict.

"Of course I'm worried!" she later said to Sam privately. "But doesn't Ethan deserve the benefit of the doubt?"

Sam demurred; he never for a moment considered that the boy would defy him outright.

But Ethan came home on his eighteenth birthday clutching a sheaf of papers bearing the US Marines insignia at the top and his newly legal signature at the bottom.

As Sam had grasped the meaning of the documents, his face grayed with shock.

"How could you do this to me?" he whispered.

"I've told you a million times, Dad, this has nothing to do with you!"

"But Ethan, you're not a ... *soldier*!" Sam said, unable to hide his disdain. "You have a terrific mind. You could do something great, something *constructive*, and instead you've gone and joined the Marines—and during a war! I don't know what you think you're proving, but this has *everything* to do with me."

Ethan slapped his papers down on the kitchen counter, his cheeks blazing.

"Wow. You never hear me, do you? This is about my *beliefs*. It's about being a citizen of this *country*."

"Do you think your *beliefs* will protect you from a roadside bomb?" Sam shouted.

"I should've known you would never give me your blessing," Ethan shouted back. "I guess that's too much to ask."

After that, Sam maintained a resolute silence until the day Ethan left. He couldn't even bear to look at him. But when his boy was standing in the front hallway in a crisp new uniform, Sam relented. He had placed his hands over Ethan's shorn head and intoned in Hebrew the blessing Jewish parents gave to their children every Shabbat and on their wedding day:

"May God bless you and keep you. May God shine His face upon you and be gracious to you. May God lift up His countenance to you and give you peace."

He had pulled Ethan into a rough hug that his son returned, the big buttons of his uniform pressing against Sam's heart.

But it was as if that decision of Ethan's, more than a year ago, had opened a sort of virtual reality for Sam that contained within it the terrible moment when he would find out his child had been critically wounded.

How could he have anticipated that his mistake lay not in the presentiment of disaster, but in the child to whom he had assigned the role of victim?

Sam became aware of the silence in the hospital room, and the nauseating truth hit him all over again: It was *Zoey* who was hurt, and Ethan and Liv were waiting for him to tell them how he would *fix this*.

"I swear, if there were anything at all to do, I'd be doing it," he said, his voice hoarse but still too loud in the cramped space. "The team will build a plan for Zoey as soon as she wakes up and we can assess the extent of her injury."

He glanced at Liv and Ethan to be sure they had heard his deliberate implication of *when* instead of *if*, but still, he knew his words sounded hollow. He had said them a thousand times to patients' families, and what comfort did it give them, if it turned out their worst fears were realized?

"Isn't there anything *I* can do?" Ethan said. "I want to help."

Sam shook his head. "I wish there—"

"Honey, just having you here is a help," Liv said.

"But you do need to get your stress test," Sam said. "Come on, I'll walk you over there."

"And that's another thing, Dad! Isn't that a little over the t—"

"No, E, it's a reasonable precaution," Liv said. "You should get that over with, and then for God's sake go home and get some rest. You look exhausted."

At her words, Ethan deflated. "Okay, I guess … but I'm coming right back."

"Of course," said Liv. "But you *have* to sleep. And forty-eight hours is long enough for you to see her out of the MIH."

"MIH?" said Ethan blankly. "Wait. We just talked about this. Mild induced hypothermia?"

"Right. Maybe she'll wake right up, and you can talk to her before you go back."

Sam blessed Liv for her hopeful nature, but he was in a different place altogether, and he had nothing good to add.

At the Cardiac Lab, Sam hugged his firstborn son for an extra moment before turning and dragging his feet back to the ICU. Purposeless waiting was not his strong suit; he was a planner and a doer. The nothingness of these days added another whole layer of misery for him, and he wished for the thousandth time in the decades since he'd fallen for Liv that a little bit of her Zen-like mindset would rub off on him.

Zoey's neurosurgeon, Peter Becker, came and went on his rounds, and pronounced Zoey *critical but stable*. Liv looked at Sam as if to ask, *Is that good?* and he mustered a reassuring smile. In theory, *stable* was certainly better than *unstable*. It was on the tip of Sam's tongue to ask Peter the same question Ethan had asked earlier: Wasn't there something more that could be done, some magic trick he could pull out of his white coat pocket? Peter was the Brain Trust. Sam always told patients' families: He had an uncanny ability to anticipate the behavior of the unpredictable, mangled brains that came under his watch. The man had reearned his nickname a hundred times over the years Sam had worked in tandem with him on those impossible cases. But he knew what his colleague would say about this one. He had seen the damning MRIs, the swollen river of blood with its insidious tributaries snaking their way through his girl's brain.

He felt diminished, as though his tall frame were shrinking by the hour.

The door opened and he looked up, his eyes red and heavy with unshed tears. Gillian, his office manager, slipped into the room.

"Dr. Sandor, I'm sorry to bother you," she whispered, "but Mr. Gladwell has been—oh, hi, Mrs. Sandor, I didn't see you back there. But of course ... where else would you be?" Her skin mottled with a quick blush and she looked abashed at her own words. "I'm so, so sorry to disturb you both, but I was hoping to borrow Dr. Sandor for a little while."

Sam rose, relieved at the prospect of getting out of there for any amount of time. "It's fine, Gillian. What's going on with the Gladwells?"

"Mr. Gladwell has called several times in an absolute lather about Hope, who's getting worse again," Gillian whispered. "And now with the new baby, I think they need to be seen." She grimaced.

The Gladwell family was a particular emotional challenge: Sam had been treating their five-year-old, Hope, for the effects of severe cerebral palsy since birth, and now it appeared their second child had been born with it, too. Since there was no family history, and no risky behavior on the part of the mother during pregnancy, Sam had been shocked at their spectacular bad luck. He thought about them often, and now he tried to imagine what comfort he could offer. Anything had to be better than this empty waiting—even someone else's train wreck.

Sam looked over at Liv, who was watching the conversation without reacting. She shrugged tiredly.

"Give me a few minutes," he said to Gillian. "I'll come find you and we'll figure something out. Okay?"

"Of course. Thanks, Dr. Sandor. And—it goes without saying, but we're all pulling for Zoey like crazy," she said, including Liv in her glance.

"I know you are, Gillian, and it means a lot," said Liv.

Gillian slipped out as quietly as she had come in, and Sam turned to Liv. "Is it absurd for me to see a patient today?"

"No, it's not absurd." She paused. "This waiting is killing you. I can see it. And they're not even reversing the MIH until tomorrow. Plus, you'll be right here in the building if anything changes."

"I'm probably driving you insane."

"No, Sam. You're driving *yourself* insane. And there will be plenty to do once she's awake."

"Are you sure you'll be okay alone here?"

He put his hand to the side of her face. Her skin was soft and a little hot, as always when she was overtired. They were both beyond exhausted, but the thought of seeing a patient gave him a little burst of energy.

"As long as nothing's happening, we'll be fine for a few hours." Liv held up her copy of *Little Women* with a tiny smile. "We've got Jo March and her whole family to keep us busy, don't we, Zoey?" She laid her hand on Zoey's foot and left it there like an anchor.

•

Sam stood in the door of Exam Room 1 and watched as Hope Gladwell moved jerkily past him. Mr. and Mrs. Gladwell followed slowly behind, looking like the survivors of a natural disaster. Sam tried to maintain his clinical focus on Hope's jarring walk, still worsening despite his best efforts.

Fear flickered in his peripheral vision. Maybe this wasn't such a good idea.

"Mr. and Mrs. Gladwell. It's good to see you again."

They stared at him balefully, and he turned to his five-year-old patient, whose enormous brown eyes looked at him through thick glasses. "And Hope! A big sister now. You've grown a lot. So, tell me, who do we have here?"

"Gwace, umm, Gwacie Webecca," said Hope.

Her mother broke into wrenching sobs, and her father looked away and swiped at his eyes. Anything Sam could think of to say was pointless. Grace and Hope. He wished for the parents' sakes they had picked different names for their children.

He had to take several deep breaths himself as he took the infant from her mother.

"Hello there, Gracie Rebecca," said Sam. He gently unwrapped the infant's swaddling and performed his physical assessment without speaking. Her condition appeared to be remarkably similar to Hope's. Though he tried to be sensitive, the parents continued to cry throughout the exam.

When Sam had swaddled the baby again and handed her back to Mrs. Gladwell, her husband pulled him aside and asked in a hoarse whisper, "Can't you do something, doc? I'm at my wits' end. All she ever does anymore is cry and pray." He cocked a thumb toward his wife, who was fingering a set of rosary beads as she clutched Gracie.

Sam wished he could offer the man some reason to believe in God, or medicine, or anything at all.

"Let me take a look at Hope, then we'll talk a little," he said. But he knew his exam would confirm that the older sister's condition was worsening. Why did he have the feeling he was missing something here? He searched his exhausted mind for an explanation, but it wouldn't come. Still, after he finished with the older girl's exam, Sam addressed the parents with as much confidence as he could muster.

"I want to increase the girls' visits to monthly—can you manage that?"

The Gladwells nodded woodenly.

"Good. We need to stay on top of the spasticity, and I want to try out some other ideas. Okay? Have Gillian set up the next three appointments now, before my schedule gets full."

As he showed them out, he knew he had failed to deliver what they needed. But something about these two girls was teasing his brain. He had to keep them coming back. Maybe after things settled down with Zoey …

He rushed back to the ICU and found everything exactly how he'd left it, with Liv reading and Zoey still as a statue. What was he expecting, with forced hypothermia?

"Sam." Liv smiled wanly up at him. "Got your patient all squared away?"

"Something like that," he muttered. "For all the help I can offer, which is …"

Liv waited for him to finish, and when he didn't, she said, "You know what would be a big help to me? Go home for dinner tonight. Check on the kids. They're stranded with Mother all day, and Zev's climbing the walls. He says she's making things … difficult." She smiled wryly at Sam. "I can only imagine. I bet even Lottie is feeling the strain by now."

"I can do that," he said, grateful at the prospect of going home. He went to the nurses' station and told Gillian he was leaving, his eyes sliding away from her sympathetic grimace. His chart notes would have to wait. He drove the familiar route in a trance, his mind circling around the Gladwell girls, only noticing he'd arrived when he was parking in his own driveway.

Unfolding his long legs from the car, he looked up and was arrested by the sight of his house in the golden light of late afternoon. His chest filled with emotion, a boggy stew of love and fear, memory and joy and ownership.

How many times would he come home to this place with his life irretrievably altered? Births, deaths, celebrations, catastrophes, all were layered onto the ancient clapboard siding. He had tried his best to keep the house exactly as it was when his parents had left it to him, having received his inheritance in a state of bewilderment, certain only of the fact that he had no business being a teenage homeowner. Through the years, he and Liv had continued to make repairs only as they were needed, but he'd never allowed any other changes. It had cost his parents years of savings to buy this house and had been a source of deep pride for them. Unnecessary "improvements" would be disrespectful to their memory. This preservation was far more important to him than he would admit, and he had hewn to his policy with a certain degree of myopia, cherishing a secret superstition that maintaining the sameness of the old place would act as a counterweight to the unpredictability of the lives sheltered within its walls.

But now he was again confronted with this truth: An abiding fear of disaster didn't serve as any kind of preventative against it. Liv had pointed this out to him more than once over the years, whenever his stubbornness about the house had won out over practical considerations or comfort.

Zoey's accident was proof of the fact that if you waited long enough for catastrophe to strike, it surely would oblige.

The door opened to reveal his mother-in-law's trademark frown.

"My goodness, Samuel. You drove up ages ago. What is keeping you? Is there news?"

Somehow Hinda always managed to sound annoyed, though Sam knew she wasn't angry now; she was distraught. It was no secret that she was very fond of Zoey. Liv would say—never in earshot of the kids—that Zoey was the only Sandor impressive enough to meet her mother's rigorous standards. In spite of himself, Sam had been touched to see Hinda at Zoey's bedside in the ICU. She had taken her granddaughter's limp hand in both of her own and whispered in her ear, wiping tears off her cheeks with one finger when she thought no one was looking.

"There wouldn't be any news today, Hinda. The nature of Zoey's treatment regimen is such that we don't expect any change in her status until at least tomorrow," he said, noticing that he had slipped into his usual habit of matching her formal tone. "How are the children faring?"

"Charlotte has once again been playing all day with her Barbie dolls." Hinda sniffed, clucking her tongue.

"Well, perhaps *Lottie* can be forgiven, at the age of eight," he said with a shrug, falling far flat of the breezy tone he was aiming for. "And Zev?"

"Zev has been entombed in the basement since he woke up—after one o'clock in the afternoon, I might add. Presumably he's been doing some sort of artwork down there, in spite of my repeated suggestion that he get some fresh air."

Cluck.

"Ethan is looking good, though, isn't he?"

"Ethan has claimed jet lag and gone to bed. Though I can't imagine how sleeping in the afternoon will act as a corrective."

"Teenagers." Sam shrugged again.

Cluck.

Sam imagined the two of them caught in an absurd dance of clucks and shrugs.

"Yes. Well, I need a quick shower before dinner," he said, sidling past her into the house.

He had hoped the hot water would sluice away his fractured perceptions, but when he sat down twenty minutes later at the silent dinner table, nothing felt right. Dinner at the Sandor house—when he was able to be home—was usually a noisy affair, with the children telling anecdotes about the latest school melodramas or Sam telling them stories about his own patients. Tonight, he was at a loss for even minimal conversation to break up the gloom, and he was aware he wasn't keeping up his side of the bargain with Liv.

Zev was even quieter than usual, but then, Zoey had always been the one to draw him out. Sam tried to catch his eye and give him a reassuring smile; he was rearranging his rice and chicken without getting any of it into his skinny body. Ordinarily, his astounding appetite was a subject of some amusement at dinner. Now only Lottie chattered on, either unaffected by the disposition of her tablemates or, more likely, trying to cover her own uneasiness.

"Camp Artemis starts on Monday, Daddy. I can't wait! Who's bringing me? Is Ethan still going to be here?"

Sam conjured a smile. "I don't think so, cookie. He only has two days off."

Lottie turned to Hinda. "What about you, Nana? Can you bring me to camp?"

"Samuel, what is to be done about these comings and goings?" Hinda asked, somehow finding a way to ignore Lottie but not her question. "Isn't there some sort of bus the child could take?"

Sam caught himself about to shrug again. Logistics had always been Liv's bailiwick, and in the present circumstances, Sam couldn't summon even a cursory interest in next week.

"Oh, I never ride the bus, Nana," said Lottie. "It makes me sick. Mommy always takes me instead."

"Yes, child, but your mother is not available now to indulge these whims."

There was silence around the table. Zev looked up as if he meant to object, but didn't.

"Will you be physically ill on the bus?" asked Hinda, with Lottie now fully in her sights.

Lottie considered for a moment. "Ummm, n-n-n-o, I don't think I'll *actually* throw up …"

"Well, then, I am certain you will find it a growing experience to endure a little bit of discomfort in order to lighten your parents' burden. And don't start your sentences with *ummm*, dear," she added. "It makes you sound far less intelligent than you are."

Zev looked over at Sam as if to say: *Are you going to let her get away with that?* And Sam girded himself to advocate on Lottie's behalf. But in the end, there was no need; she spoke up for herself without a trace of hesitation.

"Oh, I only say *ummm* when I'm *really* not sure of something," Lottie said, putting an affectionate hand on Hinda's arm. "Which isn't much, Nana, I promise! But what if I did throw up? One time, Tommy Brio puked on the bus, and it reeked for days."

Sam detected a hint of a smile beneath Hinda's frown; he had never been able to break into the locked vault that was his mother-in-law (despite Liv's early hopefulness that Sam and Hinda would find common ground in their love of music) but if Lottie continued like this, she might win a place in her grandmother's heart alongside her big sister. Zoey had coached Lottie well, making no secret of the fact that she meant to ensure that Lottie, too, would grow up intrepid. She had hung a sign on their bedroom door years ago: *The Fearless Sisters Live Here*, and in smaller letters, *No shrinking violets allowed*. She had set out to teach Lottie how to do everything that might have slowed her down in the world: climb a tree in a skirt, answer a mean retort with a smart one, dress well without ever being uncomfortable, correct people who thought girls were weak.

Two winters ago, in honor of Lottie's sixth birthday, thirteen-year-old Zoey had lobbied for Zev to be allowed to cover the girls' bedroom walls with murals she had conceived.

"I've designed them for maximum psychological impact, and Zev will be my commissioned artist. It's first grade, guys. The big time. Lottie needs ammo!" Zoey said, precocious and confident as always. Sam had not been able to deny her, though Liv had expressed a private concern that Zoey might incite in Lottie an unnecessary aggressiveness, a trait Sam knew she didn't admire. But she needn't have worried. Lottie remained as sweet as ever, and soon the walls bloomed with a flowering tree that said, *You can do anything that you dream*. A river flowed beneath it, trailing the words, *Weak is a state of mind*, and on the shore of the river was Sam's personal favorite: a hot-pink flamingo declaring that *Well-behaved women rarely make history*.

Now, Sam was glad to see that Lottie had prevailed in the battle of wills with her grandmother. Hinda didn't even correct her use of *reeked* and *puked*; she rose to clear the table, clucking at each of their full plates. There was no doubt her plain, sensible food couldn't compare to Liv's delectable creations—but anything would've tasted like sawdust tonight. Sam made a half-hearted attempt to help Hinda in the kitchen, but her umbrage rolled off her in waves, and he was all out of compassion.

"I've got to check on Zoey," he muttered. "I'll be back to put Lottie to bed." He was intensely relieved to walk out the front door, until he remembered that he had felt the same way when he left the ICU before lunch, and again when he fled the hospital after his torturous afternoon. How could this have happened? He was a refugee from his own life.

EXCERPT FROM

THE MEMORY BOOK OF ZOEY SANDOR

Running in the park with Daddy we fly over rocks and fences we laugh at the wind no one can catch us. My legs are pumping, I am a machine an engine a bullet, I can hear my feet pounding the ground. Whoosh we pass by a runner, a blurry shape we are moving too fast to see who but we have lots of friends to wave to when we run. Faster Zoey faster says Daddy. I am running as fast as the wind but I can't catch him, where are you going Daddy? He won't stop. It hurts like a big stitch it clamps tighter and tighter, I want to keep up but all the sounds get loud the wind is blowing the trees are rustling Daddy is laughing, he doesn't know that the pain is much too big I have to stop. When I fall down all the sounds go away at once, no more wind in the trees no more feet pounding no more Daddy laughing.

(Transcribed by Francesca Garibaldi, SLP)

DAY 3

After seventy-two hours, a flurry of nurses began the process of returning Zoey's core temperature to normal. Liv watched Sam pacing again at the foot of her bed, but she tried to keep her gaze soft and her mind quiet. She knew if she allowed herself to *see* what was happening, she would be unable to bear the suspense.

But as it turned out, the whole event was an anticlimax. Zoey's temperature ticked upward over the course of many hours, then hovered indifferently at 98.5 degrees Fahrenheit. When Ethan came back to sit with her before his leave ended, Liv had to tell him nothing had changed.

"She's showed no signs of awakening," she whispered, not wanting to upset Zoey as well as Ethan.

Dr. Becker strode in, his Einsteinian halo of white hair waving, his air of abstraction unchanged even as he pronounced Zoey "still stable at a GCS of four."

"What does that mean, that she's *stable* with a Glasgow Coma Scale of four?" Ethan asked, and Liv was impressed that he already knew these medical terms.

"We just have to wait and see," the neurosurgeon said, which meant nothing.

Still, Liv found the ICU less frightening now that Zoey was no longer being frozen from the inside out, and breathed a little easier. When it became clear that she wasn't going to awaken right away, Liv saw a shift in Sam's demeanor, too, but in the opposite direction from her. He talked about Zoey in increasingly clinical language and spent even less time in her room than before. Liv understood his reasons, but she missed him all the same.

She missed her sister more than usual, too, and wished she could be here. But Shula was on her third pregnancy in four years, and since she'd had early labor with her other two, her doctors had advised against the long flight from Israel. Liv tried to console herself with the image of new life growing inside her little sister, and though they had spoken a few days ago when Liv called to tell her what happened, she decided to step out and phone Shula again, let Ethan have a little time alone with Zoey.

It was seven hours later in Israel—nighttime in Connecticut, morning in Jerusalem—and as she waited for the lines to connect, Liv imagined Zoey caught in the ether between these time zones.

When Shula picked up, Liv could hear the sounds of breakfast dishes rattling and the flute-tones of small children's voices.

"How are you holding up, habibi?" asked Shula, using a term of endearment she usually reserved for her babies.

"I don't know." Liv sighed. "We're living in suspended animation. Sometimes it all feels like science fiction."

"I can imagine. Well, no I can't. Tell me."

"Well, once they induced the hypothermia," Liv said, "I couldn't get it out of my head that Zoey was being frozen to death. When I fell asleep for a little while, I dreamed that a blizzard was howling around my wonderful house, filling the windows and doorways with so much snow that no one could get out and no air could get in. I woke up next to her, gasping and shivering, and it turned out that Zoey was shivering, too. It seemed like I was still dreaming, like her room was tilting and breaking apart—but it was her body, shuddering hard enough to move the bed. I grabbed onto her frigid hands and tried to hold them still until they hung the first bag of pancuronium bromide from her IV pole—that's a medicine to suppress the shiver reflex, Sam told me. But the IV pole was already so full of swollen bags of liquid that they dangled over Zoey in this kind of menacing way. It never occurred to me before that medicine could be so … barbaric."

"Well. That all sounds terrifying," said Shula. "I wish I could be there with you. Nothing could keep me away except for this pregnancy. You know that, right, Livie?"

"Of course I know that. Only … it's strange and—I don't know—*unfair* that normal life is still going on everywhere, while I'm trapped in this impossible scene."

Shula made a small sound. "You have the best clinical team working on her, right? And Sam is at the helm?"

"Well, not yet, exactly. It's still neurosurgery right now. And it's … complicated."

"I bet. Is he the only guy around who can treat her once she wakes?"

"Not the *only*, but the best, by far."

"So, it's a miserable choice. I'm sure he's leaning on you while he's figuring it out. But don't be afraid to lean on him, too, Livie. He's a strong person." She paused. "And don't let Mother push you around."

Liv laughed mirthlessly. "I've barely *seen* Mother. But you're right about Sam. Thanks, Shula. I've been missing you."

"Oh?" she said, sounding surprised. "I miss you, too. But since you have no choice other than to stay strong, I'm grateful this is a skill you already possess."

Liv loved her sister's tough exterior, her uberpragmatism, and now found it comforting. Shula's life in Israel was a constant reminder that the human spirit endured. It had been no surprise to Liv that her plucky little sister had fallen in love with the troubled country as a teenager, after enduring eight years alone under Mother's critical eye once Liv had left home.

Liv was not as tough as Shula, but she patrolled Zoey's bedside, understanding that after a catastrophe such as this, people in their close-knit community would swarm like bees, oozing ill-concealed nosiness even as they offered genuine sympathy and support. She was grateful for the heaps of casseroles that Sam said had begun appearing at the house, organized by their synagogue's Chesed committee, but she insisted on receiving most visitors in the family waiting room, unwilling to let them see Zoey in such a vulnerable state.

Mikayla Slovnik was an exception. Twice a day in the past forty-eight hours she'd come to the door of the ICU in the company of her Russian-speaking mother and begged to be allowed to sit by Zoey's side. Today, the third day, Liv relented; after all, Mikayla and Zoey had been best friends since kindergarten—ever since the Slovniks had emigrated from the former Soviet Union and bought the house next door—and the girl had already turned sixteen, so she wouldn't be breaking any hospital rules.

"They only allow two visitors at a time," Liv said, "but Ethan's gone to the cafeteria. Can your mother wait out here, too?" She gave Sasha Slovnik a conciliatory smile, too exhausted to try to bridge the linguistic gap.

Mikayla turned and spoke to her mother in their native tongue, then took Liv's arm with a nervous smile. "Thank you. I've missed her so much," she said in a shy whisper.

Liv hoped Mikayla's presence would elicit some response from Zoey, but once they were standing by the bed, she rued her decision, as the poor, sweet child took one look at her friend and began to weep.

"She looks so—so little!" Mikayla cried. "It's like there's less of her already, like she's not all in there. Oh, how could this *happen*?"

Liv didn't know what to say. It was true. Her larger-than-life girl was shrinking. She made soothing noises despite her own aching throat and rubbed Mikayla's back until her sobs slowed.

"Can I touch her? Can I hold her hand?"

"Of course, sweetheart. I'm sure she'd like that," Liv said. "They say she can hear us."

Mikayla clung to Zoey for a little while, letting her eyes roam up and down the length of her motionless form. Then, without taking her eyes off the bed, she said in a hushed voice, "It's so good that Ethan was able to come back so fast. But—where's Zev?"

"Oh, honey, he hasn't come yet."

Mikayla turned to look at Liv, her river-green eyes round with surprise.

"But—why not?"

"Well, he's *supposed* to be sixteen. We could get around that, but Sam feels …"

It was ridiculous. Liv could never explain Sam's thinking on this. "Sam thinks it would be upsetting for him, in the same way you're upset now."

"But still, I'm glad I'm here." Mikayla was still whispering, though Liv spoke in a regular voice. "I mean, sure it's …"—she swept a hand through the air over Zoey's immobile form—"… awful. Sad and so scary. But if she has to be here, I do, too. And Zev? That's a no-brainer." She was silent for a moment, staring at Zoey before turning to Liv. "I mean, no disrespect intended or anything."

"I know, sweetie. None taken."

Zev *should* be here. Why hadn't he been more insistent? Why hadn't she thought it through? And why did Sam have to be so absolute? Zev was strong enough to stand by Zoey's side during this mess. Ethan had said the same thing, asking whether the twins' intense bond could help bring Zoey back. Maybe it could. And if it didn't, it would be unforgivable to have kept Zev from saying goodbye.

But there wasn't going to be a goodbye, Liv told herself again. There couldn't be. She would know it on a visceral level if Zoey was never coming back. Wouldn't she? Still, there was something obscenely vivid about Mikayla's strong, braceleted hand clasping Zoey's limp one, and standing next to the bed, Liv was nauseated by a wave of resentment for the perfect, unmarred body of this girl whom she had loved like a daughter for ten years.

She felt hollowed out after Mikayla left, as if she were the one who had the crying jag. She was grateful to sit quietly with Ethan again, and doubly chagrined when, later that same day, several of the older women from the synagogue somehow made it past the nurses' station and crowded into the ICU all at once, wearing solemn expressions and speaking in hushed voices like mediums at a séance.

"Mom, what's going on?" Ethan whispered.

Liv shook her head. "I wish I knew!" The smell of their face powder in the little room made her claustrophobic.

Ethan stepped forward. "Ladies, it's good of you to come, but the ICU restricts visitors, and this is my last hour with my sister before I have to return to Afghanistan," he said.

Amazed at her nineteen-year-old's poise, Liv ushered the women out to the waiting area where they clustered around her and proffered their misguided wisdom.

"What a shame this had to happen. And to a doctor's family, no less."

"Whatever will be, will be. We are all part of God's plan."

"His will is sometimes hidden from us."

It was this sort of thinking that put Liv in the secular camp, where she could maintain her own simple belief system that didn't try to explain away rotten luck with mystical hoo-hah. Still, she knew they meant well.

"Thank you for visiting," she said, and saw them out as fast as she could without being rude.

"Mom, I'd better go back home and spend a little time with Zev and Lottie before I fly out," Ethan said. "I'm worried about Zev."

"I know. Me too. And there's no guidebook for this territory. But we'll keep a close eye on him. Will you be able to stay for Shabbat dinner?"

He nodded. "The timing should work out. Will I see you at home?"

Liv shrugged. "I hope so, but I don't know if …" She waved a hand over Zoey's sleeping form.

He nodded. "Okay. And … I know this is a stupid question, but—Mom, are you okay?"

"I will be, E. We'll all be okay, one way or another," she said, knowing it might not be true. "We're holding onto each other, and we'll get through this somehow."

Ethan left to find Sam, who was driving him home, and Liv returned to the ICU's robotic serenade, interrupted only by visits from the clinical staff—doctors, nurses, and therapists.

Francesca Garibaldi, the hospital's senior speech pathologist and cognitive rehabilitation expert, came in daily to check on Zoey, bringing with her the warmth and expansiveness of her birthplace, and somehow putting Liv at ease despite the circumstances.

"How are you doing today, *bella*?" Francesca asked Zoey with every visit, sitting down on the plastic chair next to Liv and taking Zoey's hand. "Still on your Sleeping Beauty act, I see. Don't you want to join us for Shabbat?"

Liv let out a surprised laugh. "How did you—how do you know about Shabbat?"

"Well, I've been working with your husband for a long time, no? And in my line of work, I must observe *everything*. There is little that escapes my notice," she said, smiling at Liv. "You are going home tonight to join your family?"

It was true; on any other Friday night, they would all be gathered around the dining room table, the children scrubbed clean, the candles glowing from the sideboard, and her fragrant homemade challah awaiting her blessing.

Liv shook her head. "I can't leave her right now. But at least Sam is home with the other kids—and my mother. It's comforting to imagine them together as the sun is setting on this awful week."

Why was she telling Francesca this? Somehow, she felt she could trust her, although they were only acquaintances. Liv had enjoyed meeting her at holiday parties and had always had what Zoey would call a "girl crush" on the charming therapist, with her beautiful clothes and her musical Italian accent. She was too glamorous to work in this quotidian place.

What Liv couldn't bring herself to say was that she longed for her kitchen, for the meditative rhythm of chopping vegetables, the satisfying tiny perfections of pastry making. That she missed the way the kids drifted in and out of the fragrant space while she was preparing dinner.

"It would be good for you to take a little break," Francesca said. "And I'm sure they are all missing you, too. Why don't you go for a couple of hours? I can stay until you get back."

It was true—the other kids needed her, too; their lives hadn't stopped because their sister was hurt. And she could say a proper goodbye to Ethan. A couple of hours at home sounded to Liv like the best thing in the world.

"Really?"

"*Certo.* My shift is over. I won't go anywhere until you get back."

"Oh, Francesca, that's so kind of you. And, well, okay. I will. Thank you."

"It's my pleasure," Francesca said, clasping her hand.

Liv got up and left the room before she could change her mind. She stopped at the nurses' station to tell Clementine where she was going and hurried out to the parking garage, but no sooner had she pulled her musty car out into the street than she felt the urge to turn around and go back, as if the mere fact of her absence could cause something important to happen.

Zoey called this phenomenon FOMO: fear of missing out.

Liv smiled at the memory as she drove. Zoey was always up on the latest slang, though despite her popularity—or maybe because of it—she remained philosophical about peer pressure.

•

Liv pulled into her driveway with a strange feeling of dislocation. How would Zoey react when she woke up and realized how many days of her teenage life she had missed?

She unlatched the massive olive-wood front door and was startled by the sight of Lottie looking so robust. She had to keep reminding herself: The rest of the world hadn't been reduced to piles of dormant muscle and damaged tissue surrounded by a husk of papery skin.

"Mama! You're here! Are you home for Shabbat?"

Liv bent down and opened her arms, and Lottie flew into them. "I wish I could be, Lottie my love, but I've got to go back to Zoey in a couple of hours. Did you make the challahs?"

"No. Nana said it would take too long, so we went to Dafna's bakery instead."

Liv's face flushed with annoyance, and she buried it in Lottie's hair, holding her for a long time. The whole point had been to give Lottie the semblance of a normal routine. If Mother had bothered to ask, Liv could have explained. Or, at worst, she could have told her there were always extra homemade challahs in the freezer. Store-bought challahs were not the same.

Zev came in and leaned against the wall, and Liv rose and hugged him hard. He said nothing, and Liv didn't try to force it.

Sam appeared, wearing a look of hollow fatigue. She gave him a kiss and a pale smile. "I missed you all so much. And don't worry!" she said, throwing a glance at Sam. "Francesca is with Zoey while I'm here."

Liv had told herself she was going to sit down and give the kids her full attention, but she couldn't stay still.

"You know, while I'm here I could use a few things. Can you help me, guys?"

Liv took a duffel bag from the front hall closet and went from room to room, throwing in everything she might need to continue her vigil: an extra pillow, another sweater, a battered copy of *Anne of Green Gables* that Zoey had read a dozen times. Lottie, Zev, and even Sam trailed along behind her like three unraveling spools of yarn.

"Can I help you find something, Livie?" Sam said.

"I-I'll let you know. Not sure what I need," she muttered.

"Is Zoey better yet? When can I see her?" Lottie said.

Liv paused to smooth her daughter's hair, still damp and fragrant from her pre-Shabbat shower. "Sweetheart, Zoey's still—asleep. But I'm sure when she wakes up, yours is the first face she'll want to see."

Realizing what she'd said, she grimaced an apology at Zev over Lottie's head, but he was silent as midnight.

"But why can't they wake her from the coma, Mama? Why can't Daddy fix her?" Lottie went on.

Poor baby. She shouldn't know such words. And it must be extra hard on her, sleeping alone in the room she and Zoey shared, with the sign on the door declaring her to be one of the Fearless Sisters.

She wished Sam hadn't heard Lottie's question; he must have been asking himself the same thing a hundred times a day.

"Everyone is doing their best, Lottie. Not all problems can be fixed right away," she said. "Who brushed your hair so nicely after your shower?"

"Ethan! He's good at it! And he gave me this," she said, showing off a colorful yarn bracelet. "He said I should keep it on while he's gone and turn it in a circle every time I miss him."

"Oh, I love that!" said Liv. How did her oldest know, without any sort of prompting, to offer that kind of reassurance? "Where *is* Ethan?"

"He's in the kitchen, talking with your mother," said Sam.

Zev still wasn't talking, and Liv knew she'd have to get him alone if she had any hope of making a connection. But first she had to talk to Sam.

She asked both kids to find some obscure item for her in the basement, and turned to him.

"Mikayla came to visit today."

"Oh? How'd it go?" Sam asked, as if they were talking about a trip to the dentist.

"It was hard, but she said she was glad she came. She couldn't imagine *not* coming. And she thought it was important for Zev to be there, too. I'm wondering if she's right," she said, as she spotted Ethan coming up behind him.

Sam was silent, but a muscle in his jaw twitched.

"Sam?"

"He hasn't asked me."

"I know. It's a little strange, don't you think?"

"Well, this is scary stuff for a kid his age. Let me think about it. Okay?"

"Dad! Why do you baby him like that?" Ethan broke in. "He's almost sixteen! He needs to deal with this." Liv wished he'd moderate his tone, which could push Sam in the opposite direction.

"Yes. But he doesn't need it rammed down his throat. Plenty of time yet for him to wrestle with what's happened," Sam said grimly. "They are twins, after all."

"And that's *exactly* why—" Ethan shot back, but Lottie and Zev came up from the basement then, and Liv was glad Ethan knew it was time to back down. She didn't have the energy to referee a sparring match.

"Come on, Lottie. Let's go look in on Nana, and we'll come back and light our Shabbat candles, which I'm sure Zev and Daddy will set up for us in the meantime. Okay?"

Zev and Lottie nodded, and Lottie patted Liv's back. "Okay, Mama."

They found Mother bustling about the kitchen, looking harried. "Olivia. Dinner is almost ready. Is everything set? If we don't start soon, what with all of Sam's rituals, the food will get cold. Will you be eating with us?" She finally stopped to look at Liv. "I take it there has been no change in Zoey's status?"

Sam was right: Mother was locked up even tighter than usual. "No, no change. I can sit down with you all for a little while and then I need to return to the hospital."

As soon as Liv lit the Shabbat candles and covered her eyes to make the blessing, she started to cry. The children and Sam, who were standing around her in a little cluster, moved in closer all at once, leaning against one another as if to hold each other up. As though by prior agreement, they stayed within this little huddle as she and Sam turned and laid their hands on the children's heads and said the weekly blessing in unison.

They listened somberly as Sam sang "Kiddush" for the wine; Liv indicated that he should go ahead and bless the foreign challah, too—usually her job, but she couldn't bring herself to do it. Hinda brought a nondescript pea soup to the table as a first course, but no one was hungry.

When Liv could no longer ignore the feeling of dread gathering like a storm in her gut, she got up and kissed them all once more. She held Ethan for an extra moment.

"Oh, please don't get up!" she said to the others, but they all went to see her out anyway. She left Sam sagging in the doorway, one arm around each of the boys, and Lottie nestled into their reassuring mass.

She drove back to the hospital with her heart juddering, but when she arrived at Zoey's doorway, all was as she had left it.

"Ah, you're back already?" said Francesca, looking up from the book she was reading.

"Yes, I didn't want to keep you for too long, and …"—she squinted at the indifferent monitors beeping their mysterious codes—"I-I kept thinking that my absence was going to—I don't know—"

"—cause something bad to happen?"

"Yes." Why was she confiding in this near stranger? She couldn't seem to stop. "Is that super weird?"

"Not at all. You'd be amazed at how many times I've heard this from people holding a vigil for a loved one."

"Huh. Yeah. I guess it's not an original thought."

"Maybe not original, but still natural. Only try to be kind to yourself, *per favore*. Okay?"

"Yes, okay. I'll try." Liv couldn't help answering the woman's smile with her own.

"Excellent. *Ciao*, then. Good night."

"Good night, Francesca."

•

By the fifth day, Liv's physical universe had shrunk again to fit the rigid bedside chair, which resembled some medieval dining room furniture designed for a long-extinct body type. She was used to standing all day in her kitchen, moving between counter and cabinets, oven and sink; now, her back and left hip screamed their objections to this unremitting idleness.

And she hated the cafeteria food. Sometimes when her mind wandered, she made a shopping list in her head, her taste buds springing to life at the prospect of all the fresh summer food becoming available: peaches and nectarines; goat cheese from the dairy farm in Derby; kalamata olives and manchego cheese from the little Sephardic vendor; blackberries and currants for making jam; salted baguettes from Judie's Bakery. These were the little luxuries of her life, and she missed them with a dull ache.

Her fingers felt itchy with disuse. But here she had a single task to focus on: She waited. She waited for Zoey to wake up. She waited for Sam to make an appearance. She waited for the insane bursts of frigid air to stop blowing from the vents above her head and waited for her mind to release her from the image of Ethan, roasting in his uniform in the desert sun. When he'd left—was that yesterday morning?—she'd had to bite down hard on her lower lip to stop herself from begging, *Please, oh please, don't go back.* He had hugged her for a long time, as if he was trying to help her hold the words in.

She waited for lunch, though it tasted like straw, and when it was done, she waited for dinner. In the early morning and the late afternoon, she waited to catch the doctors in that elusive five-minute window during their clinical rounds. Her vigilance toward that end took up a surprising amount of time. When Peter Becker or one of the other specialists did put in an appearance, she would rouse herself from her reverie and begin her battery of questions.

"Is there anything new?"

No, they said each day, there was no change.

"Is she getting the right amount of physical therapy?"

Yes, they assured her, Zoey's idle muscles were being kept as limber as possible.

"Could her body be shutting down?"

There was no sign of that; all her organ systems were functioning.

Liv ignored the fugitive look in the doctors' eyes when she caught them. She had to make sure Zoey got what she needed, had to get enough from them to gain a temporary respite from her worst fears. And wasn't she owed at least a modicum of extra attention, given that Sam was their colleague, and she knew all of them personally? Hadn't she spent dozens of hours preparing her best food and pastries to serve them every year at holiday parties? It was her one advantage in this bewildering world where she had taken up residence.

When it came to Zoey's medical care, she couldn't shake the constant feeling she was missing something, and Sam was no help. Liv appreciated the implicit optimism of Francesca's visits: She continued to check on Zoey every day, going through her routine of ringing bells and snapping fingers—"coma stim," she called it—though Zoey never responded. As an added bonus, Francesca brought her frank humor even into this humorless setting.

"I will not ask how you are doing, Olivia. Your hair, it tells me everything."

Liv couldn't help smiling, though the muscles of her face felt strange. "I know, it's hopeless," she said, cringing at her own choice of words. "And please, call me Liv. Most everyone does. Or even Livie, if you like."

"I will try to remember. I know Americans are fond of their nicknames. Call me Fran, if you must, but not Franny, please."

She smiled as she spoke, and Liv couldn't help smiling back again.

"I'll stick to Francesca then. Did … did you have something to tell me?"

"Yes, I do. I hope you will pardon me, Liv, but this is not your coma, you know what I am saying? When did you last take a proper break, have a shower?" She pushed her leggy frame past the array of machines that were Zoey's other constant companions.

Liv assumed the question was rhetorical, but she had to laugh, and was warmed that someone was looking out for her.

"You laugh, but I am not joking."

"Thanks. I guess … it was when you sat with her. I—I don't want to miss anything, you know?"

"But that was days ago! When therapists are here is always a good time for a break. Did you ask Dr. Becker to assign Derek and Emma to Zoey's case?" Francesca asked.

"Yes, I did. Well, Sam—Dr. Sandor—my husband made sure they're on Zoey's team."

Liv never could work out how to refer to Sam when she spoke to the staff.

"Have they come yet today? No? *Madonna mia.* What is this, a cocktail party? They need to be here twice a day doing range of motion, arms and legs. Don't let them tell you otherwise. It is not a waste of time. Zoey will thank you when she wakes up."

"Thanks for the *when* instead of *if*," Liv said.

Francesca nodded. "Please, it is my pleasure. We will see a great deal of each other in the next few months. Count on it."

Tears stung Liv's eyes, because of the woman's kindness, but also because of what these next few months might hold.

Francesca scanned the printouts from the machines as she stroked Zoey's limp hand. "I have a little extra time now. You run home and freshen up."

"Thanks, Francesca. But I don't feel like I can leave her. And I'm always afraid I'll miss my window with Dr. Becker."

"Ah, yes. The doctors, they are invisible—you must wait and pounce, right? Okay. Have the nurses page me after you see him, and if you want, you can shower down the hall in the staff locker room. I'll give you the key. I mean it. You'll feel much better."

When Liv remained silent, Francesca added, "I will stay with her while you're gone, and see if I can piss her off enough to wake her up."

She jerked her thumb in Zoey's direction.

Liv laughed again, then welled up with fresh tears, wishing Francesca might be able to bring about this miracle through sheer audacity.

"Thank you. A shower would be wonderful after I see the doctor."

When Dr. Becker came in on his evening rounds, he, too, examined the strip of printer paper feeding in an endless spool into the EEG machine and out onto the floor, like so much fresh lasagna from Liv's pasta maker. Again, she was struck by the strangeness of the doctor's confidence that in this confetti was encoded the mysterious language of Zoey's future.

"What do you see? Has there been any change at all?" she asked the Brain Trust. When he glanced up, he appeared startled. Francesca must have been right; she must look wild. But she persisted.

"Dr. Becker—Peter—can you give me some idea of how Zoey's *really* doing? Sam is seeing patients now. But I know the lingo, so please, don't hold back."

"Well, I'm afraid there's nothing much new … Her GCS hasn't changed at all since she was brought in …"

GCS. Liv had heard this acronym so many times in the last few days, she couldn't believe she had to search her mind to remember what it stood for—and there was no way she was going to ask him after her boast about "knowing the lingo."

GCS … It was something to do with Scotland …

"Is that a good thing?" she asked while her brain scrabbled around. "I mean, are you seeing ongoing brain activity? What's your best estimate of her prognosis?"

Liv knew she was trying too hard, but she would do almost anything to get Dr. Becker to stay and talk to her a little bit.

"I know it's not easy to hear," he said, "but as I've been saying, we can only wait and see." He paused. "I'm sure Sam has told you, her chances of awakening from the coma will decline over time."

Sam hadn't told her that—he hadn't said much of anything. She tried to keep her face neutral, but she could feel her eye twitching.

As if her mind knew she needed some reassurance, it released the words she had been searching for: Glasgow Coma Scale. That was it! A way of "scoring consciousness" from three to fifteen, Sam had explained. Zoey was a four only because she'd seemed to open her eyes once or twice when her fingernails were pressed.

"And if she does awaken, Liv, there is no doubt now that there will be long-term effects, as I'm sure you're aware. Zoey's PET scan shows diffuse areas of bilateral brain damage. There was a great deal of swelling, though it abated somewhat during the MIH."

Had she been aware? Or had her insistence on optimism at all costs led her to miss this critical information?

"But the extent of her cognitive deficits, and the question of other permanent physical sequelae, is anyone's guess at this point," he went on. "It's still a waiting game. I'm sorry. I wish I had better news."

"I know you do," Liv said, patting his arm. Maybe it was ridiculous for her to comfort the doctor, but she was hoping he would be more forthcoming if she stopped thinking of him as the Brain Trust and let her own humanity show through. After all, he was here to help. "This is hard for everyone. Thanks for taking the time, Peter."

"No trouble at all, Liv. And of course, you should have me paged right away if you see any change," he said as he headed toward the door.

He hadn't told her to stop hoping. She would focus on that. As for his almost casual allusion to "cognitive deficits," nothing was certain, he had said, and Liv felt it was impossible that Zoey would emerge from this catastrophe without the full use of her keen mind. Of all the children, Zoey had been the one with what Sam called *manifest synapses*—a lightning-quick brain that could make and retain connections so fast you could almost hear it crackling as it worked. What was more, she had a gift for recalling obscure details of family history. Their collective stories couldn't vanish now, into the dark places Peter had pointed to in those strangely beautiful pictures of Zoey's brain.

On the evening of the sixth day, when Francesca came for her daily visit, Liv made another quick trip home to satisfy herself that the other children hadn't melted into puddles under her mother's care. She worried over Zev's gauntness and Lottie's whine, but the pull of the ICU was stronger. On the way out, she grabbed some family photos—candids that she'd taken in recent years, trying to capture the essence of each of the kids as she realized how quickly they were growing up. Now they'd have to serve as two-dimensional surrogates on the windowsill in Zoey's tiny room.

In that sterile space, her children's faces glowed as if backlit. Ethan: standing in the doorway of his room, pale like Liv, but with dark, thoughtful, bespectacled eyes and a quirky mouth, as though he had been saying something important. Zev: looking up from his sketchbook, his features like Sam's, with the curls and the olive complexion and the angled jawbone, but with Liv's odd-colored eyes and his expression turned inward. Lottie: blonde curls poking out in every direction and freckles marching across her little nose, the image of Liv as a girl, but with Sam's brown eyes and a good dose of mischief all her own. Zoey, from a few months ago: interrupted mid-note with her cello bow raised, a look of impatience in her luminous eyes but smiling anyway, and photogenic as ever.

The last photo was a picture of all six of them from years ago, when the children were much smaller, and Lottie was a toddler. They were tangled up together and laughing in a big pile under the apple tree in the front yard. Who had taken it? Who had witnessed such a happy moment for her family? She had no idea. Looking at it now, Liv wished they had laughed together more often. But that was the thing about living your life, wasn't it? You could never know which moments were important until they were already past. Liv told herself the photos were for Zoey's sake, but she knew that she was the one who needed to see them every day, as a reminder that she had enjoyed a different sort of existence before. Once she was back in the hospital's hypnotic undertow, it was easy to forget.

DAY 6

It's late afternoon and Zev wakes up from another freaky dream and grabs his sketchbook from under the bed. He rushes to get it all down, the flood of images speeding up his heart as if he's the one running. He finishes the sketch—it's sloppy—and goes to add the date, like putting a period at the end of a sentence, but he has to look it up. Any little task is a welcome distraction from the way, even when he's asleep, his brain is telling him he has to go to East Rock Park to see where it happened. It's been building in him for days. It won't let him go. Now the dream is replaying on a closed loop like a malfunctioning video.

I'm way on top of East Rock, watching her run with Dad. They fly over rocks and fences, she is a machine an engine a bullet and Dad is laughing trying to keep up. When she falls, he doesn't see it he keeps on running and I try to yell to him, but I'm too far away he can't hear me, he can only hear the wind in the trees. Inside Zoey, there is no sound at all.

He sneaks out of the house and crosses toward the park, bracing himself for the pain he felt when he visited Zoey in the hospital. But instead, the breeze picks up and washes him from head to toe in fragrant evening air, bringing childhood memories in place of the dream. As he makes his way toward the running path, he sees Mikayla in the distance. He should be dismayed but his heart jumps in his chest as if he is the one being shocked back to life.

"Hey! What are you doing here?" When he reaches her, his voice is louder than he intended. She looks both startled and spaced out.

"Oh, Zev! I needed to see where it happened. Now that I'm here, though, my brain is flooding with a million memories."

"Same," he says. "Weird."

"That *is* weird. What are you remembering right now?"

Her presence is comforting, and he only hesitates for a moment.

"I'm remembering our baby days when we shared a room, and a bed, even. I guess we were, like, two or three, because we were already talking. Well, mostly she was." He smiles at Mikayla, and she smiles back. She gets it. "And I must've been falling asleep before Zoey and waking up after her. I'd stare at the swirls and knots of our wooden crib and trace the shapes with my finger while she talked to me. She kept talking and talking ... It was like, like my own personal music to fall asleep to."

Mikayla smiles all the way to her river-green eyes. "Oh! I love that!"

"And when I woke up, she'd be talking again, about all the adventures we had together while we were sleeping. Or, at least, that's how I remember it—I don't know if it's actually possible. But she'd tell me that in these dreams, we would fly through the stars, or we'd be swimming through warm water, or running in the softest grass with a million flowers, and I was as brave and fast as she was. I couldn't remember the dreams myself, but I believed her. It was a—a thread that ran between us, so faint, like a shimmer in the air, but so strong that nothing could fray the edges."

Zev is standing in the middle of the park, blinking and looking around as if he's not sure how he got here. He grasps at the memory—baby room with Zoey, old wooden crib, flying through the stars—but it floats away like a dandelion puff on the wind. He's glad he has said it aloud, though he can't believe that many words spilled out of him.

Mikayla puts her hand on his arm, and they watch the wind in the trees. She begins to speak, so softly that he has to lean down to hear her over the breeze and the birds.

"I'm thinking about the first day of kindergarten. English was still so hard for me, and I felt sort of lost after my mom dropped me off, like I might cry any minute. Then you Sandors arrived, and I recognized you from next door. We must've just moved in. You stood in the doorway of the classroom with your mom on one side and Zoey on the other, holding Zoey's hand. Your mom knelt down and looked at your face and said, *You're okay, Zev. You two have each other. And Ethan is two turns of the hall away. Turn left, then right, like he told you when we dropped him off. Okay?* She smiled at you both, her slow, calm smile, and Zoey nodded once in that superconfident way she had, even then. Your mom stood up and walked away, and you didn't cry at all. I could tell you were scared but you could still feel your family around you. Such an amazing family—Zoey and I weren't even friends yet, but I felt better, too."

Zev lets out a giant sigh, and when he inhales, he catches a whiff of chocolate from the French bakery down the street. Out of the corner of his eye, he sees the blinking sign from the video store that used to be Magda's Grocery.

"Want to hear another one?"

"Yes, please," Mikayla says. Without talking about it, they start walking.

"When we were eight years old, Mom let us walk to Magda's store alone for the first time. Remember that place?"

"Of course! I was so sad when it closed."

"Me too. That day, we were going to buy bread and blackberry jam. Who knows why I remember that. Mom was holding Lottie in one arm—oh man, she was tiny!—and she handed me the money. I remember how proud I felt, stuffing it in my pocket. As we walked, Zoey was waving her hands in the air and talking about the comic book we were making. *The Ball of Fire.* Did she ever tell you about it?"

Mikayla laughs. "I think what you mean is, did she ever shut up about it? You guys didn't talk about anything else for a whole summer!"

"Yeah, well, I gotta say, it was pretty cool," Zev says, trying not to sound defensive.

"It was a story about your twin powers, right? And a ball of fire you conjured with your minds, that could stop all the bad guys in the streets, to keep the world safe forever."

"Jeez. I can't believe you remember all that!"

"How could I ever forget?"

"You know, I—I appreciate that," he says, the heat of his blush starting. "It helps to know you're holding this stuff in your mind, too." He's silent for a minute, and all the things they aren't saying about Zoey fill the space between them.

"So, on that day, when we walked to Magda's for the first time," he goes on, "I remember how we got to the corner and I held her hand while we waited for the flashing little man to turn white so we could cross, and how I smiled at her, and she smiled back, and it was good, even though I knew we were happy for different reasons: I loved going to Magda's because of that treat jar. And Zoey loved doing things on her own—but I could never get her to try Magda's treats. And then the little man flashed on the walk sign, and we crossed over."

Zev stops, realizing they've come to the part of the running path where the accident happened, in the shadow of the craggy triangle that is East Rock. They both stand still.

Is this where she fell? Did she know what was happening?

Mikayla whispers, "Do you think it hurt, or was it instant blackout?" Her voice is trembling.

Zev is startled at how in sync they are. He has always assumed he could only have that feeling with Zoey. But if he speaks now, he'll lose it. He looks up at the giant oaks and sees the sunlight through the leaves, and behind them the sky, so blue today that he can almost reach out and grab a handful. They stand there together, and it's like they're praying to the trees.

"You know what this reminds me of?" says Mikayla in a hushed voice, still looking up at the towering leaves.

"What?" he whispers.

"How we used to come here so Zoey could climb higher than the apple tree in your backyard. Remember? And that one time, when she picked the biggest oak she could find and started climbing. She moved so fast. But I was staring up at the leaves and noticing how the sunlight and shadows made a hundred shades of green, how I would need red and brown and yellow and blue to paint all of those greens."

Zev thinks, *Crazy. That's the kind of thing I think about.* But he still can't say a word.

"And Zoey called, *Come on, you guys, don't leave me up here alone!* I looked up, up, up and saw how the sun in the clear blue sky made the light bounce off everything. And a minute later, her voice was so small when she said, *I think I'm stuck.* And we could only see the bottoms of her feet. And you said, *No you're not, Zo. Listen, I'll tell you how to get down.* You walked all around the tree and told her how the fat branches made a winding path from the bottom to the top, how her shoes would stick to the elephant hide of the bark. And in no time, you talked her down from there. Remember?"

Zev walks the circumference of the giant oak as he once did, his eyes on the sun-painted leaves as he tries to find this memory. But he doesn't remember it that way.

"Are you sure she wasn't the one rescuing me?" He's still looking up, until he collides with Mikayla, jarring him out of his reverie. Sound of silver bangles. Honeysuckle scent.

"Hey, watch where you're going, Sandor!" she says with a laugh.

"Oh, man! Are you, like—did I crush any parts?" He purples at his idiotic words.

"Nope." She looks down at her small self, then way up into his face, shading her eyes from the sun. "All my parts are good. Though my neck is getting a crick. You'd better stop growing soon, Zev, or we're going to need to have all our future conversations sitting down."

"I know," he says, glancing down at his clumsy-giant self. "It's getting sort of ridiculous."

Mikayla is tiny as a hummingbird. What does Mom call that? *Petite.* She's petite, unlike the women in his family, who are tall and broad-shouldered and solid.

"That's okay. You can be the early warning system for us ordinary humans down here. And—no, Zev, you were the one doing the rescuing. I promise," she says.

Has he always had the urge to rescue people? He was so impatient to get his lifeguarding certification this summer, now that he was finally old enough. But he's distracted by the dozens of silver bracelets on Mikayla's wrists. Zev follows their motion as she tucks her short black hair behind her seashell ears, a ducking, tentative movement she repeats all the time, he now realizes. Is it possible that she's shy, too?

He takes in those deep green eyes, the heart-shaped face, the smooth skin that looks flushed but is actually dusted all over with freckles.

I need to paint that face. Zev realizes he's staring at her, his palms sweating.

Mikayla is staring back at him and scrunching up her forehead.

"Your eyes are exactly like hers, you know?" Her river eyes overflow with tears. "The ICU was so freaky—she didn't even look like herself."

His hand twitches to wipe her tears away, but he just stands there like a giraffe. He nods in what he hopes is a sympathetic way, then realizes what she has said.

"Wait. You were *there*?"

She nods. "I was practically camping outside the door the first couple of days. Every day I'd cry until my mom brought me, and I'd beg your mom to let me in. I guess I wore her down," she says, smiling a little before the tears take over again. "Only I didn't expect—she looks so *small*."

Zev nods. "I know. It's the weirdest thing, right? How fast that happened."

Now it's Mikayla who's startled. "But—your mom said you haven't been in."

Zev finds that he has no wish to lie to her. "That's what she thinks. I went the day after it happened. Alone. It was … awful. I never told them. My mom might not have minded, but my dad is kind of—you know."

She nods a few times. "Yeah. He's like—my mom calls him *sterejhevoi*, the watchdog."

"Exactly."

It's strange to think of Mikayla's family talking about Dad's overprotectiveness. But it's also great. He doesn't have to explain anything to her. She knows him, knows everything about Zoey. She's known them all for so long.

Zoey has always been their family historian, the memory keeper. But while she's sleeping, maybe Mikayla can help him keep things from slipping away.

"I'm going back tomorrow," she says. Her face is alight with something like hope.

Zev nods, and without another word, they head toward home. He can't account for it, but he feels better, too. He still can't find the thread to Zoey, but it's as if the light from Mikayla's face has gotten inside him. Or maybe it's the light from the sky. Either way, he takes it as a sign that somewhere in him is the strength to visit that cold, colorless room again. He will go back and find the end of the thread and drag Zoey back with him from wherever she lies dreaming.

EXCERPT FROM

THE MEMORY BOOK OF ZOEY SANDOR

I am in the stars in the inky black sky and cold is all around me but my house is a speck far below and I hear Mommy's voice so faint she calls Come home it's getting late. I try to float down but I can't move and there is a whooshing sound coming from my body it is a big hole where my heart was and cold air rushes through the hole. I see the stars on the other side of me and I am afraid I will disappear and I look for help and there is Zev floating in the distance and I call Look I have a hole in me. But now I see he has a hole where his heart was too and I can see stars on the other side of him and they are leaking out of us both and Zev floats sideways to get near me. We are afraid but his eyes get wide and he knows what to do and he shows me the way. Our hands reach across to cover the empty places and stop the stars from leaking out into the sky. See he says we have to stay together I can fix yours and you can fix mine and he is right the whooshing sound ends and it is quiet and now we can go home.

(Transcribed by Francesca Garibaldi, SLP)

DAY 6, CONTINUED

In Liv's absence, Sam endeavored to keep the other parts of their life limping along. He wandered the aisles of the grocery store placing random items in a cart to supplement the casseroles that kept materializing on their kitchen counters, courtesy of the synagogue ladies; he maintained a cautious peace with Hinda at breakfast and dinner, tried to ensure Zev ate something every day, tucked a ginger ale into Lottie's lunch box for the long ride home on the camp bus. Without Liv at home, everything came down to food.

He saw patients every day, telling himself he was saving his days off for when Zoey woke up. He folded her into a tiny square of paper he carried around in his pocket.

But every evening, the quiet dinner table brought a fresh rush of guilt: What had he done for Zoey today? He always ended up making the twelve-minute drive back to the hospital; he had to see her chart, to look for any signs the rest of her team might have missed. Every night, Liv looked on with hope in her face, and every night Sam came away empty.

On the evening of the sixth day, Sam dragged his feet down the corridor of the Critical Care Unit. He was surprised and relieved to find Liv gone from Zoey's room; at least she wouldn't have to witness another failure.

Maybe because Liv wasn't there to anchor him, or because he had slept so little in the last week, Sam—standing at the foot of Zoey's bed—somehow forgot that the medical chart he was holding was about his child. He flipped through the thick pile of test results and leapfrogged over phrases like *severe brain hemorrhage* and *cognitive deficits*. He was looking for something solid on which to pin future rehabilitation plans, as was his custom with any new patient. Over the years, he had developed a sharp instinct for predicting the chances of meaningful recovery, though from time to time he was pleased to be proven wrong by a "miracle patient" who awoke from a long coma to stage a comeback. Those were the patients who kept him on his toes. Could this one be a miracle patient? After almost a week of coma, the prognosis was worsening, and he rated her chances of full recovery as falling somewhere in the fractions of a percentage point.

This familiar mental calculus took place in a matter of seconds. When Sam's mind cleared and it came back to him that he was viewing his own daughter's vital information, he flung the chart away, his nerve endings on fire at the thought of Zoey's battered heart and brain. He crumpled into a chair and curled his arms around himself to ward off the onslaught, but he was breathless with pain, and his chest became tight, as if he, too, were having a heart attack. Deep down, he knew he was manifesting symptoms of panic. But he was afraid to move.

What if Zoey never woke up? What if he had to tell Zev and the others she wasn't coming back? What if she died?

But what if she lived? What if her body remained, while her mind was submerged in a swamp of mangled tissue? This possibility left him even more panicked. His breath came in short, sharp gasps and his vision grew dim.

He was both grateful and embarrassed that Rabbi Friedman came into the room then.

"Sam! Are you okay? How can I help?"

The rabbi sat down next to him and covered Sam's cold, sweaty hands with his warm, dry ones. "Are you ill, Semeleh?"

Sam shook his head. "I … think …" he said, panting between words, "… I'm having … a panic attack."

"Ah. Your old enemy. Good thing I brought a sandwich with me today," he said, pulling a now-empty paper bag out of his ancient briefcase. "Come on, Sam. You know what to do. Breathe. In and out. In and out," he said, holding the bag over Sam's nose and mouth, waiting for it to inflate.

Gradually, Sam's body's inexplicable resilience asserted itself. His breathing became more measured, the nausea passed, and the spasm of pain loosened its grip. He unfolded himself and sat up.

"Good that we had that old routine down pat, right, my boy?" said Rabbi Friedman with a rueful smile.

Sam nodded and squeezed his hand. "Thanks, Rabbi. Good you came in when you did. I wouldn't have wanted anyone else to find me like that."

"Oh, Sam. What an impossibly difficult situation this must be for you."

"The worst," said Sam. "Well, maybe the second worst." He smiled shakily.

"Yes. You're no stranger to sorrow—nor were your parents, along with so many others in our community …" He grasped Sam's arm with his warm, leathery hand. "But I want to remind you, as I did back then, that there is nothing you did to bring this on and nothing you can do to reverse it. And that despite everything your parents endured in their lifetime, they were able to hold onto their faith. I hope you can derive some comfort and hope from yours."

As the only child of Holocaust survivors, Sam had been coddled and protected in his growing years, living proof to his parents that hope abides. They had never shared with him the harrowing details of their time at Auschwitz, except to say that their love for each other had sustained them. When they died together in that pointless crash, the irrevocability of it had derailed him. He had turned to Rabbi Friedman for help, knowing his parents had trusted the man. Maybe he possessed some secret that would help Sam understand. The rabbi was kind and infinitely patient with seventeen-year-old Sam but maintained that there was no secret.

"Well, in this case, I'm not sure it's true that I have no control," said Sam. "There might actually be something I can—and should—do here. But you're right. This"—he waved a hand in Zoey's direction but kept his eyes averted—"is bringing up a lot of old fears."

"I hope you're turning to your colleagues and your family as much as possible for support. As you well know, a crisis such as this is not a good time to make major decisions."

"But I don't regret the decisions I made back then!" Sam said hotly. "It was the right thing! How could I have spent my days making pretty sounds on the piano, when the last sound my parents heard was the screech of metal and shattering glass? I honored their wishes by keeping my music scholarship at Yale—and I honor their memory by spending my life rehabilitating accident victims."

"And by making such a beautiful family. Your parents would be so proud of you."

"I don't know. My choice of career feels like a cruel joke now."

"You can choose to see it that way, Sam," the rabbi said. "But it is also a *gift* that you are able to understand and respond to this terrible accident in a way that most parents could not."

In the hospital ward where he had once been king, Sam began to cry. "How can you say that? It's not a gift! No more than it felt like a gift to inherit their house," he sobbed.

"*Shah*, Semeleh. I know. It's more than anyone should have to bear. But I am here for you. Liv is here, and the children. We will get through this together."

The rabbi stayed until Sam stopped crying, then hugged him and wished him good night. Sam was grateful that Liv had not returned in the interim. As he bent to retrieve his daughter's ever-growing medical file from the floor, he understood that the clinical detachment for which he had berated himself would be his best weapon, the white coat his shield. As a father he might be helpless, but as an expert in traumatic brain injury, he had a crucial role here: With the help of his team, he could bring Zoey back. She just had to wake up first.

When Liv came into the room, she crouched down in front of his chair and put her hand on his wet cheek. He hadn't even realized he was crying again. She embraced him, burying her head in his shoulder.

"She'll come out of this. I know it in my bones, Sam." Her muffled voice was hoarse but strong. "She's a fighter, our Zoey. She has been since the day she was born."

Sam nodded into her hair. "True. She is a fighter. Zoey is … fierce." He lifted his head to look at Liv. "She's a … a force of nature."

"Exactly." Liv sat down in the chair next to Sam, never letting go of his hand. She rubbed the knuckle of his right index finger, a tiny massage she had been giving him since medical school, in hopes of defusing his wired body. Even now, it worked its magic on him.

Together they looked at Zoey, lying so still, already a wisp of her old effervescent self.

"Why has she always been your favorite?"

Sam was surprised to hear her say it out loud. The idea of "favorites" went against their parenting philosophy. But he couldn't deny it.

"Oh God, Livie, I don't know. She's different from the other kids. She was fun to watch, even when she was little. I didn't worry about her the same way because she was always ready for the next challenge. I'm somehow always lighter when she's around."

Liv squeezed Sam's hand and continued to stare at Zoey as if trying to calculate something. She could never see Zoey quite the way he did. Not that she couldn't recognize their daughter's gifts, but she thought Zoey was a little too sure of herself, too ready to impose her agenda on others. Liv even speculated that this intransigence might point to an underlying insecurity. But Sam said Liv was projecting. They would argue about it from time to time: Liv would say Sam failed to discipline Zoey for behavior he would never tolerate from the other children, and Sam would say Zoey already had an exceptional grasp of her actions and their consequences.

"Maybe it's because I was an only child," he said now.

"How so?"

"Well, I don't *try* to single her out, but it's the parenting model I know. Maybe some part of me is trying to recreate my family of origin, my parents' single-minded devotion."

She said nothing, but he caught her startled glance.

"Oh, come on, Liv. I adore *all* the kids, you know I do."

"I do, but—"

"It's just, Zoey has … the ideal combination of our strengths, with none of the weaknesses. She's so bright—yes, of course, they all are!—but she doesn't have my worry gene or your dreaminess. She could take on anything."

"You make her sound superhuman. That's a lot of pressure to put on a kid."

Sam knew she was right. Had Zoey resented his high expectations? If so, she'd never said so. If anything, she seemed to relish them. But Sam knew what it was to shoulder the burden of your parents' hopes.

"It reminds me of the last conversation I had with Papa before he died," he said.

"What conversation? You always said you couldn't remember anything from the weeks around their accident."

Sam was startled. Liv was right—these memories were fresh, unprecedented. It was as if the new terror had reversed the amnesia of the old.

"Well, I never could before. But now I can. Isn't that strange?"

She nodded and took his hand again.

"I was getting ready for my Yale audition," Sam said, his eyes fixed on the wall as the memory tumbled out. "There was one piano scholarship a year, and as far as I knew, it had never been given to a local boy. But my parents were sure I could get it. The day before, Papa took me aside and put his arm around my shoulders. He said, *Semeleh, you are a lucky child. Somehow, God has seen fit to grace you with your mother's brains and good looks, and my mulishness and grit. This and your great talent will take you far, much further than we could go.*

"You see?" he said, turning to Liv. "My parents' faith in me never wavered. I wish I could've shown that kind of faith to all of our kids—but instead I've been operating under some kind of old-world, evil-eye superstition. As if by thinking of them with humility, I could shield them from harm. Only Zoey shone so bright, it was like she created her own shield. Like her gifts were enough to propel her straight out of harm's way. Oh God, the irony of it!"

"Sam, you can't think that way—"

"I know, but how can I not?"

Was he saying Zoey's gifts should have protected her from what happened? Or that those gifts were forever lost to her now? He didn't know anymore. But the longer she lay there, the more certain he was that history was repeating itself in this twisted way. His life would once again be engulfed by sorrow.

Liv made her inevitable bid for optimism. "But we don't know anything, do we, until she wakes up? We have to keep hoping, don't we?"

Sam waved his hands as if to dispel his gloom. "Of course you're right, Livie. I just can't stop thinking about Mama and Papa. It's hard not to jump to conclusions. Ignore me, okay?"

"Okay, love." Liv leaned her head on his shoulder with a sigh.

No matter what he said, Sam knew Zoey's shining future was receding into the distance. And another thing: Since her injury, he'd become aware of a deep hypocrisy within himself. It was all very well to apply ideas of compromise and accommodation to his patients and their families, yet he couldn't accept them when it came to Zoey's life. He knew these were loathsome thoughts. But still, there was no paradigm shift Sam was willing to apply to his own daughter.

Was he being punished for his excessive pride? He had always been sure he didn't figure into the cosmic equation, but now guilt chased him down like an animal. He scrabbled through his mind for some telltale sign he had missed but found only this inescapable truth: He could not make Zoey whole again. He tried to stop himself from reaching his unthinkable conclusion, but it was all he could do not to say it out loud:

She'd be better off dead.

EXCERPT FROM

THE MEMORY BOOK OF ZOEY SANDOR

It is beyond cold here like waiting at the bus stop in deep winter when the air creaks and groans. I am in an igloo the walls round and smooth and gleaming white I sit on the floor and reach my arms out to touch the sides I start to shiver there is ice in my hair and snow falling all around me I am a snow angel. The world goes quiet. I am drowsy. I lie down and spread my wings and the snow is a blanket I can wrap around myself until I am warm. I sleep.

(Transcribed by Francesca Garibaldi, SLP)

DAY 7

As time slipped by—the sixth day, the seventh day, a bizarre reversal of the story of creation—it began to dawn on Liv that her optimism might be irrelevant. She'd never imagined things would continue for so long. Since the end of the MIH, she had been expecting Zoey to awaken and resume her life. But all of Liv's hopeful anticipation could not change the fact that Zoey's GCS hadn't progressed past four.

The answer to the terrible question of Zoey's future was not within her. So, where was it?

Her eyes followed the wavy lines on the screens of the critical care monitors as their mysterious messages moved from right to left—like reading Hebrew, she realized. She was taken with the idea that these codes somehow mimicked the holy language of her ancestors. Maybe they did know the secrets of the universe.

She remembered Zoey at eleven years old, preparing diligently for her bat mitzvah by chanting her biblical portion over and over from an enormous book. Months later, when she had learned it by heart and was allowed to practice it straight from the Torah scrolls at the synagogue, she stood poised with the silver pointer in her hand and looked up at Liv and Sam with shining eyes.

"It's so *holy*, isn't it? Look how perfect the letters are!" she'd whispered.

Sam had nodded solemnly. "It's true. A scribe forms every letter by hand, and if he makes a mistake, he has to start the page over."

Zoey's eyes filled with tears. "But that means I have to *read* it perfectly, too. I can't mess up even once."

"No, sweetie. That's not what it means," Liv said, laying a hand on top of Zoey's. "Scribes spend years learning their craft, but you're only at the beginning! And you know, nobody's *perfect*. Everyone makes mistakes, even grown-ups. Dad and I make *lots* of mistakes."

Zoey pulled her hand out from under Liv's and looked from her to Sam and back again, her lion eyes swimming. "But Mom! If you're not perfect, how are you supposed to teach *me* to be perfect?"

Liv smiled now at the memory. Zoey's exacting standards were not such a surprise, she supposed, given Sam's own perfectionism, but they were startlingly entrenched in one so young.

She turned back to reading aloud from *Little Women*, cherishing the familiar words of Zoey's favorite book. She could see why her daughter identified with the character of Jo March: They were both idealistic, headstrong young women, with equal parts creativity and native intelligence. Liv realized that she was already forgetting the less appealing aspects of Zoey's personality, as if she were dead and never to be thought ill of again. She tried to enumerate her daughter's flaws—she was pushy and sure of herself, a perfectionist yet unreceptive to criticism—but it seemed an unconscionable exercise in the present circumstances, and she went back to reading.

She didn't falter until the part in chapter 13, where Jo hopes she and her sisters will one day realize their childhood dreams: *If we are all alive ten years hence, let's meet, and see how many of us have got our wishes, or how much nearer we are then than now.*

Zoey had loved the idea that, like the March girls, the Sandor children might gather in the future to share their tales of fulfillment. She had never doubted that all their dreams would be realized: Ethan would save many lives on the battlefield and go on to discover a cure for cancer; Zev would become a cross between Jackson Pollock, Bill Watterson, and Cormac McCarthy—a reclusive genius of written and rendered tales; Lottie would be a famous explorer and discover a new, unspoiled part of the world. As for herself, Zoey wasn't sure yet which path she wanted to travel down. Olympic athlete? Avant-garde cellist? World leader? The future was a perfect bright sphere she cradled in her arms.

Liv read on with clenched fists, as though she could keep the promise of Zoey's future safe in her hands. When she reached the chapter about the death of one of the sisters, Beth, she decided to skip over it altogether, even as she told herself the story had no relevance for her own life. Zoey's siblings would never have to gather and say goodbye to her; Liv would never have to be as strong as Marmee in facing the loss of her daughter; she would *not* have to stand bravely over Zoey's grave. She thumbed past the pages, still certain that there would be some primitive signal in her own body if Zoey were lost to her forever.

To her surprise, the ICU nurses took great pains to support Liv's bid for optimism, especially Clementine, the tall Trinidadian woman with the long gray braids who produced a stream of cheerful banter whenever she attended Zoey.

"Hmmm, hmmm, look at those quads. You must be some sorta runner, Miss Zoey," she said while doing her sponge bath. And while rubbing ointment into Zoey's dry, cracked lips: "You don't strike me as the heavy makeup sort, so I'm gonna stick to these neutral colors till you wake up and tell me different," she said.

Now Clementine found Liv staring into space, flexing her fists as the volume of *Little Women* rested on the corner of Zoey's bed. Clementine jutted her chin in Zoey's direction. "Go on! She can hear you, Mama," she said. "Believe it." She picked up the book and placed it back into Liv's hands.

How long could Liv keep up reading to the shell of Zoey's body while the spirit seemed to be leaking away? But the nurse's words were soothing, and Liv read on for a long time after that, clenching and unclenching her fists. She only stopped because she was distracted by a movement in her peripheral vision; she raised her head in time to see Zoey's left hand open and close in startling imitation of her own.

Liv jumped up and stood over her bed. "Zoey! Do that again!"

Zoey was motionless, and Liv rubbed her eyes. Was she hallucinating? But no, she was certain of what she'd seen. She pressed the Call button, and Clementine took Zoey's vital signs and had Dr. Becker and Sam paged. Liv paced the floor and eyed Zoey, who lay there, hands resting on the covers, breathing evenly while the machines continued their techno-symphony.

Sam came rushing from his clinic, his eyes darting this way and that. But when Liv explained why she'd had him paged, he slumped against the doorway like a deflated life raft.

"Honey. It could've been … anything. A spasm, a change of light." His voice was dull.

"But she opened and closed her hand!" Liv said. "I was reading and trying to uncramp my own hands. It was like she was imitating me or letting me know she was listening! I saw her. Stay with me and watch. I know she'll do it again."

Zoey didn't do it again. For an interminable stretch, Sam and Liv kept watch over her unchanging form, and all the while, Liv had the uneasy sense that Sam was humoring her.

"Well, what do you think?" she asked for the third time.

"I think it was a reflex," he said in a monotone. Liv's eyes filled with tears, and he added, "But let's hear from Peter. Can you page me as soon as he arrives?"

Sam looked desperate to leave. What was keeping Dr. Becker? Liv was outraged that he wasn't making Zoey his top priority. But it was a good thing that Sam went back to seeing patients, because more than two hours passed before the neurosurgeon appeared.

"So sorry. I was tied up with a complex surgery."

Liv's outrage dissolved as she envisioned him slicing into a brain even more wounded than Zoey's. What difference did it make anyway? She hadn't shown any further signs of waking up, and Liv was beginning to feel embarrassed. She sighed and paged Sam anyway.

"Now, tell me what happened," said Dr. Becker, listening while he went through what he called his "neuroroutine," a pantomime she had seen repeated so many times over the past week that she was sure she could perform it herself: He scraped at Zoey's feet with the back of his pen to look for reflex responses, shone his light into her face to see if she would open her eyes, peeled back her eyelids and shone it again, pressed her fingernails, lifted her arm, let it drop back onto the bed, spoke her name, and waited for any change in her level of alertness.

Sam returned in the middle of the exam and when Peter was done, he turned to them both with a small shake of his head. "I'm not suggesting you didn't see her move, Liv. I'm just not seeing anything now. Likely it was a spontaneous movement, not intentional. Even so, I'm upgrading her GCS to a five. Call it an aspirational adjustment. Sam, anything you want to add?"

Liv knew Peter's question was nothing more than a half-hearted show of respect for his colleague. What was there for Sam to add? He shook his head, his lips compressed. She watched his fingers curl and uncurl at the end of his long arms.

Today's Anatomy Lesson: The Human Fist in Open and Closed Position.

"Okay, then. We can agree she's not showing any signs of rousing right now. But sometimes these little events are precursors. Let's see what tomorrow brings, okay?"

Liv nodded, fighting to maintain her composure. She felt humiliated and didn't trust herself to speak. She was afraid she would start to cry before Peter left the room. And she was so confused. Should she despair that Zoey's GCS was still only a five, or should she rejoice that her status had been upgraded? She felt eroded, friable, and she reached for Sam's hand. But he was radiating a force field of mute anguish, and before long, Liv was begging him to go home to check on Lottie and Zev. She stayed where she was, still expecting to see Zoey move her hand again. She would hold on to what Dr. Becker had said: It was a precursor.

Precursor. She repeated the word to herself. It had a hopeful ring.

Rabbi Friedman looked in every other day. She was surprised at how glad she was to see him in this state of mind. She had known him for decades, but it was Sam who enjoyed a close relationship with the man. Liv liked him well enough, though she never quite knew what to say to him. She was always afraid her agnosticism would show, even if she managed the basic traditions at home for Sam's sake. She'd known when she married him that those things were important to him—the kosher kitchen, the Friday night candles and dinner, the holiday celebrations—and over time, she had learned to value the historical continuity they represented, to appreciate the rhythm they lent to her weeks and years, and the community that showed up for every occasion of joy and grief. But she had never been able to override the secular influences of her own upbringing.

A week ago, the rabbi had asked for Zoey's Hebrew name so the congregation could mention her in their prayers. "The whole community will pray for her," he promised, and his air of quiet purpose was comforting.

"*Zahava Sarah*," Liv answered, remembering Sam's insistence on Hebrew names for all the children, inexplicably superstitious in his belief that these names were somehow linked to their fortunes. *Zahava* meant *gold*—after Sam's mother, known to everyone as Goldie—and *Sarah*, the name of the first Jewish matriarch, meant *princess*. Sam wanted to leave no doubt that he treasured his daughter, as well as his sons. As it turned out, Zoey's sense of her own agency was as much a part of her DNA as her dark beauty.

Rabbi Friedman gave Liv the same reassurances day after day: "We are praying. Her name is on our lips."

Now she felt bound to ask him: "Is it okay if I don't believe in a divine being to whom prayers on Zoey's behalf will have any impact?"

The rabbi responded with a smile and his usual equanimity. "An event such as this could undermine the faith of even the staunchest believer. You are doing what God requires of you—standing by your child in her hour of need, holding your family together, and responding to the advice of the experts. Let *us* support you with *our* faith. We will continue to pray for Zoey, and you continue to be the wonderful mother we all know you are."

His kindness touched her, and she was relieved to leave the work of "having faith" to Sam and the rabbi and the community. Her own optimism, she knew, was a knee-jerk response to any form of adversity, one that Liv had cultivated while growing up in her mother's house. Shula called it her Grim Gratitude, but it served its purpose of bringing light where Liv needed it.

It was near midnight when Sam appeared in the room with Zev standing beside him. Liv rubbed her eyes and looked from Sam to Zev and back again, wondering for the second time that day if she was imagining things.

"What's going on, guys?" she asked hoarsely.

"Well, Zev made a pretty good argument for coming, now that Mikayla's been here." Sam paused. "We weren't sleeping anyway—and it's not as if it'll bother Zoey."

He might have given her a little warning. And did he have to say that in front of Zev? Liv looked at her son's face to see if Sam's comment had upset him, but Zev was in a sort of trance. He moved as close to the bed as the paraphernalia of Zoey's coma would allow but said nothing for several minutes. When he began to sway, Liv put her hand out to steady him. But he shook his head, and she stepped back. From the way his eyes darted between Zoey and the machines, he appeared to be making some sort of mental calculation.

"You can touch her if you want," Liv said.

"But wash your hands first, son," Sam said—unnecessarily, Liv thought.

"No, that's okay," said Zev in a small voice. He leaned over and whispered something into Zoey's ear and appeared to be waiting for a response. He whispered again. It sounded urgent; Liv could hear the sibilants but couldn't begin to guess their contents. He straightened up and held himself still. No one breathed a word.

"Can you take me home now?" Zev said, his voice as dull as coal.

Liv's throat was swollen with useless words of comfort. Would it help to tell him what Clementine said—that Zoey could hear them? But it would sound hollow, she knew, and Zev didn't appreciate platitudes. She settled for reaching up and resting her hand on his shoulder as he turned to leave. He paused for the briefest of seconds under her touch before continuing out of the room, a robot. There was nothing to say.

Defeated and sad, Liv lay down on her cot and fell deeply asleep. Dawn came quickly to the stuffy space, and she was certain she was having another bad dream: Someone was moaning in pain, and she was powerless to help. The awful sound filled her head, and she struggled to wake up so she could escape it. But when she opened her eyes, the moaning got worse.

"Zoey!" she shouted, stumbling out of bed, still not certain she was awake herself. Zoey moaned again, louder this time, and Liv grabbed her hand and squeezed.

"Honey, it's okay. I'm here, you're safe," she said. With her free hand, she pressed the Call button, and watched, transfixed, as Zoey began to move her head back and forth. The monitors above her bed flashed all at once: Numbers changed; lines became spikier, the beeping urgent now, as if the machines themselves were saying: *What is happening here?* Liv grew lightheaded and had to remind herself to keep breathing.

She let go of Zoey's hand to page Sam. This was no false alarm. She felt a frisson of triumph: *See? I wasn't imagining things. It* was *a precursor.*

Zoey progressed from moaning to a sort of hoarse croaking, but she couldn't speak around her breathing tube, which she scrabbled at with her free hand.

"Leave that, sweetie. Let the nurses—"

Zoey flailed her arms and legs and Liv took a step back, startled by this show of strength. Clementine rushed in and tried to check her vital signs but couldn't navigate around her thrashing. Zoey banged her hand against the railing and soon got tangled in the sheets, which moments ago had lain smooth and cool over her inert limbs.

"Be calm, child, we've got you," said Clementine, but Zoey didn't respond to the nurse's firm touch or her voice. She somehow managed to add an extra layer of tape on Zoey's IV sites, but Zoey showed no sign of calming down.

Liv took another step back, dumbfounded by Zoey's battering furor. The initial thrill of realizing she was conscious and able to move her limbs was soon replaced by worry that she would hurt herself.

Sam barreled into the room but stopped short at the foot of Zoey's bed. Liv grabbed his arm. He didn't move, and when he opened his mouth, he uttered an animal noise deep in the back of his throat. A flash of dread silvered Liv's blood.

The moment passed, and Sam moved forward, speaking authoritatively to the nurse, asking the right questions, looking at the monitors with comprehension. He addressed Zoey in the bedside voice he reserved for his patients.

"Zoey, don't try to talk. You have a tube in your throat. We'll take it out soon, but right now, can you open your eyes for me?"

Liv exhaled a sigh of relief. Dr. Sandor was back. Sam held Zoey's wrist for as long he could to take her pulse, and tried to quiet her kicking by laying his hands over her shrunken legs.

"Zoey! Can you open your eyes?" Sam said again, but she screwed up her face and squeezed her eyes shut even tighter, making harsh croaking noises as she continued bucking. Her hand started to swell from being slammed against the wall and she was developing a red welt on her head from the bed rail. Liv and Sam's communication dropped to sporadic whispers, as if they could stop her noise with a counterweight of stillness.

"Shhh, Zoey. Honey. It's okay. We're here," Liv said, moving to the other side of the bed to mirror Sam's gentle restraint. "Will this stop her from hurting herself?" she asked Sam futilely. They were no match for Zoey, who continued to thrash.

Dr. Becker arrived and went through all the steps of his neuropantomime that Zoey's agitation would allow. He turned to them with an expression Liv couldn't read.

"Well, she's awake, and that's good news. We'll extubate her after we get her quieted down," he said, signaling Clementine, who departed to gather the materials she would need to take the breathing tube out.

"Her eyes are tracking, and I see no paralysis of the extremities, though she's heavily favoring her right side, and I saw in the chart she's left-handed, so we'll have to watch that."

Sam and Liv both nodded, though Liv had no idea what half of it meant.

"I am upgrading her GCS to an eleven, also good news. I'm glad for you both."

He gave them a grim smile, a nod to the primacy of the endless Glasgow Coma Scale.

"The bad news is, it looks like a rough awakening, and she's a little too agitated for my money. You know the drill, Sam. We need to tranquilize her until she's ready to make an easier reentry. We'll use IV Valium for the next twelve hours, and see where we're at. Have me paged if anything changes."

He was already headed for the door. Liv was stunned by his summary dismissal.

"Is that *it*? Are you *kidding* me?"

Sam's head swiveled around at the furor in her voice, and Dr. Becker, too, threw a startled look over his shoulder, but he didn't break his stride. Sam stepped out the door with him and Liv was left alone with Zoey and Clementine, her adrenaline surging. The nurse gave her a sympathetic glance but remained silent.

Sam returned, unfazed.

"Livie, you need to understand, Valium is standard in situations like this. TBI patients often wake up agitated, and we need to keep her quiet."

"What *situations like this*?" Liv knew she was being bizarrely loud, but she couldn't stop herself. "Sam! This is Zoey! And she's been nothing *but* quiet for a week!"

"I know, but it won't help if she throws herself off the bed or gives herself a black eye on top of everything else. We want to keep her calm, let her adjust to consciousness gradually." Sam spoke in the even tones he reserved for his patients' families. "It's a positive sign that she's vocalizing and moving around. We don't want to have to put her in restraints. It can be pretty traumatizing."

Well, Liv had wanted Sam the doctor, and she had got him. The adrenaline left her like air from a slashed tire, and she collapsed back into her medieval chair.

Clementine was watching the whole exchange in complete stillness, holding the syringe that would rescue Zoey from her tortured return to consciousness, waiting for a sign from them. Sam nodded, and Clemetine pushed the plunger into the IV. In less time than it took Liv to draw a full breath, Zoey's frenzy evaporated, and she sank back into the world of her dreams.

EXCERPT FROM THE MEMORY BOOK OF ZOEY SANDOR

We are high above the big city there are towers everywhere like building blocks and way down below us in the street there are bad guys and bad choices and bad luck and we can stop them with our powers we can make it all go away. We look out the window and press our foreheads together and we are one person we have a supermind we are magic. You say let's start like smoke and I say okay and we leak out the window and take off we go faster and faster till we turn into the Ball of Fire red and hot as strong as our minds. Fire is pure and fire can burn away everything we don't want and it is all us we have the power we can vanish the bad guys and the bad choices and all the bad luck and the world will be safe.

(Transcribed by Francesca Garibaldi, SLP)

DAY 10

It's after midnight, and Mom is sleeping at home for the second night in a row. This should make it easier for Zev to sleep, but it doesn't. His freaky Zoey dreams are always there, and it's getting so he can't quite remember what's real. So, he puts off sleep for as long as he can. He's on his way upstairs with one of Mom's Mexican hot chocolate brownies and a glass of milk when he overhears her and Dad talking in the library:

"... and the harder we hit her symptoms now, the better her chances are for a good outcome. She'll be inpatient for at least three months. That's the most critical time, though the whole first year is key."

Three months! A year! Does that mean she won't be coming back to school in the fall?

He continues up to his room and, without turning on the light, he slams down the glass of milk and throws himself onto his bed. He will not think about what he has heard. Instead, he replays his walk home from the park with Mikayla in frame-by-frame detail, as he's done every day since. This is the only thing that can ease his feeling of spinning alone in outer space.

These are details he can't get out of his mind: the way she tucked her hair behind her little pink ear, the cool feel of her hand on his arm, her bottomless green eyes filled with tears that trembled on her eyelashes as she looked up at him. Also, the way she said, *Call me anytime, Zev*, smiling over her shoulder before she went into her house.

He wishes he had an excuse to call her, or that he could go over there and throw pebbles at her window, like Romeo. But that would be idiotic. What would he say? He sits up in bed and, using the moonlight coming through his window, writes out a list of beautiful things he can say to her:

1. *Your face is lodged like a tiny pebble in my heart.*
2. *Your green eyes are made of fresh morning sky and burnished gold sparks of hope.*
3. *Childish friendships can be forged into the strongest bonds of love.*
4. *I am gobsmacked by the fact of your existence.*

Why is it that his writing chops desert him when he needs them the most? He crumples up the paper and lobs it into the trash. And he refuses to use Zoey as an excuse to see Mikayla. It would be disloyal, wimpy. Inexcusable.

Since Zoey's official emergence from the coma, he can't even summon up the courage to go back there—and he can tell that Mikayla is unimpressed.

"But *why not*?" she asked, the last time they talked. "Don't you think it was your visit that woke her up?"

"Nah. It was a coincidence. She doesn't even know who's in the room."

"I disagree! How can you ignore the connection? She may not be herself yet, but … but this is the most important time to see her."

Zev touches his chest. He can still feel the phantom pain of the hole that ripped open when he went back to the ICU with Dad in the middle of that last night before Zoey woke up. But he can't talk to Mikayla about that, not while she's on this crusade. Mom tells him the same thing every day, too: She's sure it was Zev who brought Zoey out of the coma. But he knows that can't be true. It was all he could do not to cry out at the shock of that pain. The closest he's been able to come to Zoey since then is the hammock on the front porch—where she could be found at all hours, in the before-times—and even that's pushing it, because Zoey's cat, Willow, sits beneath it, mewing all the time. The tiny sad sound gives him the willies.

He gets up and turns on the light. In the mirror, he looks scrawny and pale.

"Wimp," he says to his reflection.

He goes downstairs, skipping the creaky eighth stair. He will force himself to lie in the hammock and come up with a Zoey-worthy plan to go back to the hospital without his parents looking on like spectators at the circus.

He will ignore the ragged hole, into which his good intentions keep disappearing like a black star. He will be as brave as Zoey would be if the roles were reversed. Which they should have been. Nobody would've been surprised if something like this happened to him. He's always been a bumbler. But who would ever, in a million years, think that the invincible Zoey Sandor would have a faulty heart muscle and a spike of bad luck that could fuck her up so completely?

He unlocks the front door in slow motion, slipping the bolt like butter, not making a sound—a Zoey trick, so they could hang out on the porch late at night without alerting their "terminally watchful" dad, as she would say. He steps out, and before turning toward the hammock, allows himself a single longing glance toward Mikayla's house.

She is there.

He has to look again to be sure he didn't conjure her. But there she is, sitting on the old aluminum glider on her own front porch. She glances up and sees him looking over, and she stands up. She gestures at herself and at him, her bare arms glowing like a mermaid in the moonlight. He nods and makes a small movement with his hand. *Come over.*

She nods back, and in a matter of seconds she is in front of him.

"Hi."

"Hi. I guess the Sleep Fairy didn't visit you either, huh?" she says with a little smile.

"Nah. We're not on the best terms right now. I think she's pissed at me."

Mikayla lets out her little laugh, then tries to rearrange her face into a scowl. "Fairies don't get pissed, Zev. You must've really stepped out of line."

"It was a case of wrong place, wrong time, but she took it personally."

They both smile at their joke and then fall silent. Zev's violent blush, which has been absent for the first forty seconds of this little exchange, comes roaring up now, and he's thankful for the darkness. As if to confirm that playtime is over, Zoey's cat comes out of the darkness and cries.

"Oh, poor Willow!" Mikayla bends down to pick her up, burying her head in the soft fur.

"You must be so lonely!" She sits down on the edge of the hammock, still stroking the cat. "I went to visit her tonight."

"You did?"

Mikayla nods but doesn't say anything else.

"What was it like?"

His blush begins to subside as he waits for her to answer.

"It was kind of awful." She pauses, her mouth all pinched up. "Well, I mean, when I got there, it was okay. She was pretty dopey, staring into space and stuff. I kept talking to her like an idiot the whole time, about nothing, and sometimes she would turn her head in my direction. And that was okay … until it was like a switch flipped, and she acted like she was having a nightmare, except she was still awake. She was moaning and kicking and banging her hand on the railing …"

Her voice gets higher and higher as she talks. Zev comes over and sits next to her on the hammock. The cat mews and jumps off. Mikayla searches his face while she wipes her eyes. "I'm sorry. Should I stop?"

"No, go on," he says, but he has to look down to confirm the hole in his chest is not real.

"Well, she started yelling something, but it wasn't anything I could understand, not words at all, and I stood there the whole time. I didn't even try to grab her hands—she seemed sort of crazy, you know? All these alarms went off and a nurse came in and injected something and she fell back to sleep in, like, one second." She stops talking and looks down at her hands. "Oh, God. Poor Zoey. What are we going to do?"

She looks at him again, tears unchecked now, and Zev doesn't know what to say. He wants to make a speech about how he is going to be there every step of the way, he wants to promise to be Zoey's coach and healer and everything—but he's pretty sure it would be a lie. And wouldn't it be worse if he says those things and doesn't end up doing them, than if he never makes the promise in the first place?

"My dad says it's going to get better," he says. "I heard him tell my mom that this is normal for a TBI, and even though her progress right now looks slow, they're upgrading her status every day."

"Sorry, I should know this already, but what's a TBI again?"

"Traumatic brain injury. And please, don't apologize. You shouldn't have to know that."

"Well, your dad has been talking about this stuff for as long as I can remember. Only—there was never any reason for me to pay much attention before. But now I want to know everything. I figure that's the best way for us to help her, right?"

"Right," he says. He tells her all the new vocabulary he's been learning, Dad's words that—like she said—he might have been using forever, but Zev never registered them before, and now they keep popping up everywhere.

"**Etiology**," he says, thinking *(noun) [ee.tee.ol.uh.jee]*, "is the study of the causes of diseases, or the origin of a disease." (*Synonyms: analysis, diagnosis, morphology, causation.*)

"**Prognosis**," he goes on, *(noun) [prog.no.ssiss.]*, "is forecasting the probable course and outcome of a disease, the chances of recovery." (*Synonyms: forecast, prediction, prospects.*)

"That's a big one they use all the time, and I guess it's still sort of a moving target," he says. "Should I keep going?"

"Definitely."

"**<u>Sequelae.</u>**" *(Noun) [see.kwell.ay]* "It's, like, the diseases or disorders resulting from an existing medical condition. Like a sequel, you know?" (*Synonyms: consequences, ramifications, results.*)

She nods after each word, and mouths it to herself to help her remember, as if she's learning a foreign language. Which, in a way, she is. What else does he want to tell her?

"I heard my dad telling my mom tonight that Zoey's going to be in the hospital for at least three months. And her recovery could take up to a year."

Mikayla is silent for a little while, reaching her foot down and rocking the hammock while she looks out at the street. She turns back to him, her eyes huge.

"Thanks, Zev. This is all so helpful. I want you to keep telling me this stuff. But, I mean, what I *really* want to know is, is she ever going to get *better*?"

He could tell her how his mom, who used to talk about novels and apricots and Swiss chocolate, talks about how Zoey *might* have permanent memory loss, or *might* have poor impulse control, or *might* be unable to read social cues. This last one is inconceivable: Zoey's always been the one to translate the bewildering language of humans for him. But none of it seems possible. Not for Zoey. And Mikayla doesn't need to hear all that, not until they know for sure whether it turns out to be true. Zev feels the urge to protect her, which is funny, since she's the one who's been brave enough to keep visiting, and he's been a gutless wonder.

"I wish I knew," he says.

Her tiny hand flutters between them like a hummingbird as she tucks her hair behind her ear. Even though this is the worst thing that's ever happened to him or her or anyone they know, Zev can feel part of himself leaning into her nearness. He is mortified that he would ever think to take advantage of this awful thing to get closer to Mikayla, but he has to shove his hands under his legs to stop from reaching out and grabbing hers. To cover, he keeps talking, though he's not saying anything.

"My dad says it's much too soon to know anything. And he's supposed to be the one with all the answers. So, I guess we wait."

She nods. "When are you going back?"

"In a few hours," he says on impulse. "Before my folks wake up. I'll bike."

"Why not go with them?"

"I can't stand when they watch me with her. You know? It's … it's hard enough."

The nurses will be changing shifts soon—it's always 7:00 a.m. and 7:00 p.m. How does he know that?—and Mom's at home, so Zev figures he has a little time before the world starts to crowd in on Zoey today.

He's quiet for a minute. "Hey, Mikayla? Remember how we were talking about the Ball of Fire? I don't know why, but I've been wondering where that comic book could be. We were so careless with our stuff when we were kids. We still are. We always count on Mom to save whatever's worth saving. So, I was thinking, if she can help me find it, maybe I'll bring it in for Zoey," he says.

"That's such a great idea," Mikayla says, grabbing his arm. "Maybe I can dig some stuff up, too. From when we were little."

"That'd be good."

What he doesn't say is that when you're a kid, you never think your little art project might one day have to serve as a reminder of a life you used to have, a life where the power of your perfect friendship with your twin sister granted you the strength of a superhero. You never think that your peaceful nights might change forever, that you might long for oblivion but instead be swamped by strange dreams that never let up.

But then, without meaning to, Zev is telling Mikayla about the Zoey dreams, and how weird it feels to remember *any* of his dreams when he never has before.

"There's this one where I'm floating with Zoey in a black sky, but neither of us can move from our spot because there's a hole where each of our hearts should be and it hurts to breathe. I can see stars on the other side of Zoey, right through the middle of her, and she's waiting for me to find a way to fix it before she disappears forever."

He breaks off talking because he can feel himself getting dangerously close to crying, and that's not something he can do with Mikayla looking on.

She nods and sighs. "Your twin connection was always crazy amazing. I think your sleeping brain is trying to figure out what's going on, like where did she go?" She's quiet for a minute. "I miss her so much, too—but then, she's still right there, you know? It's so *confusing*. I just want her to come back."

For the first time since Zoey's accident, hope surges in Zev. He promises himself that he will bring her back for Mikayla. For both of them. But he doesn't say it aloud in case he fails. That would be worst of all.

At 4:30 a.m., the sun's first rays come streaming through the atmosphere, glancing off the droplets of dew that have gathered on the grass as they talked through the night. Zev takes this as an affirmation of his bid for hope. He says goodbye to Mikayla, wheels his bike from the shed, buckles his helmet, and starts pedaling fast, grateful for the empty streets.

As he locks his bike up in the hospital parking lot, he feels the first fingers of pain in his gut. It spreads like poison, but he's decided he can take it. He's got a mission, and as Zoey would say, *Determination is ninety percent of the battle.*

He forces himself to breathe *through* the pain instead of around it, like Dad taught him when he was eleven and had to get stitches in his cheek after falling out of a rickety tree Zoey talked him into climbing.

He slips through a side door of the hospital and walks down the corridor fast.

The trick is to act like you know what you're doing.

The halls are quiet and no one even looks at him sideways. He stands in the doorway of ICU3 and watches for a little while. Her bruises have faded to yellow-gray smudges, and she appears to be a normal, sleeping teenager—if you ignore the futuristic doomscape of her room.

Making his way through the spaghetti of monitor wires, he holds his long arms at his sides, trying not to even breathe, so he doesn't startle her. But the chair squeaks as he sits down next to the bed, and in slow motion she turns her head in the direction of the sound, her eyes half open. Zev's face is right in front of hers now, and when he looks into her eyes, it's as if he's looking in a mirror: a nebula of bright amber ringed in deep brown.

As her pupils focus on his face, Zoey's eyes blaze open, and Zev's adrenaline surges to superhero levels. Like the Ball of Fire, he focuses all that energy and sends it out to her, from his icy fingertips and his seething stomach and his disbelieving mind and his untethered heart. But even before he's done making all that cosmic noise—maybe more noise than he's tried to make in his whole life—the golden mirrors of Zoey's eyes are going dull and cloudy, and her huge black pupils expand. Is there even room for a person in there with all that blackness?

Zev's eyes burn as he holds his breath and waits for the spark to return.

"I'm here, Zoey. Everything's okay."

Did he say that out loud? There is something jarring about the sound of his warm, human voice in the outer space of this room. But maybe that's what it will take to jump-start someone who's been sort of … dead.

"Hey," he says, louder this time. "I'm here, but you've got to meet me halfway."

He tries not to move or blink.

"Come on, Zo. Come back now."

He waits for an answer, a smile, or a sound from her slack mouth. He can be patient. He breathes in and out, through the poisonous pain, watching her eyes that are his eyes. Waiting.

No spark. No glimmer. No smile. No sound.

She's not even in there.

All his freakish energy leaks away. There's no superpower. She isn't going to meet him halfway. In the emptiness between their eyes, the hole rips wide open, sharp fragments implode inside him, and the pain lacerates. He cries out, his tears splashing onto the white sheet. The sound of his voice makes him jump as if it's coming from somewhere else, but her huge black pupils don't even register his shout. Instead, her eyelids sag, and she slips back into sleep.

The whole thing takes less than a minute. It is so fast that in the months to come, as he replays it over and over—*amber eyes flaring with light, glazing over, slipping away*—a hundred times, a thousand times, even as he makes major decisions based on that one memory, Zev will sometimes think he imagined the whole thing.

But on this July morning, it's all too real. He wipes his eyes, sits back, sucks in a shuddering breath. She can't come back, can she? It's impossible. The coma lasted too long. And he can't stay, even though he knows that once he leaves, it will be impossible for him to return.

The coma. It sounds like fiction. He wants it to be fiction, more than he's ever wanted anything. He can't find the thread anywhere, and without it, he's half of nothing.

He doesn't know he's left until he's riding away, his face blazing in the morning sun.

DAY 10, CONTINUED

"Even factoring in her drowsiness, I'm not sure why her walk is so uneven. She's not dragging so much as, well, going off the rails, for lack of a better phrase. There might be some neglect."

Liv concentrated as Derek, the physical therapist, talked about his latest session with Zoey, trying to decide whether to ask him to explain what he meant by "neglect" or whether to wait and ask Sam. She decided in favor of waiting—she could extrapolate the general idea. Given how much of the day Zoey was still sleeping, Liv was thrilled she was walking at all, though that was already old news around here. She knew she should be glad the therapy team had high expectations—Sam had told her as much—but she kept wanting to tell them all just to let Zoey sleep.

"It'll be easier when we get her talking," Derek said. "We can ask her what's going on. For now, we're flying blind. But she's super fit! And that's working to her advantage."

"Yes, she's quite an athlete—a runner—or, well … she was …" Liv trailed off. "Could she be again?"

"Oh, it's much too soon to tell, Mrs. S. But we'll do our best!"

"Please, call me Liv," she said, as she did every day, knowing he probably never would. Her interactions with the staff would always be skewed by the fact that Liv was their boss's wife.

She was doing far better with Francesca. Their exchanges felt more like a friendship every day, even as Liv admired the smooth integration of the speech therapist's bedside manner with her clinical skills.

"*Buongiorno*, beautiful Sandor ladies," Francesca sang, gliding into the room on her impossible high heels. How did she manage that combination of elegance, warmth, and down-to-earth humor and still maintain her clinical acuity? Liv was never able to work it out.

"How are things going, my dear?" Francesca asked Liv.

"Okay, I think. She's still pretty sleepy," said Liv, gesturing at Zoey, whose eyes had been at half-mast since Derek left.

"But this is natural after brain trauma. Sleep is when the healing happens." She turned to Zoey and changed the pitch of her voice. "Good morning, Zoey! You're looking good! How is your day going?"

She received nothing in return but a flutter of eyelids and a slight upward turn of Zoey's lips, a sort of quirk of her mouth.

"That is a lovely smile you are giving me. Can you say 'Hi' too? Come on, try it with me. Deep breath, and H-H-I-I-I."

Zoey stared at her, as she'd done day after day, never opening her mouth. But Francesca had a deep bag of tricks to stimulate Zoey's speech and was always asking Liv for details about her life.

"Your mom says you have a cat named Willow," she said today, holding up a photo Liv had brought from home. "Is Willow in this picture?"

Zoey looked at her with glazed eyes. Liv was swamped with frustration, but the therapist was undeterred.

When Liv's cell phone vibrated, she looked at the screen and stepped into the hallway to take the call. It was Dafna at the Kol Tov Bakery. She braced herself.

"*Nu*, Liv, what should I tell the customers? They ask about Zoey, they ask about tarts, and I've got nothing to say."

Liv reported on Zoey's progress in the most pleasant voice she could muster.

"So, I should tell them what—check back next week? Next month? What?"

Liv winced. Dafna's brusqueness could be intimidating, but the store owner had told her many times how the customers raved about her apricot tarts and her peanut butter silk pies, which gave her a sense of agency in these uncomfortable exchanges; she knew no one else in town made such sophisticated kosher pastries.

"Dafna, I honestly have no idea when I'll start baking again. There is so much to do here ... I will keep you posted, though. It's the best I can offer." She hoped even Dafna would see the futility of arguing with her.

Last time Liv had been to the Kol Tov Bakery, Zoey had been with her; she had pulled Liv into one of the narrow grocery aisles, and said in an outraged whisper: "Mom, she's so *rude*! Why do you let her talk to you like that?"

Liv had to reflect for a moment before answering. She knew Zoey saw her as a pushover, and it was true she was averse to conflict, but she also had legitimate reasons for keeping out of Dafna's line of fire.

"It doesn't bother me because she's like that with everyone. It makes her feel important."

Zoey folded her arms but said nothing. They stood looking at the bars of baking chocolate and rolls of marzipan.

Liv added, "It wouldn't make me feel better to confront her."

"Yes, but Mom, it's the principle of the thing!"

Liv smiled and put a hand on her daughter's arm. "Useless wars are fought on those *principles* all the time, sweetheart, and a lot of lives are lost that way."

With a clink of fear she had envisioned Ethan then, somewhere in the hottest region of Afghanistan.

"Sometimes it's best to leave it alone," she'd said. "You know, honey? It's business, and as long as I'm satisfied with my own actions, I don't need to worry about hers."

Zoey wasn't convinced; she shook off Liv's arm, obviously disappointed in her.

Still, Liv had kept quiet with Dafna then, as she did again now. She knew she was lucky not to be dependent on her baking for income. She couldn't imagine trying to work during this crisis. Had it been a mistake to encourage Sam to return to his patients so soon? But she and Sam were different people, and she was sure he couldn't have borne the empty time of waiting.

Liv came back into the room and apologized to Francesca.

"No need, no need, *bella*," said the speech therapist. "While I'm here you should feel free to roam about. And I can see that we are making progress here. It's only a matter of time before Zoey won't be able to keep her opinions to herself."

As Zoey dozed off again, Liv signaled to Francesca that she wanted to step into the hall for a moment, where she asked, "Are you sure? About the talking, I mean. I'm starting to worry."

"Yes, I'm pretty sure. I've seen this before. After what's happened, her mind is like a, like a cold motor. It needs time to run smooth again. But the damage to her brain is not in an area that would lead to expressive aphasia."

"Expressive what?"

"*Aphasia*—this is the clinical term for the loss of ability to make language. And I would bet anything that Zoey understands me already. It doesn't look like her language comprehension or production centers were injured. We have to be patient with her. It will come. Okay?"

"Okay. *Thank you*, Francesca, for explaining it to me. That helps."

"You are most welcome."

With a sigh, she sat back down in the medieval chair to keep watch. Although Zoey was no longer precariously balanced between life and death, Liv found that the quality of time in this room hadn't lost its agonizing pace. The silence was louder than ever in her head. *Where are you, my girl?* She watched Zoey float in and out of consciousness.

Liv missed the way Zoey would tease her and then laugh at how she couldn't help defending herself, even though she knew Zoey was kidding. Wouldn't she sit up any minute now, her old self, and say something like, *What's up with your hair, Mom?*

She couldn't account for it, but Liv continued to miss Shula, too. Maybe it was her guilt at not being there for Zev and Lottie. But she had to be here, didn't she?

Like Lottie and the twins, Liv and Shula were eight years apart, and Liv had always felt like more of an aunt than a sibling to her.

She had gone off to college when Shula was ten, all too aware that their kind but diffident father could never be a foil for their mother's autocratic rule. At opposite ends of their respective childhoods, Liv and Shula had shared the experience of surviving eight years under Mother's glare without each other's mitigating presence. Liv had cultivated a Gandhi-like stance as her strategy for self-preservation, but Shula became a tough teen. Sam, studying adolescent psychology during his pediatric rotation, had remarked on Shula's thick-skinned independence, nicknaming her the Little Refugee.

Liv needed that toughness now. She reached for her phone and called Shula again. Her sister wanted to know how Liv was filling her time.

"I don't know. I'm in a sort of limbo. There's far too much time to think."

"What are you thinking about, besides the obvious?"

"Well, the other kids, of course. I'm trying not to feel too guilty, leaving them with Mother. But I figure, we survived all those years, right?"

Shula laughed. "Your kids will be fine, Livie. They're tougher than you think."

"I guess so … Besides that, I'm obsessing over baking, believe it or not. But even that's no comfort—it's making me anxious."

"It's what you love to do. Why should it make you anxious?" There was an indignant squeal on the line. "Sorry, Livie, I'm nursing Udi. Still. There should be nothing left in there for him, what with this new pregnancy, but *somehow*—so, anyway, why the anxiety?"

Liv wished for the simple worries that had loomed so large when her children were small. Breastfeeding, tantrums, sleeping through the night.

"No, of course, I love to cook. My poor hands have never been so idle as these last ten days. But it's hard to imagine ever getting back to my old routine. It was so … I don't know, mundane."

"Well, that's irrational," said Shula mildly. "Even in the worst of circumstances, you can't devote every moment to suffering. People continue to do their work, irrespective of—or even because of—their personal troubles."

"Okay. But why should I spend time laboring to produce something no one needs to survive? My apricot tarts won't make a lasting contribution to posterity."

"Ugh. You sound like Mother. Isn't that why you *chose* baking? For the joy of it? Screw posterity! Just make sure you're raising mensches—your kids are all the posterity you need. We have to stick together, make the world safe for ordinary mortals! Besides, no one in this world makes pastries like yours."

Liv was silent.

"Or have you suddenly decided to buy into Mother's crap?"

Liv had to laugh. "No, of course not!"

"Whew! That's a relief! But seriously, Livie, I'm envious of the way you dream up those confections of yours. And Oren raves about them after every visit."

"Oh, that's so nice." She sighed. "I don't even know what I'm saying. I'm wiped out. So, thanks for the reality check. You're the best."

She ended the call. How odd it was to be taking advice from her baby sister! Still, in the wake of Zoey's injury, it was her mother's perspective that was gaining ground. Who cared about the type of honey in her baklava, the lightness of her caramel breakfast rolls, the sunset hue of the apricots for her much-loved tarts? They were irrelevant next to the heart and brain monitors that beeped out their rhythms in the sterile air of Zoey's hospital room. Sam's career was so much more consequential than hers, and however painful it was for him, he was in possession of knowledge that could make a difference to their injured daughter. All Liv could do was sit and ponder pastry.

Sam came in after his rounds and sat down on the side of Zoey's bed, facing Liv. She tried to arrange her face into a mask of calm, but she couldn't quite get there. He spread his big hand over Zoey's hands, and turned his body so he could lean into Liv for a second.

"Are you okay?" he asked.

"I guess so. I was just thinking."

She could feel him waiting for her to continue, but patience was never his strong suit.

"About what?"

"Well … what's next, I guess," she said.

He sat up and nodded. "I know. This part is hard in a different way. It goes slowly. But even now, there's a lot you can do."

"Like what?" She didn't want to ask why he said *you* and not *we*.

"The patients who do best are the ones who have a family member advocating for them all the time. Making sure they get their therapies. Fighting for every service. Watching for signs of improvement, or even regression. It's not always possible. But when it is …"

"What if I miss something critical?"

He shook his head. "It's not a medical thing. You use your instincts. The staff will do the rest. I'm sure they'll be extra careful with Zoey. But you're her mother. You've always had a killer radar when it comes to the kids."

"But, speaking of the kids, I can't keep leaving Zev and Lottie with Mother. It's not fair."

"I know, Livie. It's an imperfect situation. You have to trust yourself. You'll find a balance."

Liv tried to ignore the whine of resentment in her head. Why did this have to be up to her?

"What about you?" She hoped Sam would know what she was asking.

"Me? I've been trying to ride my own fence. They keep asking me what I want to do," he said, cocking a thumb over his shoulder toward the corridor. "How involved do I want to be as a clinician? But in the end, it's not about what I want, Livie. I'm too close to be effective."

Well, there was her answer: It was impossible for him. She knew it was the right thing, the only answer, but still she felt alone. She and Zoey were at the top of a vast and treacherous slope they would have to navigate by themselves. She looked down the slope in her mind's eye, but the bottom disappeared in a haze of white.

"I've got to get out of here."

She jumped up and rushed down the corridor and into the waiting elevator. She ran out the front doors of the hospital into a wall of midsummer heat, where the screech of resentment leaked out of her and into the stifling air. She slowed down and walked around the side of the building toward the Healing Garden and sat down on a bench.

Why am I so exhausted? I've been sitting still for days. This reminded her of the time right before the twins were born: She could hardly move, and every day felt like a marathon. She would put little Ethan to bed and often fall asleep herself waiting for Sam to come home from work. She'd reawaken later and find Sam asleep with Ethan, cramped and teetering on the edge of the toddler's bed. In those days, Sam was on call every third night, and overcome with fatigue the minute he got home. Liv remembered looking across the room to where they lay, Ethan and Sam—both as exhausted as she was from the effort of getting through their day. How would they all manage once the twins came?

She had tried to ground herself in the important truths about her life with Sam. She was awed by his energy and drive, his seriousness about his work; she adored his long, lean body, the sculptural angle of his jaw, his chocolate eyes, his black hair and olive complexion. She was impressed by his easy athleticism and delighted in the look of jubilation that overcame him at the piano. She loved this old house, his parents' legacy, the way it stood against time and weather and mood, as if it had been there forever just for them, and would continue to be. She respected his endless concern for their safety, the way he watched over their growing boy as Ethan ventured out in an ever-widening arc. She loved being pregnant with his children, the idea that, together, they were creating these wonderful little beings who, they'd make sure, would add a measure of goodness to the world.

Feeling restless on that summer night, she had left Sam sleeping with Ethan and wandered into the library. The air carried the metallic smell of thunder through the open window. She had hauled herself onto the stepladder to organize some books on a shelf when the wind picked up, stirring through the room.

When her water broke, she thought for a second that rain was coming in the window.

In Liv's mind, the twins' love of words would forever be bound up with the start of her labor in that book-lined room. It was as if they got one inky whiff and couldn't wait. Zoey's opening act as a twin had been to convince Zev it was time to go; she came out first, of course, working her way into the world with astounding efficiency. From the beginning, Zev was quiet, passive—the complement to Zoey's energy and drive.

"There you are!" Sam's voice came from behind the bench where she was sitting, interrupting the avalanche of nostalgia. He sat down next to her, laying a cool hand on her flushed cheek. "Livie? I didn't mean to make things harder ..."

"It's okay, Sam. I'm okay. Or I will be," she said. "It's just—a lot. You know?"

"I know, love."

They sat there quietly for a breath.

"I was remembering when the twins were born, and how, when they were babies, every time they were in the crib together, Zoey would babble at Zev, incessantly, and Zev would answer her with those short chirps, and only in her pauses. Remember that? And we would stand over their crib and watch them, blown away by their connection. Doesn't that have to count for something?"

"Yes. I remember," Sam said. And Liv tried not to get stuck on the fact that he hadn't answered her second, more important question. They sat side-by-side in the Healing Garden, surrounded by their memories, and she told herself again that somehow everything would be okay. Whatever had happened to Zoey's brain, her soul was still intact, and it was too fierce to be overcome.

DAY 12

In the days after Zoey's awakening, Sam returned again and again to the puzzle of Hope and Gracie Gladwell. He spent an inordinate amount of time reading case studies of multisibling CP, coming up against the same brick wall: *Why?* There was almost always some increased maternal risk factor. But he'd questioned Mrs. Gladwell again, almost to the point of offensiveness, and come up empty. He started a new research file, took copious notes, felt himself to be on the verge of … something. Experience had taught him to listen to these signals, as they had preceded the most satisfying breakthroughs of his career. It was a perfect distraction.

But at home, there was a gap growing between Sam and Liv, mounded like a landfill with logistical details, concerns about the other children, fear and confusion over Zoey, and profound physical exhaustion. He had witnessed this distancing so many times in his patients' families—he mustn't allow it to happen in his own. He needed to keep Liv close. He believed her calm optimism would help him survive the fractured chaos he lived in now.

When Sam first glimpsed Liv in the center of the freshman quad at Yale, she appeared illuminated from within. He'd been mesmerized by the alchemy of crinkly golden hair, serene brow, sweet smile, and something … other. Up close, the effect was even stronger: The honeyed glow of the oak trees paled in comparison to her amber eyes.

"Who *are* you?" he'd asked, wonder in his voice.

Liv took one look at his face and laughed. "I'm Liv."

Her handshake was firmer than he expected, her voice at once musical and calm.

"Liv." Her name struck him as a joyful command meant for him alone: *Live!* Live more and worry less, she seemed to say with one handshake. Live authentically. Live because your parents didn't.

"And who are you?" she'd asked, still laughing. Weeks later, she admitted that his open admiration had brought out a rare daring in her.

"I am … Sam," he said, kicking himself for sounding like an idiot, until he saw the potential for a little levity to offset his embarrassing start with this golden girl. "Sam I am." He grinned.

"I love Dr. Seuss!" She grinned back.

Their fate was written and sealed on the spot.

Liv and Sam shared a sense of mutual bemusement in finding themselves at Yale.

"Don't you kind of hate it here?" she whispered to Sam as they walked through the campus holding hands. "The wholesale snobbery of it, the ponderous buildings, the air of privilege wafting from the gates"—she'd waved her hands at the gated quad they were passing—"like it's designed to hold us in our towers and keep everyone else out!"

"Don't hold back, Livie. Tell me how you really feel!"

"But Sam! Are we such throwbacks that we're here *just because our parents approve*?"

"Well, that's rich coming from the girl who was an academic wunderkind in high school!" said Sam. "You don't get a 4.0 to please your mother. You get it because you're that effing smart."

Liv laughed. "But what's it all for, when what I really want is to go to Le Cordon Bleu? Why did I let Mother stop me by calling it *little more than a trade school*?"

"It might be easier to finish your degree than to fight with her about it for the rest of your life. After that, you can do whatever you want, right? And … I mean, okay, it's true that I can practically feel my parents smiling down at me here," Sam went on, "but that's a good thing. And don't forget, I'm on scholarship, so I'm not going anywhere."

Sam was always more practical than Liv, but she had a surfeit of patience. Still, he had to acknowledge that, Ivy League or no, she was not where she should be. She'd confessed in the early days of their love: "When I dream, I see jewel-toned fruits and rich chocolates and cool, creamy, vanilla egg custards. I can feel them melting on my tongue."

"Oh, man, you're killing me here!" Sam said, becoming aroused whenever she talked about food. "You have no choice. You've got to pursue this dream of being a pastry chef! Just ... please, can you wait for me? If you leave now, Livie—I'd be lost."

So, Liv finished her degree at Yale for Sam's sake, majoring in literature because she loved to read, arranging her schedule so she could take the train into Manhattan one day a week for cooking classes, and spending her summers working in a series of patisseries, to her mother's growing dismay. Liv was determined not to let her creative vision get sucked away by what she called the "Ivy League Stress Machine," but she was also careful to support Sam's decision to trade music for medicine. "Even though it kills me to think of the pleasure your choice will give Mother," she'd joked, and Sam laughed along, knowing that in truth, Liv didn't have a resentful bone in her body.

Long before senior year, Sam knew they were a perfect match: He was in need of a family, and she was eager to provide a cosmic corrective to the one she'd been raised in. He knew his world would be bleak without the glow she cast.

"You've *got* to marry me, Liv. When I'm with you, I'm Superman! You're perfect for me, and you'll see. I'll be perfect for you, too."

Liv laughed and said, in her serene way, "You don't have to be perfect, Sam. You just have to be mine."

They had married right after graduation, on a wave of hope so powerful it would surely wash away Hinda's predictable objections and annul Sam's loneliness and sorrow.

Twenty-seven years and four lives later, Sam still counted on Liv to soothe him with her confidence in the world's essential goodness. He couldn't allow his anguish to break down their bond, he told himself again as he turned his car into the driveway. He trudged up the front steps of his house, kicked aside a soccer ball that had rolled in front of the door, and concentrated on ignoring the empty hammock in his peripheral vision, where in summers before, he could almost always find Zoey reading when he came home from work. He had his hand on the latch when the door opened from the inside. Did Hinda stand all day by the window, waiting for him?

"Hello, Samuel. I wasn't expecting you so soon."

"Oh! Yes, sorry, I didn't call ahead. But I was no good at work, and I wanted to see the children."

Why did she always make him want to apologize?

"Hmmm. Yes … I was about to get dinner going—I bought a nice filet of sole at the market, only to find that yet another nondescript casserole had been deposited on your front porch by a member of your synagogue's 'crisis committee' or whatever they call it."

"*Chesed* committee, Hinda. It means *kindness*," said Sam as he dropped his keys on the front hall table.

Hinda sniffed. "Hmmm. I don't believe in casseroles, Samuel. They are nothing but homogenous glop. Foods should be recognizable."

Sam had no idea what to say to this latest pronouncement. His mother-in-law appeared to be on the warpath; he would do best to keep quiet. And Liv was right—she needed to start coming home for dinner. He went about setting the table for four, thinking again how reduced they were in their ranks.

His spirits lifted when Zev and Lottie were facing him across the big table.

"What's going on with Zoey today, Daddy? Is she better?" Lottie asked around a mouthful of food. Sam was glad to see her eating well and wished the same could be said for Zev, whose enormous appetite was usually the subject of much sibling mirth.

"Zoey's doing better every day, sweetheart. She's still sleeping a lot, but she's starting to heal. She's already up and walking with support, and I think she'll start talking any day now."

"But when is she coming home?"

"She'll be moved out of ICU and into the inpatient TBI Rehab wing soon, where she'll work on relearning some of the things she's … forgotten. And you can visit her there. I know she'd like that. But it'll be a long time yet before she comes home."

Zev said nothing, and Hinda, too, was quiet at first; she watched him with her head tilted to the side in a manner that reminded Sam of Liv.

"But—why does she have to move to an impatient place?" Lottie asked, always one to fill a silence. "Is that 'cause she's impatient to come home too?"

"No, sweetie"—Sam smiled—"the *in*patient wing. The part of the hospital where patients go when they still need to live *in* it, but they're not so sick that they need extra intensive care."

"Why does she have to live in the hospital? Why can't we take care of her?"

"Well, she's not ready for that yet. And neither are we. She needs more help than we can give her here. But soon—"

"When do I get to see her?" Lottie's voice was suddenly tremulous, and Sam was grateful when Zev saved him the trouble of searching for another politic answer.

"The thing is, Zoey's pretty confused right now, peanut, because she's been unconscious for such a long time," said Zev. "Imagine sleeping for a whole week too long, how grumpy and confused you'd be when you woke up. You know how you feel when you're sick—remember the strep throat?—and you want everyone to leave you alone so the room's quiet? That's what Zoey needs right now."

Sometimes Zev surprised the devil out of Sam. At the same time, he felt a twinge of wistfulness at Zev's easy camaraderie with his siblings and Liv. Why was he always so distant with Sam? Lottie was looking to him for confirmation, and he nodded at her and smiled, then turned his smile on Zev, squeezing his skinny arm and leaving his hand where it was for as long as the boy would allow it. He was glad, too, that Zev had used such hopeful language. There was little about this situation he could control, but at least he could protect his kids from the chilling facts for a while longer.

Hinda, though, had no such scruples. "Truly, Samuel, what *are* Zoey's chances for meaningful recovery, given the brain damage? What of her intellectual capacities? Will she recover those? Will she even be capable of lucid communication? She was the *most* promising child."

Sam could see Zev's face reddening as he absorbed his grandmother's words and he tried to send Hinda a message with his eyes. Was it possible she was unaware of the effect she was having? She didn't even look at him.

"Hinda, this is not the—"

"It is such an *imprecise* field, isn't it? Is there nothing your people can do to intervene? It would be a terrible shame if her intelligence were compromised, and all that potential lost through medical incompetence."

It was galling. There they were: his hateful private thoughts, laid out for the kids to hear.

"Look, my department is doing *everything* possible, along with neurosurgery and cardiology. What you call *imprecise* is the reality that we can't know anything definitive yet. And we *must not* jump to conclusions. The brain is remarkably elastic, but this is a slow process. And it's true that Zoey hasn't spoken yet, but there's no neurological indication she won't recover her verb—" He stopped himself, wanting to make sure Lottie understood him. "She will be talking again soon, we're sure. There are many different paths to meaningful recovery, and Zoey will forge her own path, as she always has."

He had to stop. He could taste the bitter alloy of his own hypocrisy. He knew the children were listening hard, though they picked at their food and avoided making eye contact.

Hinda sniffed, and Sam hoped it was a sniff of repressed tears and not one of disdain.

"Hmmm. Time will tell, I am sure," she said, her face a mask, though he could hear a faint tremor in her voice.

Sam rose and began to clear the supper dishes. He knew that many people, including Hinda, maintained that most of his patients would "never make a significant contribution to society." They were calculating worth in economic terms. But wasn't every person—irrespective of the condition of their body or mind—someone's parent or spouse, son or daughter? Someone worthy of receiving—and usually, capable of giving—love and kindness?

Over the years, he and Hinda had had many heated discussions on the subject. Her doctorate in human evolution, obtained when she was in her forties, dovetailed with her personal worldview; from the earliest days, she had kept their interactions obsessively trained on his career, at first praising him for his "sensible ambitions" (as Liv had predicted), but soon becoming as critical of him as she was of everyone else. She had even gone so far as to term his work "Humpty-Dumpty medicine." In Hinda's skewed view of his patients, they either adapted or they died off; no amount of prayer or medical expertise could conjure a miracle. She was not alone in her attitude; Sam was all too aware of the widespread dehumanization of disabled people. But he also knew better than most how strong their spirits could be, how much they could contribute—as much as anyone, maybe more, if you used a less mercenary calculus. Who better to expand people's capacity for consideration and empathy? To break us out of our materialistic mindset, so pervasive in the United States? Who else could meet daily pain and adversity with joy, resilience, creativity?

Hinda had a certain gift for making him feel as if, despite all his good work, he wasn't doing enough for posterity. And now it wasn't even about posterity anymore. It was personal.

Sam groaned inwardly as she appeared in the kitchen to help with the washing up. He had been hoping for a truce, but he was too angry.

"I would *appreciate* it if you would keep your negativity to yourself in front of Zev and Lottie." His words came out in a fricative hiss. "They've been through enough, don't you think?"

"What I think is clearly immaterial to you, Samuel."

No apology? No sign of contrition? Sam was incensed.

"You know what *I* think, Hinda? As much as we appreciate your *help*, you should go back to Chicago. You've made no secret of the fact that you're missing some important departmental meetings, not to mention your … your symphony subscription. So don't let us keep you any longer."

His mother-in-law looked shocked and suddenly old, but he held her gaze, one frightened animal staring down another. Finally she looked away, compressed her lips in a thin line, and stalked out of the room, her back as straight as a mantis.

Sam returned to his washing up as Zev wandered into the kitchen with his head down and almost collided with his grandmother in the doorway. He blushed and muttered an apology, then began drying pots and dishes, stacking them on the counter with care. Even Sam, with all the things he didn't know about his most inscrutable child, knew Zev would never volunteer to do kitchen chores. Was he trying to reach out, or looking for something to do? Liv could have answered that, and so could Zoey. Why was it so hard for Sam to connect? He was afraid to make a wrong move at such a fragile time. But the silence between them grew louder and louder, taking on the mass and density of steam that hung in the air.

It was Zev who turned to him: "Dad, what's *really* going on with Zoey? Is Nana right?"

He blushed nearly purple, and Sam wanted to put a cool hand on his cheek. But he supposed that would only embarrass him more.

"I need *details*," Zev was saying. "It can't be worse than what I'm imagining."

Oh, yes it can. But the boy was so enmeshed with his twin, maybe keeping him in the dark hadn't been such a good idea.

"You're right, Zev. What do you want to know?"

Zev looked surprised and started talking fast, as though afraid Sam would change his mind.

"Will she ever be Zoey again, like, you know, the way she was before? Some people are saying she could be like a—a baby forever, or even—a vegetable. So, what's really happening? And aren't you going to take over now that she's out of the coma? I thought you were the major go-to guy for people with TBIs. And how long will it take before she comes home ...?"

His voice trailed off and his eyes filled with tears.

Shame and confusion rose up in Sam again. How could he answer Zev when he didn't know any of the answers himself? How could Zev ever understand the nuances of Zoey's situation? He was waiting for Sam to perform a miracle, and that wasn't in the cards.

"Well, here's what we know for sure: Zoey is *not* a *vegetable*. She's out of her coma. The swelling on her brain is going down. There *is* a TBI, but it'll be a good while before we know the full implications. Though it's slow going with her verbal skills right now, they *will* return, and once it happens, it could happen quickly. As for her personality—it might not be *unchanged*, but glimmers of the old Zoey are back already! She's got some mischief in her. And what I told Nana is true: The brain is super elastic. It's way too soon to know where she'll end up."

Sam watched as Zev's shoulders slumped more and more. He couldn't take back his words, so instead he continued to speak from the all-too-familiar script he used for family meetings with the bewildered and grief-stricken at work.

"Zev, you have an important role to play in all this. Zoey will need you to bring her back to herself as much as possible. You two are connected in a special way, and those connections count for a great deal here. The more involved you are, the better. Do you understand?"

"But Dad, you're the one who wouldn't let me come earlier. And now—"

"Now?"

Zev shook his head but didn't continue.

"Listen. This is only the beginning of her recovery. There will be lots to do, I promise." Sam stopped and softened his voice. "And meanwhile, you've got to take care of yourself, too—because we can't be around Zoey if we're sick. So, I want you to remember to eat, and sleep, and get some fresh air and exercise every day. Can I count on you to do that?"

Zev nodded, opened his mouth, and closed it again. He looked at Sam, and there were questions in his eyes that Sam didn't have the energy to tease out.

"Also—when will Mom be around again?"

"Hmmm. I'm afraid that might be my fault. I asked her to keep a close watch during these days, while we're still working out my role in all this. But we were talking about that earlier today, and we're all realizing she needs to spend more time at home. I'll mention it again. Okay?"

Zev nodded again and stared at his hands.

"I miss her, too, Zev. It's hard on all of us," Sam said, resting a hand on Zev's alarmingly bony shoulder.

Zev was still waiting for something, though Sam couldn't be sure whether it was to ask or to tell. Anyway, he had nothing left to give. He squeezed Zev's shoulder and watched him leave.

That night, Liv came home to sleep for only the third time since it happened.

"Oh! I need my own bed." She sighed. "But I would hate for her to wake up and find me gone."

"Of course you should sleep at home. She's so drowsy still, she's unlikely to wake up during the night."

Already Zoey was reduced to a pronoun, as though it was understood between them that she was the only person they could be referring to. "I'm glad you're here."

He hugged Liv, missing her perpetual scent of cake batter and summer jam that only the ICU could eradicate. They climbed into bed and turned to face each other, Liv's luminous eyes drooping already.

"Livie?"

"Hmmm?" She tried to focus her gaze.

"I've asked Peter to meet us tomorrow to have a talk. I know he's always running out of the room, and you've been unbelievably patient, but he at least owes us the courtesy of fifteen or twenty minutes of his precious time. We'll meet with him at noon."

"That's great," she said, yawning hugely. "I'll make a list of questions first thing."

Sam was about to say he already knew what he wanted to ask the Brain Trust, but he refrained. He needed Liv's insights to augment his own myopic clinical perspective.

"Good idea," he said. Her eyes had drifted shut again. "I've missed you," he whispered.

"I've missed you too, honey," she mumbled.

"And the kids. Zev asked when you could be home more."

Liv opened her eyes and sat up. "What did you tell him? I mean, didn't you say I need to be vigilant at the hospital, especially now that she's awake?"

Sam put out an arm to pull her back down. He felt guilty keeping her up, but he badly needed their ritual of whispering on the same pillow their postmortem of the day.

"I told him that it's my fault you've been gone so much, that I can see you need to be here, too. Zoey has other people watching over her, and the kids at home only have Hinda."

"And you," said Liv.

"Yes, but even together, we make a poor substitute for you. I don't know their routines, what they need. And with Zev and me … well, you know how that goes. Plus, Hinda is tough."

Liv grimaced. "I know. But at least she can drive. I'm not sure errands and car pools are a good use of my time right now."

"Well, it may seem trivial, but it would give the kids some semblance of normalcy. Which is missing with Hinda here." He paused. "I'm afraid we went at it tonight."

"Oh, no. Sam! I was counting on you to keep the peace! What happened?"

"She ... she pushed all my buttons."

"Is that why she was talking about leaving? When I checked in with her before coming upstairs, she said something about getting back to Chicago before her next date at the symphony! Which was a bit much, even for her."

Sam nodded. "That's on me, too, I'm afraid. Even your mother wouldn't leave at a time like this for the *symphony*. I—I told her to go."

Liv's eyes widened. "But, no! We needed—"

"She went on and on tonight about Zoey's *damaged intellectual faculties*. In front of the kids. It's bad for them—and I can't keep my cool."

"Oh, God. She really is awful," Liv said.

"It's not worth it, Livie. We don't need the added stress of trying to get along with her!"

"So, what should I do, then? About watching over Zoey? About getting Lottie to camp and keeping an eye on Zev?"

She was close to tears, and the guilt made Sam angry. He had hoped Liv could make sense of things. "I don't know, dammit. Do you want me to apologize and ask her to stay?"

She sighed. "No, she should go back. She's making you all crazy."

"It's true." He sighed. "I'm sorry."

"Never mind. It can't be helped. It's nothing new. I wish we had *one* person between us who we could ask for—"

"I know. We'll figure all this out tomorrow. Okay?" said Sam, brushing her matted curls away from her face.

"Okay." She sighed and closed her eyes again.

"Oh, and Livie?"

For the third time her eyes opened. She raised an eyebrow, as if to say, *Are you going to keep me up all night?* Sam smiled. Thank God she was such a patient woman. "You do get why I'm not her treating physician, right?"

Liv turned toward him, one knee over his legs, her hands between her face and the pillow. It was her customary position during their pillow talks.

"Of course, I do. It's the right thing. But … if you won't be there to interpret all the gobbledygook for me, I'll have to be extremely careful. I'm afraid I'll miss something. Like, she can understand me pretty well now, when she's not spaced out, so why isn't she talking? Francesca said her bleed wasn't in the area that causes expressive aphasia and if that's the case—is there something I should be doing differently?"

"Oh boy, you're really getting a crash course, aren't you? What did Francesca say?"

"She said Zoey needs more time. That her brain is still recovering from the trauma. But what if I'm missing something? You know me, Sam. I'm not a detail person."

It was true. Liv's approach to their busy household had always been somewhat vague; she assumed if she remained calm in the face of chaos, things would work themselves out one way or another. It wasn't efficient, but it was benign, and most of the time she was right. And since Sam was so often absent during waking hours, he was not in a position to criticize.

"Maybe details aren't your strong suit, but you always manage to do what needs doing."

"Yes, but this is different. The stakes are too high." Liv looked on the verge of tears again. They were both too tired to think.

"I—I don't mean to make things harder for you."

"It's not you. The whole *situation* is impossible. We'll try again to figure it all out tomorrow." She patted his arm, and turned out the light.

Her breath slowed instantaneously, while Sam lay awake, marveling at how she could relinquish her grasp on consciousness. But then, Liv didn't indulge in fits of harsh self-analysis, whereas Sam replayed every interaction. Soon his clinical musings began to intrude, nowadays indistinguishable from everything else. *Look at*

Zoey's chart again … Maybe review her old pediatric files? No family history of cardiac problems … No family history—like the Gladwell sisters. No risk factors. Why should they both be born with CP? Why are Hope's symptoms worse instead of better?

He sat up in bed. The *symptoms*. That was it! It wasn't about the Gladwells' history: The symptoms were the key. What else could cause them? He grabbed a notepad from the bedside table and jotted down the words *dopa-responsive dystonia*. He would have Gillian call the Gladwells first thing, bring them back for more testing.

He fell asleep at daybreak and awoke a few short hours later to the smell of challah wafting up from the kitchen. He permitted himself a single moan of fatigue: The whole world wasn't going to hell today if Livie woke up with enough heart to bake her remarkable braided brioche. Come Friday night, they could once again light Shabbat candles and break bread together with her sweet, buttery loaves.

EXCERPT FROM

THE MEMORY BOOK OF ZOEY SANDOR

I am safe and warm in my bed. I am an angel the clouds are my bed, I am my cat Willow sleeping in the sun in the rocking chair, I am a baby and Mama is holding me. I hear voices saying wake up wake up, they are talking and poking me but I say go away and let me sleep. Sleep is good, sleep is calm and quiet and my head doesn't hurt. I want to sleep forever but I smell Mama's challah baking and the smell comes up to my room sweet and eggy it says wake up wake up. I dig deeper into my blankets to go back to sleep but I'm so hungry the challah won't leave me alone, hungry is winning over sleepy. I need to wake up.

(Transcribed by Francesca Garibaldi, SLP)

DAY 17

High up on his lifeguard tower, Zev is in control, looking out for all the little people who've got no idea what sort of mishaps await them. He's like the Ball of Fire up here. Why does he keep coming back to that stupid comic strip? And talk about a ball of fire: It is ridiculously hot out here. It's so hot today, it's—he digs around in his brain for an obscure word—it's *pyretic.*

Pyretic (adjective) [pahy.ret.ik]: of, pertaining to, affected by, or producing fever. Synonyms*:* hot, blazing, febrile, feverish.

He's glad for the inferno, though, because he's getting the best tan of his life, and the sun is bleaching away all meaningful thought. He's not, for example, thinking about Mikayla every minute of the day, and how she hasn't noticed his tan and doesn't care about that sort of thing anyway. Or how he can tell that she's kind of disappointed he hasn't gone with her to see Zoey.

He's not thinking about how Nana left in near-total silence one morning last week, how she looked sad and shrunken, and how he felt sorry for her even though he was hugely relieved. He's not thinking about how it's been ten days now since Zoey woke from her coma and Mom keeps saying his twin needs him, but Zev figures Zoey has no idea whether he's there or not, and instead of showing up, he sends whimsical little drawings for Mom to hang in her room. It's good that Zoey's up and walking again, but he's not thinking about how her walk is "wobbly," as Mom says. So much for running sprints. Mikayla says Zoey uses his drawings as a target to focus on, something to walk toward, and that she's sure Zoey understands her now "because otherwise, how would she know to walk toward your sketches, right?"

But as long as she's not talking, how does anyone know?

And Zev is definitely not thinking about the fact that today is their sixteenth birthday, the day they've waited for and planned together for years, over a hundred late-night cups of hot cocoa. It's been years since Zev and Zoey started lobbying for a new car for their sixteenth birthday and dubbed the campaign Project Sixteen. It started out being about the car, but over time it turned into a grand plan—a road trip around the US, stops at all the great sights, midnight feasts at strategically located diners.

Now, instead of the twins going to the DMV to get their learner's permits together, Zev has to go solo before they all bring cupcakes to Zoey in the ICU Stepdown.

No, Zev is thinking about *this moment only*, and there are about three hundred souls counting on him to pay attention. The pool is crammed with kids from the day camp, a mob of bored teenagers looking for trouble, a clutch of mothers already tired from toting around restless miniatures of themselves for these long days of summer.

Behind his sunglasses, Zev scans back and forth over his end of the huge, L-shaped pool—he's got the shallow end, but also the first part of the deeper end before the elbow—trying to pick out the problem kids who don't know their own limitations, and the wise guys who can't resist doing something stupid: splashing toddlers in the face, untying straps of floaties, holding their friends under for too long. It's a fool's paradise, and Zev is king of the fools for four hours today. His shift is almost over, which is too bad—he would stay all day and night to avoid going home and dealing with what his parents have planned. He is ... *pusillanimous.*

Pusillanimous (adjective) [pyoo.si.lah.nuh.muhss]: lacking courage or resolution; indicating a cowardly spirit. Synonyms: timid, fearful, spineless, nervous, faint-hearted.

These recitations are doing nothing for him now. His mind is not fooled anymore. As he scans and scans again through the hordes for unusual movements, his stomach rumbles. Did he forget to eat again? As he scrolls back through the day, he realizes they'd skipped the family ritual of "birthday breakfast" this morning. It's one of Mom's few unbreakable rules: If you're anywhere on the continent on the date of a family birthday, you must present yourself for birthday breakfast by 7:00 a.m. or suffer the consequences. And who would want to miss her chocolate bread pudding? But this morning, no one even mentioned it. Not that he's surprised. It has taken him all these hours to notice.

Zev looks at his watch: *Twenty more minutes.* He wipes a bead of sweat from his forehead before it can get to his eyes, and spots three big kids who are dunking a puny fourth kid and aren't stopping even when he's struggling for air. They're not in Zev's part of the pool, but the lifeguard on the other end is Carrie Landers, and she's too busy flirting with Glenn, the head lifeguard, to notice. Glenn should at least know better. But no. Zev leans forward, holding his breath, and waits fifteen seconds for either of them to react. He blows his own whistle and points at the kids. Carrie looks up, adds her whistle to the mix, the kids stop their horseplay, and Carrie waves at Zev: *Thanks for saving my butt.* Sure thing, Carrie. Anything to make you look good.

That puny kid struggling to catch his breath sets off a dream flashback. Zev has been dogged by them, instant replays of a recurring nightmare his messed-up brain has invented. In these horror shows, he is standing next to Zoey's bed when the jagged hole he feels in his chest whenever he's with her—if he even *thinks* of her—becomes real. He looks down, sees his guts, starts gushing blood. It drips onto the floor, becomes a lake of red that rises around him. He knows he is bleeding to death. He refuses to put this one on paper, though he's still compulsive about recording the other dreams of Zoey that keep coming, night after night. He's often petrified, beset by random frenzies of terror.

He shakes his head to clear it, looks at his watch. *Ten more minutes. Pay attention.* He scans the crowd, which has swelled even more. A group of moms with babies wades into the shallow end, a lone little girl jumping around next to them on the deck, arms flapping. She is wearing a cerulean blue swimsuit and she has long, auburn hair that gleams in the sun. Zoey's hair.

Zoey. Zoey. Zoey. He should be there helping her, but he can't get around the pain in his gut. If it would only let him finish his shift …

The auburn girl scampers off to the deep end of the pool. The moms are not paying attention. Zev sits forward, keeps his eye on the kid. Cerulean blue, moving too fast.

No running, kid. It's slippery. Come on, Carrie, blow your whistle.

A picture comes into his mind of Zoey and Mikayla, six years old, giggling inside a tent in the living room, playing mother (always Zoey) and daughter (always Mikayla).

"Come on, Zev! You can be the dad," Mikayla had said. She was always so gentle. He never felt left out. Well, not by her, anyway. Zoey's other friends are a different story. Carrie, for instance …

Sometimes he tells Mikayla about the weird dreams—not the slashers, but the nicer ones—and last night he even showed her his latest drawing.

"Is that Zoey curled up in bed, with Willow at her feet? And what is this, at the bottom?"

"A cloud of Mom's challah mist wafting up the staircase and under her door."

Mikayla laughed. "Yes! See? Your sleeping brain is protecting you, trying to get you back to normal life before Zoey's injury. That's how I see my life now like it's divided into the time Before Zoey's Injury, and the time after. In my mind it's an acronym: BZI."

"Oh, man, that's brilliant. BZI. A shorthand for the train wreck," he said.

Mikayla looked pleased. "You can use it, too," she said. "Our private code for everything we don't want to say."

Zev looks at his watch again. *Time's up. Get over yourself. It's only a birthday, and there's no point missing her. That part of your life is BZI, and it's gone.*

He sees his replacement coming out of the guardhouse, gets ready to climb down, scans the bobbing mass once more, looking for the auburn-and-blue flash of the little girl. She's way over in the corner of the L, at the ten-foot end where nobody swims when it's this crowded, and she's jumping up and down in a puddle. *Shit.* Carrie is still flirting, and Zev blows his whistle as he's climbing down, two short, sharp blasts to get her attention again, but Glenn is showing Carrie his new tattoo and they never even look up.

On the ground Zev turns, whistle poised in his mouth for another blast, but the little girl is gone. She's in the water. He knows it, even though he can't see her, even though it makes more sense that she is in the crowd on deck, headed back to the moms. Zev knows.

He grabs the red rescue float and runs. *Every second counts*, he hears his lifeguard instructor saying.

"Move, move!" he yells, tearing around the right side of the pool. He is running as fast as possible, but still it feels like the longest trip he's ever taken, like the corner of the L is getting farther away instead of closer. Has everyone stopped talking? All he hears is the sound of his feet slapping the wet cement, his chafing breath.

When at last he reaches the place where the two arms of the pool come together, he looks over the edge for long enough to see auburn hair, waving like seaweed, ten feet under. He throws the float in the water, sucks in a huge breath, and dives deep, using his hands like an arrow and kicking as hard as he can to get past the other wriggling bodies. *Every second counts.* The water offers no resistance until he reaches his long arm way out in front of him to grab the girl by her blue swimsuit. He yanks upward, but she is deadweight, her head lolling forward. A hundred years pass before he can get his arm around her chest. He kicks them both toward the surface, her head bouncing against him, his biceps straining to hold her close. A muscle twitches on either side of his jaw as he fights the impulse to open his mouth.

He bursts out of the water, tipping his head for air, gasping like a fish. The little girl is limp. A marionette. He hears screaming from all sides, sees arms reaching to pull them both out. Carrie is standing nearby, not moving, wearing a look of terror.

Zev hands the girl up to waiting arms and hears himself rasping: "Lay her down flat." He flings himself out of the water and confirms that she has no pulse. He begins CPR, lining up his fingers on her bony little chest.

One, two, three, four, five. Breathe. Again: one, two, three, four, five. Breathe.

He pauses. Her lips are cold and white, his fingers tangled in the strings of her long hair. The mom is crying and screaming the girl's name: "Rosie! Rosie!"

Don't push too hard. She has a tiny heart. One, two, three, four, five. Breathe.

Zev keeps pumping on her heart. *Come on, Zoey. Come on! You've got this. One, two, three, four, five. Breathe.*

A muted gurgling sound comes from the girl, and he reaches a hand up and swivels her head to the side just before she vomits water all over the place. Her lungs retract with her breath, and she starts to cry. In three seconds, she's sitting up and the mom is all over her, crying and laughing.

Zev slumps back onto the cement, sucking wind. He is disconnected from his own body. Everything looks a little hazy, as if he needs glasses.

Words are flying around him, fast and jubilant. … *saved her!* … *amazing!* … *so close!*

"Are you okay?" he hears again and again.

"I'm fine," he rasps.

"I can't believe it. You were so fast! Absolutely incredible. How can I ever thank you?" the mom sobs, hugging him with shaking arms.

"No need. I was just doing my job," he says, his voice still ragged.

"I'm sorry, Zev, I … I'm … sorry," Carrie whispers in his ear.

He sees Rosie, standing there on her little faun legs steady as can be, as if nothing ever happened. Zev stands, too, smiles down at the girl and lays a hand on her auburn hair.

He walks over to the guardhouse to file an incident report with Glenn. The pool has been cleared, and Zev guesses it'll be fifteen minutes before people forget what happened and get on with the day.

He changes his clothes in the employee locker room, waves off the many offers of a ride home, and gets on his bike, a little shaky still, but glad for the chance to replay the whole thing. By the time he passes East Rock Park, it already doesn't seem real, and when he sees Mikayla sitting on her porch swing, he knows he's not telling her about what happened. That would be cheap.

When she sees him, she gets up and comes down the stairs, wiping her eyes. Is she crying? Of course: She knows what day this is. Zev has forgotten for a little while.

She comes right up to him and puts her arms around him for a hug, sniffling into his shirt. He hugs her hard but fast, knowing he's leaching chlorine and sweat, though what he wants is to settle his hand in the gentle curve at the small of her back, to rest his head in the soft skin of her neck. His body aches. It's as if he vibrates at a different frequency when Mikayla is around.

"Jeez. Some happy birthday," she says, laughing a little through her tears. "I miss her so much right now." She peers into his face. "You must be having such a shitty day."

Zev manages a little shrug, knowing that any movement bigger than that would make room for the scary sob that's building in his chest.

"Well, at least there's the DMV," he manages with almost no tremor in his voice.

She steps back, puts her hand up to her mouth, her bottle-green eyes huge and bloodshot. "Oh, God. I forgot. Project Sixteen. That *sucks*," she whispers.

"Yep. All gone. Not that we ever had much hope of bringing Mom and Dad around to the idea. But BZI, we could still hope, at least. Now? Forget it."

Mikayla's quiet for a minute. "But you're going ahead with your permit?" she says.

Zev nods.

"She's gonna be so pissed at you!" She punches him in the arm.

"Ow!" Zev smiles, feeling disloyal. "I know. Me, going ahead? It's a first." If it were anyone but Mikayla, he would never be talking like this.

"But you know, Zev, she'd be even more pissed if you didn't."

She's right, and he should say so. But there's that mess in his chest; he can't be trusted to say anything that matters.

He nods. "I'd better go. There's a whole … birthday thing at the hospital."

"Okay. Call me later. Tell me how it went. If you want, I mean."

"Sure."

If I want? It's the only birthday present he cares about. Despite the dread of the hospital that sits in his stomach like a lump of clay, despite the lost dream of Project Sixteen, despite the fact that saving Rosie feels more like a karmic correction than an act of bravery—Mikayla makes everything a bit less dreadful. He is swamped by a giant wave of feeling. He might love her.

She is standing there looking at him as if she can read his mind. He flees indoors and almost runs over Lottie in the foyer, doing her dance of impatience. When she sees him, her face breaks into a huge grin.

"Zev!" she shouts, grabbing his arm. "Finally! I thought you'd never get home."

"What's the deal? Is there some big news? Did Zoey talk or something?"

Lottie does another little jig. "No, silly! It's your *birthdays*, and you won't believe what Mom and Dad—"

Mom comes into the hallway with her finger to her lips. "Lottie, shush. What did we talk about?"

Mom is wearing a mischievous smile as she puts a hand on Lottie's curly head. Zev looks from one to the other, and the wheels of his mind start to turn. *What was Lottie trying to tell me? And why is Mom grinning like the Cheshire cat when she hasn't smiled since Zoey ... ?*

His stupid brain keeps circling back to Project Sixteen. *What if?* It's undeniable that Mom's eyes are twinkling like they haven't in weeks. Zev summons his most casual and measured tone. "So, what's the schedule?"

"Dad is coming home early, so we can get to the DMV for your four o'clock spot and we can make it to the hospital for Zoey's dinnertime. She seems excited about our visit."

And just like that, the mirage vanishes. *What am I thinking?* This whole year has been a series of events designed to cancel Project Sixteen. When Ethan joined the Marines, it already put Dad on Danger Overload for the next decade. And any remaining hopes Zev had evaporated on the last day of school. He lurches past Mom into the kitchen, blinking back idiotic tears.

"I'm starved," he mumbles, sticking his head into the refrigerator.

"Well, yeah," Mom says. "You need fuel for that test!"

There is one thing he has control over for the rest of today: He's good at taking tests. *Thank the goddesses for small favors*, as Zoey would say. The trip to the DMV goes off without a hitch, and though his photo looks ghastly, and Zoey's absence pokes him like a fat splinter, his heart lightens a little when he tucks the laminated driver's permit into his wallet.

"Passed." He grins into the driver's-side window.

"Way to go, Zev!" says Dad, sounding surprised.

"Not that we're surprised," says Mom, as if she's reading his mind, as usual. "Do you want to drive us to the hospital?"

"Nah, that's okay. It's ... it's rush hour. Later is good."

They get to the hospital at 5:00 p.m., when the halls are buzzing with orderlies bringing dinner trays to the patients. As if they're all babies, needing to be fed so early. Mom is clutching her box of cupcakes, and it takes them a good fifteen minutes to make it through the throngs of well-wishing scrubs clustered around them.

"Hi, Dr. Sandor. Hi, Mrs. S. Good to see you. How are you holding up?"

"We're doing okay," says Mom, smiling her new, tired smile. "Zoey's making progress. And today's a special day: It's the twins' sixteenth birthday."

A special day. Zev feels like he's six instead of sixteen.

"Wow! Happy birthday!" the scrubs clamor.

"We're all rooting for Zoey. She's doing so great! Up and about already!"

"We're praying for you."

"We're holding a good thought."

What does any of that mean? As if their "good thoughts" could have any impact on Zoey's derailed life. All their talk is designed to make them feel better about themselves. Zev keeps his head down.

Things don't get any better in Zoey's room. She's sitting up in front of her dinner tray with a bib tucked under her chin.

"A bib? Seriously?" he mutters, accidentally out loud. But in the hubbub of wishing Zoey happy birthday and showing her the cupcakes, no one hears. He hangs back in the doorway.

He senses the edges of the hole tearing open again. It's coming. It's a freight train. In desperation he closes his eyes, grabs a virtual pencil, and draws a virtual suit of armor around his inner organs. He locks the armor in place with a key, a shield against the horror-movie gash. He knows it's the power of suggestion, at least that's what Mom told him when she taught him this stuff a few years ago: It's called *positive visualization*. But sometimes it helps with talking to people. Now, it's helping him feel one millimeter less freaked. He concentrates on keeping his face neutral.

Zev risks a glance at Zoey. The nurse—Mom talks about her all the time, calling her "my darling Clementine"—is helping Zoey to get the spoon of yogurt from the tray to her mouth, but Zoey's hand is jittering all over the place. Maybe that's what Mom means by "wobbly." Besides that, she doesn't look too bad. The bruising on her face is gone, and she looks sleepy and dull, as if she pulled an all-nighter.

Zoey finally takes a break from the marathon sport of getting food to her mouth and looks up. She sees him standing in the doorway and everything changes: Her eyes go wide, her face opens like an umbrella, and her lips form a wavy smile. She drops the spoon.

"Zev," she whispers.

The whole room inhales at this—her first coherent word since the coma. Zev lurches forward, palms sweating, and grabs Zoey's fisted left hand. She startles at his touch and her breath comes in short gasps. Her eyes get even wider, a swirl of amber shot through with sunlight. Zev's identical eyes are locked on hers.

"Hey, Zoey." His voice matches hers. He clears his throat and squeezes her hand. "Welcome back!"

She's trembling and she flinches a little, so he loosens his grip, remembering the purple half-moons he left that first time.

"Zev," she says, louder now, looking surprised at the sound of her own voice, which is whispery and high. "Want ..."—she clears her throat, too—"want ... a cupcake?"

Zev unlocks the suit of armor.

"Oh, yeah, sure," he says, trying for nonchalant. "I'll have one if you do."

Lottie pushes forward and hands him two cupcakes. "Here!" she practically yells. Zoey flinches again, and Mom and Dad shush her quickly.

"But why can't I talk to her too?" Lottie whispers.

"We don't want to overwhelm her," Mom whispers back. "You'll get your turn."

Zev focuses all his energy on Zoey.

"I'll put the cupcake here, on your tray. And, hey! Happy birthday to us, right? Can you believe it? We made it to sixteen! And guess where I'm coming from? The DMV. I got my permit. Look."

He pulls out his wallet, flashes the ID card, and waits.

"Per-per-mit?"

"Yeah. Don't feel bad, you'll get there soon. I know it's gotta be frustrating for you, stuck in here. But you're doing great. You'll be out running sprints again in no time. And I can track you in Mom's car, if she ever lets me drive it. But anyway, first I have to get my license. When you get outta here, I'll drive you wherever you want while you're working on yours. Deal?"

The room is silent, as stunned as he is by the verbal torrent that has fallen from his mouth. But he's been saving up for a while. This is only the beginning of all the things he wants to say to her. He catches his breath and waits for her to answer, squeezing her hand.

She retracts her hand with a jerk, startling him. A mercury flush spreads across his face.

"Zev," she whispers again, smiling crookedly.

She's looking right at him, so he sees the change in her eyes as they grow dull. As if someone pulled down a shade. She's gone again.

Amber eyes flaring with light, glazing over, slipping away.

Zev stands there for the four or five seconds it takes him to understand that there won't be a conversation. He stares around the room. Everything blurs. There is an echo in his head. When his focus returns, it's wrapped around a core of burning pain. The black hole. He grits his teeth against the spasm, dropping into the plastic chair behind him.

Mom and Dad both talk at once, in semihushed voices, about Zoey's "amazing breakthrough," and Lottie comes and sits at the end of Zoey's bed.

He gets it now: There's nothing magical about this day, and Zoey is not coming back. He needs to get used to being alone, which he's never been in his life.

He clenches his fists and forces himself to breathe. No amount of positive visualization will stop this wound from opening every time he's near her.

If she won't come back, he won't either.

When Zoey finishes the interminable process of eating her mutilated cupcake, Mom wipes her chin and hands, and Zoey turns her head away again and again, like Lottie in the high chair when she was two. Zev can't stand the sight and turns his own head away. Dad helps Zoey into a wheelchair for a "birthday ride" since she's not quite ready for the long walk down the hall. Zev keeps his face averted. He doesn't need to see her floppy body sliding off the bed.

Lottie is wild about the expedition. "Can I ride in Zoey's lap?"

"No, sweetheart, she's not ready for that," says Dad. "But you can help push her."

Lottie dances a little ballet of glee, and "helps" wheel Zoey down the hall. Zev shuffles behind them, wishing he was eight years old and could shake off the last half hour. They jostle through the front doors of the hospital into the muggy air and make their way out to the emptying parking lot. Dad does an end run around the wheelchair and whispers something to Mom.

Everyone stops. Lottie is jumping up and down. "Happy birthday!" she screams.

Zev looks past her bouncing curls to see what she's so excited about now. He blinks and rubs his eyes to be sure he isn't hallucinating the tableau at the end of the parking lot: Ethan is grinning and waving as he leans up against an old VW Bug covered with bumper stickers. Zev starts toward his brother, waving back. Where could Ethan have gotten the wheels, and how has he come back so soon again from Kabul?

Zev stops in his tracks as he realizes this is a *red car* with an enormous white bow on top. It doesn't have a scratch on it, just a bunch of bumper stickers about *peace* and *love*. Zev looks over at Mom and Dad, who are smiling and nodding at him.

Dad hands him a key tied with a red ribbon. "Happy birthday, son."

He stares at Dad's outstretched hand.

"Go on. Take it."

Zev reaches out and takes the key.

"We decided long before all of this." Dad waves a hand over Zoey's head. "It's Mrs. Mishkin's, from the synagogue. It's been in her garage for thirty years, so we had her keep it there for us a little while longer. Only fourteen thousand miles on it. Isn't it a beauty?"

"We trust you, honey," Mom chimes in. "We know you'll use it well."

Zev nods. He squints at his brother, who waves him over to their car—no, *his* car, at least for now—glowing a juicy candy-apple red in the late-afternoon light.

"Come on, little brother! What're you waiting for?" Ethan says.

Zev bows his head for a moment, grateful for the benediction of hope restored. Then he lets out an enormous whoop and goes to collect his consolation prize.

DAY 17, CONTINUED

Liv pulled her van into the driveway with a small thrill. Her spirits had been buoyed by Zoey's breakthrough, but even so, she was surprised to feel like she was coming home to her house for the first time. She pushed open the door and stopped, breathing in as the walls exhaled their welcome. Garlic. Basil. Caramelized sugar. She walked down the long central corridor to the kitchen, passing the little library to the right and the living room through the French doors to the left, where the worn baby grand waited for Sam to come and charm sweet sounds from its keys. Zoey's cello stood next to it, a film of dust already collecting on its feminine curves.

That room had been filled with music every Friday night for as long as Liv could remember—music Sam called forth with joy from the piano, and with even greater glee from his children. Their weekly jam sessions often lasted for hours. Zoey on the cello, Ethan and Zev switching between guitar and ukelele. Then Lottie on bongos and djembes. Even Liv hadn't been able to resist and was assigned the tambourines and bells. All of them singing, laughing. Now the room had a forlorn air, as if it knew the silent Fridays it had already endured were the beginning of a long dry spell.

The house at East Rock was the center of Liv's life, the cradle of her family. It was true she'd loved Sam from the moment they met, as though there had been a vacancy in her life and he was the one to fill it, but the fact of this house had been a thrilling bonus, and she'd slipped into it with the certainty of homecoming.

Now Liv could feel her house waiting for normal life to resume, the walls asking their questions: What happened to the sounds of laughter and arguing, the clumps of teenagers who left piles of sweatshirts and bracelets everywhere? What happened to the music, that great noise we have come to love? Where are the scents of soups and sauces, rich cakes and yeasty breads that once suffused every corner?

Liv couldn't put to rights all that had been lost in these last weeks. She couldn't bring back the music or the knots of young people. But she could do something about the food.

First, she had to find out what was in her refrigerator—she had no idea, another unprecedented situation. She watched Zev pulling his little red car into the driveway behind the minivan, with Sam riding shotgun and looking like a skittish hound. Zev ran inside and hung his new keys on the hook next to Liv's with a quick grin in her direction.

"How'd it go?" she asked.

"Good! I call the shower!" He bounded up the stairs.

Sam came inside and stared at Liv as if he wasn't sure why she was there.

"We could all do with a little snack," she said.

He nodded and sat down at the kitchen table, running his hands through his hair.

Liv stood in front of the open fridge trying to make sense out of the abundance of nothing. Had they been subsisting on Chesed casseroles alone? Well, no matter. At least there was fresh mozzarella to work with. She grabbed it along with a jar of her fig jam and a day-old baguette that should have been in the bread box.

Ethan came in with Lottie. "Ugh. This jet lag is a killer," he said, collapsing into a chair next to Sam.

"With two trips from Afghanistan in less than three weeks? It's no wonder," said Sam, looking as if he had made the trips himself.

"Yep, I'm *wrung out* from all this excitement," said Lottie, and plopped herself down with the men. Liv kept her back to the group, concealing her amusement as she assessed her indoor herb garden and busied herself at the cutting board.

"Well, my CO said I'm no good to anyone this distracted. He ordered me to get my head straight before I come back." Ethan paused. "Is there a snack?"

"What do you think?" said Liv with a smile, checking the temperature of her panini pan. "Give me about—six more minutes."

She was unaccountably happy as she set down her "snack" in the middle of the table: grilled panini with fresh mozzarella, rosemary, and fig jam. Not bad, considering.

"Oooh! It's like—toasted-cheese-pizza-dessert," said Lottie, grinning up at Liv.

"Amazing, Livie," said Sam, shaking his head.

"Oh, my God, Mom. You are a freaking genius!" said Ethan. "I try to tell my friends about your magic tricks in the kitchen, but they've got no idea. Now that I've been living on army rations, I'm even more impressed. How do you do it?"

"How does she do what?" asked Zev as he shuffled in, looking like a little boy fresh from his bath.

"This. Taste it and weep, birthday boy," said Ethan, handing him a sandwich.

Zev took a bite, grunted appreciatively, and raised his eyebrows in her direction. She shrugged modestly, but her heart swelled. She didn't know how it worked, though she had once heard Zoey describe her to a friend as "a cross between Julia Child and Amelia Bedelia." In fact, she went almost completely on instinct in the kitchen. All that mattered tonight was that she had done her small part to repair the torn fabric of their world.

"Did you know that we missed birthday breakfast this morning?" said Lottie.

"What? Oh no! We did, didn't we? Why didn't you say something, sweetie?" said Liv.

"I forgot! I'm always half asleep when I get on the bus."

"I guess we've all been half asleep," said Liv.

Zev shrugged. "It doesn't matter. We're here now."

"But it's not the same!" Lottie said. "And I got your present *ages* ago. Can't we do it tomorrow? Please oh please?"

"Oh, yes, let's do that. I would feel terrible if we didn't!" Liv said.

Somehow, Lottie managed to extract a promise from her brothers to be up again at 7:00 a.m. the next day. Zev looked glum, but Liv was pleased, another chance for redemption. "Well done, Lottie. Now off to bed!" She steered her baby's sleepy little body up the stairs.

•

Liv's alarm woke her at 5:30 a.m. She must be nuts, getting up at dawn to bake; she figured the last time she was this exhausted was when the twins were infants. But no birthday breakfast was complete without her chocolate bread pudding, and right now, she was willing to trade sleep for even a moment of normalcy.

She went downstairs and turned on the coffeemaker and the oven in her quiet house, giving herself over to routine. She tore up a loaf of challah, bathed it in the sweet egg-and-milk mixture that would turn to custard in the oven, and dusted it all over with shards of dark chocolate. She slipped it in the oven, poured herself a cup of coffee, and started on the vanilla rum sauce.

Ninety minutes later, true to their word, they all stumbled back down the stairs, bullied into consciousness by an insistent Lottie, and further persuaded by the smell of bread pudding. Heaven. They deposited gifts and cards in front of Zev on the barn door that served as a kitchen table, poured giant mugs of coffee, and slumped into their seats. Sam smiled at Liv as she set the bread pudding before Zev in its usual blue ceramic dish, stuck with sixteen candles and one for good luck. He blew them out without so much as closing his eyes.

There was an awkward silence while no one mentioned the Wish. Even Lottie understood that the situation called for restraint. The Wish was Zoey's favorite part of the birthday ritual, and Liv was sure they could all hear her voice in their heads.

"No matter how old I get," Zoey would say every year, "when I close my eyes and make my Wish, I feel like anything's possible." She would give a little shiver of delight and that secret smile of hers.

It didn't bear thinking about now, but Liv couldn't help it. She sank down in her seat at the table in time to see Zev close his eyes after all, in the moment that first bite of bread pudding landed on his tongue. He swallowed, opened his eyes, and looked at Liv with a sweet, little boy grin, and she answered him with the brightest smile she could manage.

He turned his attention to his presents. "When did you guys even have time …?"

"Oh," Liv said, "it was pure luck that we all planned ahead for once."

From Ethan, there was a frame for the license plate of Zev's car, engraved with the saying *A Good Driver Is Quick on the Draw.*

Zev grinned at Ethan. "Thanks, E. Clever! Where'd you find it?"

"I found it in an airport, but I can't tell you where or I'd have to kill you."

Everyone laughed.

"Ha-ha. Such a wise guy." Zev grinned, tearing into his gift from Lottie, a spectacular set of drawing pencils he had been eyeing on his last trip to the art supply store.

"Wow. Thanks, Lottie. These are awesome. How did you know?"

"A little birdie told me." Lottie giggled and eyed Liv sideways.

"I can't wait to try them out. You rock, peanut."

From Sam and Liv, there was a card that went with last night's surprise. Liv had bought it months ago and was glad, now, that it was humorous instead of sentimental. Zev read it aloud, their family custom.

"*Now that you're sixteen, you can do all kinds of things you never did before …*"—he opened the card—"*… like backing over your own bike in the driveway. Happy birthday, Zev. We love you always.*" He smirked. "Oh, ha-ha. Everyone's a wise guy today."

They all laughed again, and Liv stood up, squeezing Sam's shoulder as she passed on her way to clean up the detritus of her sunrise cooking project.

Sam rose as well. "Happy birthday, son. I've got to get to work. Stay out of trouble, kids." He came over to Liv and murmured, "I'll look in on her this morning. Why don't you take your time with the boys?"

Liv nodded. "Thanks, love," she said as he bent to kiss her. She wrapped herself around him and held him there for a moment, wishing to prolong the illusion of normalcy though she could feel the restlessness in every part of him. He went back to the table and kissed Lottie on the head, placed a hand on Zev's shoulder, and tousled Ethan's hair on his way out. But she watched Sam's heavy walk down the hall and saw him stop to stare at the piano as he passed. It was the look of a poor man at the cafe window: He knew he wouldn't play today, or anytime soon.

Liv ran the sponge ineffectually over pots and mixing bowls and stared out at her garden, which had the air of a vacant lot. She felt the weight of all that was missing from the twins' "sweet sixteen," two years in the making. She remembered how, the night before their fourteenth birthday, she had come upon them hatching one of their fanciful plots while Ethan played devil's advocate.

"So, what's this grand plan, guys?" she had asked with a smile.

Zoey's eyes shone. "The plan is, when we turn sixteen, we'll come down for birthday breakfast and there'll be a brand-new car in the driveway. Candy-apple red, of course. There'll be two sets of keys hanging on the key rack by the door."

"Oh? And what then?"

"We'll hop in, roll down all the windows, and take off. You guys will all be standing in the driveway with your mouths open, and you'll have to just wave goodbye."

"Yeah, right!" Ethan put in. "Dad'll never go for it." In those days, Ethan and Sam had been fighting nonstop over Ethan's plans. "I was practically in lockdown right after I turned sixteen. You know, Dad might be going on about this family's *environmental footprint*"—he smirked at Liv—"but the real reason you guys'll never get your birthday wish is Dad's paranoia about car crashes. After what happened to Papa and Goldie? Plus, what does he do all day at the hospital? He patches up people who've been crushed to a pulp in their cars! Forget about it. Never gonna happen, little sister."

"Never say never, E," Zoey said. "Dad might give in, if I keep working on him. If I ask him *super nicely*."

"It's true, you do kind of have a private request line with Dad," Zev had said, with a touch of hope and not a hint of resentment.

"Yeah, but even Mom buys into his paranoia."

"Hey, E, don't put me in the middle of this!" Liv had said, laughing.

"Well, what about those crazy restrictions you guys piled on me? As if the state driving laws weren't bad enough! If you pull it off, Zo, I'll eat my hat." Ethan took off his baseball cap and waved it at her.

"Okay, E. I hope you like the taste of sweaty cotton."

Zoey's eyes gleamed. She loved a challenge. If anyone could talk Sam into such a plan, Liv surmised, it was Zoey. Her potency lay in the fact that she didn't rely on charm alone. She was a diplomat; she didn't hammer at her father, but broached delicate questions with him rarely, strategically, after an exhilarating run or a Friday night jam.

Meanwhile, Zoey and Zev were busy behind the scenes. Before long, what started as a childish fantasy was transformed into an elaborate game. The twins could often be found sitting up late at night, on the hammock in warm weather or huddled around the kitchen table in winter, embellishing their plans in high whispers, talking in the shorthand only they understood. One night, Liv had come across them poring over a US road map, guidebooks and computer printouts spread all around them.

"What're you two up to now?"

"We're mapping our route for Project Sixteen," Zev said.

Liv was surprised to see they had indeed traced several possible routes in different colors.

"Wow! I'm impressed. You've put a lot of thought into this, haven't you?"

"Oh, Mom, you have no idea," Zoey said. "We've already identified our top five destinations in the continental US! Niagara Falls. The Grand Canyon. Santa Fe …"

They'd calculated how long it would take to drive between points, scheduled eating and sleeping stops, and consulted their savings accounts for budgetary limitations.

Liv had whispered to Sam during one of their pillow talks, "Did you see that Niagara image Zev worked into his latest painting?"

"I did. In fact, I was going to mention it to you. I've been thinking, Livie, that since this Project Sixteen has such a hold on Zev's imagination, maybe the car would be a kind of doorway out for him. We need to tease out his independence before the twins have to leave home, don't you think?"

"You're right, love," she said, touched by Sam's willingness to put aside his fears for Zev's sake, as he had forced himself to do in giving Ethan his blessing before he was deployed.

Why was it that parents were so often called upon to sacrifice their own peace of mind so their children could grow?

Liv watched her boys now, engaged in one of their little verbal sparring matches, the present circumstances too painful for either of them to acknowledge. It was so much easier to cultivate this atmosphere of casual hilarity.

Ethan: "Don't imagine just because you've got wheels, you'll get the girls. Let your big bro give you some pointers."

Zev: "You're not the only one with the goods. Between the new wheels and the lifeguarding, I'm going to be next-level cool. So move over, soldier."

Ethan: "Nah. The uniform rules. Besides, a mutant giraffe like you will never get a date."

Zev: "Who are you calling a mutant, Four-Eyes?"

Lottie stood by and giggled; Liv could see she wanted nothing more than to bask in the warmth of birthday breakfast and her brothers' gentle ribbing. They all lingered at the table among the gift wrapping and breakfast dishes, reluctant to break the spell.

"Will you come home for my end-of-summer play at Camp Artemis?" Lottie asked Ethan.

"We'll have to talk about that later, Lottie, time for the bus now. Quick!"

Liv gave a mental nod to Mother for having accomplished the impossible with the camp bus, glad not to be making the drive each morning and afternoon. There were, after all, some advantages to being a tyrant. As she waved Lottie off, the image of Zoey alone in the hospital flickered in Liv's mind like a migraine, but she pushed it outside and shut the door.

She poured herself another cup of coffee and sat down with her boys.

Ethan said, "Okay, Mom, so Zoey's stable now. And talking!" He saluted Zev, who blushed and said nothing. "What happens next?"

Liv smiled at her perennial pragmatist. "She's being transferred to the TBI Rehab wing sometime in the next week." She made a face to acknowledge the strangeness of it: The TBI Rehab wing had been Sam's stomping ground for the last twenty years. "And unless a miracle happens, she'll be there for two to three months at least."

The boys exchanged a glance.

"So, what is that, like, PT and cognitive retraining?" Ethan continued.

"Exactly. She'll have physical, occupational, and speech therapy every day, with Dad's most experienced team. You can bet they'll be bringing their A game while their boss's daughter is there. That's my one consolation in this whole impossible mess."

"Is there *any* chance she'll be okay, Mom?" Ethan asked. "Like you said, Dad is in charge. If everyone works overtime, could she get back to her old self?"

Zev sat up a little straighter. Liv desperately wished she could say what they wanted to hear, but she shook her head before she could stop herself. "By the fall, we'll have a better idea of where Zoey will be for the long term." She didn't say why she was shaking her head, but the spine went right out of Zev.

Ethan glanced at his brother before speaking again. "I'm not sure—" He paused and pushed his glasses up the bridge of his nose.

"What, sweetheart?"

"I was going to say, I'm not sure if you guys need me here or if it's pointless. I don't even know *what* to say about Zoey ... I see lots of TBIs in the field, so I'm learning about this stuff faster than I ever would've wanted to, but I've got no real training that could help her when she's already got Dad."

He paused again and gave Liv a distressed half smile like Zev's. Liv smiled back without speaking; she learned far more about her children by keeping quiet.

"Though I can't imagine how he's handling this," Ethan added. "Personally, I'm taking turns being repelled, hopeful, and heart-broken."

"Oh, Ethan. Count on you to say it straight," Liv said. "You might be going on twenty, but in many ways, you've been an adult for years. I guess it's the blessing and curse of being the oldest, right?"

"I guess."

"But E, you know that Dad shouldn't be treating Zoey, don't you? And he can't 'cure' her of a severe brain injury. No one can."

The phone rang as Ethan was about to respond. Liv would've liked to let the answering machine get it, but she always worried that it could be the hospital. In this case, it was Glenn, the head lifeguard at the Swim Club, calling for Zev.

"One minute, I'll get him for you," said Liv, mouthing to Zev, *It's Glenn*.

"But before you go, Mrs. Sandor, I want to congratulate you on Zev's extraordinary bravery and fast thinking yesterday," Glenn said. "It was amazing the way he rescued little Rosie Kramer. Perfect form pulling her out, and he didn't even need to ask for help with the CPR. It all happened so quickly. Everyone was super impressed with his maturity, the way he kept a cool head."

"Oh, well—gosh, thanks. I appreciate you saying that," said Liv, trying to keep the shock from her voice. She shook her head as she handed the phone to Zev. How could he have been through something so dramatic yesterday and not said a word to any of them?

When he hung up a moment later, Liv said, "Zev? Glenn just congratulated me on your act of bravery yesterday!"

Zev looked startled and turned crimson.

Ethan sat up straight and squinted at Zev. "Wait! What act of bravery?"

"Well, apparently, your brother saved a little girl from drowning," said Liv. She turned to Zev. "So, what happened? Spill it!"

"All right, all right. I-I didn't want to make a big deal out of it," Zev said, his face mottling red and white by turns. "Her name is Rosie. She's probably, like, five. She fell in the deep end. I pulled her out. I did CPR. She was fine. End of story. Okay?" He cleared his throat and picked at the scarred surface of the table.

"Jeez, Zev," Ethan breathed. "It's not a small thing, saving a life, you know?"

Liv wondered what appalling scene in the Afghan desert he was recalling.

"And why would you keep something like that to yourself?" she asked Zev. "What an incredible thing to happen—you gave a child her life back on your *birthday*."

"God, Mom, you make it sound so … I just did what they trained us to do. I'm a lifeguard. I didn't want everyone acting like I was some sort of hero."

"Honey. I know you don't like being the center of attention, but this *was* extraordinary. Even Glenn used that word." She paused. "Were you scared?"

Zev looked up at her, his lion eyes soft. "No. Well, yeah, I guess, when I first realized. But it happened so fast, I just had to go with it. It was over before I had time to freak."

"I'm surprised Rosie Kramer's mother hasn't called. Did she thank you?"

"Yeah, she thanked me a bunch of times. But like I said, it's what they hire us to do."

Ethan let out a kind of barking laugh that didn't sound like him. "You say it's no biggie," he muttered, "but you changed that little kid's future. And her parents' future, too. What if things had turned out that well for Zoey?"

Zev looked ready to bolt. Liv took a deep breath to push back her tears, wanting to say, *They still could.* But she also wanted to keep the boys talking for as long as possible; she would need to let Zev simmer down.

"So, Ethan, where were we before the phone rang? We were talking about your plans."

"Right. I was saying that on the one hand, I feel like I should come back here, help out in whatever way I can. But on the other hand, if I ask for an early release, I'll lose my scholarship for sure, and you guys would end up paying my tuition. A total waste. And, well, you might need that money for Zoey."

Zev sat up straight. "Jesus, E!"

"What? I'm just calling it like I see it."

Liv was startled, too. "Honey, you don't need to be worrying about—"

"But I do, Mom. How many stories has Dad told us about his patients who can't support themselves?"

He was so much more like Sam than he knew, his ruminations taking him far into a murky future no one else wanted to contemplate.

What if Liv encouraged him to go back to his unit, and he was injured, or worse? This was her chance to keep her boy safe. Then again, what if she told him to come home, and the loss of his scholarship derailed his plans somehow, or they ended up in financial trouble? It felt like a Solomonic dilemma.

But looking at Ethan, Liv knew what she had to say.

"Sweetie, you should go back. Life around here is a hot mess right now. The best thing you can do—for everyone's sake—is to stay on track. Don't jeopardize your goals because of what happened to Zoey. Finish your tour, go to college, and follow *your* dreams."

Ethan's brow relaxed. "Wow. I didn't expect that …"

"Wait! Were you—were you looking for me to give you an out?"

"No! No. This feels right to me. I mean, if you're sure."

"I am," she lied.

"Okay! You won't be sorry. You'll see. I'll work my ass—sorry, my butt—off and come home safe. Less than a year left! You and Dad don't have to worry about me, I swear."

If only that were true. Sam would not be pleased to hear about this conversation. But Ethan bounced out of his seat.

"I still want to stay a couple of days—but I'll call my CO and set up my flight back to base." He started out of the room, turned, and came back to kiss Liv on the head, tousled his brother's mop of hair, and hurried out.

Liv had noticed Zev's color rising again as she spoke to Ethan, and now he expelled an angry breath. "Mom, you're not seriously saying Ethan is the great hope of the family now that Zoey's brain is fried!"

"What? That's a *terrible* thing to say. And not what I told him at all!"

"Well, it sure sounded like it. That's, like, a *Nana* attitude!"

"Zev, you're mistaken. I'm not talking about some objective social standard. I want Ethan to succeed for Ethan's sake. Should I *not* encourage him to go back, even if it's the right thing for him?" She was trying to keep her voice even.

"That's not what I'm saying, Mom."

"Well, then, I guess we're both misunderstanding each other. But whatever issues we might have—and doesn't every family have them?—Dad and I've tried to be pretty evenhanded in our parenting. And I hope we've succeeded." She exhaled long and slowly. "Speaking of which, let's talk about you."

Zev shook his head. "You don't need to worry about me."

There were smudges of fatigue under his eyes.

"I know, honey. But that's the thing about worry. There's always enough to go around."

He was silent.

"You had a bunch of major art projects waiting for summer. How are those going?"

He looked pained. Liv knew he'd counted on this summer to flesh out his art portfolio and had confided to her that he'd planned a series of drawings he thought might be his ticket into the Rhode Island School of Design. She'd reported that conversation to Sam as proof that Zev was becoming more independent, glossing over the fact that Zoey had her sights on Brown University, right next door to RISD; she was glad that Zev was setting his own goals and beginning to imagine a life beyond New Haven.

But of course, that was all derailed now.

"I've been so tired. I'm still getting used to lifeguarding, you know? It's intense."

"I guess it is." Liv forced herself not to get sidetracked again by the Rosie Kramer story. "It's a great experience for you, holding down a job—and I like that you're spending more time outside. But you need to get your ducks in a row for the independent study with Mr. Vincent."

"I know," Zev said gloomily.

"What? Is there a problem? You were so flattered that he picked you!"

Mr. Vincent was the most beloved art teacher in New Haven, and he had become a local celebrity when he found a way to merge his curriculum with the city's desperate need for beautification. Now, every year he would handpick a group of advanced painting students to identify local sites in need of aesthetic improvement, then have them design a mural for the space and assemble a team of other art students to help them paint it.

"It's a lot of responsibility, Mom," said Zev, not meeting her eyes.

"Yes, it is. And when you decided it would be worth the stress, you couldn't have known what would happen. But, well, do you think it might be a good distraction? And didn't Mr. Vincent say you could paint whatever you wanted as long as you ran it by him first?"

"Yeah. And I've almost got my team together: Gideon and Ramie have mad illustrating skills." He paused, blushing, and looked down at his fidgety hands. "I think I might ask Mikayla to be the fourth," he said.

Liv kept her expression neutral as she wondered what there was to blush about. Mikayla was a great choice, with her eye for color. And Zev would be more comfortable with her than with most people, wouldn't he?

"Good idea. So, what's the problem?"

"I need a full set of sketches by the end of summer if I want to finish on the Thanksgiving deadline."

"Well, that sounds doable."

"I guess." He was silent for a long moment. "Organizing a team isn't my best thing, you know? That's Zoey's gig. Or it used to be, anyway."

Liv put a hand on his arm. "Zev. What is this really about?"

Zev swallowed. "It's—the site, Mom."

"The sight? Whose sight?"

"*S-I-T-E*. The stupid thing is supposed to go up in the courtyard outside the TBI Rehab wing, remember?"

Liv blanched. That part of the plan had slipped her mind. Zev had asked for permission to do his mural on the downtown campus of Yale New Haven Hospital, and the administration had approved. Zev had seemed happy about it, too—or at least comfortable enough in the space, and confident no one would question his right to be there.

Now she could see the whole scenario laid out before her, another personal train wreck.

"Oh, Zev! That's—that's hard, isn't it? Do you want to ask Mr. Vincent for a change of venue?"

"I can't. It's too late." His voice was thick. "The committee that meets to approve the sites is gone for the summer. Besides, I can't see moving the project to another location where I'd have to deal with people I don't even know."

"Well, maybe it won't be so bad, then. You'll get to spend some time with Zoey and Dad—"

"Oh, joy!"

"What does *that* mean?"

Zev looked away. Liv jostled his arm a little.

He looked back at her and sighed. "I don't know, Mom. Even with everything that happened, Dad's right back to status quo. He's never home, and he worries more about his other patients than about Zoey."

"I see how it could feel that way to you. But this is a complex issue, honey."

"What's so complex about it? Isn't he the biggest brain injury expert in the state?"

"I suppose he is, but—"

"And she's a ... She has a TBI now, right?"

"Right." Liv cleared her throat around a swell of sadness.

"So, then, *he* should be taking care of *her*. Simple, like I said."

"It might look simple. But you know, this is what I was saying to Ethan—it's considered a bad idea for doctors to treat *any* family members, much less their own children."

Zev thought for a moment. "Well, what does Dad say?"

"Dad is pretty conflicted. On the one hand, Zoey has a moderately severe TBI, and she's on his wing because it's the best rehab in the area. On the other hand, he knows he can't be objective about her care." She paused. "But you know, even *without* Dad treating her, she still has an advantage, since everyone on the TBI Rehab wing is under his supervision, and he's making sure they follow every lead. Can you imagine, if he *was* her doctor and he missed something?"

"When does he ever miss something with a patient? He's, like, unstoppable."

"Mistakes happen in every medical practice, Zev. He's not a superhero—he's human, like everyone else."

"People sure act like he's God. And what about the 'miracle patients' who make those inspiring speeches at the holiday parties every year? Aren't they all Dad's?"

Liv realized that Zev still believed Sam could be the architect of Zoey's miracle. She'd have to be careful what she said next.

"Of course, and we're all hoping Zoey can be one of those miracle patients. But even those people don't make a comeback only because of Dad, and it doesn't happen overnight, either. They have supportive families, and a fighting spirit, and a team of experts working for them. And time."

"Well, Zoey has all those things, doesn't she?"

"She does." Liv paused. "Although, speaking of 'supportive families,' Zev, I hate to bring it up again, but this is such a crucial time in her recovery, and you got her talking last night! Doesn't that mean something? And did I tell you she's started drawing in a notebook Francesca gave her? It's all a mess right now, none of it's making much sense yet, but if you could sit with her, do one of your sketches in person ..."

"But, Mom! If it's such a crucial time in her recovery, isn't this when Dad should be the *most* involved? What if *he's* the tipping point? What if she could have made it all the way back, but she *doesn't*? How could he live with himself then?"

Zev's voice was edging out of its recent baritone into the tenor register, and Liv couldn't bring herself to push him anymore about visiting Zoey.

"We have to trust Dad to make the best decisions he can," she said lamely.

Zev sighed and left the table without another word. Liv rose with a sigh of her own and got ready for the hospital. She was knackered, and her day was only starting.

EXCERPT FROM

THE MEMORY BOOK OF ZOEY SANDOR

We're in the living room in our tent, no boys allowed, no Mommy and Daddy to tell us what to do, just me and Mikayla best friends forever and a bubble of happiness jumping in my throat. Let's play House I get to be the Mommy and you be the Baby. No, says Mikayla, she stands over me her hands on her hips, you always get to be the Mommy now it's my turn you be the Baby, lie down here I will put a blanket over you. It's hot under the blanket and I don't want to be a baby it makes me feel little and scared. Mikayla is happy she brings me juice she reads to me "It is the time you have wasted on your rose that makes your rose so important" she says in her Mommy voice. The words make me sad, I start to cry, the blanket is heavy I can't move but I don't want to hear any more. Still she keeps on reading "You must not forget it you become responsible forever for what you have tamed you are responsible for your rose ..." Stop I try to yell but my words come out wrong and nobody can understand me anymore.

(Transcribed by Francesca Garibaldi, SLP)

DAY 28

The bathroom door slammed open, and Sam looked up from where he was waiting uneasily in the chair by Zoey's hospital bed in time to see her lurch out with her shorts all bunched up around her waist and one arm pinned underneath her T-shirt. It was true that these patient bathrooms were cramped, but that wasn't the main problem: She had clearly tried to dress with one hand again, and her nondominant one at that; she forgot she had a left hand at all.

"Do you need help?"

Zoey wavered in front of him, focused her eyes on his face, and nodded.

"You fix me?" she said in her whispery new voice.

If only I could, baby.

Zoey used to say those words when she was a little girl, maybe four years old, and learning to dress herself. Like Sam, she was an early riser, and she would always want to put on her own clothes, presenting herself to Sam afterward for adjustments.

"You fix me?" she would ask adorably, flapping her shirt with the buttons not quite right or tugging on her twisted shorts, and waiting while he put the offending item to rights.

"All set!" he would say at last.

"Thanks, my Daddy," she would reply in her clear little voice, kissing his rough cheek. They would go hand in hand down the stairs to have breakfast before anyone else was up.

He was sure he was being punished for favoritism. He bit his lip as he tried to straighten Zoey's clothing without startling her or knocking her off her precarious balance. How often had his patients' families described their injured loved one as "everybody's favorite"? Could he trust a divine presence that would mark the most beloved children for catastrophe to right the scales of cosmic justice?

"All set." He recited his next line in their old script, though he knew Zoey would never remember the last part.

She smiled crookedly at him. "Thanks, my Daddy," she whispered, then covered her mouth as if she had no idea where those words came from.

Sam hugged her harder than he should, knowing it was wrong to ignore how she flinched at the close contact. Still, he was comforted by the evidence that fragments of the old Zoey were alive inside her. He was experiencing the seesaw effect he always warned his patients' families about: despair on one side and hope on the other. You had to teeter between the two while you waited for the arc of recovery to play itself out.

"Hi, Dr. Sandor."

Sam turned toward the physical therapist in the doorway, but Zoey didn't register his arrival. She was staring into the mirror on her closet door, mesmerized by the reflection of her own small movements.

"Oh, hey, Derek. She's all ready for you. And Liv is on her way."

Sam tried not to sound apologetic, though he knew his staff was struggling to walk the line as he wavered between his roles. Parents weren't permitted to attend daily physical therapy sessions; it was considered a liability. But Liv had taken to heart his warning about "being involved" and insisted on being there. Sam had asked his employees to indulge her for now; he figured there had to be some advantage to being the boss.

Derek nodded. "Hey there, Zoey. You ready to work?"

Zoey swiveled away from the mirror and shook her head, glancing at Derek with mingled distrust and alarm. Sam suspected she had no idea who he was, though she saw him almost every day.

"What are you working on today?"

"Balance, straightening out that walk. Making those legs stronger."

"Sounds good. Derek will take good care of you, honey."

Sam hoped today would go well, that his dedicated team could continue to push things forward. At the last Team Meeting, Francesca had reported, "Zoey Sandor is regaining verbal skills daily. She is currently able to construct simple sentences and appears able to read and write, though she is limited by left neglect. Drawings are unsteady and missing all or most of the left side, indicating hemispatial as well as functional neglect. We are assembling a Memory Book but her short- and long-term memory are erratic, and she is only intermittently responsive to prompts. All in all, though, I am pleased with her progress."

At the same meeting, Emma, Zoey's occupational therapist, reported, "The patient is left-handed but, based on discussions with her mother, has some cross dominance, as she plays the cello and is also in the habit of catching a ball with her right hand. This bodes well for recovering function over the long term. We're working on her activities of daily living—her ADLs—such as dressing, eating, brushing teeth, and personal hygiene."

Emma had glanced at Sam a few times during her report, and he'd tried to look reassuring. All of them had to know how brutal it was for him to hear them speak of Zoey in this way—but if he was going to insist on attending these meetings, he had to keep it together. And on some level, it was reassuring to witness them using their advanced clinical skills to restore as much of his daughter as they could.

Sam headed to his office, thinking that from a clinical perspective, he was always amazed by the unpredictable nature of TBI recovery, and how much it depended on the patient's constitution. The fact that Zoey hadn't spoken for all those days postcoma but now was already making complete, if halting, sentences, he attributed to her confidence, her outspokenness—a primary personality trait that had survived the accident. And hadn't she surprised him just now? Maybe he had no clinical judgment at all when it came to her. As he sat down at his desk to wade through piles of accumulated paperwork, he promised himself for the tenth time that he would leave the medical assessments to his rehab team and to the Brain Trust.

The intercom buzzed. "Luisa Reyes is here for her pump check."

Sam took a deep breath, grabbed the patient's chart from his desk with one hand and tried to smooth down his tortured hair with the other. He remembered as he was going out the door that his new physiatry fellow was coming today. Great. Babysitting, on top of everything else. What was her name again? He prayed she would be wearing a badge.

"Dr. Sandor?" His admin, Gillian, was waiting for him at the door to Exam Room 1. Perfect timing. "This is your new fellow, Sima Andrapur."

He glanced at the young woman—bright eyes, straight back, serious expression, chart in hand—and breathed a sigh of relief. She didn't look like she needed babysitting.

"Dr. Andrapur. Welcome to the floor," he said, shaking her hand and speaking quietly as they watched Luisa Reyes being wheeled down the long hall by paramedics. "As you can see, I like to observe the patient approaching. A lot can be gleaned from those moments before they enter the room. This is a long-time patient, so I can get an idea of her current level of pain by the extent of her grimace. She's a smiler on a good day."

Dr. Andrapur nodded and murmured, "TBI from an assault at age fourteen, yes? And a pioneer patient for the baclofen pump?"

Sam nodded, impressed. "Very good. Now age thirty. One of my first people."

Sixteen years ago, he'd somehow had the hubris to imagine he could help this girl, who had been beaten nearly to death in downtown Bridgeport. Luisa wasn't expected to survive, but she had defied the odds, the first of a special group of Sam's patients whom he privately called the Halfway Miracles, those who Sam took on after his colleagues had failed. He saw it as his personal challenge to help them chart a pathway back to a meaningful existence—whatever that meant to them now.

He told none of this to Dr. Andrapur, only asked her, "What do you know about the pump?"

"Well, it's implanted by a neurosurgeon but can be refilled in the office through an external port. And we can program it for custom doses of antispasticity medication at the times of day when the patient's spasms are worst. When Luisa started, it was still in clinical trials, right?"

Sam chuckled. "True. I guess that makes me an old man. At any rate, it worked brilliantly. The spasticity in Luisa's hands let up enough to allow her to communicate with basic sign language."

"And the stretcher?"

"We haven't been as lucky with her leg spasms. They're still so bad, she's unable to sit in a wheelchair," he said under his breath, now that the patient was so close.

More loudly, he said, "Mr. Reyes, Luisa, how are you? This is Dr. Andrapur. This is Luisa and Mr. Reyes, her father and full-time caregiver."

Mr. Reyes, a gentle man who asked his questions in broken English, never expressed resentment about the fate of his once bright and beautiful daughter; he was nothing but grateful for his Halfway Miracle, a fact Sam had always thought extraordinary, and now found incomprehensible.

What are you doing here? How can you even call yourself a healer? said a voice in Sam's head. *I bet Mr. Reyes has never thought Luisa would be better off dead.*

Out of nowhere, Sam's stomach heaved. "Excuse me, Mr. Reyes. Luisa. Back in a moment."

He avoided looking at Dr. Andrapur's earnest face as he sprinted past the stretcher and all the way to the staff bathroom, where he vomited up his breakfast. He rinsed his mouth and splashed his face with cold water. In the mirror, he saw a man with unnaturally pale skin and the sunken eyes of a fugitive. He took a couple of deep breaths to steady himself.

Sam was sweating shame when he returned to the exam room. He couldn't bring himself to look directly at Mr. Reyes. Fortunately, interrogating Luisa's pump required a certain focus, and he bent to the task, narrating the procedure for Dr. Andrapur.

Back in his office, he changed his sweat-soaked shirt for the emergency spare he kept there and sat down at his desk. Maybe he should try to see someone in the Psych department. But he knew he wouldn't. He heard Rabbi Friedman's voice in his head. *My door is always open, Semeleh.* But could he even admit these thoughts to the rabbi?

Thirty minutes later he was back in Exam Room 1, waiting with an eager Dr. Andrapur for Billy Miller to arrive. Billy was another of Sam's longtime successes, and the son of an old friend. But when the twenty-two-year-old's wheelchair rolled into view, Sam was horrified by the familiar sight of his clawed fingers and gaping mouth, the drool bib that was part of his daily wardrobe. Leslie Miller followed close behind, oblivious to Sam's mood. He fought the urge to grab his old friend's arm and ask her how she could bear the endless heartbreak. How had she not disintegrated under the force of her despair?

Out loud, he said, "This is Billy Miller, and his mother, Leslie—a friend since high school. My fellow, Dr. Andrapur." She seemed well prepared, so he didn't need to explain that Billy was here for Botox injections to control his spasticity.

Billy had been the same age as Zoey and Zev were now when he'd hit a highway barrier at high speed and flown through the windshield. His brain injury was enormous, eradicating his ability to speak or walk, and much of his upper body function. But Sam's team had made remarkable advances with him, especially after Billy received an implanted pump like Luisa's: He'd gradually learned to navigate his own electric wheelchair, and Francesca had devised a way for him to converse using a spelling board and an electronic voice generator. Billy had become another Halfway Miracle.

"I am so pleased to meet the famous Billy Miller," said Dr. Andrapur, smiling widely. "You were my favorite case study in Boston, young man!"

"Do you hear that, Billy?" Leslie asked. "They're talking about you across state lines. And it's all thanks to Sam here."

"It's true, Dr. Sandor is a legend," Dr. Andrapur said with an easy laugh. "I am fortunate indeed to be here."

Sam was focused on Billy. Was the boy any more than a poor patch job, after all? What was the point of all that work, if he lived in perpetual pain and dependence? Sam's hands shook, and he didn't trust himself to perform the delicate injections. He stood paralyzed next to the counter, a syringe in one hand and a vial of medication in the other. Seconds passed before the others in the room noticed.

"Can I assist in some way, Dr. Sandor?" Dr. Andrapur's voice was gentle.

He smiled weakly at her and glanced at the young man. "Just rethinking your dose, Billy. I was considering tweaking it a little, but I've decided we'll stay the course for now."

Billy grinned lopsidedly, a line of drool dropping onto his bib. "Sure. Thing," his robotic voice generator said after a long pause.

"Whatever you say, Sam," Leslie said. "We're in your hands."

Sam looked down at his hands, which to his surprise, were unchanged. They were the hands of a healer who knew his craft. He took a few slow, deliberate breaths and let muscle memory guide him.

•

As the month of July ground on, Sam continued to attend every Team Meeting and to read every note in Zoey's chart as soon as it was added, but he found nothing new to pin his hopes on. He couldn't get the words of Peter Becker's latest progress note out of his head: *Struggles with processing, distractibility, and some emotional lability. Ambulation and speech are halting. Daily speech therapy has begun to address cognitive deficits.*

Sam was too stuck on the *cognitive deficits* to see the big picture. Liv had to keep reminding him of the things they could be grateful for.

"Like what?" Sam asked during one of their pillow talks.

"Well, for starters: She can walk."

"You're right, that *is* an enormous relief."

This was true for obvious reasons, but also because their old house could not easily be rendered handicap friendly, with its numerous front steps. The fact of his own home's inaccessibility to wheelchairs would have been a source of some embarrassment to Sam if his patients or staff had become aware of it, but he made a point of never holding his holiday parties there; he believed in maintaining a strict separation between his work and personal lives. Also, he still refused to consider any updates that changed the way the house looked. In his mind, it would always be his parents' place.

"The kids are hereby forbidden from breaking their legs," Sam had joked with Liv when the subject came up in the past.

Coming home from work one evening, he stood in his driveway, surveying the house, his eyes roaming over a sight so familiar it was usually invisible to him: Here was the broad, welcoming porch that wrapped the house in its embrace. Here, the richly grained olive-wood door his father had ordered from the Galilean Hills to mark the occasion of Israeli statehood, now scarred with decades of sun and snow and key scuffs and boot scuffs. Here was the stand of white birches that bent their silvery leaves over the heads of generations of Sandors, the gnarled apple trees, and the many-paned windows that let in sunlight at every time of day.

The wraparound porch was littered as always with an assortment of nonessential items, testimony to the prosperous life they had built. The hammock around the left-hand curve of the porch was a fixture, the place he used to check first when he arrived home, for the chance to spend a moment or two with Zoey. It had become her favorite perch once she gave up climbing the old apple trees; she stayed there most afternoons when the weather was fine, in a jumble with a whole group of friends, or planning one of the many school events she orchestrated using a yellow legal pad and the cell phone she'd convinced Sam to buy her and Zev years before they needed it. Or reading one of the novels she returned to again and again for the voices of their strong heroines. *Little Women. The Red Tent. Anne of Green Gables. The Handmaid's Tale.*

Would she be able to read those books again? He forced himself to look elsewhere. But the view through the living room window was no better. He could make out the shadow of his old Steinway baby grand, procured like a miracle by his parents, immigrant shopkeepers who had saved for years to buy it for their musical only child. Next to it was the arched neck of Zoey's cello, which she'd played with a precocious mix of tenderness and authority. Now the instrument waited there like the last wallflower at a school dance.

He understood as never before the ugly truth about these special patients of his, like Billy Miller and Luisa Reyes: how complacent he was about the small advances he managed to engineer for them. If he was *lucky*, his own girl would become a Halfway Miracle. How could he ever be reconciled to that irony? It was excruciating.

"Sam? Where'd you get to?" Liv looked out the door and into Sam's miserable face. "Why don't you go for a run?" she suggested—as she'd done a dozen times since the accident. "Try to work off a bit of stress."

If only to stop her asking again, he said, "Livie, those side-by-side runs with Zoey were one of the high points of my week, and I can't bring myself to go without her."

"Oh, honey. Okay. I get that."

It seemed to Sam that he and Liv had, by tacit agreement, placed whole swaths of their life on indefinite hold: baking, exercise, prayer, sex, music. He wasn't sure how she saw these things, but in Sam's mind they all fell into a single category: indulgences that were both nonessential for survival and too emotionally charged to handle.

DAY 35

A series of knocks and clatters came from Zoey's bathroom, and Liv guessed she was trying to manage her own morning routine again. Excellent. Liv could use the time to take stock of room 2113 in the TBI Rehab wing, where Zoey would be living for the next couple of months. She'd tried to make the room as homey as possible within the confines of institutional décor: A colorful Israeli bedspread from Shula covered the narrow bed, a tapestry hung on the wall, a prism dangling in the window caught the sunlight and made rainbows on the ceiling, and the windowsill was lined with photos.

Liv had opted not to include her favorite print of Sam and Zoey, running at full speed through the park during a torrential downpour; Sam was laughing as he looked at Zoey, who had tipped her head back and opened her mouth to catch the raindrops as she ran. After what Sam said, it would be cruel to display such a picture while Zoey was in here.

On the bulletin board, Liv had tacked up a selection of Lottie's sweet drawings, interspersed with some of Zev's sophisticated and comical pieces: talking flowers, fencing frogs.

Zev's drawings are here, but where is Zev?

Mikayla's art was also here, a growing collection of beautiful watercolors she had made from favorite childhood books. At a loss for what to do with Zoey on her frequent visits, Mikayla had started reading aloud from these old stories. Here was a rendering of *The Little Prince* next to a scene from *A Wrinkle in Time*. Liv's chest tightened as she remembered the last time Mikayla had read to Zoey, struggling to get the words out around her tears. "*What is essential is invisible to the eye. It is the time you have wasted on your rose that makes your rose so important.*" Was that only last week? Liv stared at Mikayla's fine artwork and realized again how the girl's nature and interests dovetailed on so many levels with Zev's: her self-deprecating shyness, her artistry, her unquestioning love of Zoey—they were like a familiar echo.

There was a knock on the door, and Liv was startled when Mikayla's elfin form appeared, as if Liv had conjured her. Mikayla smiled tentatively. "Hi, Mrs. S. I've been zooming around looking for you guys. I forgot Zoey switched rooms." She glanced around. "This looks great. How's it all going in here?"

Liv was ambushed by sorrow—these girls should be playing volleyball on a beach somewhere, not making the best of another hospital room—but she summoned a bright answering smile. "It's going fine today, sweetheart, but she's about to leave for PT, I'm afraid."

She gestured toward the whiteboard showing Zoey's rehab schedule. "New home, new schedule."

A series of loud bangs issued from the bathroom. Liv knocked on the door. "You okay in there?"

"Don't know … Stupid … pants …"

"Well, call me if you need me, honey!" She turned back to Mikayla. "We have less than five minutes, I'm afraid."

Mikayla looked crestfallen. "Oh, that's too bad. I … I hope you don't mind, but I brought Carrie with me today." She made a gesture, and the other girl came into view, looking both uneasy and pleased with herself—a suspect combination.

"Hi, Mrs. S," said Carrie. "I hope it's okay that I came!"

She didn't sound like she was genuinely asking, and Liv wasn't so sure of her answer. Carrie was one of a group of Zoey's friends who moved in a well-groomed pack; they had been to the house for countless visits but had never made any sincere effort to converse with Liv. For her part, Liv had not favored them as friends for Zoey, though on the surface there had been nothing to object to. They were never in trouble, maintained excellent grades, and were the organizers and supporters of every school event. But Carrie's crew radiated a sort of glittering anger disguised as confidence and aimed at any vulnerable creature in their path.

Zoey had possessed an innate poise that granted her automatic entry into this circle. Mikayla, on the other hand, hovered on the periphery, as if she didn't quite trust the others but was too mesmerized by the group dynamic to tear herself away. And Zoey was nonchalant when Liv questioned her about the value of spending time in such a clique.

"They're not *mean* girls, Mom. They're smart and put together, so they can get impatient with kids who aren't on the ball. There's nothing ominous here, nothing to worry about."

She had said *ominous* without a hint of sarcasm, her tone so easy that Liv was convinced to return to her default position of giving everyone the benefit of the doubt.

It was true that Mikayla was the only friend of Zoey's who had come to visit since the accident, but hadn't Liv turned them all away at the beginning? Liv asked herself whom she had been protecting as she marked her own apprehension at seeing Carrie here. She could feel the dismay like a shadow on her face.

"Not sure if you know that Zev and I are lifeguarding together this summer?" said Carrie. "People are still talking about the way he saved that girl, Rosie Kramer? You must be proud."

"Yes, we are."

An awkward silence followed, and Mikayla hastened to fill it. "Carrie's been asking me for a while now if Zoey was ready for visitors, and I've been spending a lot of time here, and she's not as nervous around people as she used to be, so maybe she'd like to see someone else, you know? I mean, she must be getting sick of me by now."

Mikayla stumbled a little, her words delivered in the self-effacing manner for which Zoey used to reproach her. But Liv had always found this quality of Mikayla's endearing. Carrie and her crew could benefit from a little bit of her humility.

Liv watched Carrie take in the large-print wall calendar next to the bed with the days crossed off in red, and the whiteboard where the staff wrote notes to Zoey. She could imagine what the girl would extrapolate from these signs, and felt defensive on Zoey's behalf, though it was undeniable that she had yet to name the day, month, or year.

Liv had been silent for too long, and Mikayla rushed in again to fill the void.

"Also, like, maybe it would help with her rehab? To see more people from high school, outside her family? Since those are, like, a different set of memories ... But of course, we can come back if this is a bad time."

Liv was impressed with Mikayla and unimpressed with herself. What was her problem with Carrie? Visits from peers could only be good for Zoey's morale and might even jog her memory.

She was about to thank Mikayla when the bathroom door banged open and Zoey tottered out, her sweatpants twisted around backward and one sleeve of her T-shirt hanging empty, as always. She stopped, looked around blankly, then continued stumbling across the room. Liv realized she was headed for trouble. Because of what the team called her "left neglect," she couldn't walk a straight line, and the tangled clothing compromised her balance. She was on a collision course with her closet door.

Liv leapt forward to intercept Zoey, forgetting how spooked she was by sudden movements. Zoey recoiled and shrieked, spinning around before losing her balance and pitching onto her bed, which was now, mercifully, right in her path.

"Shhh. It's okay, Zoey, you were just a little off course. There's no need to get upset!"

Zoey continued to squawk and moan. Mikayla blanched and turned to Carrie, who looked on with her lip-glossed, Cupid's-bow mouth agape.

"Let me help you with your clothes, sweetie, so it'll be easier to stand."

She reached out, but Zoey batted her hands away, curling into a ball.

Liv put up her hands. “Okay, okay.” She turned to address the girls. “I’m sorry. This isn’t a good time. We’ll have to try again another day.”

Carrie nodded and backed out the door, her eyes wide and blank.

Mikayla rubbed her face. “Oh, God, I’m sorry,” she whispered. “I don’t know what I was thinking—”

“It’s not your fault, honey. It was bad timing, that’s all.”

Mikayla nodded and hurried out of the room. As the girls walked away, Liv heard Carrie’s nervous laugh. “Oh my God, Mikayla, why didn’t you tell me?” she whisper-shouted. “She’s like, I dunno, like *retarded* or something. It’s so weird!”

“Shhhhhhh. Not so loud! And not that *word*,” Mikayla hissed. “Jeez. The thing is, you get used to it. She’s getting better, but it’s not—”

The girls moved out of range and Liv bowed her head. Why was it that people never understood how loud a whisper was? She went and sat by her curled-up daughter, grateful for her oblivion. Maybe Zev was right when he said most of them were motivated by voyeurism and not genuine compassion. Liv could hear her mother’s voice in her head: “Survival of the fittest is always in force, Olivia, in every age and at every stratum of society.”

Her baby was no longer among the fittest.

After that day, Liv was fierce. She never missed a therapy session, trying to anticipate Zoey’s needs and detour her around potential pitfalls. It was the only way she could keep repeating her daily creed: Everything will be okay. She needed to be able to tell herself she had done everything she could.

Zoey’s sessions with Francesca were a bright spot, and they became longer and more interesting each week. Francesca would start with a hopeful question and would wait forever to get her answer.

The first real progress had come shortly after the twins’ birthday. Liv had baked Francesca a pie, a creamy, rich peanut butter silk, to thank her for her diligence and for sitting with Zoey during the coma. Francesca, who had already confessed her love for peanut butter, was effusive in her delight.

"Look, Zoey! Do you see the beautiful PIE your mom brought me?"

To Liv's surprise, Zoey lifted her arm off the bed and pointed in the direction of the pie. In those days, every movement of Zoey's was still a revelation.

"Very good. Can you try to say it for me? P-I-I-I-E."

Zoey had pursed her lips and whispered, "Puh-I."

"Yes, Zoey. That's good! Say it one more time. P-I-I-E."

"Puh-I," Zoey croaked.

"You are working so hard. Do you want to try another one, *cara*?"

Francesca had riffled through her file of picture cards and held up a picture of a cookie. Zoey mouthed it clearly. K-U-K-EE. A picture of a loaf of bread brought a distinct BR-ED, and a photo of a wedding cake from the morning paper elicited an audible K-AY-K.

By now, Francesca had Zoey talking back regularly. Every question she asked, Zoey answered—though often, with, "Dunno."

"You don't know, Zoey? Is that what you're telling me?"

After several seconds' delay, Zoey would nod.

"That's good! It's always best to admit when you don't know. Can you say it clearly for me? I. DON'T. NOUHHHHW," Francesca enunciated, and Zoey watched her face, mouthing the words after her.

Soon this became Zoey's favorite refrain. She said it cheerfully—"I don't know!"—in a register Liv had never heard her use before, a silvery, high singsong that sounded nothing like her old, earthy alto.

"Do you notice, Liv, that this girl loves baked goods? And no wonder, with a mother like you! You must talk to her about your work. She will make more progress, and it will be meaningful for you also. You see? You can shoot two doves with one arrow."

Liv thought for a moment and laughed. "Actually, the expression is *kill two birds with one stone*. I hope you don't mind me correcting you."

"Are you kidding? I thank you! Everyone here in the US is too polite to do it. Instead, they look uncomfortable, but say nothing. As if they were passing the gas," said Francesca.

Liv laughed again. She liked this woman, but she was skeptical about the angle. Zoey had never shown any interest in food before; she had once told Liv she viewed food as "nothing more than body fuel." Liv had been stung, though it hadn't escaped her notice that Zoey was the only one of the kids too "busy" to hang around the kitchen and chat while she cooked.

But she couldn't deny Zoey's interest now. Half-heartedly, she brought in one of her challahs and forced herself to talk with Zoey about the process of making it.

"First, I proof the yeast. Do you know what that means?"

"Proof?" came Zoey's silvery voice.

"Right. It means adding … adding something sweet for the yeast to eat, so we know it's working."

"Something sweet for me to eat?"

"No, love, for the yeast!" Liv laughed. "I mix it with the dough, and when it rises, I punch it down …" she went on. Zoey's eyes went wide, her listless expression replaced with one of delight, maybe even excitement.

"And you know my favorite part?"

"I don't know!" Zoey said with her crooked smile.

"Before I bake it, I add in golden raisins, and braid the dough into loaves and brush them with egg so they'll shine."

"Golden raisins," Zoey repeated. Liv had to admit she was rapt. Liv suspected that the prospect of eating the sweet egg bread with raisins was what truly held Zoey's attention—but it made a nice change from lethargy.

Francesca saw her every weekday and persisted in her conviction that cooking stories and homemade foods were a key to her recovery. When Liv brought in a batch of white chocolate mint cookies, Zoey took one bite and volunteered: "I like cookies!"

Francesca and Liv exchanged a glance at this sign of initiative, and they again spent the session talking with Zoey about baking.

"White chocolate?" Zoey asked when Liv told her the ingredients.

"Yes! It's creamy and tastes like vanilla. And mint tastes cool and fresh."

"Creamy. Cool … Make cookies for *me*, Mommy?" she asked, clearly enthralled.

Liv smiled at Zoey. "Yes, love. I did."

Afterward, Francesca teased Liv, her eyes sparkling. "Zoey is not the one holding back, eh, Livie?"

Francesca was right. Liv was having trouble making the transition. Zoey's indifference to her cooking had always been a source of private frustration as she looked for a way into that self-reliant heart. How could things have changed so completely?

Six weeks after the injury, Zoey's recovery took another leap forward. It started during one of Francesca's regular sessions.

"Good morning!" Francesca said, taking her hand as soon as she came in. "Did you sleep well last night?"

"I floated in the ocean. It was sparkly. Mommy was there …" Zoey sounded half asleep still, but Liv was too excited by this elaborate speech to keep quiet, as she'd promised to do when Francesca was working.

"Does it feel like that when you sleep, honey?" she asked. "Like floating in the ocean?"

"No, silly!" Zoey said, giggling and shifting her gaze to Liv. "I *made* the sparkly ocean, *then* I swam. You were there. And Zev and Lottie. And Daddy."

What a glut of words! Liv exchanged an excited glance with Francesca, whose posture had shifted to high alert.

"Zoey, were you dreaming?" Francesca asked. "Was there an ocean in your dream?"

"I don't know!" Zoey said. "I saw Mom and Dad and Zev. Oh! and the rabbi …" Her voice trailed off and she stared at the wall.

"Go on. Tell me more." Francesca patted her hand.

Always give her a physical cue to bring her attention back, she'd told Liv.

"The sparkles come when I ask them. But words make them go away."

Francesca opened the Memory Book and wrote down everything Zoey said. She looked more excited than Liv could remember.

"It sounds like a dream, Zoey. Can you start from the beginning and tell me the story of the sparkly ocean?"

Zoey began to speak in a sort of monotone, as if reciting something she had memorized.

"I am standing in the middle of a circle and everybody is clapping and laughing and I have a fancy dress, long and shimmery and silver …"

Zoey stopped speaking abruptly. Francesca was scribbling to get it all down. Liv grew lightheaded and realized she was holding her breath.

Zoey picked at her bedspread. Francesca was still writing in the Memory Book when she resumed speaking in the same monotone.

"Now I'm swimming in the air and it looks like a sparkly ocean and I'm floating above all the people and they call to me "Come down, Zoey, come down" but I'm happy up here … There is glitter in the air and it lands on everyone and makes them look pretty like me but when they talk the sparkles go away and that's like bad magic I will be quiet I won't talk anymore so the magic will only be good."

She relapsed into silence.

Liv was dumbfounded at this waterfall of verbiage. What was more, it seemed that Zoey was somehow processing her injury.

"Do you know what that sounds like, Zoey?" Liv asked. "Your bat mitzvah party! Silver was your favorite color: You had a long silver dress, and we threw silver confetti."

Holding a finger up to Liv, Francesca said, "That was great! How do you feel?"

Zoey looked up. "Hungry?"

"I wrote the dream down for you. Would you like to read it?"

"I want a snack …"

"We will get you one, Zoey. Well done, *cara.*"

Liv and Francesca stepped out into the hall and Liv gripped the speech therapist's arm.

"How is this possible? All those words! What happened in there?"

"Sometimes, this is how it goes. The language comes back in a torrent. And you must realize, Liv," Francesca said, "some of this is stream of consciousness, in the same way you might experience it if you were writing down your own dreams after waking. She is not fully engaging in dialogue yet. But she's getting there, fast!"

The two women exchanged an excited smile—*she's coming back!* After that, Francesca asked Zoey about her dreams daily, and sometimes Zoey would spill one out in a single stream, like that first one. The speech therapist wrote them all down in the Memory Book, which, she explained, was a tool Sam insisted on for all TBI patients, to "anchor them in time and events."

•

Zoey's recovery was not a straight line. Two weeks after she told them that first dream story, Liv sat in the therapy gym and watched her shake her head at Derek as he tried to coax her onto the treadmill.

"I don't wanna," Zoey whined, managing to sound simultaneously weak and intractable. Liv stood up, ready to intervene, but Derek sent her a friendly warning glance, a reminder of the last Team Meeting, where the therapists had implored Liv to dial it back. They said they needed to develop their own relationships with Zoey, and if Liv stepped in whenever there was a conflict or a question, that could never happen. And Zoey had to learn to manage her obstinacy. It was part of her recovery process.

"Can I have a snack?" Zoey asked for the third time in five minutes.

"As soon as you finish your walk," Derek said. "Come on, try again."

When she finally got to the end of the railing, her left arm hanging at her side, she let go and pointed at the carts filled with food service trays. "Time for lunch?"

"What do you need to do next?" Derek asked.

"I don't know!" she answered. "When is lunch?"

Liv sighed. Progress today would have to be measured in inches. And why was every other word out of Zoey's mouth about food?

That night, Liv asked Sam about it. "Zoey hasn't showed as much interest in food in her entire life as she has since the injury. Why is she so fixated now? Is it a symptom of something? Are her nutritional needs not being met?"

"No, Livie. I'm sure she's getting everything she needs," Sam said. "I can think of two possibilities: One, she might be perceiving constant hunger, because of the brain injury. Impulse control isn't high on the list for TBIs with temporal lobe damage."

Liv winced at his clinical tone.

"And two, she might be *perseverating*, which is a common TBI behavior. They get fixated on an idea or a feeling and return to it as a sort of theme throughout recovery, especially during times of stress or anxiety."

•

Ten more days passed. Their girl was gradually becoming reanimated, like some quirky feminine Pinocchio. She was by turns obdurate and funny, lethargic and lively.

One morning, Zoey said to Liv, "I remember the broken chocolate."

"Is this one of your dream stories?"

"No." Zoey shook her head vehemently. "Maybe … but I remember the broken chocolate."

Most of the time, their biggest challenge of the day was getting her to recall what she had learned or said or done the day before, so Liv was thrilled to hear Zoey say the words *I remember*. She tried to think back to their recent discussions about baking and food—had there been a recipe where the chocolate had to be broken up, maybe for melting?

"Where was the broken chocolate, sweetie?"

"At the store, silly Mom!" Zoey smiled as if Liv had made a great joke.

Zoey hadn't been to a store in at least six weeks. "Did you eat the chocolate?"

"I don't think so! Zev ate it."

"Zev was there? Who gave you the chocolate?"

"The old lady. We could have some from the big jar if we were good. Am I good? Can I have chocolate?"

Liv nodded absently and patted her hand. "Sure, Zoey. I'll bring you some chocolate after your PT. Do you want dark or milk?"

"I don't know! What is PT?"

Had she not known what Zoey was like before, Liv might have been charmed by her lack of drive. She was so unlike her old self, with her talk of test scores and extracurriculars and internships. Sam kept saying the goal was to bring back the *old* Zoey: "Look for the cracks in the wall of her lethargy and try to pull her fighting spirit out." But there was something soothing in the way this Zoey allowed events to unfold instead of continually trying to control them. She was like the anti-Hinda. Uneasily, Liv realized this description could apply to herself; maybe she only wanted Zoey to be more like her.

These days, Liv was at least as concerned about Zev's lethargy as Zoey's. She wished he hadn't quit his lifeguarding job, though it was true the incident at the Swim Club had turned into a bit of a circus after the story of Zev's rescue ran in the local papers and the mayor of New Haven insisted on a public commendation. Zev muttered angrily that it wasn't even *about* him; it was an election year. Liv couldn't believe he knew that. He declared his intention to refuse the award, but Mother had somehow gotten wind of the whole thing and had called to set him straight.

Since then, he wasn't doing anything at all that Liv could see. He slept until noon or later. He said he was working on his mural project, but Liv could see no plans or sketches or other evidence of it, and she never saw him when she was at the hospital. About Zoey he said almost nothing, though he implied he was visiting her when no one else was around, and Sam said the nurses sometimes mentioned that they had seen him in the halls at odd hours.

"*Buongiorno!* How are my two favorite ladies this morning?"

Liv gave a guilty start. Zoey was drowsily watching the rainbows on the ceiling where the sunlight refracted through her prism. Liv hadn't started her on the arduous process of getting dressed, nor had she followed the trail of her chocolate memory.

"Hi, Francesca. Zoey was telling me a memory about a store and some chocolate." Liv turned back to Zoey. "What does the store look like, sweetie?"

"It's dark. It smells like pickles. Can I have chocolate?"

She grinned, and the two women laughed at her single-mindedness, but Liv had a feeling the memory was already irretrievable. These glimpses were like small rifts in the fabric of time: Every so often, the weight of Zoey's sixteen-year history broke through the wall of scar tissue that had built up over the last weeks.

Francesca waved goodbye. "Okay, Livie. I only came by to say hello. I will pick it up again later with her. Chocolate ... pickles ..."

Liv felt a new appreciation for the personal approach Sam required of his team. Now all those missed bedtimes with their own children made more sense. Unlike podiatry or ophthalmology, brain injury rehabilitation required an intimate knowledge of each patient's personality, quirks and fears, family supports or lack thereof; all had to be factored in.

Liv picked a pair of gym shorts out of the cabinet and tried to hand them to Zoey, who looked everywhere but at her. The shorts landed on the floor in a crumpled heap.

"Come on, Zoey, pick up the shorts and lay them out."

Zoey eyed them as if from a long distance away and stooped to pick them up with her right hand while her left dangled loosely at her side.

"Try to use both hands, sweetie. The way Em taught you."

"Who is Em?"

"Em is your OT. Her whole name is Emma. What do you need to do with the shorts?"

"I don't know!" She hadn't touched the shorts. "What's Oh-Tee?"

"OT is for occupational therapist," Liv said for the twentieth time. "Em helps you work with your hands. What do you do with the shorts? What do you need to find first?"

A long silence, but Liv could see her mind working. "Find the holes?"

"Yes, Zoey, very good!" Liv cringed at the sound of her own voice. "Find the holes and ..."

"You do it!"

This was another of Zoey's favorite refrains.

"No, honey, you need to do it. Find the holes with your hands, then put your feet in."

It was upsetting, having to reteach Zoey such childish tasks. But paradoxically, Liv also nursed a kernel of secret pleasure at being needed this way again. Caring for her small children had been so simple—dress, feed, wash, love—and that simplicity had vanished into a tangled knot as they grew up and struggled for mastery of themselves. She recalled how Zoey, at age two or three, used to push her hand away when Liv tried to help her dress. "I do it myself!" Though Liv had appreciated Zoey's independent spirit, she couldn't bridge the distance it created between them.

"I'm hungry. Need a snack."

Liv was startled to attention for the second time that morning. Zoey had plunked herself down on the bed and was staring into the mirror on the closet door as if she was looking for something.

"I'll bring you chocolate later, remember?"

Surprise and excitement crossed Zoey's face in quick succession. "Chocolate!"

"But only after therapy, and for that you've got to get dressed."

With Houdini-like contortions, Zoey eventually got her feet into the shorts, and her head and right arm into the T-shirt. But the process took over thirty minutes, and now they were late for Derek. Liv gave up and pulled the left arm through herself.

She released Zoey into Derek's custody and sat in the therapy gym, trying to pay attention as she mulled over broken chocolate and the smell of pickles. Maybe Francesca was right. Could Zoey's food fixation help them forge a new, stronger connection? She tried to imagine a day in the future when the two of them would stand side by side making cookies in her sunny, quiet bakery.

Liv was suddenly swamped with longing to be back there, playing with her kitchen toys amid the perfume of apricots and caramel. She pictured the perfect little workspace she'd designed in their old carriage house at Sam's urging, neglected now and likely covered with dust. How would it feel to go back?

Maybe it was time to find out.

As soon as she formed the thought, worry flooded in. She shouldn't get distracted when this period of Zoey's recovery was so critical. On the other hand, what if she could nurture Zoey's newfound interest in food while doing what she loved? She could hear Francesca's voice in her head: *You can shoot two doves with one arrow.* She smiled at the therapist's mangled idiom. Zoey was in excellent hands with Sam's team, and her heart leapt at the prospect of escaping into the bakery's warm, enveloping peace.

Liv stood up, filled with childish impatience.

"Derek, I need to take care of something. You've got this covered, right?"

He looked startled and pleased. "You betcha, Mrs. Sandor. Zoey and I have lots of work to do, right?"

Zoey stopped her slow march at the parallel bars. "I wanna come!"

Liv hesitated. Should she wait until the session was over? Derek shook his head and waved her away.

She patted Zoey's arm. "Derek will take good care of you. I have some work I need to do too. I'll come back later today and tell you all about it. And I'll bring you that chocolate treat."

Zoey brightened. "Can I have it now?"

Liv smiled at her. "No, love. I need to make it first. I'll see you a little later."

By the time Liv got to her van, she had compiled a shopping list: that Peruvian chocolate she loved, sweet butter, eggs, fresh fruit—what was in season? She stopped first at the farmer's market. The apricots were gorgeous, sun-hued and florally sweet. Liv's apricot tarts were her personal favorite; there was magic in them, a sort of alchemy in the rosy sweetness combined with cool custard and buttery shell—a tiny, perfectly balanced world.

She unlocked the door to the converted carriage house and set her bags down, inhaling. Here it was, her own little place, waiting for her. She set about dusting everything with a slow and deliberate hand: the cool marble countertops, the curved neck of the copper faucet leaning over her enormous yellow farmhouse sink, the worn bamboo boards for chopping fruits and herbs. She polished her beast of a stove, a six-burner black Viking cooktop where she could make sauces, melt chocolate, and pan-roast nuts all at the same time. She touched the tops of her sleek wall ovens, their interiors gleaming royal blue, ready to render up their evocative scents.

Liv never got over her romance with pastry. It was an uncomplicated, sensual pleasure: sifting together the flour and raw sugar and salt, a beautiful pale sand flowing through her fingertips; introducing the butter and feeling it soften under her touch until it began to yield and melt into the dry ingredients; kneading the mixture patiently until it came together in a smooth, elastic body. She would make a golden custard or a frangipane to line the shells, adding jewels of fresh fruit or dark chocolates that carried echoes of the jungle and watch as they were transmuted by the oven's heat into something else altogether, lush and aromatic and delectable. It couldn't be rushed or persuaded, and it couldn't mend the berserk world in which they all had to live. But she felt a flash of joy whenever she watched someone taste the first buttery morsel of one of her tarts and, with eyes closed, give a sigh of rapture. That had to be some sort of antidote, didn't it?

Apricot tarts for home and chocolate cloud cookies for Zoey. That much, at least, was within her reach.

DAY 53

Sam looked at his watch. Morning clinic was going to overrun his lunchtime with Zoey. He had been running late since he started training Dr. Andrapur; teaching always took extra time—those fresh-faced fledglings inspired him to pontificate about the true purposes and applications of rehabilitation medicine. He might lack his old sense of conviction now, but Sima still bought it. Though it had been a long morning, he was excited to see the Gladwell sisters today. Earlier, he had sent Dr. Andrapur to retrieve their genetic test results, and even his own spirits lifted when it turned out he had been right in his hunch. It would be an unusual visit.

Hope Gladwell lurched through the door, followed by her parents who had Gracie in a carrier and looked, as always, like the victims of natural disaster that they were. How could he have missed it for so long? He exchanged a smile of anticipation with Dr. Andrapur. Fortunately, this was one disaster that could be undone.

"Hello, Gladwell family. Are you ready for some great news?"

Hope flapped her arms. "Gwait news!"

Mr. and Mrs. Gladwell nodded glumly. Sam realized that, though he had explained it all before, they didn't understand the implications of the girls' tests.

"Dr. Andrapur? Will you explain?"

"Well, Hope's diagnosis of cerebral palsy was based on her weakness and muscle dystonia as a baby. But it is not typical for a child with CP to worsen so dramatically in childhood, nor did we expect, considering your excellent prenatal care"—Dr. Andrapur smiled at Mrs. Gladwell; her bedside manner was quite promising—"that your second child would be at risk. When Gracie's condition was the same, Dr. Sandor began to wonder why. The testing was meant to rule out a *different* condition. Do you understand?"

The parents nodded, looking more miserable than ever.

"But why does it matter what you call it?" Mr. Gladwell asked. "If the girls end up like this either way?"

Dr. Andrapur was smiling widely now. "Because you see, that is the good news. It turns out the girls have a genetic disease called *dopa-responsive dystonia*, which looks a lot like CP, but is largely *reversible* with medication."

At the word *reversible*, the Gladwells snapped to attention.

"What do you mean? Like, they can get *better*?" Mr. Gladwell asked.

"Yes. Exactly. They can get dramatically better."

"But they *told* us it was CP. It's incurable, they said. How could everyone at the Children's Hospital be wrong?" asked Mrs. Gladwell.

"Well, this is an easy one to miss," said Sam. "The symptoms are similar to—"

"I knew it! I told you!" The woman was staring at her husband, whispering loudly to him. "It worked!"

What worked? Sam wanted to ask. *Prayer?* He was offering nothing less than a miracle, which she could choose to interpret as the hand of God if she liked. It didn't matter who got the credit.

"We have the test results here." Sam showed them the lab report. "Of course, every patient responds at their own pace. But I'd like to start the girls on a medication trial right away, and we'll take it from there."

"You see, folks," Dr. Andrapur said, "Dr. Sandor has made a rare find indeed." Sam registered her reverent tone and was pleased in spite of himself. "This condition is only found in about three patients out of a million—that's eight *hundred* times less common than CP. But the test results confirmed his brilliant diagnosis!" She waved the labs in the air festively.

When they left, the stunned parents were clutching Sam's prescription in their hands like the lifeline it was. Dr. Andrapur looked thrilled. And Sam had to admit the win felt good.

He looked at his watch again. If he hurried, he would still have ten minutes to sit with Zoey while he ate his lunch. That was fine: Ten minutes was about all he could take these days. Whenever he saw her, there was a snarling buzz in his head. He didn't imagine for a moment that it would be silent after this morning's events.

He found Zoey sitting on her bed, staring as always into the mirror on the closet door. The television was blaring an inane children's show she wasn't watching, though when he turned down the volume, she looked up at him with startled eyes.

Right away, the infuriating buzz started up.

"Hi, cookie, whatcha doing?" said Sam, hating the fakery in his tone.

Zoey wiggled her fingers and stared at herself in the mirror. She spoke in a faraway voice. "In there"—she waved at the mirror—"my *other* hand works. Like in my mirror dream." She wiggled the fingers again.

"No, Zoey. It's still the same hand. It just looks like the opposite in the mirror."

He sat down on her bed and lifted the hand to show her. "See?"

Zoey was silent. How many hours a day was she spending alone, staring into that mirror or watching silly children's shows? And where was Liv right now? In their past life, he always knew where his wife could be found. It was a habit they fell into early in their married life, not for control, they used to assure each other, but for peace of mind.

"Can I eat lunch with you?" Sam asked.

Zoey shrugged but still said nothing. She was making him work for it. He unwrapped his sandwich. "What's in your lunch today? Anything good?"

"Pudding."

"Pudding? What kind of lunch is that? I'll have to talk to the lunch ladies."

She brightened. "There are lunch ladies at my school."

"That's right, there are. Do you miss school?"

"No. I don't like homework. I like pudding. This is vanilla."

"Hmmm. You always liked school, though!"

The buzz grew so loud in his head that he was irrationally worried about scaring her.

She gave him a slow smile. "Vanilla is *almost* as good as chocolate." She dipped her spoon awkwardly into the pudding with her right hand.

They were making no progress with her impaired left side. Sam fought to keep the anger from his eyes. He had four more minutes to get through.

"You might be coming home soon. Would you like that?"

"Is there pudding at home?"

"Yes, there's pudding. Mom can make it for you." Liv was right. She really did perseverate. "What else do you miss from home?"

"My cat Willow?"

"Your cat is still there, waiting for you. She sleeps on your bed, or under the hammock. Would you like to go back to sleeping in your own bed with Willow?"

Zoey shrugged. "Is Zev at home? I want to see Zev!"

"You see him all the time!"

Zoey shook her head. "No. Never."

So, her short-term memory was obviously still no good, either. But the cat, that was good. Long-term memory was improving.

"At home you can see him whenever you want. But you need to get well first. Will you keep working on that?"

She nodded, but he could tell she had no idea what he was talking about. He looked at his watch again: almost time to go.

"I've got to go see my patients, Zoey." He touched her knee gently so she wouldn't be startled. "But Mom's coming soon."

A memory was tickling at the edges of Sam's consciousness as he spoke.

You need to get well first … Mom's coming soon. When had he said those words to her before?

Then it came to him: Zoey had a history of Lyme disease! She had been about thirteen at the time, miserable, weak, aching all over. She had called him at work when Liv was out picking up Lottie from kindergarten and begged to be allowed to attend the first track meet of the season. "You need to get well first," Sam said, and Zoey had cried. "Shhh, it's okay. Mom's coming soon."

Why had no one considered Lyme disease as a cardiac risk factor? He searched feverishly for her old pediatric chart, tossing pillows aside and moving furniture, glancing over his shoulder from time to time to make sure his movements weren't upsetting Zoey. But she was staring off into space and picking at her comforter with her right hand while the left lay like a sleeping kitten in her lap. Sam went back to his search. What if Zoey's doctors had missed something? What if her cardiac arrhythmia was a result of their negligence?

Breathless, he stopped searching. *Then what?* Would anything change? Would they have been able to prevent the freak cardiac arrest that started this whole mess?

His pager was going off, but he ignored it and went to check on Zoey, who was looking at him quizzically. "Are you okay, honey?"

"Why are you throwing things? Are you mad?"

"No, I'm not mad," he said, and felt a new appreciation for the words *lying through my teeth*. "I … I lost something, and I was upset when I couldn't find it. Okay?"

"Okay, Daddy. Do you *have* to go?"

She sounded so very young.

Sam's pager beeped again. "Yes. I need to see my patients. That's why I'm beeping. They're calling me. But Derek is coming in—" he consulted the whiteboard "—half an hour. So sit tight until then. I'll check on you later. Okay?"

"Who is Derek?"

Oh, Zoey.

"Derek is your physical therapist. Your PT. You see him every day! He'll take you walking."

"I don't wanna walk, Daddy. It's hard. I always get crooked."

"I know, honey."

Sam's pager went off for the third time. He was fifteen minutes late for afternoon clinic. Gillian must have been going crazy.

"But this is what we were talking about. You need to work hard so you can get better and come home. Okay? That's your job right now. And I have to go do mine."

Somewhere in Sam's mind, a door of doubt had swung open a crack. What if Pediatrics *had* missed something? Shouldn't someone have followed up in the years after her bout with Lyme?

Five hours later, the door of doubt was yawning wide. It was too tempting, finding someone to blame. He would search for the old chart again. He stopped at the nurses' station to ask about it, and the charge nurse reminded him he had insisted on holding onto it after Zoey's transfer to the TBI Rehab wing.

"That's what I thought," Sam muttered, and hurried back to Zoey's room.

Liv was there, brushing Zoey's ratty hair. "This would be much easier if it were a little shorter."

"I don't wanna haircut."

"I know, but wouldn't it be great if there were less tangles?" Liv glanced up then. "Look, Dad's here!"

"Hi, Zoey. Hey, Livie." He fruitlessly scanned the room. Did he leave the chart at home?

"Hi, Daddy," Zoey said mournfully. "My hair is a mess."

"Oh, we're making good progress, sweetie!" said Liv. "Don't you worry. And how nice this is! Now we can all visit together. That doesn't happen often these days." She paused. "Sam, did you say you were already here today? How did I miss you?"

"Zoey and I had a quick lunch together. You must've gotten here later than usual."

"No, this is my new schedule, remember? We talked about it."

"I don't think so."

"Yes, we did! I promised Dafna I would start filling her weekly order again at the bakery. I come here early to get Zoey dressed, spend the morning baking while she's in therapy, and come back until I need to get Lottie off the camp bus at four-thirty. Zoey and I always have a nice long visit. And today we had extra time, right? Lottie is at a friend's house, so I decided to try to tackle Zoey's little hair problem. Did you two have a nice lunch?"

Her tone was mild, but Sam could tell he had put her on the defensive. He scrolled back in his memory. How could he have forgotten a whole conversation?

"Hello? Earth to Sam. Are you in there?" Liv laughed. "I asked if you had a good visit?"

How could she laugh about this? Her calm added to Sam's confusion. Five minutes ago, he had been a fountain of indignation, certain of his mission: find someone to blame. Now he wasn't so sure.

"It was fine. We talked about school, right?"

Zoey shrugged in her lopsided way, and Liv resumed brushing her hair. Sam sat down on the bed. "As I was leaving, I remembered about Zoey's Lyme disease. Do you remember that, Livie?"

"Of course, I remember it. She was miserable, and the follow-up visits went on forever."

"What follow-up visits?" asked Sam, jumping up again to search for the chart.

"What are you looking for?"

"Daddy lost one thing and he was throwing other things ..." Zoey said.

"Good remembering, Zoey," Liv said, stopping her brushing to look a question at Sam.

"I was trying to find her old chart, the one from Pedes. So, what kind of follow-ups did she have for the Lyme?"

"Oh, I don't even remember them all now, there were so many! Neurology, rheumatology, cardiology. They're always so overcautious with our kids. Why?"

Liv went back to brushing Zoey's hair.

"I thought ... maybe it was a clue to what happened ... You know, sometimes there are cardiac risks ..." Sam was beginning to feel silly.

How had he forgotten all the follow-ups? "Maybe someone dropped the ball—and it might be grounds for malpractice."

He strove for an easygoing tone to match Liv's, but still, she dropped the hairbrush.

"*Malpractice?* Hasn't everyone been saying from the beginning that her cardiac arrest had no known cause? What do they call it? Idiopathic."

"Right. But what if there were warning signs during her checkups? If so, there might be compensation for Zoey. For her future ..."

"Is that even conceivable, given the kind of scrutiny to which they routinely subject our kids? Or is this about something else?" She got down on the floor. "Oh, where is that silly hairbrush?"

Sam's face burned.

"Ah ha, I got it!" she crowed from under the bed. "And is this what you were looking for?" Liv emerged holding a tattered accordion file in one hand and the hairbrush in the other. At the sight of Zoey's old chart, Sam rushed forward. Liv handed it to him expressionlessly.

Sam began to pull folders from the file, glancing through each one before discarding it. For a few minutes, the silence was punctuated only by the sound of his sighs.

Liv cleared her throat. She had gone back to brushing Zoey's hair, and without looking at him, she said, "I'm sorry, Sam, but I can't help feeling this sort of undertaking is both false and foolish."

"Hmmm. False *and* foolish. You sound like Hinda. Would you mind explaining?" He didn't look up for her reaction to his uncharacteristic insult.

"Are you sure you want to hear? Because you're kind of worked up, and I don't want to argue in front of—in here."

"I'm sure."

"Okay, then." She turned to him. "It's false because if we sued anyone, we'd have to be absolutely sure someone was to blame. Which isn't likely, though I'm no expert. I've just been listening to you and your colleagues talk about Zoey for months. Is there new information?"

"No. I had a case today that got me thinking. Sometimes diagnoses *are* missed, and all kinds of faulty decisions follow. But you might as well finish. What's the foolish part?"

"Well, you'd be burning all your professional bridges, bringing a suit like that. You're a respected member of the medical community, not just because you're a good doctor, but because your integrity has never been in question. You've always prided yourself on that—you don't even take samples from pharmaceutical reps!"

"True."

"Would such an accusation be coming from a place of integrity?"

"I guess I just—"

Liv put her hand on Sam's arm and raised her voice, startling him into silence. "And I might not be a genius with numbers, but even *I* know the loss of your professional reputation will do far more damage to this family—both financially and emotionally—than the cost of Zoey's long-term care ever could."

She laid both hands on Zoey's head as if to bless her.

Zoey ducked out from under Liv's hands and looked back and forth between them "*You* take care of me, right?" she asked out of the blue.

"Of course, sweetie. We always will," said Liv. She turned back to Sam. "So, what is this really about?"

"Oh, God, Livie. I don't know. I got caught up, I guess."

There was no point in trying to explain about the angry buzzing and his momentary glee at the prospect of handing it off to someone else. Of course, she was right. He couldn't believe he'd even contemplated going down that road. Practicing medicine in such a litigious country was infuriating enough. Sam would feel like the worst sort of hypocrite, adding his voice to the greedy clamor.

"Let's forget about it. Okay?"

She searched his face for a moment. "Okay."

Sam returned the chart to the nurses' station. It would never give him what he wanted.

EXCERPT FROM
THE MEMORY BOOK OF ZOEY SANDOR

We walk holding hands, a piece of paper crumpled in my red mitten and we start to run blowing out puffs of air we are little dragons. Stay where I can see you kiddos Mom calls. Inside the store it is dark and it smells like dust and pickles and the counters are high above us. I read to Zev from the list "Milk" I say, "Car-rots" I'm a big girl and I can read them all. Zev carries the basket till it gets too heavy and he drags it across the floor. We stand in front of the counter and the old lady reaches for the jar and I squeeze his hand I know we've been good and the chocolate smells like heaven but it is all broken in little pieces and I am crying. Zev takes one anyway.

(Transcribed by Francesca Garibaldi, SLP)

DAY 60

Zev is in a fight to the death with his Snooze button, and he's winning. The latest Zoey dream is beginning to fade, but he can't let it go.

He groans and opens his eyes, reaching for his sketchbook. His heart is soggy. Without getting up, he pulls the sketchbook out from under the bed and puts the lines down on paper before he's even awake. It's almost like—what do they call it? He learned about it in English class when they were studying surrealism—*automatic writing*, that's it. This is some kind of automatic drawing—it's all stream of consciousness. He's not even in control of what gets onto the paper—in this case, a series of quick scenes like a comic strip.

We walk holding hands, a piece of paper crumpled in her red mitten.

We start to run. Mom calls a warning after us.

We make it safely inside the store, where it's dark and it smells like dust and pickles and the counters are high above us.

She reads to me from the list. "Milk" she says. "Car-rots."

I carry the basket till it gets too heavy and I drag it across the floor.

We stand in front of the counter and Magda reaches for the jar and I squeeze her hand. I know we've been good and the chocolate smells like heaven.

Zoey cries about all the broken pieces but I take one anyway.

His life feels less in control than ever, especially after that charade with the mayor. He wanted to forget the Rosie Kramer thing ever happened, but then Nana had to call and put in her two cents.

"You must accept praise when you earn it, Zev," she huffed. "It is a sign of maturity."

He couldn't argue with that. "Okay, Nana. I'll try."

At the ceremony, the mayor spoke exclusively in clichéd headlines: "A Commendation for This Fine Young Man." "A Credit to Our Great City." The insincere attention was bad enough, though when he heard the man's words, Zev was feeling kind of proud of himself, until he saw a look on Dad's face and realized that he'd been programmed to save the life of Rosie Kramer ever since he was born.

The worst thing is, that look on Dad's face could only mean he was thinking the same thing as Zev: *Why couldn't it have been Zoey?* All he sees is that flash of auburn hair, and when he replays it, he still thinks he can hear the mom screaming, *Zoey! Zoey! Save my baby!*

Maybe he's more like Dad than he ever thought.

Still, he secretly kind of likes the medal thing, hanging there on the edge of his mirror on its wide yellow ribbon. God knows Zoey has enough medals, and all he ever got before this was a couple of art prizes in middle school.

But that's long over now. Notices about junior year have started to arrive in the mail, which means Zoey has been in the hospital for almost a whole season. Today, he's supposed to drive Dad to work and spend the morning on hospital grounds, sketching the outline for a mural he hasn't even designed yet. He has got to summon the nerve to visit her.

He lets his mind drift in a much more interesting direction. Mikayla. He can't stop thinking about her, not even for five minutes. He has to paint her! He imagines himself caressing her lines and curves—oh mercy, the swell of her hip below her tiny waist—and a shiver of excitement runs through him, along with something vaguely familiar from long ago. He searches his mind and is surprised to find it's just happiness.

"Zeeeev, you've got seven minutes! Let's go!"

Dad.

He can't put it off any longer. The art project is about to go critical. There is exactly one more week to prepare before school starts, and a whole artistic team that he will be letting down if he doesn't come up with something. And as for Zoey … Mikayla says it'll get easier. He'll just have to trust her.

With a groan, he propels himself out of bed, feeling like someone stretched him on a rack. In the kitchen, he grabs two fresh muffins for breakfast—mercifully, Mom is baking again; he's basically living on her raspberry chocolate chip muffins and glasses of milk—and is heading out the door when Mom corners him.

"Zev, do the words *broken chocolate* ring a bell?" She has a funny look on her face, and for a panicked second, he's sure she has found his sketchbook. But how could she? It's safely stowed under his bed, where he was until minutes ago.

"How cub I eber fuhget dem?" he says, trying to swallow his giant mouthful of muffin. "Jeez, Mom. Senior moment? Broken chocolate was our treat from Magda's store."

Magda is the one who took over the store that used to belong to Papa and Goldie, whom Zev never met. The sick irony of them dying in that car crash after what they survived … He remembers Magda as kind of creepy, especially the numbers tattooed on her arm. Even as a small boy, Zev knew what those numbers meant: a secret password to a horrifying past they all somehow shared. But no matter how nervous Magda made him, he could always count on her to deliver what she promised, and that meant a lot when he was little.

Something else creepy: These memories aren't much of a stretch for him today. They're fresh from his latest dream.

"What else do you remember?" asks Mom, looking too psyched for him to refuse her.

"She used to say the same thing every time we came in. *If you be bahd, you no get nutting frum Magda.*"

Mom is smiling—he has always been a good mimic.

"Go on."

"*But if you be guhd, if you help you Mama, den Magda geev you shokolad.*" Zev pauses. "Weird that you're asking now, 'cause I—"

"You what?"

He shakes his head and stuffs an entire half a muffin into his mouth. "'M twying to eak in a huvvy here."

That was close. He can't believe he almost let it slip about his dream. The freaky coincidence has thrown him.

"Well, humor me. It's for a good cause. And mind you don't choke, honey."

Zev gulps down some milk and swallows. He sighs and gets on with it.

"You would let us walk ahead to the corner. Zoey would read off your shopping list and I'd lug the basket around. When we were done, Magda would open the candy jar sitting on top of the counter, and say something like: *Brrroken shokolad barrrs, they dohn't make me no moneys, but they steel make you smile, yes?* And she was right. It was the best chocolate."

He should have left out some details, so Mom doesn't wonder why his recall is so good. "Why do you want to know?"

"It's something that happened with Zoey. She said, *I remember the broken chocolate.* She also mentioned pickles, which was pretty random."

This is getting creepier by the minute.

Mom mutters, almost to herself, "I still don't get how she can remember these details from ten or more years ago and she can't remember the name of the PT she's seen dozens of times in the last two months." She looks at Zev, shrugs. "But Dad says that's how it goes with TBIs."

"Okay, Mom. Gotta go. Dad's waiting." Time to shut down his childish memories.

Dad fidgets in the passenger seat while Zev practices his driving and thinks about how he has deceived his parents. He has even been lying to Ethan, answering his brother's sporadic emails by furnishing details about Zoey that he has gotten from Mikayla. *She said something funny today, listen to this …* or *She likes to be read to, especially The Little Prince.* When he's on the base in Kabul, Ethan writes back, his letters full of praise: *That's great, man. Keep going. She needs you now*. In his life BZI, it was widely accepted that Zev was the one who couldn't manage without Zoey. Now, everyone keeps saying how much she needs him, but Zev figures she can't even remember whether she needs him or not. And doesn't that make him even more superfluous?

When they park, Dad runs into clinic, yelling over his shoulder, "Tell Zoey I said hi!"

Zev waves and nods. He's stuck here till Dad's lunch break anyway. Maybe he *should* go see her. The guilt is starting to weigh on him.

He stands staring at the blank courtyard wall where the mural is supposed to go, but his mind reflects back only blankness. He has no idea what to say to his "creative team" who are meeting him here at 11:00 a.m. Small pieces of him break off and vanish through the windows and down the hall in the direction of Zoey's room. There can be no creative flow here. All he feels is fear. Mikayla has been a steadfast friend to his sister all these weeks, and she will be here in a few hours, asking him how his visit went. He has to get it over with. A knot of dread wrenches his stomach, but he drags himself around the side of the building and through the automatic doors.

As he walks down the halls of the TBI Rehab wing, the nurses and orderlies greet him warmly. "Look, it's young Sandor. Wow, don't you look *exactly* like your father!"

They always know who he is, even if he can't remember any of their names from one holiday party to the next. He tries to be polite as he answers their questions about his summer, his artwork, his other siblings. To his consternation, they know everything about him.

Consternation (noun) [kon.ster.nay.shuhn]: alarming amazement or dread that results in utter confusion; shocked dismay. Synonyms: anxiety, bewilderment, distraction, worry.

He tries to slow his breathing as they usher him in the direction of Zoey's room. He dreads the sight of her pale face and floppy body. Crossing the threshold, he plows directly into someone who's coming out as he's going in. She steps on his foot with her high heel, grabs hold of his arm.

"*Madonna Mia!* Watch it there!"

The woman looks up and realizes who he is, her expression shifting instantly.

"Is that—little Zev? But you've grown so tall! I would not have known you, only you look like your father, and the eyes, they are the same as Zoey's, yes?"

"Y-y-yes." Zev disentangles himself from her grasp. His foot is throbbing, and he can't remember who she is, though the accent should've been some kind of clue.

"*Va bene?* Everything is all right? I didn't hurt you?" She sounds more amused than worried.

"Nope, I'm fine, but, uh, who …?"

"Of course. I am Francesca Garibaldi, your sister's speech pathologist." She sticks out her hand. "We've met at the many holiday parties, yes?"

"I'm sure we have."

Seeing that Zoey isn't in the room, he gestures at the empty space. "Do you know where she is?" He tries to keep the anxiety out of his voice. There's a muffled crash. She must be in the bathroom. "Is she—does she—need help in there?"

He starts automatically toward the door, then jerks to a halt. There's no way he's going in there. He blushes to think what that might've involved. What the hell is he doing here? He glances around wildly.

Amber eyes flaring with light, glazing over, slipping away.

He shakes his head to clear the flashback. On the whiteboard are childish reminders, always with fat exclamation points like the notes the girls pass in school—*Today is Tuesday!! PT with Derek at 2:00!* Below are these words: *Discharge Planning Meeting scheduled: Tuesday, September 6, 10:00 a.m.*

Tacked to a bulletin board are his little drawings (pathetic) and Mikayla's sketches (very good), and a Magic-Markered calendar with the days crossed off. He had one like it in first grade. His skin goes prickly and hot. It's a matter of seconds before he has to bolt.

"No, no, she is fine. She knocks into things because her balance is not—how should I say—*perfected* yet. But as long as she's not bleeding, we leave her to learn for herself, yes?"

Her smile dies as she sees Zev's pure panic looking back at her. "No, this was only a joke—" She moves toward him, but he's already backing out of the room and power walking down the long hallway.

He passes all the nosy nurses and goes right back out the door of the hospital, but he's worried: What if that Francesca lady reports him to his parents? And something else has wormed its way into his brain: the phrase *Discharge Planning Meeting*, written on that whiteboard, with a date only two-plus weeks away.

Is Zoey coming home? He can't imagine a shaky and confused and blank-eyed Zoey back at the house. That would be a whole new layer of crazy. And no way he could keep up his Invisible Man act then.

His stride falters as the wall of sweltering August heat hits him. *What am I doing? Mom and Dad will kill me.* Still, he doesn't turn back, but continues around the periphery of the building until he finds the Healing Garden. He collapses onto a bench.

Ha! That's rich! The *Healing Garden.* As if it has magical properties, like they used to think when they were kids. He remembers when Mom took them all to have lunch with Dad here, right after the garden was finished; he and Zoey thought the place worked like a fountain of youth, that it could grant an instant reprieve to all the sick and dying patients inside—which meant, in their seven-year-old minds, that their father would be out of a job.

"What will Dad do now?" Zev had asked Zoey as they sat on this bench.

"Maybe he'll be an astronaut! Or a famous musician. Or, I know! He can go on tour with me. We'll be a duet!"

She'd just taken up the cello.

But since then, so many summers have passed. If only he could still be small, spending his summer days inventing new worlds with Zoey. They could be invincible. The Ball of Fire.

Why won't his mind leave that stupid comic book alone? But it's true, that was the best summer, though it started out the worst: raining all the time, and they were so bored. Zoey started making up those fantastic stories about twins conjoined at the temples, who lived in a high rise in New York—what were their names? Albertus … and Alanna. That was it! And of course, Zev did the illustrations.

In Zoey's story, the twins' handicap wasn't a burden, it was a gift: The physical passageway between their brains doubled their mental potency, so they could perform all kinds of tricks, including a sort of astral projection. They had this avatar made of smoke that they would send out through the windows; it would become the Ball of Fire that could vanquish the bad guys and save the day.

An electric jolt of the old excitement sweeps through Zev as he remembers: It wasn't only the thrill of creativity. It was magical. That whole summer, they were invincible.

He jumps to his feet and propels himself at warp speed out of the garden and around the back of the building. He sees that his "team"—Gideon and Mikayla and Ramie—is already waiting for him at the mural site. They exchange sounds and gestures that pass for hello.

As Zev outlines the concept that somehow comes out sounding fully formed, they all stand and stare up at the white wall, trying to envision it. He permits himself a single glance at Mikayla—she is standing quietly next to him, head tilted, watching him as he speaks—and he blushes as always, but manages to finish without stumbling over his words.

"Well, what do you guys think?" He bounces on the balls of his feet a little.

"I *think* I like it?" says Gideon.

"Ummm, it's, like, a huge blank space, dude," says Ramie. "How are we ever gonna cover it all?" He sizes up the wall as if he's planning to climb it, not paint it.

Their lukewarm reactions are not exactly what Zev was hoping for, and he holds his breath, waiting for Mikayla.

"You know, Zev," she says slowly, "I think you're onto something. Everyone likes superheroes, right? And don't they always have some kind of intense problem that's the flipside of their superpowers? This could really work!" She smiles at him.

Zev wants to grab her and kiss her, but instead he grins. What if this doesn't totally suck?

"If we put in some prep time over the next week, maybe this thing won't get totally out of control during the school year. Are you guys free?"

The boys nod and shrug.

"Awesome, so I guess I'll make a mock-up, and you guys can come by whenever, and work on it on your own time."

"Actually, could we, like, make a schedule, guys?" Mikayla asks tentatively. "I've got a babysitting gig in the afternoons that I need to give at least fifteen hours to this week. Plus, I think there's a better chance everyone will show up if we've got set times to work."

She blushes and tucks her hair behind her ear. Zev finds this adorable. He stares at her, his thoughts everywhere: how sweet she smells ... why girls are always so eager to organize everything ... his amazed realization that she's shy, too.

Before she catches him staring, he shrugs. "Sure. Whatever works. I can ride in with my dad in the mornings, say, Tuesday, Thursday, and Friday at eight thirty?"

Gideon and Ramie look at him as if he's off his rocker.

"You want us to get up at *what* time now, for the last week of summer vacation?"

"For an art project? No way."

"Okay, okay. Don't freak, guys. We can make this work," he hears himself saying. It's like Zoey is talking out of his mouth. "Why don't we split into two teams? Mikayla and I'll do the mornings, and you guys work the afternoons. That way we won't be all over each other and we'll get more done. You two need to show up before twelve thirty so we can check in with each other, 'cause my dad needs to drop me home before his afternoon patients. Does that work for everyone?"

They all agree, and as the group breaks up, Zev realizes he has engineered himself a lot of time alone with Mikayla. Who *is* this guy?

He finds his father behind his desk, looking kind of wrecked, running both hands through his suddenly graying hair. When he spots Zev, he leaps to his feet.

"Good to go? All right then, let's head out." He grabs Zev and squeezes.

Zev is shoulder to shoulder with his dad now, a fact the man has failed to mention, either because he's gotten used to his kids growing a foot overnight, or because he's reliably oblivious these days.

Oblivious (adjective) [uh.bliv.ee.ess]: unmindful; without awareness or memory. Synonyms: unconscious, unaware, insensible.

Zev is grateful for Dad's silence that allows him to focus on navigating the parking garage without causing an accident. When he's safely headed toward home, he decides to bring up the subject of visiting Zoey himself, figuring he'll have better control of the conversation.

"So, I hung out in Zoey's room for a while this morning." Not an outright lie, more a sin of omission.

"How'd that go?"

"Fine," Zev says. "Oh, and I ran into that speech therapist, Francesca something? Like literally." He laughs, a bit manically. "She practically crushed my foot with those stilettos." He waves an agitated hand in the air and hits the brakes a little too hard.

Dad puts Zev's hand firmly back at the 2:00 spot. "Son. Keep your eyes on the road and your hands on the wheel."

Obviously, Dad's made his usual mental leap from momentary distraction to three-car pileup. What's the point of talking to him? Zev retreats into silence.

"You can be more relaxed about it when you've got more driving hours under your belt and you're less, well …"

"Less what?" Zev simmers.

Dad doesn't answer right away.

"What have I ever done to make you doubt my driving? Why does everything have to be a freaking emergency with you, huh, Dad?" He strives to keep his voice low and his eyes front.

"It doesn't. But you seem jumpy. And that kind of anxiety can lead to all kinds of problems on the road."

"*I'm* jumpy?"

"Looks that way to me."

Zev can't decide if he's more pissed that Dad is such a hard-ass, or that's he's right.

"Fine. Whatever."

In the driveway, he slams into park, jerks out the car keys, and jumps out, running up the front steps without a backward glance.

EXCERPT FROM
THE MEMORY BOOK OF ZOEY SANDOR

I am standing in the middle of a circle and everybody is clapping and laughing I wear a fancy dress, long and shimmery and silver. I have done something wonderful some good magic and everyone is proud of me but I don't know what it is. Now I am swimming in the air and it looks like a sparkly ocean and I am floating above all the people and they call to me "Come down, Zoey, come down" but I am happy up where it is quiet. There is glitter in the air and it lands on everyone and makes them look pretty like me but when they talk the sparkles go away and that is like bad magic so I will be quiet I won't talk anymore so the magic will only be good.

(Transcribed by Francesca Garibaldi, SLP)

DAY 77

Sam looked around the conference table at his exceptional clinical team: Francesca, Emma, Derek, Gillian. How many times had they sat here, discussing the progress of a patient? He did a quick calculation—approximately fifty Team Meetings a year, plus dozens of Discharge Meetings, multiplied by fifteen years. Over a thousand times that he had presided over this talented group of people, guiding them and pushing them and praising them. There had been a great deal of rueful laughter in this room: Team Meetings were protected time, when each of the therapists could give an honest assessment of the patient's progress or lack thereof, free from the need for diplomatic filters that had to be in place when the patient's family was around.

There had also been a fair amount of grief in this room during Discharge Meetings, when patients' caregivers had sat here with them, trying to imagine how they were going to bear the burden alone, now that their loved one was coming home. How could they wrap their already frayed lives around the mystery that used to be their son or their mother, their sister or their husband? How would they keep them safe? How would they ever take them to the supermarket? What if people stared? Sam and his team would hasten to assure these caregivers they were not alone, the team was there to help on an outpatient basis, to advise and tweak and support for as long as it was needed.

Now it was their turn: Zoey's Discharge Planning Meeting. There would only be one or two more Team Meetings after this, and she'd be home. Sam could hardly believe it. By then, it would be three months since her injury.

Liv sat next to him, wearing a look of careful concentration as she leafed through the Tentative Discharge Plan the team had compiled:

1. Target discharge date is set for the third week of September, pending final physician assessment and approval.
2. Family will install safety railing around the toilet and bathtub in patient's bathroom. (NOTE: Parents have declined home visit to assess safety measures. Dr. Sandor will assume responsibility for said assessment.)

Sam read over Liv's shoulder and thought about how rude he'd been to Emma.

"Zoey is due for discharge in a couple of weeks, right?" Em had asked him innocently in the corridor the other day. "When should I come by the house for my usual little safety roundup?"

"Are you kidding me? Thanks anyway, but we've got it covered," he'd snapped.

He couldn't bring himself to apologize, though he knew how insulted she must feel. They all must. He should've kept his mouth shut and let her do her job, which she did so well. He was the one behaving unprofessionally.

The meeting began, and each team member took a turn talking about Zoey's progress.

Francesca summed up neatly the fundamental shift in Zoey's personality since the TBI: "The Zoey who came out of the coma does not have the drive of the girl who went into it. If we wait for her to *want* to get well, it will not happen."

It was true. Where Zoey had once been taut and muscular, ready to leap forward into whatever the next moment required, now she was soft and dreamy, easily distracted and slow to respond. Everyone was too at ease with this change, Sam thought, taking it for granted that they'd all have to work within the strictures of her newly unfocused personality.

Sam's attention wandered back to the Discharge Plan:

3. Patient is ambulatory and will sleep in upstairs bedroom (with assisted ascent until no longer needed), where family's sleeping quarters are located, so they will be able to provide nighttime supervision.
4. Patient's mother is able to work at home and has agreed to be in the house whenever patient is present.
5. Family will hire an aide for respite care and has been urged to minimize rotation as patient continues to exhibit discomfort with unfamiliar people.
6. Patient will not be left in the unsupervised care of nonadult family members.
7. Patient will return for OT, PT, and SLP on an outpatient basis three times per week for at least 12 weeks, with regular assessments ongoing.

At some point, Francesca stopped speaking. Sam looked up and smiled vaguely at her. Emma cleared her throat nervously:

"*Ahem.* The most significant changes to Zoey's fine motor skills, *ahem*, continue to be caused by her left neglect, which—"

Sam knew that constant note of concern in the Discharge Plan was injected to minimize the hospital's liability, but he still found it galling. Did they imagine he and Liv would fail Zoey? He didn't realize he'd made an annoyed sound until everyone stopped talking.

"Apologies. Please, continue," he said, aiming for a blasé tone, though it came out sharper than he'd hoped. Was he expected to nod and smile at their false assurances?

"—which we have yet to resolve." She talked about the strategies they had tried to get Zoey to recruit her left hand, and about other small motor work they'd undertaken.

Em finished and waited for Sam to speak, but he knew it wasn't safe, so he just nodded. After a glance in Sam's direction, Derek took over. Sam had never seen him nervous before—usually he was the picture of heartiness. *Gung ho* was the word Sam would have used to describe him. Now he haltingly discussed Zoey's unreliable balance, her left-sided deficits, her poor muscle tone, looking up at Sam several times—for what? Confirmation? Approval?

Sam was trying to imagine bringing Zoey home. Prickles of heat traveled from the top of his head to his fingertips, and he flexed his hands helplessly to discharge the sensation. He looked over at Liv, who saw his small movement of distress and gave him a trusting smile.

Again, he tried to envision the day Zoey would come home. But every time, what arose in his mind was not the future but the past: He was seventeen at his parents' funeral, trying to hide his anger at being left alone to stand over their graves. That same prickling sensation had plagued him then, and he'd tried to release it along with the clumps of dirt he'd been asked to drop on their coffins. Only it wouldn't let go.

How could they do this to him? he'd silently asked. He wasn't even a whole person yet. He couldn't even vote. How was he supposed to parent himself through the end of his teens? Through college and beyond? He had no idea what he was supposed to do. Rabbi Friedman helped as much as he could, offering guidance about the rituals of mourning—"we wash our hands at the graveside to create a separation, a transition if you like, from the realm of death to that of the living"—which provided Sam with an anchor, a bit of ballast on which to rely. But the rest of the time, he was at sea. And he was furious.

When he came home from the funeral to his parents' house—*my house*, he repeated to himself hollowly—the entire synagogue community came with him, but he was still alone. He could not stop imagining their car accident. The scene wrapped itself around him like a suffocating cloak: the rebar jutting out of the pickup truck that crashed into them at eighty miles per hour, impaling them where they sat. The moment of impact. Their fear and pain.

He couldn't bear this ending for them, not after they had survived the worst that humanity could throw at them in the Camps and had found some way, afterward, to be as loving and optimistic and kind as anyone he knew. He asked Rabbi Friedman to explain how the universe could be so bitter, so spiteful.

"Semeleh, I wish I could understand the point of such a thing. I wish anyone could. But there is no point. If you want to make meaning, it is to be found in what they made of their lives, not in the way they suffered, or in how they died. And your life, too, Sam. It has meaning *despite* what's happened, not because of it. Your life matters because those good, loving people brought you into the world and raised you. It won't be easy, I know. But you can carry their spirit forward into the future."

So, he tried. Between infuriating meetings with Social Services, where he had to keep proving his parents had left him everything he needed to get by until he turned eighteen—he even had to pull the rabbi in to vouch for it, though he didn't really believe it himself—he tried to sit at the piano in his empty house and play for them, play away his fury and bewilderment and the avalanche of loneliness that assailed him daily. But it was futile. He had to *do* something. There was no one else. He had to be the answer to his own question.

DAY 84

An early frost was doing its best to chase away the remnants of summer when Liv left home to meet with Francesca, right after seeing the other kids off to school. Did Lottie take her lunch? Liv could only hope so; she'd been woefully distracted this morning. Zoey was due to be discharged next week, and Liv suspected her new friend was disappointed by her progress. But ready or not, the machinery of insurance would soon propel her out the doors of the hospital.

The two women smiled at each other with quiet purpose before they turned down the corridor to Zoey's room. They found her sitting in bed, arms and legs splayed in all directions, staring into her mirror. Would Liv ever get used to this soft body?

Francesca was Zoey's best defense against lethargy. To begin each session, the therapist sat next to her, rubbing her pale, limp hand between her own warm ones to bring her into the present moment.

"Good morning. How are you this fine day, Zoey?"

"I'm hungry!" Liv was getting used to Zoey's silvery soprano. It was as if even her vocal cords couldn't be recruited to their former robust levels of energy. "When is breakfast?"

"I know, *cara*, I know. We will go to breakfast soon. First, I want to talk with you a little."

A patient shuffled by in the corridor, and Zoey craned her neck. "That man walks too slow, and he smells bad."

"That man is another patient. Do you know why he's here?"

"He hurt his head like me?"

"It's possible he did, Zoey! It's good you remember that. Why do you think he smells bad?"

"He *does* smell bad."

"But why? Maybe it's hard for him to wash himself?"

"No. He's lazy. Like me."

Francesca laughed, and Zoey looked confused.

"Are you really lazy, or does your injury make you tired?"

"I am tired," Zoey answered with a wicked grin.

Liv was enthralled. These glimmers of the old Zoey that were breaking through—the sly manipulation, the storytelling, the sense of humor, the raw assessment of other people—were reassembling into a new version of her clever, articulate, confident daughter. And when had she become aware of her own brain injury?

"Time for breakfast?" Zoey asked again.

"Where do you need to look to find the answer to that question?" Francesca tapped the Memory Book, but Zoey didn't pick up her cue.

Of course, the Memory Book. If Zoey had been reading it, maybe she knew more than they thought.

"You tell me. You're smart, Franny."

"You are also smart, Zoey." Francesca smiled and patted her hand. "Use your Memory Book. This is where you find your schedule."

Zoey stared blankly at the book until Francesca reached around, pulled the daily schedule off the left inside cover of the binder, and placed it on the right, over the title page.

Zoey looked straight at it, scanning near the top of the schedule. "Eight-oh-oh-a.m. … Breakfast!" she sang out.

"Very good, Zoey. *Very* good!"

Francesca turned to Liv. "Everyone must be reminded to keep important information on the *right* where she can see it, until we find a way to beat the left neglect," she said.

She picked up the digital clock and moved it from the left to the right side of the bed. "What time is it now?"

"Seven-five-five," read Zoey.

"Right. So how long is it until breakfast?"

"Ummm. Five minutes?"

"Wow! That was great!" How many times had they mistaken Zoey's silence for incomprehension, when really she couldn't see what was being asked?

She looked on as Francesca wrote an entry in the Memory Book.

> *Sept. 13, 2005, Francesca Garibaldi, SLP*
>
> *You had a great day today! We found out you remember how to tell time and do math problems. You should practice a lot. Also, remember to keep writing down your dreams—ask someone to help you until it's easier for you. These are important! You are going home soon, and you are ready to make the change. I am proud of you, Zoey!*

As they dropped Zoey off for an OT breakfast with Em, Liv asked Francesca, "*Is* she ready to come home?"

Francesca nodded. "She will continue to progress. She has some quite useful skills. Though her short-term memory is impaired, it isn't absent. And I see the outline of the true Zoey Sandor now—she emerges from the shadows. Home is within her reach."

On an impulse, Liv said, "Speaking of home, why don't you let me cook lunch for you today?"

"Such a kind offer! I am tempted, only I am not sure I have the time." Francesca frowned at her watch. "The bad weather is traveling up from the South, yes?"

Liv, who hadn't seen a weather report in weeks, shrugged and remained hopefully silent.

"Still, you've spent much time observing me at my work. Now I would like to watch you at yours. If I take my own auto, can I make it back in ninety minutes?"

Liv grinned. "I'll work fast! I promise."

"Okay then, I accept. Do you know, in all these years, I have never seen your house?"

Liv was uncomfortably aware she'd breached Sam's ironclad separation of work and home. But this was the only way she knew to adequately convey her gratitude to Francesca.

She pulled into her driveway, her menu all planned out: a salad of field greens, toasted hazelnuts, avocado, and golden beets, which she'd roasted the other night for dinner; crostini topped with her own Vidalia onion marmalade, fresh thyme, grapes, and fontina cheese, warm from the oven in fifteen minutes; a chocolate cherry soufflé that could bake while they were eating. A little feast, and she'd have Francesca back with time to spare.

At the edges of her mind, Liv sensed there was something about this afternoon she was forgetting, but she dismissed the thought. That uneasiness was so often with her now, another by-product of this fractured life.

By the time Francesca's car appeared, Liv was rushing to pull ingredients out of the fridge. She beckoned her guest to come inside, but Francesca had stopped to look around.

"Good that Zoey is ambulatory, no? These stairs would not work for a wheelchair."

Liv winced, knowing Sam would be mortified. "Yes, it's an old house by American standards. Almost a hundred years. I'll take you on a tour later if we have time, but first I want to get you fed!"

She smiled at her guest. When was the last time she had brought home a friend?

"I would love that. It is a beautiful example of colonial architecture, yes?"

"Thanks, yes, we think so."

Lunch went brilliantly. Francesca was effusive about Liv's culinary inventiveness. "The crostini? Amazing. *Stupefacente!* You are a professional chef?"

Liv blushed. "Well, not exactly. I do love to cook and bake, and I've been trying to branch out, but—"

"But what? Where is the hesitation? Surely not among the customers!"

"No, you're right, the hesitation is mine. I want to have time for my family. I'm not"—she searched for the right word—"not positive about cooking professionally, I guess. It brings me joy to make beautiful food for the people I love, but I don't feel the need, the drive to do more. Especially now. Do you understand?"

Liv worried she came off sounding lazy.

"I understand exactly. For you, home is not in the world. Your world is in your home. Yes?"

"Yes! Exactly. My world is in my home."

They talked and laughed like old friends, but this was a new sort of companionship for Liv that she realized she'd been missing. What had held her back all these years? She could certainly use a friend now. She and Sam had never been so distant.

She recalled meeting Francesca's charming husband, Giovanni, at several of the holiday parties, and had been drawn to both of them, but had never questioned Sam's wish to keep the two parts of his life separate. Liv realized she still knew next to nothing about this woman, in spite of all their hours together over this summer. She didn't even know if Francesca had any children! When she finally made up her mind to ask, the other woman shook her head firmly.

"No. We have no children, only our work and each other," she said, sounding perfectly content. "Of course, we have many, many nieces and nephews in *Italia*, and fantastic friends who make our lives full and busy," she said, smiling at Liv to leave no doubt she was now included in that privileged circle.

Liv smiled back. "It must be wonderful to be free to spend your time as you wish."

"Yes, it is. But your life is wonderful in a different way."

Liv nodded and bent to take the chocolate soufflé out of the oven. Even with all of her recent woes and worries, she wouldn't trade her life for any other.

"*Voila!*" She set it on the table between them with two spoons. "Oops, sorry. Wrong European language."

Francesca shook her head and raised her spoon in anticipation. "No, no! Even in Italian we say *voila*. Now, may I sink in?"

"You mean *dig* in? If you wanted to *sink* in, you'd have to climb into the dish. Kind of messy!"

They laughed as they shared the rich dessert and vowed to get together again soon.

After Liv saw Francesca to the door, she made a cup of strong tea and collapsed onto the overstuffed love seat at one end of the kitchen. She sipped her tea and let her mind drift to Sam, who was withdrawing more and more, lapsing into long silences at breakfast and dinner. This was what worried Liv the most: Like his opinions, Sam had never been able to keep his troubles to himself—she could always count on him to express every little concern as it arose, and they had long since fallen into a comfortable marital routine wherein Liv agreed to listen to his endless fears, and Sam agreed to let her gently debunk them one by one.

"Okay, okay. Sorry to be such an old lady," he would say, sighing as he climbed into bed beside her. They always tried to go to bed at the same time, no matter how busy the day was.

But since June, their familiar world had been unraveling, and Liv had taken to ruminating almost as much as Sam. Who would take away their worries now? And that episode with the Lyme disease. A malpractice suit? They were still in the twilight zone.

She had to believe that life would feel more normal when Zoey came home.

She couldn't quite persuade herself to get up off the love seat. Maybe it was more than wine. She was a little chocolate-stoned, an expression she had coined when the children were small. One day when they were gorging on fresh-baked double chocolate cookies, she had noted their dazed faces and it had occurred to her that despite its caffeine content, chocolate might possess tranquilizing powers above and beyond its antioxidant load. In the evening, she had relayed her insight to Sam.

"I got the kids stoned today," she'd said with a playful smile.

"Oh? What's their drug of choice?"

"Chocolate! And after observing the effect, I've realized I have a powerful tool at my disposal: Mexican hot chocolate with shortbread; toffee chip cookies and cold milk; rocky road brownies. They'll quickly render the children powerless, and once they're chocolate-stoned they'll do whatever I ask. I'll try to use this tool judiciously, so the kids don't become immune."

So, the expression "chocolate-stoned" became part of their parenting shorthand, a small weapon in the arsenal they reserved for desperate times. Liv figured she should have been using it more lately, as a counterweight to the unending, amorphous war Sam was waging. Last night, he'd shouted at Lottie in the door of her room to "clean up this pigsty, for the love of God!" and thundered at Zev that "if I see one more sketch pad lying around this house, I'm going to confiscate them all." Was it such a catastrophe that the house was a little messy during this awful summer?

Liv sighed and looked up at the ancient grandfather clock ticking away on the wall. The old thing must have needed winding again. It couldn't possibly be 4:00 p.m. It was just 2:00 p.m. a few minutes ago. But logic finally invaded her muzzy brain. If it was ticking, it must be working.

"Oh, my God. Lottie!" she shrieked, jumping up as she remembered that she was supposed to have been at the Camp Artemis open house at 3:30 to see Lottie in the final play of summer.

She hated to be late. Mother had drummed the idea into her from an early age: *When you are late, you signal the person waiting that your time is more valuable than theirs.* Liv would never want Lottie to feel that way. These months had been hard enough on her, alone in her room with Zoey's empty bed staring back at her. As time went on, she'd needed more and more reassurance, and this wouldn't help. Liv tried not to envision a crestfallen Lottie scanning the audience for her. How could she have let this happen?

She drove at top speed through pelting rain and lightning, and then, when the thunderstorm was at its most violent, burst through the back door of the Arts and Crafts Building, all out of breath. A sea of parents turned startled faces toward her, but she ignored them as she scanned the stage, praying she would catch a few minutes of Lottie in the gorgeous Athena costume Mikayla had made for her. No such luck. The stage was empty, the room filled with applause, and minutes later, all the children crowded back out to take their final bows.

There was Lottie, curtseying and trying to maintain her warrior-like persona as she searched the audience. Liv caught her eye and smiled and clapped, but she couldn't do anything about her dripping hair and clothes. Lottie's expression grew pinched, and her chin began to tremble. Liv vowed to find a way to make this right: Lottie was her baby. It didn't matter what else was going on. She and Sam had made a promise after their fourth child was born that she would never be made to feel like an afterthought. Liv pushed through the throngs of people, her throat tightening at the slump of Lottie's gold-clad shoulders.

"Lottie, sweetheart, you look perfect."

Lottie's eyes filled with tears. "Mommy, how *could* you? Where were you? Were you with Zoey?"

"No! Don't blame Zoey for this!"

Lottie recoiled at her harsh tone, and Liv took a breath before she spoke again.

"I went home from the hospital because I was feeling … sick." Her face blazed, though there was no way Lottie could know the truth. "I sat down for a few minutes to rest, and I … I fell asleep. I messed up. Can you forgive me?"

Lottie looked doubtful, and Liv took her little arm and started to walk. "Well, it was a terrible mistake, and I can't take it back. But right now, I want to see your weaving and your jewelry. Okay?"

Lottie still wore a skeptical expression, and her arms were folded over her chest. But she nodded with compressed lips and walked on ahead. Liv exclaimed over each of her works of art, but her words sounded hollow even to her own ears.

Before long, an act of contrition presented itself. A breathless, diminutive, pigtailed Greek goddess ran up and said: "Hey, Lottie! A bunch of us are going to Wooster Square for pizza. Can you come?"

Lottie turned to Liv with a look that would only accept one response. "Please, Mommy, oh please! Can we? Everyone's going!"

Liv's mind shouted, *No! No! I'm too tired! It's raining! I have to bring Zoey chocolate!* Still, she knew Zoey would never remember her promise, whereas one word here could go far.

"Okay."

As Lottie squealed with delight, Liv reached for her cell phone to let Sam know she wouldn't make it back to the hospital today, and that she could bring home pizza if he liked.

Arriving at Pepe's Pizzeria in another spectacular downpour, Liv inhaled the warm, Mediterranean fragrance and realized she was hungry in spite of her lavish lunch with Francesca, which already felt like a distant memory. Parents and children were crammed together around the scarred tables, and Liv found it a relief to be listening to chatter about something besides speech therapy, ADLs, and left neglect. How circumscribed her world had become.

She and Lottie gobbled down the delicious pie, exclaiming over the chewy crust, the perfectly balanced sauce, and the creamy mozzarella drizzled with olive oil. They made desultory conversation about the fourth grade, and heard snatches of other conversations, all of which revolved around the weather. That was odd. Hadn't Francesca mentioned it too? The words *storm* and *surge* and *flood* recurred so many times in the babble that Liv wondered if she *had* missed something. She tuned in to the adults while Lottie chattered with her new friend.

"They're saying it's one of the worst hurricanes in US history? And the death toll might rise to over one thousand people?" said one young mother, sounding as if she wasn't sure of her own information.

Liv sat up straight. What could they be talking about? She hadn't read the papers in weeks, hadn't turned on the radio or the TV.

"New Orleans looks demolished from what I saw on the news," said another woman, her eyes such an intense blue they were almost violet. "They're saying over eighty percent is flooded. There was this horrifying footage of a man and his children clinging to their roof as the waters rose. They drowned waiting for the helicopter."

Liv was appalled. How could people be drowning on the roofs of their houses?

"I'm sorry to interrupt," she said. "Could you tell me—what you're talking about, is it current? I mean, this storm you're describing, it's happening now?"

The other women exchanged incredulous glances and began to speak all at once.

"Yes! Hurricane Katrina?"

"It's been all over the news!"

Liv blushed. She was still drawing a complete blank.

"You know, the levees in New Orleans broke? The city's flooded?" said Violet-Eyes. "They say there'll be more rain tomorrow. But the worst of the storm has already played itself out. Where have you *been*?"

"I've been at the … I haven't had …"

What could Liv say to these women, whose names she didn't even know? Her own family's misfortune was nothing compared to a disaster on this scale. But before she knew it, she had said aloud what she meant to keep to herself.

"My older daughter was in a coma, and I've been basically living at the hospital since the start of summer. This is the first time I've been anywhere in, well, months. I lost track of the news."

The atmosphere around the table shifted instantly.

"What? You poor thing! Did you say a *coma*?" asked Violet-Eyes.

Liv nodded. Could the woman's eyes get any bigger?

"Oh my God! Was it a car accident? How is she now?"

"Why haven't we heard about this? Lottie hasn't said a word to Brittany."

"She's in the TBI Rehab wing at Yale New Haven," Liv said, her face hot from the attention. "She's recovering slowly from a severe traumatic brain injury."

Her voice trembled. It was the first time she had said the words to strangers.

"Is she—will she be, like, okay?"

Liv could see the uneasy sympathy on their faces, could almost hear the unasked questions. Was Zoey intellectually impaired? Would she ever be normal again? Liv opened her mouth but couldn't find anything else to say. She supposed Zoey's injury *was* a sufficient excuse for her ignorance, but she wasn't sure she wanted to be let off the hook so easily. Hadn't she been thinking how narrow her world had become? Even now, with terrible images of drowned people and broken dams swirling around in her head, she was obsessed with bringing Zoey her promised chocolate. She had missed an entire national disaster because she was so busy trying to manage her own personal one.

Liv looked down at Lottie's head and thought about her daughter's sorrow an hour earlier. *No.* It was Liv's right, maybe even her sacred responsibility, to put the needs of her own children first. It was the best way to make a mensch, a good citizen. There was time to change the world before you became a parent, and again after the children were grown and gone. But children needed to know they mattered most to someone, so they could feel safe and loved, and confident enough to go out and have their own turn at changing the world.

It was Lottie who rescued her from the silence growing around the other mothers' questions. "Zoey's doing great, right Mom? Right now she's impatient—I mean *inpatient*, which means she still has to live at the hospital, 'cause she has therapy practically All. Day. Long. Physical therapy and speech therapy and oppu—occu—the other one, for her hands and stuff." She rolled her eyes and the moms around the table smiled sympathetically. "But that'll be over soon and she'll be back at home. Not like those poor Katrina people. My counselors say it's gonna be a looooong time before they get their lives back. But we still have our house and our toys and, well, *everything*. Hey! I should send some of my Barbies to New Orleans. Can I, Mom?"

They all turned to Liv, who stammered, "I—I—I don't see why not."

"Yay! After Zoey gets back, she can help me decide which ones. Everything'll be back to normal. Right, Mom?"

"Right, love," she said, her face stiff with the smile she required of herself.

There was no doubt that a bigger sorrow waited for Lottie, as she came to understand how radically the landscape of their own family had changed. But that could damn well wait for another day.

DAY 88

"I'm going to Zoey's room for a quick visit. Wanna come?" Mikayla asks, trying and failing to sound casual as she cleans their brushes, and they replace the tarp that hangs over their mural whenever they're not working on it. Now that school has started again, they come in the afternoons a few times a week. Zev looks forward to these hours with Mikayla, though he has to work hard to ignore Zoey's nearness.

Zev shakes his head. He's held firm in his resolve: no visiting. Mikayla's disappointment makes him feel bad, but not bad enough to go back there. He waits for her on the bench outside, facing the mural wall, tapping his feet impatiently as he considers the progress of his project, or the lack of it—everything has taken longer than he expected, and now that school has started, Gideon and Ramie are here less and less. He's worried it won't be done in time—scary, but not as scary as what's going on down the hall.

Mikayla returns from Zoey's room crying, which isn't unusual, and Zev hugs her and rubs her back for a minute. He guiltily welcomes these chances to make physical contact. He doesn't ask her what's wrong, because he already knows the answer. Anyway, she'll want to talk about it when she calms down. She doesn't shy away from things or pretend they're not happening; she's kind of an open book. Nothing like other girls. Well, except Zoey, of course. She was a big one for honesty. *No artifice*, said a sticker on her locker. She got away with it, too—and somehow it never compromised her popularity. She was that good. At least, he thinks that's how it used to be. The legend of Zoey is fading fast.

"Oh, my God. Sometimes I miss her so much!" Mikayla sighs, letting go of him and scrubbing her eyes. "But she was so funny today, Zev. She said I look like Tinker Bell, and she begged me to teach her to fly. She says she had a dream about flying … or, well, *swimming in the air* is what she called it."

With a jolt, he remembers his latest dream-sketch.

She stands in the middle of a circle, everybody clapping and laughing, she wears a fancy dress, long and shimmery and silver. She is swimming in the air among the glitter, it looks like the ocean sparkling, she is floating above all the people, they call to her "Come down, Zoey, come down" but she is happy up there where it is quiet. The silver glitter lands on everyone and makes them all look pretty like her …

It reminds him of their bar and bat mitzvahs—how all Zoey wanted for the party was a silver dress and iridescent confetti. He should share the memory with Mikayla, maybe even tell her about the eerie coincidence—a sort of peace offering—but the words won't come.

"Huh. She's right. You do look a little like Tinker Bell," he says instead, smiling at her with surprising ease.

"Yeah, I get that a lot, but what does Tinker Bell even *look* like? I mean, besides a cartoon one inch tall." She's smiling back at him. Zev's smile widens to a smirk. "Hey! I'm not that short." She punches him lightly on the arm and grins. "Anyway, I was surprised because I didn't know she could even *remember* her dreams. It's progress."

His smile disappears. That's today's big deal? So, she remembered a dream. Zev wishes he could forget his. What other people keep calling Zoey's *progress* turns out to be nothing more than these tiny baby steps that will never get her back to where she was before. He doesn't want to know, but Mikayla's just getting warmed up.

"Sometimes it's hard for me to figure out how to treat her," she muses. "Because, you know, it seems pretty advanced for her to be able to remember dreams. But these are things we talked about when we were six or seven, too. So, is she a little kid? Or one of us, still? Or something in between?"

Zev stays silent, sure she wouldn't want to know what he's thinking.

"So, I promised I would read to her from *Peter Pan* tomorrow." She grimaces. "I know she loves it, but it's so *depressing* for me."

Zev is embarrassed by his silence.

"I wish you'd come with me. She misses you. How long has it been, anyway?"

He shakes his head. "I can't, Mikayla. I. Just. Can't."

Mikayla nods. She's not mad; she has told him before. She's just lonely, and Zoey is, too. What about Zev? Isn't he lonely? *Not so much, anymore*, he wants to say, allowing his mind to glide away from Zoey and toward Mikayla. Holding her. Or at least being alone with her.

"Hey, I've got an idea. Why don't we take a break tomorrow, skip the hospital? Let's go to my house instead," he says.

"I don't know."

"Come on! I need another subject for my portrait series, and you promised you would think about it."

He has brought it up as many times as he dared, but she has demurred each time, pointing a finger at her own chest and raising her eyebrows as if to say, *Why would you want to paint my portrait?*

"Shouldn't we put our energy into the mural right now?" Mikayla gestures at the wall in front of them with a sweep of her braceleted arm. "The way we're going, it'll never get done in time! And what about Zoey? I promised."

"It's just, I need to build my portfolio this year, and, and portraits are popular with admissions committees. C'mon, Mikayla, do this for me and let me worry about the mural. Okay?" He doesn't stammer with her anymore—its own miracle.

"Okay," she sighs. "Tomorrow after school."

"Awesome! You won't regret it!"

In the morning, Zev tells Mom he'll be painting after school and doesn't want to be disturbed. His classes pass in a blur. This year, he's made a new art form of keeping under the radar, ignoring any lingering whispers from classmates, ducking away from teachers who talk to him in syrupy voices. When they get home, he's grateful that the high school lets out earlier than the elementary. Before Mom can arrive with Lottie, he hustles Mikayla into the part of the basement where he paints—the part with the high windows that used to be a speakeasy, which he secretly thinks has infused his work with a subversive note he might not otherwise have access to.

Now, she perches delicately on the edge of the barstool where he has placed her. She looks a little ill at ease at first, but he's in no position to reassure her. His mouth has gone dry as sandpaper and his palms are so slippery he can barely hold the charcoal. He starts to work in silence, with only the sweet sounds coming from his old stereo. He knows his taste in music isn't normal for a kid—all those oldies; Zoey used to tease him about it—and he hopes Mikayla doesn't think it's uncool.

Soon she looks more relaxed, and the flow overtakes Zev. Making art is like stepping into a river; ideas and feelings trickle from his mind into the pencil and straight out on the canvas. In the world of images, he's keen and articulate. He believes in himself. The pencil is an extension of his heart, and he maps her outline on the thick, nubby fabric in a fog of adoration.

He can't remember anything they talked about, but when he's done for the day, he knows the painting will be good.

"Can you come back tomorrow afternoon so I can finish?"

"Can I see?" she asks shyly after she slides off the stool.

"Not till tomorrow. I promise you can, as soon as I feel like it's mostly done. Deal?"

"Deal."

That night, Zev tosses in bed for hours, debating. If he tells Mikayla about his feelings, he will almost certainly be humiliated and rejected. Still, there have been small moments between them, a burst of energy when their hands brush against each other, a sort of heat radiating from her body when they work side by side on the mural.

He knows now what she is to him. She's his muse, a word he's especially fond of because it does more than its fair share. It is both noun and verb, concept and action.

Muse (noun, verb) [myooz]: 1. N: a goddess who inspires an artist; 2. V: to think or meditate in silence, as on some subject. Synonyms: cogitate, ruminate, think, dream, contemplate, meditate, mull, ponder.

No synonyms for the noun, but the verb more than makes up for it.

He knows what Mom would say about this, too: If only human beings were as thoughtful as this bounty of alternatives would suggest, the world would be a much better place. He wishes Zoey were here to give him advice about Mikayla. What would she tell him to do?

Alone in his room, he resists the most important thing he already knows. If he wants Zoey, he'll have to be the one to go to her. For her part, she'll only visit him in his dreams.

Sleep overtakes him again.

She stands in front of a mirror looking at herself there is bright light everywhere she holds up her hands to shield her eyes but her hand in the mirror never moves. She reaches out to touch it and her image vanishes now it's a door she's standing in front of, she is carrying an armload of books her eyes send out golden sparks she tries to come out the door but meets herself coming in, only her left hand is curled and useless her eyes are wide and staring she can't get past herself but she wants to more than anything. "It's okay, Zoey," she says to herself. "You can have your Heart's Desire."

Zev opens his eyes. He wishes for once he would dream about Mikayla instead of Zoey, but still, he puts everything down in pencil: the light, the mirror, the two Zoeys standing in the doorway. His hand pauses as he draws the second Zoey, staring back at the first. It was only a dream, but he still hears her voice saying the words. *Heart's Desire.* It's one of her favorite expressions; there's a whole line from a Yeats poem, "The Land of Heart's Desire." This is her private shorthand for the single-mindedness of teenage romance, something Zoey was immune to, despite—or because of?—the bottomless well of her admirers. "I'll know when I'm ready, Zev. And I'm not ready yet."

Zev knows he's living in the land of Heart's Desire. And even though it's weird and sad, and it makes no sense that he should've gotten there before his twin, he's pretty sure he's ready.

The next afternoon, when he opens the heavy olive-wood door he has opened a thousand times and sees Mikayla standing there, smiling for him, he understands that Zoey was right about the single-mindedness thing: No amount of rational thinking, or shyness or fear or even misery, could stop the love he feels for this girl. This is more than attraction. It's become part of him. He's almost rude as he ushers her back to the barstool in the basement, hurrying her past the 1920s writing on the walls that she likes to stop and read. He's desperate to avoid any interruption in their rapport. But once she's set, he slows down and paints with tenderness, caressing the planes of her face with his brush, tracing her curves with confidence. He pours it all onto the canvas: his deep physical yearning for her, his wish to protect her from harm, from sorrow, his admiration for her courage, his gratitude for her kindness, her loyalty. The layers of paint on the canvas are a textural record of his feelings: complicated, heavy, alive.

When he's finished, he puts down his brush and steps back to look at his work. Even he knows the painting is powerful and honest and beautiful.

He realizes he hasn't spoken in a while, maybe even for the whole afternoon, content to let music fill the space between them. He glances at Mikayla and she smiles and stretches, yawning and covering her mouth with an embarrassed duck of her head. Her voice comes out a little hoarse.

"Whoa, you were really in the flow there," she says. Her eyes are shining. "Can I see it now?"

Zev knows he has to do it. He can't wait or he will lose his courage. He bows, sweeping his hand toward the easel, then toward her.

"It's all you," he says, summoning bravado to cover the tremor in his voice.

She hops off the barstool and approaches the easel with a nervous smile. When she sees the portrait, she lets out a gasp. Her smile vanishes.

The words are out of his mouth before he can stop them. "Oh, no. Do you hate it?"

When Mikayla turns toward him, she looks serious. Some kind of understanding has dawned on her face. In agony, he waits.

"Zev! I *love* it," she says.

•

For the next few days, Zev is paralyzed. He doesn't approach Mikayla at school, though he can't prevent a slow smile from creeping to his lips every time he sees her, and he replays her words often in his mind. *I love it.* He pictures himself tracing her mouth with his finger as she pronounces the word with that slight Slavic thickening of the L. *Love.*

She doesn't avoid him, but neither does she seek him out, and Zev understands that she's waiting. He must be the one to act. But there's a sort of harrowing joy in his longing, as fragile as a silk thread. If he speaks to her and is rebuffed, he'll be crushed. If he doesn't, he'll know that he's been held back from his Heart's Desire by a wisp, a filament.

On September 20, the fall equinox, the day of the upperclassmen's end-of-summer beach party, Zev stands at Mikayla's front door, his knuckles not quite making contact with the wood. He glances over his shoulder—he doesn't want Mom to spot him. He doesn't want any witnesses to his humiliation if he flubs it and is rejected. Finally, he raps hard on the door.

He knows she's home, but only silence comes from inside.

This is a terrible idea. She isn't coming. She knows what he wants and is avoiding him. He should go. He turns to leave. But what if she didn't hear him knock? Maybe he should ring the doorbell. He turns back. Once she opens the door, though, once he opens his mouth, there will be no undoing it, and unless the world has suddenly turned into a much kinder place, things between them will become awkward. He turns to leave again.

When the door opens behind him, he nearly trips as he turns back again, blushing purple.

Her glass-green eyes are full of laughter, she's smudged with colors, and her bracelets jingle on her slim wrist. "Hey, Zev. What's up?"

"Hey, Mikayla. You busy?" He comes back up the stairs, slowwwly, sending a prayer to Zoey's goddesses that he won't trip, sweat, or stammer.

Mercy comes in the form of distraction: Mikayla's not looking at his blushing face, but back over her shoulder, into the house. "I was working on a complicated batik, and I need to get right back in there. Got to keep up on my own art projects, too, you know? That's why it took me so long to answer."

"Umm, well, if this is a bad time—"

"Wanna help?"

"Oh! Sure."

He steps inside. He can practically hear Zoey laughing in the next room; he has been to this house so many times to collect her at dinnertime. Everything is so familiar that in ordinary circumstances it would be nearly invisible: the modular furniture purchased hastily from Ikea when the Slovniks arrived from Moscow, the woven rugs, the faded wall hangings, the ancient nesting dolls lined up on the mantel.

Now, under his feverish gaze, the house's contents look fluorescent, and those dolls—what are they called? Something with an *M*, *Matroika? Marushka?*—all seem to be smiling and cackling at him like a group of little shtetl grandmothers. "Go on, *boychik*! Tell her your Heart's Desire!"

Breathe! he commands himself. It's a simple process, as his science teacher would say. *Expiration* followed by *inspiration*. He loves the homonym.

Inspiration (noun) [in.spuh.rey.shun]: 1. stimulation or arousal of the mind/emotions to a creative or special act. 2. the act or process of inhaling, breathing in.

He follows Mikayla into a sunroom she has clearly commandeered for her art-making—one advantage of being an only child. There are easels and stretching racks and pots of dye and pallets everywhere, with half-opened boxes of charcoals and pastels strewn on a long folding table, and paint-soaked rags in varying states of dryness. Interesting! She's organized with her schoolwork, but a bit of a slob at home. So different from his own austere workspace.

"I know what you're thinking!" she says. "You're surprised it's such a mess in here, right?"

"No, I-I don't—"

"Don't try to deny it! I see it in your face. It's okay. I was surprised too, when I saw yours. I didn't expect it to be so neat. Most guys are slobs. Goes to show, you never know."

"Yeah, well, my bedroom's a disaster. But my studio? I've always been kind of a nut about recapping paints and putting pastels in spectrum order in their boxes. Because of something my dad said to me when I got my first set of paints."

"Which was?"

"He said, 'These are your instruments of creativity, son. Treat them with respect and care, and they will treat you the same way.' He's always so serious about everything. At the time, I was, I don't know, six or seven, and he made it sound as if my paints were on a par with his medical instruments. Like we were both doing important work."

He remembers thinking they might one day be equals. Instead, they've remained poorly matched competitors in a pointless tug-of-war.

"He's right. It *is* important work," Mikayla says. "But once I'm in the flow I can't be bothered to keep it all straight."

"Well, whatever. There's no right way. That's what my mom always says." He smiles at her. There's something appealing about the chaos in Mikayla's studio—a kind of exuberance. As if she's too excited by the work to be neat and methodical. Or maybe she doesn't need to take herself so damn seriously every second. Maybe she knows it's all practice right now.

His eyes come to rest on a series of fabric panels stretched on wooden racks against one wall. He walks over to take a closer look.

"Whoa, Mikayla, these are insane."

"Like, in a good way?"

He turns in time to see her blush and smile.

"In the best way. They're totally hypnotizing, like the inside of a prism. Or, or the way light would look if you could take a picture of it through water."

His clumsy words will never do justice to her work. Mikayla has figured out how to saturate large swaths of silk with jewel tones—emerald and topaz and ruby and amethyst—all intense and translucent at the same time. The colors twist and bend over the fabric like fantastic tree roots and iridescent cobwebs.

"How d'you do it?"

"It's wax-resist dyeing. Batik!" she says happily. "I'll give you a crash course while we work."

For the next hour, she chatters away while she pulls Zev here and there by the wrists or the shirt. Zev remains mostly silent, electrified by the contact and glad for an excuse not to ask the question he has come for.

When the fabric is drying on a rack in the sun and they've slurped down glasses of lemonade in the kitchen, he can't put his mission off any longer.

"Mikayla, I was wondering—"

"So, I meant to ask you—" she starts to say at the same time.

"Oh, okay, you first."

"No, I was wondering why you came over. Did you need something? Exciting that Zoey's coming home!"

"Yeah." He swipes the thought away. "I mean no, I didn't exactly *need* anything ..." The blush and stammer are setting in again, and he forces another deep breath. *Inspiration.* He looks down into Mikayla's eyes, a river on a sunny day. He has to shove his hands in his pockets to stop himself from reaching out and touching her face.

"Well, uh, it's that beach party tonight, and, umm, well, you know I don't usually go to those sorts of things unless Zoey drags me to them, but she's not here to drag me now, you know? And for some dumb reason I still feel like I should go. So, I thought ... if you don't have any plans, umm, maybe you'd like to go? With me?" he ends on a near-squeak. Pathetic. He hadn't meant to mention Zoey at all.

Mikayla raises her eyebrows at this deluge of words. He braces himself for the rejection.

"Sure, Zev. Sounds like fun. What time?"

"Yeah, I get it. It's no—what? I'm sorry. *What* did you say?"

"I said sure."

"You'll come?"

"Why not? I was thinking about going anyway, but I was worried about finishing this project. Who knew I'd have an assistant?" She grins. "But I still need to know what time."

"Hmmm. Seven o'clock in my driveway? We can ride with Gideon. He's already legal. Will that work?"

"Perfect. It'll give me time to clean up my studio ... and myself," she says, holding up her dye-stained hands. She looks happy, even excited.

Walking up the driveway to the house he has lived in for his entire life, he thinks about the way his center of awareness has shifted. Where once he had to use all his energy not to see the empty hammock on the porch, the cello collecting dust in the living room, now every nerve ending in Zev's body is crackling and straining toward the house next door, as if he and Mikayla are two halves of a powerful magnet.

This is different from the easy sense of belonging he has known since before birth. With Zoey, there was always this instinctive understanding. They didn't even have to speak. With Mikayla, it's hard work, confusing and nerve-wracking but charged with possibility. Now he has to communicate like every other human. And he's actually doing it.

He bounds up his front steps two at a time.

"Is that you, Zev?" His mother is in the kitchen with Lottie, but he doesn't want to get her radar going, so he races up the stairs and ducks into the bathroom, hollering as he goes.

"Yup, taking a shower." He hesitates. "Hey, Mom?"

"Yes?"

He can hear the stairs creaking as she comes partway up.

"I'm going to that beach party tonight. Don't worry, I'll get a ride."

He can feel her silence through the door and knows she's wondering if she has heard him right. Zev voluntarily attending a party? He turns on the shower full blast before she can ask for details. When he reappears in the kitchen forty-five minutes later, his curly hair is washed, his face is clean-shaven, and he's wearing cargo shorts and a nondisintegrating T-shirt. Mom sniffs the air, and he knows she recognizes Dad's cologne.

He avoids making eye contact, sure she's dying to ask him what seismic shift has propelled him to attend a social event without Zoey there to cajole, wheedle, or torment him into it. In the face of Zev's steadfast silence, Mom draws her own conclusion—which, judging from the look on her face, is that they've entered the Twilight Zone.

"Did—did you say you had a ride to the party?"

"Ooh, a party! Can I come?" Lottie asks.

"No, bunny. This one's for older high school kids," says Mom, turning her attention back to Zev. "Who else is going?"

He's got to give her props. The effort of holding back her real questions is making her eye twitch, but she is not giving in.

"Yep. Gideon—and probably Ramie," he says, suppressing a smile. "And yes, he's legal to drive me—he passed the one-year mark with his license—and before you say it, I know it's a school night. We'll be back before ten thirty, 'cause the beach closes at ten."

"Well then. My work here is done," Mom says, sounding bemused.

"I bet I know who else is going!" says Lottie with a mischievous grin that reminds him unnervingly of Zoey. Could his baby sister also have his twin's gift of prescience?

"Lots of people!" says Zev hastily, as a horn honks outside. "Okay, that's me. Bye, Mom. Bye, peanut." He turns to shut the front door. Maybe they won't see who's getting into the car with him.

Mikayla emerges from next door in perfect tandem. It's serendipity.

Serendipity (noun) [seh.run.dip.eh.tee]: an aptitude or faculty for making desirable discoveries by accident; the fortune of making such discoveries. Synonyms: destiny, luck, kismet.

Since Ramie is riding shotgun, Zev holds the back door for Mikayla, goes around the other side, and slides in cozily next to her. They exchange a smile as Gideon zooms off. Now he just has to keep from making a fool of himself for the next three hours.

If only it were that easy. At school he keeps to himself, focuses on classes, practices selective deafness when voices follow him down the halls. He knows nothing about going on dates. And *is* this a date? When they arrive at Hammonasset Beach State Park, he's so busy debating whether he should take Mikayla's hand as they walk along the beach that he barely remembers to get out of the car. The wind is whipping the surf, and whitecaps dot the ocean. He glances at her sideways as they walk; she looks perfect here, in a flowing white skirt and blue-green shirt that tumble all around her, those bangle bracelets tinkling on her arm. She's like a perpetual painting.

Though he's got a few weeks of the school year behind him and he should've known what he was in for, the mob of high school juniors and seniors in the distance catches him off guard. In an instant, he's flushed with panic. *Chill. You can do this.* But keeping a low profile is a lot harder out here than in the corridors and classrooms, especially with a girl by his side. Especially with all the beer and other stuff that's already being passed around. The heat is ripe and overpowering. He starts to sweat. She grabs his slippery hand and squeezes. *Inspiration. Expiration. Focus on Mikayla.*

Mikayla spots some friends, and before he knows it, they are absorbed into the amoeba's teeming center. Words come at them from every side. Selective deafness isn't working here. The hissing whispers are like splinters under his skin. His sweat turns cold and his hand slips out of hers.

"I can't believe *HE'S* here ..."

"Hey, wait, did you come with ZEV? What's THAT about?"

"I heard the two of you've been working on an 'art project.' Nice code."

"He looks awful. So skinny!"

"Yeah, my mom says he's like, brokenhearted and refuses to eat."

"Well can you blame him? I mean, Zoey Sandor? She was, like, Supergirl."

Zev is horrified. They're all so clueless. So frighteningly gleeful.

What happens next will never make sense: His mind goes blank. He forgets where he is and why he came. He forgets Mikayla standing next to him. He forgets everything except the tidal wave of voices. He bolts, running faster and faster until the sounds fall away, stumbling over the uneven beach until he can't run anymore, until his heart is going to burst. He has no idea how far he's run, but he can't even see the crowd.

He drops to his knees behind the dunes, gasping for air and crying, making noises that sound like they are coming from someone else.

Is this how it felt before your heart stopped, Zo, like you were being torn into pieces? Why'd you have to go running on the last day of school? Why didn't you wait for me? Why did it have to be you? What the fuck am I supposed to do now?

Zev burrows into the sand, curled into a tight ball, hands over his ears to shut out the voice in his head. He closes his eyes. His breathing slows. The sun makes an orange kaleidoscope that dances on the insides of his eyelids. He sleeps.

She stands in the garden the air smells like cookies she walks down the path toward the little house there is the sweet scent of vanilla sugar. She opens the door and Mom smiles at her, let's make more cookies she says. The counter is cold under her hands the dough is warm and sticky the flour is dusty and dry. She tries to roll the cookies into little balls but her hands won't hold them she starts to cry a bell is ringing it won't stop her tears fall on the cookies one by one they melt away.

"Zev! Wake up, Zev. Shhh. It's okay. I've got you."

Someone is shaking his shoulder, talking close to his ear. He wipes sand and salt streaks from his face. He can still smell vanilla sugar. When he understands where he is and who's beside him, he sits up and it all rushes back at him. What can he say to Mikayla now? He drops his head into his hands, waits for her to get up and walk away. Instead, she sits down next to him and lays her sweet little hand on his back. She says nothing, but he can feel her warmth through his sweat-soaked T-shirt. When he turns his head to look at her, she appears serene.

He wants to apologize but what comes out is a hoarse croak. He clears his throat and tries again. "I'm so sorry, Mikayla. It was too much, you know?"

"I know, Zev." She is silent for a little, looking at the sun as it sets over the water. "It was a lot for me, too."

"Oh, God. Of course, it was. I never should've left you alone to deal with everyone. They're like—vampires, feeding on other people's misery. But I'm the worst! Are you okay?"

"Yeah, I guess. It's hard to know what to say. People don't get it."

"No shit."

"But Zev, *I* do."

It's true. She does get it. She loved—loves—Zoey, too. She knows how much they've lost. And she's the only one who knows the awful truth about him, that for months he has forsaken his twin.

"And I miss her, too. All the time. You know?" Mikayla's voice breaks a little.

Zev nods, unsure what to say.

"Why didn't you … I don't know, say something? You didn't have to disappear for an hour. We could've left the party together, gone for a walk or something. It's like you think you're all alone, Zev, but you're *not*. Or at least, you don't have to be. We can miss her together. Okay?"

She looks right at him, and Zev looks back, into the clear, calm green of her eyes. A small, wavering space opens inside him, and he reaches out to take her hand.

"Okay."

DAY 91

The buzz of the intercom startled Sam, and since his hands were occupied, he used the foot pedal to answer.

"Yes?"

His hand hovered above the port in Luisa's abdomen, into which he had just inserted a long needle attached to a syringe filled with medication.

"Dr. Sandor? We need you out here for a moment, please."

Gillian's voice had a strange tremor to it.

He depressed the plunger on the syringe. "Can't it wait? I'm doing a pump refill."

"No, I'm sorry, it can't."

Sam dropped the needle in the sharps container, peeled off his gloves, and gave Mr. Reyes an apologetic smile. He opened the door to find Gillian right outside.

"What's the big emergency?"

"Sorry, but Zoey's having some sort of meltdown, and we can't find Mrs. Sandor anywhere," she whispered.

"A *meltdown*?" Sam whispered back. "Is this about her discharge coming up?"

"That's all I know. The duty nurse asked me to come get you immediately."

"Well, I can't leave Luisa. Tell them I'll be there in five minutes. Okay?"

"Uh … Okay."

It wasn't like Gillian to be so unprofessional. Sam returned to the exam room and smiled apologetically at Mr. Reyes again. Where was he? Right, Luisa's pump refill. He put on a fresh pair of gloves, took the syringe filled with medication from the counter, and bent over Luisa's stretcher.

"Dr. Sandor—" Mr. Reyes began.

"Hmmm?" Sam didn't look up.

"I—I—Didn't you …?" The needle went smoothly into the port and the girl didn't squirm. "Never mind," the man said, more quietly than usual.

Sam was relieved. For once, Luisa appeared to be in no pain. He wouldn't feel so bad about bolting. "Well, that's done. Sorry, I have to run—emergency. I will see you in six weeks, as usual, right, Mr. Reyes?"

Sam had one foot out the door as he handed him the follow-up slip. He could see the man still wanted to say something, but it would have to wait.

Sam stuck his head into the front office. "Going to Zoey now, Gillian." Without waiting for a reply, he pushed through the double doors of the inpatient wing, trying Liv's cell phone as he walked. He left an angrier message than he intended.

Zoey's charge nurse, Debbie, met him at the doorway to her room. "Zoey isn't herself, Dr. Sandor. She's been agitated—Derek said she was downright combative during PT—but she hasn't been able to tell me what's bothering her."

"That doesn't sound like our Zoey!" Sam cringed—he didn't sound like himself, either. But Zoey wouldn't have noticed. She was moaning and crying, wild-eyed. "Have you paged Dr. Becker? If there's a change in her mental status—"

"I've paged him, but he's out of town."

"Shit." He chose to ignore Debbie's startled look at the expletive. "What about Dr. Andrapur?"

He tried to take Zoey's pulse, but every time he touched her, she snatched her hand away.

"She hasn't answered. I've paged twice."

"How are her vitals? Does she have a fever?"

"I-I'm sorry," Debbie stammered. "I haven't been able to get close enough to take her temp. She keeps batting my hands away."

Sam grabbed Zoey's wrist more forcefully than he meant to. She whimpered as he counted the beats—her pulse was hammering at 150, twice the normal rate.

"Hey, cookie, how're you feeling?"

Zoey started crying and tossing her head back and forth on the pillow.

"It hurts. I want Mommy!"

"What hurts, Zoey?"

"Smmmhhp," she moaned.

"Honey, can you tell me where it hurts?" Sam's pager went off. He let go of Zoey's hand to see who was calling. Gillian. *Jesus.* She knew where he was. Couldn't she leave him alone for even five minutes?

"I can try again for the temp, Dr. Sandor, if you need to get that."

"Yes, you do that, Debbie." Was a simple temperature reading too much to ask from a nurse? "I'll also order blood work. I'll have the phlebotomist come up here, and maybe the two of you can work together to get us some useful information."

Debbie looked mortified. What was he doing? He took no comfort from further humiliating an already embarrassed employee. Sam's pager went off again.

"What the fuck?" he muttered, then noticed Debbie's startled face. Expletive number two—he'd better get ahold of himself. "I'll—I'll be right back."

He hurried back to the clinic.

"What was so important it couldn't wait for five minutes while I checked on my daughter?" Sam thundered at Gillian, who reddened and blanched in quick succession—the second employee he had embarrassed in the past two minutes. What was the matter with him? He tried to soften his expression. Gillian crossed her arms and pursed her lips.

"Enzo Battali's pump is nearly empty, and you were, well, tied up, and Dr. Andrapur said she would do the refill, since you told her the other day she was ready to try one on her own."

Sam nodded. Of course. This was why Sima hadn't answered Debbie's page—she was covering for him on Mr. Battali's refill.

"And?"

"Well, Dr. Andrapur couldn't find the meds anywhere. We ended up using the emergency spare. But I know I put that vial on the counter in Exam Room 3, right next to Luisa Reyes's meds. Did you see a second syringe?"

Dread bloomed in Sam's chest like a virus as he tried to envision the two vials of medication on the counter. He grabbed Luisa's chart and stared at it uncomprehendingly as he went over his movements one by one. Ready the syringe. Refill Luis's pump. Intercom buzzes—no, wait, didn't he do the refill *after* Gillian's first interruption?

Nausea swept through him as he realized his mistake. He had filled the same pump twice, once before the call about Zoey, and again after, with the meds that had been left on the counter for his next patient. He could see Mr. Reyes trying to stop him and realizing it was too late. Oh, God, how he wished he'd given the man enough time to speak up! Sam had overdosed Luisa, and it could kill her.

He grabbed Gillian's arm. He could feel her muscles tense under his panicked grasp. "Gillian, listen to me. You need to get in touch with Mr. Reyes right away and tell him to bring Luisa back. And I mean *immediately*. I've overdosed her. I can probably still reverse it, but it has to be *right now*. So, you get her back, even if you have to drive over there yourself."

Gillian turned as pale as milk but nodded and moved immediately to the door.

"Wait a minute! You'd better cancel my afternoon, too," said Sam.

"But what should I tell the Gladwells, who are already waiting?"

Sam waved a hand. "Dr. Andrapur can see them. Hope is walking better than she has since she was two, and Gracie is raising her head unassisted. Tell them whatever you want—they don't need me right now. I have to deal with Luisa, and we can't reach Liv, so I've got to go back and manage Zoey, too. Page me the minute Reyes gets here. *Go!*"

Gillian left the room at a run. Still clutching Luisa's chart, Sam started back toward Zoey's room, stopped, and thumbed quickly through the pages. Nothing there could illuminate his actions. How could he have made such a terrible mistake? He would have to tell Mr. Reyes what he had done. It could be the end of Sam's career, and what was infinitely worse, a man could lose his daughter.

Where the hell was Liv? He had never needed her more. But she was MIA, and he couldn't afford to stand here any longer. He would have to clean up this mess alone.

EXCERPT FROM
THE MEMORY BOOK OF ZOEY SANDOR

It's a sunny day and it's warm and pretty in my garden and the air smells like cookies. I walk down the path from the big house I smell vanilla and sugar so sweet and I open the door of the little house and Mom is there smiling at me. Such a big girl, she says, here's a spot for you let's make cookies. The counter is cold and hard the dough is warm and sticky the flour is dusty and it makes me sneeze. I try to roll the cookies into little balls but my hands won't hold still and I say It's too hard for me don't you know that and aren't Moms supposed to know everything? But Mom says you can do it Zoey like this I will show you and the bell is ringing and ringing and I say please Mommy please I want my cookies I'm not a good helper and tears fall on the cookies they melt away and now they are all gone.

(Transcribed by Francesca Garibaldi, SLP)

DAY 91, CONTINUED

Liv finished frosting the last batch of maple toffee cupcakes and wiped her hands on her apron. She took a bite of her tester-cake and was pleased with the moist crumb, the way the toffee bits melted on her tongue, the spicy kick of the ginger in her maple buttercream frosting.

She smiled at her reflection in the copper faucet as she wiped it down with a rag.

"You're good!"

She needed to keep reassuring herself—this sort of work was less instinctive than cooking for her family; she found it painful to write down every minute change she made in her recipes, but it was the only way to achieve the consistency expected in a commercial product. Maybe it wasn't the best idea to have promised Dafna two new varieties of baked goods before the High Holidays, but Sam had encouraged her. "You need to keep branching out if you want the business to grow."

She glanced at the clock on the wall. It was past 2:00 p.m., and she hadn't been to the hospital yet today. She was hoarding her time right now, with Zoey coming home tomorrow, and Rosh Hashanah in two weeks. Liv was worried there would never be enough time to do everything, but she was determined that her family have a good holiday. She wished Ethan was coming home. He had called earlier that morning, sounding much too far away as he said that he was going out on a mission and might not be able to call again for a while. Liv had tried to keep the tremor out of her voice as she told him she loved him and to *take care*. Such empty words.

She wished Sam hadn't missed Ethan's call, though in his present state, it might have done him more harm than good. Maybe she would stop by his office with a cupcake. Her little treats used to bring him such pleasure. She chewed her lip while she swept the floor. Something was definitely wrong with Sam; he was flailing, scrambling to prevent a disaster that had already happened. If only he would talk to her. How could he forget she was his sounding board? It was as if Zoey's injury had robbed him of his memory, too.

She picked up her cell phone to call him, but the screen was blank—she must have used up her battery talking to Kabul and missed the warning chime as it powered off. She felt a tiny chill of alarm at having been incommunicado for so long. But wasn't everyone accounted for and under reliable supervision? Zev and Lottie were safely back in school, and if Zoey needed immediate attention, Sam was within arm's reach, wasn't he?

But after she plugged in, the screen displayed six missed calls and four new messages. With trembling fingers, she punched in her access code and pressed the cool little square to her ear. The first message was a puzzled-sounding Francesca, telling her Zoey had had a difficult last session. She began to relax as she listened to the second message, a reminder from the discharge coordinator about their meeting at 11:00 a.m. tomorrow to go over the paperwork for Zoey. As if she could forget! She locked the door of the bakery, went back up the garden path to the house, took her sweater and purse off the hook inside the back door, and climbed into her minivan.

The third message was the nurse, Debbie, saying that something was "very wrong with Zoey." Liv jammed the phone against her ear to be sure she heard right "… disoriented and agitated … combative behavior … crying for you … tried the house phone … Please come or call when you get this message." With icy hands, she set the phone on speaker so she could drive and listen to the last message, where Sam was telling her Zoey was in the grip of some sort of delirium.

"Where *are* you?" He had canceled his afternoon, and she should call him "for God's sake" as soon as she got this message. He sounded more angry than scared, but Liv knew it had to be bad if he'd canceled clinic.

She drove to the hospital at top speed, cursing the traffic and the full parking garage. She parked illegally, got out of her car, and ran, not even stopping to get the obligatory visitor's pass. When she came to the deserted nurses' station on the TBI Rehab wing, she could hear urgent voices, punctuated by Sam's heavy baritone and the sound of Zoey crying. She sprinted down the hall and stopped. Zoey's room was crowded with staff and equipment, and Zoey was thrashing about on the bed, screaming and crying.

Sam had his hands on her arms, presumably to calm her, while at the same time barking orders at three different nurses who were scurrying around. Zoey's face was splotched and red, and her hair was tangled, her forehead wet with sweat. She looked terrified.

Debbie caught sight of Liv during a fruitless attempt to get a thermometer into Zoey's ear. "Oh! Mrs. Sandor!"

Zoey screamed. "No, don't touch me! You're hurting me. You're—ow!" She screamed again. "It hurts. It hurts. I want my mom! I want my mom!"

"Liv! Jesus, where have you been?" Sam blurted.

Swallowing the urge to apologize to everyone in the room, Liv stepped forward and put her ice-cold hand on Zoey's forehead.

"What's all this, Zoey? It's okay now. I'm here, I've got you. Shhhh. You're fine, baby. Shhhhh."

Zoey was thrashing so hard it took her a moment to register Liv's presence.

"Mommy!" she sobbed, and Liv's eyes filled up too.

"Debbie, can you *please* administer the IM Ativan and update Mrs. Sandor on the events of the last hour?" Sam said.

The nurse looked mortified but did as she was told, sidling in next to Liv and—Liv was certain—pleading for help with her eyes. Liv continued to speak softly to Zoey, urging her to hold still for the injection, which, it turned out, her poor girl hardly noticed.

Debbie started her update in a near-whisper, her eyes turned down. "Zoey was brought back to her room in the middle of PT because she was too agitated to continue. That's when I left you those messages on your cell and home phones. Her pulse is elevated, and she's disoriented, as you can see. Dr. Sandor ordered Ativan, which she's getting now by injection because she was too agitated to swallow it. We haven't been able to put in an IV or do a complete exam."

"Thank you. Is that all?" Sam sounded formidable.

Liv held her breath as Debbie started and looked up at Sam.

"Actually, no. Dr. Sandor, you left the room so quickly before, I never got to tell you the rest. Derek said he left her in her bed, but when I came in, she was sitting on the floor. Maybe she fell out of bed? I managed to get her back into it, and I paged Dr. Becker right away, but—"

"And I'm only hearing this *now*? It should've been the first thing you told me!" Sam thundered. Everyone froze, and Debbie looked almost as terrified as Zoey, who continued to cry as Liv stroked her hair. Liv wanted to tell him to keep his voice down, but she knew that wouldn't do at all.

"I know. I'm *so sorry*," Debbie said. "I've been trying to stop her from hurting herself again, to get a temp on her, like you said." She looked up. "But, well, maybe Mrs. Sandor can get her to calm down so Phlebotomy can do some blood work and get an IV into her?"

Zoey was weeping piteously and tossing her head from side to side.

"Can you tell me where it hurts, sweetheart?" Liv asked.

"Mm, mm." Zoey moaned, smearing mucus all over her face in a feeble attempt to wipe her own nose. She was somewhere that Liv couldn't reach her and Sam looked like a lost, angry little boy. She put her palm on Zoey's forehead again and realized that, even correcting for her own nerves, the difference in their temperatures wasn't normal. Zoey had a high fever.

She quieted a little under the cool of Liv's touch. "Debbie, can you squeeze in here next to me and try again with the thermometer now?"

Sam made a gesture like Moses parting the Red Sea, and everyone moved out of the way. Debbie inserted the instrument into Zoey's slack mouth, and it beeped its end-signal as Zoey tried to bat it away. The nurse made a small, involuntary sound of triumph and held the instrument up to read the result.

"Well, *that's* something. 104.4."

"Can we get her some ibuprofen?" Liv asked. Sam was staring at Zoey and running his hands repeatedly though his hair. He looked up quickly when she spoke.

"Sure we can," he said sarcastically, "but she won't be safe to swallow it." He included both women in a withering glance, and stepped forward, only to stop at the end of Zoey's bed and begin pacing. They were all losing it, but Sam most of all.

Debbie whispered, "There's no injectable ibuprofen, and we still don't have an IV."

Liv nodded her thanks.

"She has to be transferred," Sam muttered. "Some sort of infection—"

"Oh, no, do we have to? She'll get even more disoriented. Couldn't we treat her here?"

The minute she said it, Liv knew it was a mistake.

"Well, Liv, have you got a better idea?" There was acid in Sam's voice. Liv looked away.

Zoey started kicking again—and swearing.

"Ow! Get the fuck *off* me!" She lunged sideways and nearly succeeded in throwing herself out of the bed. Everyone in the room jumped forward, arms outstretched.

"That's it. No more discussion! We need to get her tranquilized now," Sam shouted. "Debbie, push two milligrams of Ativan IM. We'll transfer her to Stepdown and wait for Dr. Becker, who I *trust* is en route back to Connecticut?"

Now Liv understood why Sam had been thrust into the middle of things again.

Debbie nodded and left the room immediately, and when she returned, Sam pinned Zoey's arms down as she injected the tranquilizer. Zoey screamed. Though Liv could see he had no choice, it was all she could do to keep herself from yelling at Sam to *stop it*. Even as Zoey's movements slowed and her eyes began to droop, she continued to whimper, and when an orderly tried to transfer her to a stretcher, she cried out, more weakly this time. Liv started forward again. Sam put a restraining hand on her arm.

"Everyone, give me a minute. I want to take another look. If she fell, she might have a fracture."

He raised and lowered Zoey's arms easily one at a time, but when he went to raise the right leg, she gave a piercing scream, and her eyes flew open. Liv could see the whites bulging, nearly blue in the fluorescent light of the room.

"Ow, ow! Help me, Mommy!" She pushed at Sam's hands and looked around wildly.

He stepped back. His voice, finally, was soft. "Okay, I know, sweetie. I won't touch you again. I can see it hurts."

Zoey squeezed her eyes shut and the tears rolled off the sides of her face and onto her pillow, leaving damp little puddles on either side of her. Liv took her hand and whispered whatever came into her head.

Sam said, "All right, Debbie, this is what we need to do. Put in the IV now and give her a shot of morphine. Take her straight to X-ray, and page Dr. Montez in Orthopedics. Pretty sure she broke her hip, but they need to film the whole right side, from hip to ankle. I'll call the order down, but I want you to go with her and make sure they get all of it, right?"

Debbie nodded once but hesitated as if unsure if he was done.

"Go!"

She flew out the door, and Sam turned and spoke into the wall phone. Liv watched him as if from a slight distance; she should have been grateful—but when did he get so *mean*?

Standing in the middle of Zoey's calamity-littered room, she understood she'd been fooling herself. Everything would *not* be okay.

Life would not return to normal. Sam's professional life was in jeopardy. And Zoey's discharge would not be happening anytime soon.

Sam hung up, but he still wasn't looking at her. As an orderly wheeled Zoey out with Debbie at her side, Liv's mood shifted again, and she swayed under a wave of guilt, barely able to resist the urge to plead her case with Sam. *My phone died! I didn't do this to her!* she wailed silently.

She waited for him to turn his anger on her again, but he sank into a chair and put his hands over his face. Liv kneeled on the floor next to him and touched his arm. He raised his head to look into her eyes, and with no warning, his face crumpled like a piece of onion skin. He slipped onto his knees in front of her and his shoulders shook as he wrapped his arms around her waist and clung there. He was drowning. The sounds coming out of him frightened her, and she fought to keep them both from coming apart. He cried on and on, not even looking up when the door opened and slammed shut again.

The world went away and they drifted along on the tide of his tears. Even after the terrible noises stopped, Sam stayed there, curled around Liv like a question mark. She tried not to move.

Finally, Sam sat up with a shuddering sigh. He said nothing, only took her hand. They rose and walked to the elevator, and Liv could feel him straightening up as they descended. At one point, he gave her a small grimace of chagrin. Liv made a moue back, trying to telegraph the words of comfort she knew would be inadequate.

Zoey's right hip was, indeed, broken. She would need surgery, and a pin would have to be placed in the bone to keep it stable. There would be weeks, possibly months, of additional physical therapy to restore her walk. *Not fair.* Liv bit her tongue to keep from saying it aloud. *Especially with the left neglect.* How relieved Sam had been that Zoey was ambulatory! Now he was being denied even that consolation.

But Sam had retreated into his clinical persona. "I'll call Mustafa. I'm sure he'll stay tonight to do the surgery."

Mustafa Marrakech, the head of Orthopedics, was pressed into service at the tail end of his workday, and Sam thanked him solemnly for his personal attention.

Sam kept his cool after that, though he kept getting paged and several times left to check on another patient, leaving Liv to ruminate alone. After he returned from one such absence, she burst out: "I can't believe this happened!" What she wanted to say was: *What could be so important that you have to keep leaving me?*

"I know. It's a big setback," Sam said, his tone subdued though he kept shoving his hands through his hair. "These things happen. It could've been worse—she could have hit her head."

Even as they waited through the interminable surgery, Sam continued to come and go at regular intervals. Liv was on the verge of asking him what could possibly be so urgent when Francesca stuck her head in the door.

"Oh, good! You're both here. Dr. Sandor, I wanted to ask you about the Luisa situation."

Sam looked up, wearing a strange expression. "How did you …?"

"I ran into Mr. Reyes in the hall when I was looking for Zoey," she said, pointing over her shoulder with her thumb. "What a thing to happen! Will she pull through?"

Liv, startled, thought she was talking about Zoey. "Oh, no, there was never any—"

But Sam said, "I think we caught it in time. Unbelievably close call. I'm monitoring her constantly." He looked down at his watch, and muttered to himself, "I'll go again in a few minutes." Liv realized the "Luisa situation" must be critical, and she was glad she hadn't given him a hard time about it.

"Poor thing. Please, let me know if I can help when she wakes," said Francesca.

Sam nodded mutely. Was the "poor thing" the patient or Sam?

Francesca turned to Liv. "In the first place I was looking for Zoey, and they told me you were here. What's happened, Livie?"

Now it was Sam's turn to be startled, Liv saw. She was sure he was reacting to Francesca's use of the nickname that only a handful of people ever called her. But she didn't have the energy to worry about that now.

"Zoey's in surgery for a badly broken hip," said Liv.

"*Che cosa?* I don't believe it." Francesca came and sat beside Liv and held her hand.

"I know. I can't either. We think she fell out of bed, but she was alone so we can't be sure." She glanced guiltily at Sam, who didn't appear to be listening.

"Out of bed! But how?"

Sam remained silent.

"Well, she spiked a fever because of a urinary tract infection. They say she was delirious. From there, it was an avalanche of bad luck."

"Oh, those UTIs, they are the devil!"

"Yes, that's what Sam was saying. They seem to be common around here. And she was doing so *well.*" Liv had an idea. "The thing is, Dr. Marrakech is doing her surgery now, so we'll be here for a while. Could you possibly fetch Lottie from her friend's house and stay with the kids for a few hours? Zev can hold the fort overnight, if need be, but it's a long evening, and the across-the-street neighbor who usually pinch-hits for us is out of town. Can you do it? Will Giovanni mind?"

Sam was looking at her oddly, but she didn't meet his gaze. Still, she could almost hear his questions: When did she get so cozy with his best speech pathologist? And was she really asking Francesca to spend the evening at their house?

"You don't worry about Giovanni, he is a grown man," said Francesca. "Of course, I will get Lottie. And where is Zev?"

"I think he's home, but I can't reach him." Liv blushed. She should know where her children were. "I guess you should tell them what happened. I wouldn't ask, only he's not answering his cell and—"

"I understand, Livie. You can trust me. I will call you later, okay?" She kissed Liv on both cheeks, and Liv kissed her back.

Francesca turned once more to Sam. "So, I am not so free, to help if Luisa wakes. But you can call me at your house, yes?"

"Yes …" said Sam uncertainly.

Liv was sure it was the sanest thing to do. They needed friends to help them through this. And if everything had to revolve around the hospital, that's where they would find their friends, too. Sam would have to get over it.

DAY 105

... *She reaches out to touch the mirror and her image vanishes she shakes her head at herself it's not a mirror it's a door she's standing in front of—*

"Zev! Wake up, son."

Dad's voice. But it's not *him* in the mirror. The same dream that has been repeating for weeks is getting even weirder.

"Zev! Wake up. You're talking to yourself."

He swims out of sleep with great difficulty. He opens his eyes and looks right into his father's face. "Dad? Wass happ'ning?"

"It's time for shul."

"Did I say to wake me?" Zev croaks.

He tries to get his bearings. He doesn't remember any such conversation.

"Zev. It's Rosh Hashanah. Don't tell me you forgot?"

Zev says nothing.

"You need to get up now," Dad says, pacing the floor. "It'll be a mob scene later."

Zev clambers out of bed. Right. Rosh Hashanah. What a perfect time for repentance and renewal. He doesn't get Dad's whole thing about praying: You'd think the sudden death of his parents would've knocked the faith right out of him, but it's the opposite. Dad once told him that he figured if Papa and Goldie came out of Auschwitz with their faith intact, the least he could do was carry on the tradition. Now, as far as he knows, Dad hasn't gone to services at all since June, though he used to go all the time in the mornings. He would say he was "giving something back," since Rabbi Friedman had become a sort of surrogate father to him.

He stands and stares blankly at his closet until Dad walks over, pulls out a dress shirt and his suit, and hands them to him silently before leaving the room.

Maybe Dad has finally realized there is no benevolent presence keeping an eye on his family. It's the biblical New Year, but there's nothing for them to celebrate. And the ten days between Rosh Hashanah and Yom Kippur—the Days of Awe leading up to the Day of Atonement—are supposed to be when you make amends for wrongdoing and renounce any hastily made vows, so you can be "Inscribed in the Book of Life."

Some life.

All this thinking makes his teeth hurt. He goes to wash up and put on his suit, his dread rising with every button he fastens. Zev has no desire to parade before the prying eyes of the whole congregation, but he can't face arguing with Dad, who's already pacing the front hall when he gets downstairs.

"Hey, son. Ready to go?"

Why is he always so impatient? And how come the girls get to waltz in two hours later? Girl, he corrects himself. *One* girl waltzing in with Mom. Zoey isn't going anywhere.

He shrugs into his coat and notices the sleeves are two inches too short, but he doesn't care. Mikayla's out of town with her parents, and she's the only one he wants to impress. Not that he's succeeding there, either—he's been a complete klutz around her ever since the beach party. He's not even making what Zoey and her friends on the track team would call a "good effort."

He takes the short walk to synagogue with Dad in silence, eating a couple of Mom's muffins, without which he figures he would've starved to death by now. Zev can practically hear Dad grinding his teeth, but he doesn't ask what's wrong. "Want some?" he offers instead. But Dad shakes his head.

If it's possible, things have gotten even worse since the broken hip fiasco. Last week, Zev had listened from the top of the stairs as the last vestiges of the old Sandor family rules of engagement disappeared …

"Sam!" Mom's voice, with a newly familiar edge. "We need to talk about wheelchair modifications."

"Modifications? For what?"

"For the house! Once Zoey's discharged—"

"Zoey's discharge is a long way off." Dad's dismissive tone had scalded Zev's brain. He never used to talk to Mom like that. "I should be able to make a case for several more weeks on the inpatient wing. PT and OT and gait training for a start."

"Several *weeks*? Is that what's best for Zoey?"

"Are you really *asking* me that?"

"You don't have to shout, I was only saying—"

"I know what you were saying," Dad had continued to yell. "*I'm* saying, I've got it covered. It makes no sense to schlep her back and forth to the hospital, as often as she needs therapy. And when she starts to heal, we'll be able to get her up and walking again. You'll see how pointless this conversation is. For the love of God, leave it alone!"

That had been the end of it. Dad had come stomping up the stairs, and Zev had run for cover, trying to remember why he and Zoey used to joke about their parents' telepathic marriage. Mom and Dad were now officially speaking two different brands of English.

What's worse, Zev suspects Mom's right, that Dad is embarrassed to put a wheelchair ramp on his own house. Like that story about the shoemaker's kids who go barefoot. But what happens to Dad's reputation as king of rehab if the whole world can see his own kid's in a wheelchair?

Rabbi Friedman nods at them as they slip into the sanctuary. The congregation's launching into the *Vidu'i*, the part of High Holiday services that's like a public confession of all the sins humans might commit against one another in a year. They're all supposed to read the words together, tapping their hearts with their fists for each transgression, whether it applies to them personally or not. In years past, Zev found this ritual comforting—he liked the idea that the whole community assumed responsibility for individual weakness, and it felt like the only time he could say something so personal in a room full of people without fear. This year, though, his sins are missing from the list. What's the Hebrew for "I-have-abandoned-my-twin-in-her-hour-of-need"? How do you say, "I-am-too-fucking-sad-to-notice-the-suffering-of-others"?

As every head bends to the *Vidu'i*, Zev looks up and sees Dad staring off into space. Why are they even here?

But he plays their game of Simon Says, standing up and sitting down with the people around him, holding the prayer book without ever looking at it. He fails to notice a hush falling over the crowd and realizes too late that he's missed his chance to leave before the rabbi begins his sermon.

"My friends, in these Days of Awe, as you go through your process of *t'shuvah*, of repentance, I would like you to ponder this passage from the beginning of the Torah: *God created mankind in his own image. In the image of God, He created them; male and female He created them.* If we accept the idea that there are no wasted words in the Torah, what reason could there be for this repetition, this circularity?"

He pauses and looks out at the sea of people. Zev shifts in his seat.

"We are reminded from the beginning that we are *all* made in God's image. We are the self-doubting adolescents and God is the wise parent. Here we have two important lessons. First, if we are all made in the image of God, we can take heart, for God understands us and knows we are destined to lose our way sometimes. But second, we also contain within us the kernel of perfection that makes us God's children, and we can each strive toward that perfection, safe in the knowledge that, like any good parent, God wants, above all, for us to find joy in our lives."

Anger is rolling off Zev's body in hot waves. He can't stop his knee from jiggling, and from time to time he lets out an involuntary sigh-huff. He refuses to look at Dad though he can feel his stare. But when the old lady in front of him turns around to give him the beady eye, he shoots out of his seat and slams through the door at the back.

He breaks into a run, pumping his legs until he rounds the building and hits the preschool playground. This is getting to be a bad habit. First the beach party, now shul. He slumps onto one of the little swings, scuffling his feet on the gravel, his long legs jackknifed up to his chest. He doesn't know how much time goes by. He feels like a baby, kicking the pebbles beneath his feet, clenching his fists around the chains and swinging back and forth.

"Zev?"

Ugh. How could Dad know where to find him?

"What's going on with you? What happened in there? It's not like you to make a scene."

"Seriously, Dad?" Zev says to his knees. "That's what you're worried about? Me making a scene? All eyes were on us anyway. Those old biddies were practically clucking, for fuck's sake. But you're worried that *I* might attract attention?"

"I know it's awkward in there right now," Dad says. "There's this compulsive fascination when others are in trouble. I hate it, too, that feeling of being watched—"

"No! Don't give me your soothing doctor-speak. Anyway, I don't even give a shit about that! I could've sat there and dealt with it, if it hadn't been for the … the unbelievable … Oh, forget it, you wouldn't understand!"

"What wouldn't I understand? What happened? I can listen, Zev. We don't have to agree on everything, but I can listen."

"No, you can't, Dad! And you, you *love* that guy. You think he shits pearls of wisdom! And today, he was so, so—oh *fuck*!"

"Are you talking about Rabbi Friedman? What's the difference what I think of him? You matter more to me than he ever did! Don't you know that? Would you look at me for a minute?"

Zev doesn't move. If he looks at Dad, he'll totally lose it.

"I hate to see you so upset. Tell me what this is about. Please, Zev? I promise, I won't judge and I—I won't interrupt you."

Zev lifts his head, and sees his father is sincere. He takes in a deep breath and blows it out.

"Okay, Dad. You want to know what this is about?"

"I do, son."

"This is about hypocrisy! This is about parents and their colossal ego! We're made in God's image? What a crock! What does it even mean? If there is a God, which I seriously doubt, He has no ego, right? And if He's above ego, He has no need for people to be like him. Or Her, if you like Zoey's version. But either way, that's a totally human idea. It's *people* who want to have control, and when they realize they can't control their own lives, they have kids! It's all a big ego trip. See? You have kids so you can point to them and say, look what a perfect thing I made. So, what happens when the thing you made isn't so perfect anymore? Huh, Dad? What happens when the apple of your eye, your Supergirl, with all the talent, all the brains, all the beauty—what happens when she's none of that anymore? Or maybe that's why you and Mom had so many of us, so you'd have plenty of backups? But where are you gonna look, huh? I mean, maybe I'm marginally artistic, but I can't even string two words together. So not me. I'm sloppy seconds."

Dad opens his mouth to say something.

"Breaking your promise already? Go ahead!"

Dad closes his mouth in a tight line.

"So, I get why you were never too impressed with me. But what about Ethan? Too bookish for you? Or is he too hawkish now? And what, no hope for Lottie in the future? Oh, right, there's no point—she can't possibly compare to Zoey! Right, Dad?"

Zev is on a roll, and adrenaline has sharpened his mind.

"Parents want their kids to be made in *their* image—it has nothing to do with God! Does it? So, what I want to know is, how come none of us gets your vote for most favored Sandor child, now that there's a vacancy in the lineup?"

Dad looks like he's in pain, but he's not talking.

"*Exactly.* Only Zoey was good enough to be the Sam Sandor upgrade. Only she could improve on Superman."

Zev's beginning to lose the thread, but he doesn't care. It's as if a switch has been flipped, and now he can't flip it back again.

"So where does that leave Zoey, huh? Is she a waste of space now that she won't be taking over the world? At least she didn't die. The only thing that died was your dream of her great shining future. But what about *our* future? You can't even *see* any of us! We might as well not *exist*!"

He gestures wildly, his body on fire. He doesn't know when he stood up, but the chains of the tiny kids' swing are squealing.

"You're such a hypocrite! You tell yourself you buy in to all that *God* shit, and there's all those inspiring stories about your patients and how you see the potential in every one of them, no matter how *damaged* they are. Now the shoe's on the other foot, and it doesn't work that way, does it?"

"Oh, no, Zev. I don't—It's not—"

Talk about the shoe on the other foot. Dad can't even form a coherent sentence, while words are flowing out of Zev like he's the next prophet.

"See? It's true! You can't even argue 'cause you know it! And you know the worst part? The worst part is, you keep on seeing your patients, but you're not even taking care of your own *kid*. As if Zoey doesn't deserve your *time!* Don't you even owe her that much anymore? Why can't you fix her, Dad? Why not? *Why not?*"

Dad hangs his head and says nothing.

Zev's voice is doing this weird thing, getting higher and higher till it's in the stratosphere, and he can't get it back down to earth.

"No? No answer? Well, *mazel tov*! I got your message anyway. I haven't been back to see her. Not even once. Not since our birthday! What do you think of that?"

Dad's head snaps up and he goggles at Zev, his mouth open.

A final surge of adrenaline spikes his blood, even as he knows he's coming apart. "Oh, you're surprised? Well, you shouldn't be. Why *should* I go see her? I've got no more interest in getting to know the new Zoey than you do. The old Zoey's gone, and if *you* can't bring her back, she—she—she might as well be dead!"

Dad flinches as if he's been slapped, and his recoil breaks Zev's rhythm. There is a high moaning sound, and when he realizes it has come from his own mouth, he freezes, his face twisted into a mask of horror.

Dad steps forward and winds his long arms around the whole rigid column of Zev's body. A keening sob bounces against the stucco walls of the courtyard—is it him, or Dad?—and like a demolished building, he collapses against his father's shoulder. Together, they weep.

They stand there for a long time, crying, silent, leaning into each other. The trees don't stir. Even when they move apart and start walking home, they don't speak. The streets, too, are quiet. It's late morning, an ordinary weekday, but all the sound in the world has been used up.

DAY 111

In the days after Rosh Hashanah, the gift of sleep was lost to Sam, and on the few occasions he was granted a brief respite, he was always visited by the same dream:

He is running side by side with Zoey through East Rock Park, laughing and talking as they fly down the trails. She clutches her chest and falls to the ground, but his dream self keeps right on running. When he notices her absence, he turns around to find her, blanches as she strikes her head on a jagged boulder, runs back at full speed. Too late. He sees himself standing by the rock as her blood seeps into the ground.

Each time, he woke to his own shout of fear, his pulse like a beating drum.

Liv awoke each time, too, and asked him what the dream was about, but Sam couldn't bring himself to speak the words. She begged him to talk to her. What happened on Rosh Hashanah? Finally, he held her in the crook of his arm and whispered the story of Zev's outburst into her ear. He was too ashamed to look at her.

"That must've been so hard," she whispered when he'd finished. "I'm glad you held onto him, Sam."

There was no denial or even surprise in her words, and soon afterward, she went right back to sleep. Sam curled in on himself. Surely her reaction was a further indictment. He had failed his family in every way. Zev's accusations called for a response, but what could Sam do?

After the holiday, Zev went mutely back and forth to school, even more impenetrable than before. Liv divided her time between the hospital, the bakery, and the house and kids. Zoey improved by millimeters. Lottie got fed and read to and tucked in at night—but her sweet, pinched little face told Sam that was not nearly enough.

As exhausted as an intern, Sam continued to see patients, though he knew he shouldn't: Luisa Reyes had been his warning sign. He had watched her even more closely than Zoey in the days following the two incidents, even after he was sure his patient would survive his critical error with no lasting damage. He knew that he had been given a reprieve. But he couldn't bring himself to tell that story to Liv, and on the advice of the hospital attorney, whom Sam had no choice but to bring into the situation, he resisted begging forgiveness from Mr. Reyes as well, though he desperately wanted to. There would be no atonement for him here.

These omissions ratcheted up his shame all the more, and even the steady improvement of Hope and Gracie Gladwell did nothing to assuage his guilt. After a week of tortured nights, of listening to the sound of Liv's tidal breathing in the dark, he rose before dawn and stumbled out of the house, got into his car, and started to drive. Fifteen minutes later, he was holding a sleeping Zoey's hand.

"Can you forgive me, baby? I never meant to abandon you," he whispered. "I was protecting myself when I should've been protecting you. I'm a bad doctor, and a worse father." As atonements went, it was pretty cheap. Zoey wouldn't answer one way or the other, and Sam didn't have the courage to make a similar plea to his other children. He turned to go and found Debbie standing behind him. How long had she been there?

Suddenly, he was furious. She'd been the charge nurse on the floor when Zoey broke her hip. She was as much to blame for this situation as he.

"And where were *you* when she needed you?" His voice was a low growl.

"What? I-I'm sorry. I really didn't—"

She backed away, shaking her head. Sam followed her into the hall, unable to stop himself. "Why the *hell* was she left alone that day?"

"I don't know," Debbie whispered. "*We* couldn't. She should have been—"

Sam's fury expanded, flowing noxiously down the hall.

"Should have been *what*?"

"I don't know. Maybe she should have been with a sitter?"

There was a flash of red behind Sam's eyes, and the scene before him vanished. He heard his voice shouting, but the sound seemed to be coming from somewhere beneath his feet.

"What she *should* have been is a healthy, laughing, sixteen-year-old! What she *should* have been is a gifted cellist! A fucking Olympic sprinter! What she *should* have been is the child of a doctor who didn't miss critical information about his own daughter! Nobody gives a goddamn what she *should* have been, now that she's a broken, frightened child who will never, ever be any of those things again!"

He stopped when he ran out of breath. He didn't see Debbie cover her face with her hands and cry, didn't notice the crowd of night nurses and orderlies who had come to see what the commotion was about and stayed to witness his disintegration. When his vision cleared, an assembly stared at him in open shock.

He stared back at them, and after an eternity of silence, left the building.

He pulled out of the parking lot, knowing with some part of his brain that he shouldn't be behind the wheel, any more than he should go home in this state of mind. But he couldn't take his foot off the gas. As he was passing the synagogue parking lot, something in him yanked the wheel to the right, and the car shuddered to a stop next to the rabbi's old Escort. It was the only other car in sight. Sam banged on the bolted door, but the sound echoed back at him. He stood and stared for a long time—it might have been forty seconds or forty minutes—waiting for a clue.

A disheveled Rabbi Friedman appeared at the door. "Sam! My goodness, it's early. Come in, come in."

He held the door wide, and Sam stepped through. The rabbi was holding a yellow legal pad covered with scribbles and cross outs, and Sam realized it must be his Yom Kippur sermon.

"I'm sorry for bothering you at this hour, and at such a busy time of the year."

The Day of Atonement would begin at sundown the next day, but Sam was accumulating sins far too fast for it to matter.

"I'm never too busy for you." The rabbi smiled and put an arm around Sam's shoulder, steering him into the office. The door closed with a quiet click. "Sit down, sit down. I'm glad to see you. How are you faring these days?" He peered into Sam's face. "You look exhausted, I must say, Semeleh."

At the sound of the affectionate nickname, Sam's eyes filled. "I'm not good, Rabbi."

"How can I help?"

"I don't even know where to start."

"Start anywhere. As the story unravels, we'll surely find the beginning together."

Sam told him about his outburst at the hospital and about Zoey's setback. He told him about the confusion and awkwardness with his staff. Haltingly, he recounted his mistake with Luisa Reyes. "I thought she would die, and I felt so ... *guilty*. What if I did it on purpose, you know, on some subconscious level? I kept hearing a small voice asking, what if she would be better off dead?"

"Do you really believe that?"

"Not professionally. I'm appalled at myself. Still, I can't stop thinking it on a personal level. As it applies to-to Zoey." He stopped. "Uch, I can't believe I'm saying this out loud!"

"But it's natural to have such thoughts. And it must take a superhuman effort for you to continue seeing patients while Zoey is suffering. You're too hard on yourself."

"No, I'm not! It's one thing to hear those things expressed by my patients' families, but it's horrifying to hear them in my head, and coming from my mouth, about my own child."

"Now that you've said the words, do you think they're true? Is there nothing to be gained from Zoey's life, which God has chosen to spare?"

"I know the right answer to that question, but I'm not sure I feel it, in *here*." He pounded his chest. "And Zev has clearly picked up on my ambivalence." Finally, he talked about the thing he was most ashamed of: the scene with Zev on Rosh Hashanah, and the implied indictment in Liv's lack of surprise about all of it.

Rabbi Friedman listened, his fingers steepled, his elbows leaning on the desk. His eyes never left Sam's face. When he finished, the rabbi stroked his beard several times with a broad, open palm, a familiar and comforting gesture.

"I'm so *sorry*, Semeleh. You and your family have enough on your plate right now, without being provoked by my sermon. But it sounds to me as if you're responding as well as you can to a difficult situation."

Sam shook his head. "I don't trust my own judgment. It's—spectacularly impaired."

"Maybe so. But, at Zev's age, he can't appreciate all your motivations, either."

"But he's right! I've been burying myself in my work to survive these last months, figuring Liv could carry things, like she always does. This is such a critical time for us all—I know that only too well. And even before any of this … looking back, I'm not sure I've ever given my family my full attention." He paused, then mumbled, "Well, except for Zoey, if Zev is to be believed."

"Whether or not Zev's argument has merit, what matters is that *you* are compelled by it. You do have the right, maybe even the duty, to respond to this terrible situation as a parent, not just as a doctor. In the end, that's what keeps you up at night, am I right?"

Sam nodded.

"This is a knotty situation, but you appear to have reached a sort of crossroads. How can you best provide for your family?"

It was true; Sam was on the verge of something. But he was silent, bewildered.

"When congregants come to me with these sorts of big questions, I often ask them to apply what I call the Deathbed Test. Surely I've mentioned this to you before?"

"No, I don't think so. The Deathbed Test. I'd remember that."

"No? I'd have thought, after your parents … Well, maybe you were too young then. But no matter. The Deathbed Test is simple enough, though you'd be surprised how many people never consider it when they are debating a seemingly unresolvable question. Here is the essence of it: If—God forbid—you were on your deathbed, what would you wish to have done, or not done, in the situation in question? Usually, there's only one answer. Take a moment to consider."

Sam's mind stretched itself around the rabbi's idea. The Deathbed Test. What would he wish to have done? He knew immediately. Was it that simple? Well, maybe not simple, but certainly clear.

DAY 112

Liv rose while it was still dark and padded through the quiet house. After yesterday's revelations, she hadn't expected a good night's sleep. It was all a bit surreal. She needed to talk to Shula. When had she become such a talker? She switched on the coffee machine. What happened to the introvert that happily worked things out in her own head? But this stuff was too hard. And honestly, Sam couldn't be the only person she turned to. Reaching out to the women in her life was starting to grow on her.

She pulled up Shula's name on her mobile. "Hi, it's me. Time to talk?"

"Of course, habibi. I'll make time. *Oren!*" she shouted for her husband, and a stream of Hebrew followed.

Liv waited for her sister to get organized, getting teary at the mere anticipation of recounting the latest turn.

"So, what's going on, Liv? Is Zoey okay?"

"Yes, nothing new since the whole hip fracture UTI mess. She's recovering slowly. But, well, Sam is taking a leave of absence from work"—she realized her voice had gone all shaky—"which, for some reason, came as a shock. Though it really shouldn't have."

"It's true, he's in an untenable situation. But I can see how you'd be taken by surprise."

"Well, what shocked me is that he made this decision and even spoke to the hospital board without ever discussing it with me." She started to cry, but she didn't want to stop talking until she got it all out. "He's going to invoke the Family Medical Leave Act, and his new fellow, Dr. Andrapur, will take over seeing his patients, and call him only in emergencies. In fact, he's come up with a whole new Life Plan, as he called it, without a single conversation involving me. And get this! He says he's going to be the 'at-home' guy for a while. He says, if he spends some time being 'a real parent,' things will fall into balance for everyone."

"And where are you in this new Life Plan?"

"Me? I get to focus on expanding my bakery business. Isn't that great?"

"Do you *want* to expand your bakery business?"

"Well, I don't know! Certainly not *now*, of all times. But Shula—we didn't even talk about it! Not even once!"

"Yeah. Psssht." Shula pushed out a long, hissing breath. "That's a lot, Livie. I guess this is part of the fallout of everything that's happened."

"I know. And on some level, I get it. This has all been so painful for Sam, in ways that none of us can understand. But presenting this new Plan to me as a fait accompli—it made me realize"—she sobbed—"how much of *us* we've lost in all this!"

"What do you mean?"

"I mean, we used to wait for each other to go to bed every night, so we could talk things through together before sleep."

"Really? That's—that's amazing."

"Well, it was! But there's no more of that. And no more Shabbat sex on Friday nights—or any nights! No more little conversations about the children's quirks and quibbles. No more bringing him little treats at his office and watching his face light up. I know that these luxuries of intimacy go by the wayside in a crisis. But for how long? It's been months! When did this become normal? And how will we ever find our way back?"

She sucked in a trembling breath and tried to calm herself. With the phone jammed between her ear and her shoulder, she got up and poured herself a cup of coffee, looking out the kitchen window at the carriage house behind, where they had invested a tidy sum to create her bakery the year before. It would take an awful lot of apricot tarts to justify that expense now.

"And well, you know, FMLA doesn't include a salary after he uses up his paid time off. We have some savings, but they won't last long if we have to live on them. And I said as much to Sam, who said something about, quote, unquote, 'making other money available.' After a minute, I realized he must be thinking of Zoey's college fund! And I couldn't continue the conversation. I mean, don't you think that's jumping the gun?"

"I don't know," Shula said. "Is it?"

"Is there more coffee?" said Sam.

Liv startled to see him standing before her. "Hang on, Shula, Sam just came in." To Sam, she said, "Yes! But no breakfast. Sorry, I lost track of time talking to my sister."

"Okay. I'll pick up something at the caf. I've got to get to work early. Tons to do before I turn over the reins. And of course, I've got a short clinic this afternoon. What time's dinner?"

"What? Oh, regular dinnertime, I guess," Liv said, annoyed he was asking when she clearly wanted to get back to her call.

"That seems late. But I've got to run now. Sorry."

"No worries."

He turned away and started gathering his things.

No kiss goodbye? Oh, Sam.

Into the phone, she said, "I'm back. He gave no sign that he heard me. But what do you think?"

"Well, I'm the last person to know what's 'jumping the gun' where Zoey is concerned. But I have to admit, I'm surprised. I didn't think Sam would do anything to jeopardize your Big American Life," Shula said wryly. Liv could hear the capitalization. "That said, I'd think he'd know best whether Zoey could ever hope to go to college, unless he's just catastrophizing. Beyond that, I don't think it's terrible for your family to adjust to having less imported chocolate for a while. As far as I know, this has never caused anyone irreparable harm."

Leave it to Shula to put things into perspective.

"No one knows how long Sam's big Plan will last," her sister went on. "I mean, it could be over in a month or two, so maybe save your worries about money until they're needed? And meanwhile, it's a good thing for him to be a more involved father, right? Even if his reasons are all mixed up. You and I both know how hard it is to live with a parent who's there but might as well be absent. It's got to be better for the kids to see him at least *trying*, don't you think?"

"I guess so. Though it's not as if he didn't *try* before, he—"

"Hang on, Livie," Shula broke in. When she came back on the line she said, "Sorry, sorry. Chaos here—we're about to sit down to eat before the fast. Well, of course the kids and I aren't fasting, but Oren is. No matter how secular we are, Yom Kippur is still Yom Kippur, right?"

Liv was aghast. She'd completely forgotten—or blocked it out. Ordinarily, she welcomed the opportunity to clear the air of petty family resentments that had built up over the year, but now she found she had no patience for the idea of atonement. And fasting was the last thing any of them needed now—on the contrary, they'd need extra nourishment to get through this.

"Would you believe it slipped my mind that Yom Kippur starts tonight?"

"That's impressive!"

"I know." Liv sighed. "Sign of the times, I suppose. But please, go, enjoy your *yom tov* meal. And tell Oren I hope he has an easy fast. And kiss your beautiful babies for me, Shula."

"I will, Livie. You, too. And while you're at it, get Sam to give you a kiss for me, too."

"Okay," said Liv, though she knew she wouldn't. She couldn't remember the last time Sam had kissed her. And as if things weren't hard enough already, he now seemed determined to finish the job of turning their lives upside down.

DAY 124

Sam's new Life Plan moved forward with surprising ease. None of his colleagues and employees had looked too taken aback when he announced his decision. And though the children might have been a bit shell-shocked, Liv seemed to understand why this was so important to him, even if he was a little short on details when it came to the day-to-day. He didn't share with her the secret part of the Plan, the part where his extra time with Zoey would bring about her miraculous transformation. He wasn't exactly admitting to himself that he hadn't let go of that part, either.

He would make a fair househusband, though: He was organized and methodical and good with details. How hard could it be? The more he thought about it, the more sense it made. Liv was a gifted baker, but not such a gifted organizer—a fact she often mentioned herself. He thought she would jump at the chance to grow the business, but she had been uneasy when the manager of the busy Edge of the Woods health food store called to ask whether she would begin supplying them with a weekly order of apricot tarts and mocha mousses. Sam had told her of course she should do it: He couldn't help seeing it as a sign that they were on the right track. He would gladly be the "morning guy" at home, he said, and she could get to her baking earlier.

On the first day of his strange new routine, Sam's alarm rang at 6:00 a.m., and when he reached out to wake Liv, she was already gone. As the warmth dissipated from her side of the bed, he had the odd feeling that a piece of his marriage was going with it, and he didn't know if he could get it back.

No, he told himself, *no time to stew today*. He swung his legs out of bed and jumped in the shower. He tried to imagine what it would be like to spend hours a day with Zoey, as Liv had done for the past several months. How would the staff act after his recent outburst? How would Zoey respond to him? He dried off, gave himself an encouraging smile in the bathroom mirror, threw on jeans and a T-shirt, and galloped down the stairs.

"So, what do you want for breakfast, Lottie the Lovely?" he asked as he skidded into the kitchen. "Pickle and peanut butter quiche? Marshmallow fluff soufflé? Or my special, olive and chocolate crepes?"

"Eww, Daddy, none of those! Mommy mostly makes me oatmeal with maple syrup and cinnamon and raisins and apple slices on top."

"Oh, is that all? That should be easy then."

How would Livie make the oatmeal—stovetop? Microwave? How much water would he need? He scanned the back of the box for intelligence and opted for the microwave. Zev slunk into the room, his expression forbidding any conversation. Was Sam supposed to do something to get him ready? He hesitated, trying to recall Liv's instructions as the microwave beeped.

He shook his head, opened the microwave door, and grabbed the hot bowl of oatmeal with his bare hand, yelping as he spilled it all over the counter. He wiped up the mess and tried to make the dish a second time to Lottie's specifications. When he set it before her, she made a face. Sam wanted to ask her what he should do differently, but Zev was on his way out the back door, mumbling something incoherent, and Sam was busy trying to decipher it when Lottie jumped up and grabbed her schoolbag.

"Time for the bus! Where's my lunch?"

Sam turned to her, open-mouthed. She hadn't eaten a thing, and he had forgotten to make her lunch. Liv had offered to do it last night, but he had declined. Lottie would miss her bus if he stopped to make it now.

"Didn't I tell you? I'm driving you to school today!"

"Um, no, Daddy. You didn't tell me that!" Lottie smiled and folded her arms, and he smiled sheepishly back at her.

"So, what kind of sandwich? And how about some cereal while I'm making it?"

The strange new day whirled around him and swept him up in its tide.

When Sam arrived at the hospital, he went straight to the reception desk but wasn't sure how to proceed. He'd made a point of leaving his hospital badge at home and only now realized that security regulations prohibited him from walking the halls without some sort of identifying tag.

George, the desk guard who'd been working there for a hundred years, looked at him quizzically. "Hey, doc. Forgot your badge today?"

"Not exactly, George. To tell the truth, I'm taking a leave of absence to spend some time here with my daughter. I need an ordinary visitor pass today."

"Whatcha mean, doc? You quit doctoring?"

"No, no, nothing like that. I'm taking a … a sort of break." He was growing impatient. "So, what does a fellow need to do to get in the door around here? Do I need to fill out some sort of form or something?"

He tapped his foot and waited for the confusion to clear from the guard's face.

"Oh, okay, yessir. I wanted to axe you one more thing, though—did you say you have a child who's a patient here?"

Sam stopped tapping his foot. Didn't everyone here already know about his family's misfortune?

"Yes, my daughter, Zoey. She's been here since June."

Almost four months. And what did they have to show for it? He needed to get moving. He resumed tapping his foot.

"Well, doc, I am sorry as can be to hear that. I'll pray for her in church this Sunday."

"Thanks, George. That's very kind."

There was an awkward silence as the guard looked at Sam expectantly, hands poised over a keyboard.

"I just need your first name, doc, to put on the visitor pass?"

"Oh, sure! It's Sam," he said, blushing.

While the guard tapped on a keyboard and waited for the printer to spit something out, Sam mused about the inequities of the hospital hierarchy that would allow him to know nothing about George except his first name, while he expected George to know personal information about him and his family that the man never had reason to learn.

George handed him a sticker that Sam affixed to his shirtfront.

"You hand it in when you leave for the day, and we do this all again tomorrow. You have a good day, now."

"You, too, George, and thanks for the info." Sam hurried down the hallway with a glance at his watch. It was 8:00 a.m., and his neck was already tight.

"Hey, Derek."

"Oh, hi, Dr. Sandor." Derek stood over Zoey's bed with the railing down. "Good to see you," he said awkwardly. "Zoey and I were working on her hip range of motion. Sometimes she starts in bed, so she gets warmed up before attempting her first transfer of the day."

"Oh, okay. Good to know. And hey, feel free to call me Sam."

His employee of eighteen years looked up with a wry smile. "Well, I'll try, if that's what you want."

"I do." Sam turned his attention to Zoey, who had not registered his arrival. "Hi, sweetheart, how's it going today?"

"It hurts. I want Mommy."

He was expecting that. "Mom will come tomorrow, Zoey. She sent me to help today. I'm sorry it hurts. What does Derek say?"

Zoey didn't answer; she looked dully back and forth between the two men.

"Zoey's brave," said Derek. "We're making progress with your hip, aren't we?"

"So, what's on the schedule for today?"

"Today she's got all her therapies. OT again tomorrow, and I'll be back, too. Our biggest challenge now—besides the lethargy, which is at least somewhat temporary—is the combination of left neglect and right hip pain. She can't steer a walker with one hand, and her gait is too uneven for a cane right now; she's too weak for unassisted wheelchair transfers too, so she needs a lot of support."

He paused and grimaced at Sam. "The hip is healing well, though. She's making progress with her strengthening exercises, aren't you, kiddo?"

Zoey looked a little anxious. Maybe Derek was pushing her too hard. Or not hard enough. Either way, Sam hated to see her upset.

"Ready?"

Zoey shook her head, but Derek kept on moving. "Let's show your dad how you've been getting from the bed to the wheelchair. Dr. Sandor, do you want a refresher on the transfer technique we've been using? Not that you need it."

"It's *Sam*, remember? And actually, I do need it. I'll watch this one and do the next one myself. Sound okay?"

Derek nodded, leaning in to grasp her under the arms. "Arms around my neck, Zoey. If you help me, neither of us gets hurt."

Did Derek have to repeat these instructions every day? The physical therapist's well-muscled body strained as he lifted the near deadweight of Zoey off the bed, pivoted on both feet, and deposited her into the wheelchair. Sam wasn't happy to see how passive Zoey was, and how startled she looked, as if the entire operation had happened without warning. Had they been neglecting her short-term memory work?

He started a mental list: He had to get in better shape if he wanted to transfer Zoey without hurting himself, and this meant finding time to exercise; he had to talk to Francesca about how to improve Zoey's cognitive function; also, he needed to tackle the left-neglect problem. It was the key to her recovery. The devil growled into his left ear and the voice of hope whispered into his right; the result was a familiar, dismal buzzing in his head.

While Sam walked at a turtle's pace behind Derek and Zoey down the hall to the therapy gym, his mind rocketed ahead. He hoped he wouldn't run into a patient or see Sima Andrapur. On the other hand, why hadn't he gotten a single panic-stricken question from her since he'd made this decision? Maybe he wasn't so indispensable. Now that he had only one patient to focus on, he had to come up with the best Halfway Miracle of his life. He glanced at his watch and realized that only fifteen minutes had passed since he arrived at the hospital. It was going to be a long day.

Seven hours later, an exhausted Sam raced home to meet Lottie off the school bus. If he was lucky, if all the traffic lights were green between the hospital and home, he would just make it. He'd been caught up in a conversation with Francesca and had lost track of the time again.

"Red light stop, green light go. Red light stop, green light go." Manically, Sam chanted the children's jingle as a mantra under his breath at every stoplight. He had something to prove to his family, and being late for Lottie on his first day wouldn't win him their vote of confidence.

Sam felt chastened after his talk with Francesca. He had assumed he would be bringing all kinds of new ideas to her—but found that she had already tried them. Zoey simply wasn't responding the way they hoped. The conversation had been an eye-opener in other respects as well; he had asked Francesca to explain her comment about getting back to "the baked-goods strategy," since this was a concept as yet unfamiliar to him.

"We talked about this in Team Meeting. And hasn't Livie mentioned it? Though it's true: She doesn't believe she is making a difference with Zoey, despite her gifts, yes? But you know how Zoey loves to eat, how the sight and smell of her mother's pastries get her going. And why not? Your Livie can cook!"

Francesca appeared to know a lot more about his family than he would expect from an employee. Even with the perseverating, he couldn't believe Zoey gave a damn about food as anything other than rocket fuel. The entire day was an exercise in ego control for Sam: He no longer had his doctor's badge to hide behind, and he'd been so quick to take over Zoey-duty from Liv, it had never occurred to him that she might have some unique angle that could help—maybe even more than his bottomless research.

He pulled up to the bus stop in the nick of time, and once they were home, Sam stayed in the driveway and surveyed the front of his house. Would it be so bad if they had to make it wheelchair accessible? But the idea made him burn. He refused to deface his parents' legacy with evidence of his own failure. He had to get Zoey home on her feet.

Late that night, as Liv was dropping her clothes onto his reading chair, Sam said, "I was surprised how close you and Francesca have become. She knew an awful lot of personal info."

Liv blushed. Sam hadn't meant to accuse—he had meant to offer some reassurance about her time at the hospital. But the wall of unsaid things was growing taller every day.

"She thinks highly of you," he offered. "And the first thing Zoey did this morning was ask for you. Francesca said she had some sort of strategy involving your baking?"

Liv looked up with an enigmatic expression. What was she holding back? Sam began pacing the room. "They're getting ready to transfer her back to the rehab floor."

"Oh, Sam! Do you think she's ready? That's great news!"

"Ready or not, it's happening. Insurance. Got to get her out of that wheelchair."

"Oh. Well, if they're pushing for an early discharge, we're going to need that ramp."

"I'm sure I could tweak her discharge date if I needed to."

"I'm sure you could, but—"

"Let's see what happens in the next couple of weeks. Okay?"

Liv put her hands up. "Okay, okay." She got into bed and turned toward him, her eyes already at half-mast. "I meant to tell you, Dafna wants to double my order." She looked less pleased than he would've expected. “So, things are moving fast, and I want to make sure it’s okay before I say yes.”

“Livie, that’s wonderful! Of course, you should say yes,” he said, ignoring the voice in his head that shouted *No!* They would all get used to these new roles, wouldn’t they?

Liv nodded and closed her eyes.

EXCERPT FROM
THE MEMORY BOOK OF ZOEY SANDOR

It is quiet in Nana's house, the big clock is tick-tick-ticking and the couch is hard, I'm squirming and my legs are dangling down. Nana sits in her big chair and her back is straight like a ruler and everything here is shiny and stiff, not like my house it is dark here the window shades are always down. Open the shades Nana I like the sun but she shakes her head No, it fades the furniture dear. I want to play with Gramps but Nana is watching and she says make the games harder she says Zoey needs to learn, but playing is for fun not for learning Gramps says and he winks at me when Nana's not looking. My hands don't work right and I drop the stupid little game pieces and they disappear, tut tut Zoey have a care she says why is Nana always mad? All the pieces are disappearing and Gramps disappears and only Nana is left and she shakes her head tut tut Zoey, I sit on the hard sofa and I'm shrinking and soon I will disappear too.

(Transcribed by Francesca Garibaldi, SLP)

DAY 135

Zev pulls into the driveway and parks behind the minivan, grateful to have passed his road test. It feels good to drive himself to and from school, with no antsy Dad riding shotgun. Just Zev, alone in his car, keeping track of his own life. Now he has five minutes before he's supposed to meet Mikayla at their prearranged spot in the park and he doesn't want to keep her waiting.

It's weird to have to worry about dodging Dad and his endless questions in the middle of the afternoon. But then, what isn't weird these days? He races past the hall table cluttered with unopened mail, and into the kitchen to grab a granola bar, wishing instead for one of Mom's coconut carrot muffins, a distant memory now that she's baking for money. He barrels out the front door again and comes face-to-face with the person he's most trying to avoid. Dad, lugging a garden hose from the back to the front. On a Thursday. Weird.

"Whoa, Zev, slow down for a sec. I never see you anymore. How'd the driving go?"

"Fine, Dad. No problems." He concocts a cover story while trying to signal his hurry with body language. He focuses his gaze on the ancient bumper stickers on the front of his car. *Visualize whirled peas* and *Peace is patriotic* and especially *Love your neighbor*, which inevitably makes him smile.

"Where are you running off to now?"

"What?" Zev tries to focus. "Oh. Ramie's. Calculus quiz."

He starts moving again so Dad won't see him blush. He's always been a bad liar, though he's getting better all the time.

"Oh. Okay. Did you leave your keys on the hook so I can move your car? I have to get Lottie to dance class."

"Yup. See ya later, Dad," Zev calls over his shoulder. He waves a hand as he lopes off down the street. He shakes his head. Dad's running car pool while Mom works in her bakery at all hours. Everything's a mess, and as far as he knows nobody here is getting any extra "quality time" with Dad, who spends every spare moment squirreled away in his office, reading medical journals as if his life depended on it. Which, come to think of it, maybe it does.

Zev misses the old familiar routines, but he can't complain, since he knows it's his fault. If he hadn't thrown that tantrum on Rosh Hashanah, Dad would never have spun off on this track. Even Lottie knows things aren't right. He's surprised to be thinking of her as an ally, to see how these months have changed her, wounded her—she's got her own jagged hole to fill in. She doesn't seem so little anymore. As he waits for Mikayla, he thinks about how quickly life can change directions—unlike when he was small and everything seemed absolute.

This fact—the inevitability of change—has been jumping out at him everywhere. At school, the gossip about Zoey has already been replaced by the next scandals: A girl in their class is pregnant; a guy has been arrested for drunk driving. The juggernaut of high school is unstoppable, and where this fact used to terrify him, now it's a bonus. He's grateful to be almost invisible again. So, he keeps things cool with Mikayla at school. *Be undetectable*, he keeps telling himself.

He knows he should make the effort to be more sociable so he can sit with Mikayla and her friends at lunch. But it's not worth the risk. If people get wind of his fixation on Zoey's best friend, all the talk will ramp up again. He can't have that, no matter how much he wants to spend time with her. Instead, he has become the king of organized, keeping careful schedules and rearranging obligations so he can spend as much time as possible with her outside of school. This behavior doesn't go unnoticed by his parents—he sometimes catches Mom looking at him with her head cocked to the side, as if trying to place what doesn't fit in this picture.

Zev and Mikayla meet most days after school at the far end of East Rock Park, out of sight of their houses but within walking distance—a necessity, since Mikayla has her license but no car, and until yesterday, Zev had a car but no license. As long as he's with her, he's content. That afternoon, they walk a long way together in the woods, holding hands and kicking at the incandescent leaves and talking about books and people. He longs for her painfully, with a wildness that gallops through him whenever they're together. He turns and smiles at her every few minutes, and she smiles back. Sometimes when they're holding hands, he thinks, *You are all I will ever need.*

But one morning his period of contentment begins to expire, as if—like in one of those Yiddish folktales—by being happy, he's attracted the attention of an ancient Evil Eye.

"Meet me in our usual spot?" he whispers to her by the lockers when the halls empty out during lunch. He tries to look nonchalant, but his face flushes and his palms sweat.

"Why are we slinking off every day?" she whispers back. "Is this still about the beach?"

"No, I like hanging at the park," he lies. "Don't you?"

"It's getting a little old, Zev."

"I'm sorry. About the sneaking around," he whispers, looking over his shoulder.

"So why are we doing it?"

"The truth is, I don't want everybody at school talking about us, saying we're hanging out because of, you know, what happened. They'll get all cranked up again."

"Who cares what everybody thinks? I used to worry about fitting in, but if you're confident about what you're doing, it doesn't matter what people think. Zoey taught me that."

"Well, I wish it was true."

"*She* believed it, didn't she? It's one of the things about her I envy. How she believes in herself. That's still true, even now. But here, it was like people assumed whatever she was doing was cool, 'cause that's how she acted. And you know, you get more like her all the time."

"I don't know, Mikayla," he says. But he does know. How is it possible that he has become more like Zoey as she becomes someone else? What does it mean? Sometimes it feels like he's stealing her life.

"Besides, you and me, we're just friends, right?" she says, her expression unreadable, though her eyes are kind of laughing at him. "What's there to talk about, anyway?"

He's not stepping in that one. "So, will you meet me?"

"Why don't we study at my house today? We can prep for the AP English exam on *The Cherry Orchard*. No one'll be home," she says.

He knows this is meant to put him at ease, but the thought of being home alone with Mikayla makes him ache all over. Is this some sort of test? He gives the only answer he can.

The tension gets worse when they're trying to study together in her dining room. There's a chill draft in there, but heat is rising off both of them and shimmering in the space between. Zev tries to come up with a way to cross the divide, but he can only imagine being rebuffed, mortified, gutted. He'd rather play it safe and hold on to his fantasies. So instead of kissing her, or even broaching the subject, he picks a fight about the theme of the play, then apologizes.

Mikayla chortles. "Are you kidding? You're the calmest person I've ever known! My family's Russian, remember? Around here, everything's like a Chekhov play."

"But—your mom never talks! And, well, you're kind of quiet, too."

"Oh, she talks, just not to you! She still doesn't know much English, and as far as I know, you don't know Russian."

She makes a face. He knows she finds it hard being her parents' translator all the time.

"And I speak my share at home, too. Not that there's anything wrong with being quiet," she says, tapping his forehead with her pencil. "I just don't have telepathy, you know? I can't hear what you're thinking."

Lately they've been on the phone every night, sometimes for hours at a stretch, though they spend most of their time talking about nothing. He remembers how Zoey used to rail against this aspect of high school relationships—that need to relay every tiny detail of your day to someone else. But now he understands it on a cellular level. Ha-ha.

"What are you thinking about?" Mikayla asks him over the phone that night, though they've spent the whole afternoon together.

He tells her everything except what matters most: that the desire to kiss her has become a fact of his existence, like breathing, or dreaming. That he wishes she *could* read his mind, or that they could share a secret language like the one he had with Zoey, so he wouldn't need to sweat it out trying to find the right words. But as much as he tries to telegraph his feelings to Mikayla, he can feel her frustration growing.

The next day, to show her he's trying, he suggests they meet at the stop sign at the end of their street instead of the one by the park. When she arrives, he greets her with a smile of berserk joy. She hasn't given up on him yet.

"Hey."

"Hey. You look tired," she says. So sweet.

Zev steers her toward the park, trying for subtlety. When they round the corner, he breathes an internal sigh of relief.

"I'm okay. Had another Zoey dream last night."

Mikayla is still the only one who knows about the dreams, though he often hesitates to tell her what they're about. He can see they upset her. In the latest sad scene he has committed to paper, Zoey is trying frantically to play a game with Gramps, but her fingers aren't working and she drops all the game pieces, which keep vanishing until Gramps vanishes too, while Nana sits there, clucking. He can still hear the echo of her *tut tut* in his head.

"Won't you tell me what it was about?" Mikayla asks, as if she can read his mind. "I won't break, you know. Do you think I can't handle it?"

She looks up at him as they walk, and their arms brush against each other. His fingertips tingle. He has imagined kissing her so many times: He would put one hand behind her head the way he has seen in the movies, the silky cap of her dark hair under his hand like a little bird. He would lower his head to meet hers, they would close their eyes, and he would press his lips to hers so, so gently. She would taste the same way she smells, like lemon and honeysuckle.

Mikayla has stopped to look at him; he never answered her question.

"What? No, I'm sure you can handle it. I'd rather not think about it is all. The more time I spend with you, the more I dream about Zoey. It's depressing."

Shit. He has made it sound like he doesn't want this time with her. But he hopes it's obvious: It's the dreams he doesn't want.

Still, she looks hurt. "Why?"

He's not sure what she's asking and trying to clarify will prolong the conversation. "It—it doesn't matter. I wish it would stop."

"I can't believe you're saying that." She sounds angry. "I *wish* I dreamed about Zoey. Maybe I wouldn't miss her so much. I mean, the old her … Oh, forget it."

She kicks at the piles of leaves collected at the side of the path, and looks up at Zev. "So, if you don't even want it, why do you think it's happening?"

"I don't know … Hey, aren't these leaves the perfect shade of yellow for the mural? Not too pale or too eggy. Let's collect some and match them at Hull's Paints."

He hopes she'll get the hint, but she sighs and barely glances at the leaves.

"Whatever you want." She's silent for a few paces. "Maybe Zoey's trying to tell you something. Maybe you *should* go see her. Maybe that'll stop the dreams."

He has told himself Mikayla of all people understands his need to stay away. She's the only one who has stopped bugging him about it. He slows to a halt. There is a bench under a nearby giant oak. "Want to sit?"

Mikayla shakes her head and looks down at her hands, changes her mind, and swerves off the path. "Zev, we need to talk." She sits down hard.

Fear robs him of his voice for a moment. He knows what she's going to say: She doesn't want to do this anymore. Whatever "this" even is. Oh, God, she's getting ready to say it. He has to stop her.

"All right! I'll do it!" His voice is harsh. "If it's that important to you, I'll go! Okay?"

Mikayla looks startled but not pleased. "That's great, but it's not about me. You need to figure this stuff out for yourself."

"I thought it was what you wanted."

"Well, I do, but like I said, it's not about me." There's a tremor in her voice. "It's about you and Zoey. What I need? I need us to stop sneaking around."

"I know. I'm being an idiot."

"You're *not*, and it doesn't make me feel any better when you're down on yourself. I'm just ... frustrated! And it's not only the secrecy thing, though that's driving me crazy. But if we're always hiding out, how am I supposed to ever see my other friends? And even more than that—hmmm, how can I say this?"

She swivels on the bench to look him right in the face and he braces himself, but she doesn't say what he expects. "As much as we talk, I feel like you're not saying anything. It's like you're always holding back, waiting for me to guess what you're thinking. You say I'm not a stand-in for Zoey, but sometimes that's how it feels. I know you guys practically shared a brain, but the thing is, *I'm not her*."

"I know! I know."

"Yes—but is that really true? Because I spend enough of my time translating for my mom and dad. I don't want to put words in your mouth, too."

She waves her fine little hands in the air for emphasis, and all he wants is to grab them and hold on.

"People don't finish each other's thoughts like you and Zoey do—did. Us ordinary mortals have to work at it." She smiles her shy little smile, which is trembling a little now. "And I don't know what you want—with me. So, what do you want, Zev?"

She waits for him to answer, looking up at him with her jewel eyes of malachite, of emerald, of jade. He wants to fall into them, all the way in. He wants those eyes to look at him with wonder, with adoration. He wants to hurtle himself into her heart.

He opens his mouth to say all the words he has rehearsed in his mind a thousand times, but he is frozen. The silence stretches between them, growing louder and louder.

I'm trying, his mind says; *hang in there with me.*

Mikayla shakes her head and stands up to leave. "Nobody can wait forever, Zev."

He nods miserably.

"Are you coming? I've got homework."

She sounds upset, but her eyes are not accusing. Her expression is as wide open as ever. Another thing he loves about her: She never holds a grudge. Still, he can tell this golden time with her is running out. He's got to do something.

That night Zev comes to the dinner table thinking he's too worked up to eat. But Mom has cooked for a change, has in fact made all his favorites: butternut squash lasagna, salad with goat cheese and walnuts. It's like the end-of-school dinner they never had, and he's ravenous. Fancy meals like this have become a rarity. He doesn't notice his parents' loaded glances. He wolfs his food and jiggles his knee, only half listening to Lottie's chatter.

Where's the Rewind button? If he could go back to this afternoon and make himself speak. If he could go back a little further—maybe even all the way back to the second-to-last day of sophomore year, he'd tell Zoey not to go running. She'd be here now, to give him advice about Mikayla. Except, back then, he would never, not in a million years, have dared to fall in love with his sister's best friend. There goes that line of thinking.

He tries to tune in on the dinner conversation. Lottie is whining:

"Zoey was always the one who helped me with my dance steps for the recital! When is she ever coming home?"

"It'll be a little while still, love," says Dad, making a goofy face to try to distract her from being sad. Why can't parents ever deliver bad news straight?

"But Daddy! Even if she misses my recital, she's not gonna miss my birthday, is she?"

"I hope not. She's working hard to get stronger, and your birthday's still over a month away. At your next visit, why don't you tell her how much you want her to come home? That will matter more to her than anything I say."

Zev is surprised. It isn't like Dad to make empty promises. Does that mean Zoey might be home in a month? He doesn't want to think about this. He needs to create a distraction.

"So, speaking of birthdays, Mikayla's is next week, and I need some advice about presents ..." Zev trails off as his parents' heads swivel in his direction.

"What a lovely thought!" says Mom. "Zoey always made such a big deal out of Mikayla's birthday. She'd appreciate the gesture."

"This has nothing to do with Zoey," Zev says, and instantly wants to take it back. Mom gives Dad a meaningful look. *There goes Zev again, refusing to deal with the Zoey Issue.* Dad sits forward and opens his mouth, but Mom grabs his hand as if to say, *I've got this.*

"Zev! How does it have nothing to do with Zoey?" That new, spiky voice he hates.

"Never mind," he mumbles.

"Well, Dad and I need to talk to you about—"

"Lottie, you're a girl," Zev interrupts.

"Duh." She swats his arm.

"So, you must know what girls want. What should I get her?"

"Why don't you get her something at Hull's?" Mom says.

But art supplies are way too impersonal. This present has to be *good.*

"I've got an idea. Buy her a sweetheart necklace!" says Lottie.

"No, Lottie, I don't think—" Mom starts.

"What's a sweetheart necklace?"

Zev tries to ignore the change in Mom's posture as she figures some things out. He doesn't care anymore, as long as she gets off the Zoey Issue.

"It's a silver heart on a chain with writing on it, and you pick the writing. Usually it says something like ..." Zev listens to Lottie's detailed answer. How does his eight-year-old sister know more about this stuff than he does? And how'd she know he needed such a gift?

"Thanks, peanut. I'll go check it out."

She pats his arm. "You can ask me for girl advice anytime."

Mom looks like she still has something to say, and Zev is trying to figure how to finagle a little of her time to take him to the mall when he realizes he doesn't need anyone's help with this errand. He can drive himself—and he's got lifeguarding money. Pride swells inside him. Maybe he'll survive this year after all.

Feeling generous toward the world, Zev tells Lottie as she's heading upstairs to get ready for bed that she should pick a video for them to watch together this weekend—anything she wants. Energized by her supergrin, he stands and begins to clear the table.

Dad wraps a hand around Zev's wrist. "Hold up a minute, son. Mom and I want to talk with you about something."

Zev looks up and sees his parents' faces hold nothing but worry. What now? This can't all be about Mikayla, can it? Whatever. He doesn't want to fight. He sits down.

"I'm betting you know what this is about, so I won't beat around the bush," Dad says.

"I've got no excuses left. Zoey asks for you all the time," Mom adds.

Zev becomes a statue.

Dad slaps the table. "This ridiculous standoff can't continue—"

Mom holds up a finger. "Can I put in my two cents?" The old, gentle voice.

Dad makes a gesture. Be my guest.

"We want to know if there's something we can do to help you over this hurdle. I'm sure it's painful for you to see Zoey, but you can't avoid her forever, honey."

Zev shakes his head.

"I know you've been reluctant to talk about this," Mom continues, "and we've tried to give you space, but this is not healthy. Zoey is coming home soon, Zev."

It sounds like a threat, even in Mom's old voice. Maybe *she's* not ready for it either.

"It's time for you to see a thera—" Dad says.

"Not this again! I'm not going to—"

"Zev! This isn't optional anymore," Mom says. "You need to see a counselor. Whether at school or somewhere else is up to you. The school social worker is fine, as long as she calls to let us know you've been in."

There's no way he'll walk in and out of the school shrink's door. Talk about grist for the rumor mill. How can he get out of this?

"Or you can see someone at Yale," Dad puts in. "I know some great people. There's no shame in it, you know. Anyone in your situation would—"

"And what if I refuse?" He crosses his arms, holding Dad's gaze.

"Well, son, if you can't take responsibility for your mental health, maybe you're not ready for the responsibility of driving your own car, either." Dad stares him down.

"Blackmail, *seriously*?" He looks at Mom, who makes a face. No rescue there.

He should've known they'd use the car as leverage. Anger scalds him. "Are *you* seeing a therapist, Dad? Is Mom? Is *Lottie* seeing a therapist?"

His parents give each other a look. They're not used to him fighting back.

"Right. This is everyone's *issue* in this family, but I'm the only one who needs a shrink? Thanks a lot for the vote of confidence."

"No one else is her twin, Zev," Mom says quietly.

He looks from one to the other. They are determined, perversely united once again over their total lack of faith in him. His face is hot, and orange spots dance in front of his eyes.

"So, you're saying I don't get to decide? That's, like, totally unfair! Just *leave me alone* and let me deal with it. I don't need to talk to anyone. You can't make me!"

He bangs his fist on the table, and the plates and silverware jump. Mom flinches. Dad sits up as if he's been goosed. Good! Zev stands up so fast his chair falls over and makes a splintering sound.

He tries to shut out the déjà vu as he takes the stairs two at a time and slams his bedroom door—but he can't stop the flashback to that gutting first day of summer: the bizarre stillness when he woke up; staring at his bifurcated ceiling as Mom's call about Zoey reassembled itself in his disjointed brain; the miserable scene with Nana and Lottie that ended when he knocked over the patio chair and ran.

Flinging himself down on his bed, he stares up again at that ceiling crack. The lines fly off in opposite directions, like him and Dad. What he can't understand is, *why*? If he and Zoey always got each other without even talking, and Zoey and Dad had no trouble communicating, how come he and Dad are like immigrants from two foreign countries? Something about this doesn't compute. The *Y* on the ceiling echoes in his head. *Why? Why? Why?* As dusk falls, the image grows blurry and fades out, and he's asleep.

She lies on the hammock and looks out at the apple trees glowing in the dark. The wind blows and the blossoms drift around in the air like nightlights. She is drowsy swingingfalling asleep and there is Dad standing by her. He doesn't talk, and something wet lands on her hand. Is it raining? She asks but Dad shakes his head no and he wipes the water off his face. She says why are you crying Daddy but he doesn't answer. Her arms and legs are so heavy she can't move she lies in the hammock and Dad holds onto her hand and he is quiet. The wind starts to blow and the apple blossoms fill the air like sweet snow.

Zev wakes up to a dark room. He turns on the light and makes a careful record in his sketchbook and scribbles the date at the bottom, though it hurts him to draw this timeline of a vanishing Zoey, to outline his sorrow with the tip of a pencil.

DAY 135, CONTINUED

Liv didn't need to say a word. It was all over Sam's face—he knew he had blown it again with Zev. But assigning blame wouldn't be productive, and was her silence any better? She got up from the table and began to clear the dishes, her hands still trembling from the jolt she got when Zev broke that chair. Sometimes she didn't even recognize her younger son anymore.

Was it purely a function of this cataclysmic year, or would all of her children become unrecognizable for a time as they were passing into adulthood? Ethan had certainly been at loggerheads with Sam at that age—but that was a particular sort of conflict. At his core, he was still Ethan. And Zoey had always been at ease with authority; for her it was a question of navigation, either through or around. She had never doubted her own internal compass, a fact Liv should've found comforting, but instead had questioned, even resented.

She shook her head and plunged her hands into the warm dishwater. She didn't trust her memory when it came to Zoey. Had her fifteen-year-old girl been as impressive as all that? Maybe they were all starting to forget. For that matter, maybe the act of raising teenagers—much like the act of giving birth—induced a certain level of traumatic amnesia in all parents.

She turned to the question of Zev and Mikayla: a romance? That was a surprise. But hadn't she been remarking recently how many interests they shared? And now they had their grief in common, too.

The real surprise was Zev's willingness to take a social risk of such magnitude. Glad as she was to see him grow, it worried Liv that he manifested new courage in every arena except where Zoey was concerned.

Sam came into the kitchen and pulled a wry face. Liv could see he was smarting. She would be careful not to rub salt in his wounds—an image she always found particularly apt. She scrubbed instead at the lasagna pan.

"So, it looks as if Zev and Mikayla might be … something," she said.

"You think so?" said Sam. "It's hard to tell. I can't read him."

"Who can, these days?" said Liv, trying to be extra kind. She paused. "But—do you think we've somehow signaled him that he can't go it alone?"

"What do you mean?"

Sam started drying pots. How strange it was to have him working side by side with her—and on a weeknight! Until recently, it had been part of their tacit understanding that she was in charge of household maintenance, and in truth, it never bothered her. She found washing dishes peaceful, enjoyed the quiet splashing, the feel of soapsuds and warm water. Dirty dishes only had to be cleaned, whereas small children needed to be sung to and played with, listened to and read to and taught about the world. And it was getting harder. Her children were traveling further out of her orbit all the time.

"It bothers me that, instead of trying to reconnect with Zoey"—Liv lowered her voice—"it's like he's chosen a different primary person, as if he doesn't trust himself to go through the world without some sort of 'other' to keep him anchored. So now he's clinging to Mikayla—or to the idea of her, at any rate. Hard to tell if she feels the same way, or how that would be, if she did. Not that it matters hugely. I mean, they're so young."

Liv tried to trace the path of the last few months, but it was a mystery to her how she and Sam had gotten so far away from the life they had planned in their early years together. The ground was shifting and there were new cracks dividing them all from each other.

"I've been thinking about the choices we made when *we* were young," she went on. "We met when we were hardly more than children ourselves—two years older than Zev and Mikayla are now! And I'm not sure our motives for getting together were so different. We were both running away from our own loneliness, weren't we?"

"I guess, but that worked out well—and I'm not quite getting the connection."

Sam sounded tired all the time. In their old life, armchair analysis had been his favorite activity at the end of the day, no matter how worn out he was, and Liv had been content to listen most of the time. She couldn't explain her nostalgic loop to him because she didn't understand it herself. One minute she was thinking about the children, then her and Sam, and now she was remembering when *she* was eighteen, and how, while she was away at school, eleven-year-old Shula had toughened like some sort of street urchin.

"Do you remember how worried I was about Shula while we were in college?" She paused. "And Lottie ... Sam, we need to make sure Lottie isn't left too much on her own when the other kids are grown and gone."

Sam set down the dish towel. "Wow, you're sorta all over the place. I'm not sure where all of this is coming from. But Livie, honey?"

His change of tone made Liv look up.

"Zoey might *never* be grown and gone, or not the way we envisioned, anyway. There's a chance she might not even be able to live on her own. You know that, right?"

"Of course I do," said Liv. She tried to cover her surprise but she had to sit down on the kitchen love seat. She hadn't thought that far ahead. But Sam was right: It was likely that Zoey would never complete her natural arc, the slow transformation from dependence to self-reliance. Sam had often talked about the disconcerting family dynamic of the perpetually dependent adult child, but until now, Liv had never appreciated the implications.

A look passed between them. She didn't fool him for a second. He knew he had startled her. More than that: She was afraid. She might tell herself she wanted to keep the children with her always, but that was when she believed things would someday return to the way they started—just her and Sam, alone again.

Now, everything was different.

A barrage of questions created a logjam in her brain. No matter how she looked at it, she couldn't see how these ingredients would form themselves into something palatable.

Sam was waiting more patiently than usual to continue their conversation, but she stood up and started washing dishes that were already clean, afraid if she opened her mouth, these terrible, selfish thoughts would spill out.

The phone rang. Liv hesitated, started toward it, stopped again.

"Don't answer it, Livie. We should talk this through."

She didn't want to answer, but neither was she ready to admit what she was thinking. "But what if it's the hospital?" She picked up the receiver. "Hello?"

Sam put a warm hand on her shoulder as if to say, *I'm still here, ready to talk.*

"Hello. It is I."

Liv sighed. "Oh. Mother. Hello."

"How are you, Olivia? You sound exhausted."

Liv hadn't told her mother about Sam's Plan, feebly hoping that things would right themselves before she ever had to. And now, she didn't have the energy to explain.

"I suppose I am."

"How is Zoey coming along?"

"She's making progress. We're hoping she'll be home soonish."

"Well, that is precisely why I'm calling. I'd like to come back. It feels wrong to be going about my business, with everything that's happened. I know Sam and I had our differences, but tensions were high. And you will be run off your head, preparing to bring Zoey home. I want to help in whatever way I can. We should all be sensible about this. What do you say, dear?"

Liv was surprised into silence. Mother sounded kind, and nearly apologetic—even a bit tremulous—which she could not remember ever happening. And her timing! Liv couldn't imagine turning her down now that things were about to get truly messy. But that meant she'd have to put up with Mother's opinions about Sam, and her, and Zoey. All the kids. Was it worth it, just for another pair of competent hands?

"Hello? Olivia? Are you still there?"

"Yes. I'm here. And it's good of you to offer. We could use the help. But let me talk to Sam about it first, okay?"

"Well, all right then, if you think that's best," she said, sniffing.

"I do. I'll call you tomorrow. Good night, Mother."

"What was that about?" Sam had been hovering in her peripheral vision during the call.

"She wants to come back and ... and help out."

"Oh, honey! The last thing we need is her nosing into everything during this transition!"

"I know, but—this was *weird*, Sam! She was—softer! She didn't apologize in so many words, but she might as well have. And we can't afford to turn down the only steady help we can get right now. I think we'll need it. Don't you?"

"Won't you at least let me have a real try at all this"—he waved his arm around the room—"before we call in the cavalry?"

Liv was close to tears. "I ... I can't think about this anymore tonight. I have to be up early. Can we talk in the morning?"

At 5:00 the next morning, Liv stole out of bed and drew a sweatshirt over her nightgown. She shivered in the chill air as she went down the walk to proof her first batch of yeast for the day. Everywhere she looked, the lines wavered and melted. She couldn't recognize any part of the life she loved. It was as though a giant hand had come down and torn the roof off her beloved house.

She longed with a physical ache for the comfort of her old routines. Once upon a time, she would wake up and feel the pulse of her family surging around her. She would get breakfast for her children, their faces still bathed in the milky skin of sleep; she would drink her coffee while she conjured bold new confections that would quicken Sam's blood. She would cook dinner for her family every night, noting with care the ebb and flow of their tastes and moods.

She missed Zoey, too, with an unfamiliar fierceness. Not the old Zoey whom they were all so busy mourning, but the new one—the dreamy, stubborn, funny, indolent girl emerging from the chrysalis of room 2113. Liv had been getting through to her; they had been working well together. Why did Sam have to come in and turn it all on its head?

Still, didn't she owe Sam the chance to forge a new way forward? But it was hard to see the path he was carving out as something they could sustain. Their old life together had emerged organically; it had made some sort of sense. This felt like an impossible mess.

Liv contemplated her image in the copper faucet. She had always been certain of her role in the family: She was the optimist, the patient one, the one at home. But Sam's unilateral decision had erased any remaining shred of clarity, and she could no longer understand her life.

She chewed her lip and kneaded her bread dough irritably, certain on top of everything else that her fierce emotions would yield a tough and unappetizing loaf. The door opened and there was Sam, looking rumpled and sleepy and sweet.

"There you are! I was worried."

This only increased Liv's irritation. "Where else would I be?" She'd tried for sarcasm, but she was mortified to hear a sob escaping. She put the back of her sticky hand over her mouth to keep the sound in, but Sam came to her and tried to take her hands.

"Don't! You'll get all doughy," she cried, pulling away. She was angry with herself for crying, and even angrier at him for being so kind. She was too dependent on him. She didn't want him here now.

"Who cares about a little dough? Honey, won't you tell me what's wrong?"

"Oh God, Sam. I—I miss our old life. And Zoey. I miss her so much! She would've helped us with all this, wouldn't she?"

"She would, Livie," he answered, as if she hadn't said something ridiculous, impossible.

Now that Liv had started to cry, she couldn't stop. She cried so hard her stomach cramped, but still, she couldn't stem the sobs. She punched her wooden cutting board in frustration, which only added pain to the mix.

"Ssshhhh." Sam folded his hands around her fist and kissed her reddened knuckles. "You're exhausted from taking care of us. Who wouldn't be? It's a lot, Livie, for anyone." He wrapped his arms around her and held her until she finally quieted.

"Listen, let's tell Hinda to come on ahead. Okay? We'll tag team things at home. You can spend more time out here, in your bakery, where it's quiet. You'll see. It'll all be okay."

How could he not understand? Of course she loved it out here, but his Plan would never work. Had she told him that? She wasn't sure anymore what she'd said out loud. The truth was they were lost, all of them. How would they ever find their way?

EXCERPT FROM THE MEMORY BOOK OF ZOEY SANDOR

We're in school all around the square table with the sheets of rough pebbly paper and the big box of crayons and the dusty wax smell. So many pretty colors and the teacher says, Take them out and draw a field of flowers and I see the colors like a rainbow and the sun is shining I am happy. Zev draws a picture too and his picture is perfect and all the kids call out to him and they say good job Zev but nobody calls out to me. My hand won't go where I want it to and the colors are all wrong my leaves are purple not green and everyone is laughing at me. I'm crying and I say help me make it right but Zev doesn't answer and I can't find him where'd he go? I cry louder and I say Teacher won't you help me fix it Zev won't help me and he doesn't want to be twins anymore because my colors are all wrong but then I see that's not how it is. Zev is the tall man at the front of the room he is the teacher now.

(Transcribed by Francesca Garibaldi, SLP)

DAY 147

Sam exhaled with relief as the bus pulled away from the curb. Lottie was off to school and Zev had driven away in his car without a word. Sam went inside and made some attempt to clean up from breakfast, but Hinda shooed him out. "We agreed on a clear division of labor, remember, Samuel?" There were bills to pay and groceries to buy, but he was impatient to get to the hospital. Thank goodness Hinda was taking care of dinner. He had to admit bringing her back was a good idea. She was being exceptionally helpful, almost kind. What had gotten into her?

On the other hand, his connection with Liv had never felt so tenuous. They had always been in accord before, had always been able to talk. Now who was left to stop him from steering them all off a cliff?

To make matters worse, all his desperate searching hadn't yielded a single new idea for bringing Zoey home on her feet in time for Lottie's birthday. The team was doing everything right, but Zoey was following her own path, as his patients tended to do.

When he got to the hospital, Sam found her room empty and her Memory Book lying open on the bed. He was irritated: Why hadn't they made sure she had it with her? It was true what they said about rehab—you had to advocate constantly. It was exhausting. He had told them all again and again: The Memory Book should be with Zoey always.

Sitting down on the bed, he leafed through the book and was reminded why he insisted on Memory Books for his TBI patients: to provide a crucial historical record of their journey—to remind them where they came from and where they were trying to go.

It dawned on Sam that his own voice was absent from Zoey's book, and he took out a pen and began to write. But he was surprised by what came out—not a record of these last months, but memories of when she was young.

Even when you were little, you were always looking for a challenge. You used to love climbing our old apple trees and shaking the blossoms down to the ground in the springtime. "I'm making history!" you'd say. "These blossoms will make baby apple trees so the old trees can live forever!" When you got bigger, you would take your friends down to the basement and show them the scribbles on the walls from the 1920s, when it was a speakeasy, and you would say, "See? History in the walls! This house is special." You were the historian for our family—our memory keeper. Now, we can return the favor by helping you keep track of your memories.

Sam saw that much of the story of Zoey's initial injury was also missing, and he promised himself he would go back and write it out for her. It had to be done. He tucked the Memory Book under his arm, straightening her covers before he left the room. As he was going into the therapy gym, Sam was chagrined to meet Mr. Reyes coming out. He had tried to avoid mingling with his patients or their families while he was on leave, but there was nowhere for him to hide now.

"Dr. Sandor! I almost did no' recognize you without the white coat. It is good to see you," said the man, with a firm handshake.

"How are you, Mr. Reyes?"

"I am well. How are you? How is the child—it is your daughter who was ill?"

"Yes, my daughter Zoey. She's over there." Sam pointed. "She's been here since June."

Mr. Reyes's eyes widened. "June? Ai, she must have a bad eenjury." He placed a sympathetic hand on Sam's arm, and he had to fight the impulse to brush it away.

"Yes. Well. She's making good progress now," he said, not quite achieving eye contact. "We hope to bring her home soon. But tell me, how is Luisa doing?"

On solid ground again, he allowed their eyes to meet, though he already knew the answer. He had been tracking Luisa's progress like a hound.

"She is the same as before, Dottor Sandor, the same. She is *fine*, my Luisa."

Mr. Reyes was being deliberately kind, Sam saw. Not that he should be surprised. He strove for a warmer tone in his own voice. "That's terrific news."

"Yes. But is true, what I say before—she meesses you, Dottor. Even if she can no' tell me so, I see how she looks around when we go into your room and the lady dottor is waiting for her. When are you coming back to your patients?"

How could he answer the man when he didn't know himself? Out of nowhere, Zoey's voice came into his head. *Try honesty. It's always a good bet.*

"I'm not sure, Mr. Reyes. I need to take care of my family first, you understand?"

Mr. Reyes nodded. "Thees I do understain. Your family must always come first. When my Luisa got hurt, I made this choice also. But I am no' like you. To care for my Luisa, I only gave up fixing thee water pipes. Was no loss for thee world. But is great work you do, important work for many people who can no' do it themselves. Do *you* understain?"

Sam met his eyes. "Yes. I do, and I'll think about what you've said. It was a pleasure to see you. Please send my best wishes to Luisa and the family."

"You do the same, Dottor. *Adios.*"

Sam was comforted that Mr. Reyes had treated him—at least somewhat—as a peer, when he had felt so alone moments before. He realized again how condescending he used to be toward his patients and their families—maybe still was.

He found Zoey chattering brightly with Derek.

"Hi, guys. How's it going?"

"It's going well today! Right, Zoey?"

"Derek makes me sweat."

Derek and Sam both laughed, and Zoey smiled. Did she know she was being funny? Sometimes he could see a glimmer of his old girl in her sly humor and her talent for getting what she wanted.

"Well, sweating is a good thing. It means you're working hard," said Sam.

"I don't like it." She pulled her mouth into a clown frown. "I like Franny. She lets me write stories! No sweating allowed."

The men laughed again. Noting how the physical therapist kept looking at his watch, Sam waved him off, mouthing a thank-you. What would it take for his staff to treat him as a parent? Maybe it required a more convincing shift in his own mindset: If he were a regular parent, they wouldn't be *his staff*, would they?

"Okay, cookie. You ready to see Francesca?"

"I'm not a cookie, silly Daddy!" Zoey giggled. "Did you bring me a cookie? I'm hungry."

"I like cookies too. What's your favorite flavor?"

"I don't know! My mom makes cookies."

"That's right, she does."

"Daddy, I wanna cookie now!"

The slump of her shoulders and her distracted gaze told Sam her energy was beginning to flag, but he wasn't ready for Zoey to recede back into that fretful, lethargic version of herself. He detoured to the cafeteria on the way to Francesca's office and bought her a giant chocolate chip cookie—it would raise her blood sugar enough to get her through the next session. He handed her the cookie from the left, but he had to move it to her midline before she saw it, and she reached across her body from the right, leaving the left hand curled in her lap as always.

"Can you take the cookie with your other hand?"

Zoey dropped her right hand, hesitated, shook her head, and put the same hand out again. He could see from the set of her jaw there was no point pushing, so he gave in. Feeling glum, he wheeled her back toward the elevator.

"Yoohoo! Sam Sandor? Is that you?"

He turned with a sinking heart to see Leslie Miller, Billy's mother. His patients' families were stalking him today.

"It *is* you. Where've you been? They told us you were on some sort of family leave." She looked down at Zoey, and said, "Oh, wait! Are you back? Is this a patient?"

Sam debated how to answer, but in the end, he reasoned he would be more ashamed of lying than telling the truth. "This is Zoey, my daughter."

"Oh! How nice. Hi there, Zoey! I didn't recognize you. Your father's an old friend of mine. He takes care of my son."

Zoey was absorbed in her cookie. Leslie bent down to shake her hand, and when she straightened up, her expression had changed. "I'm so sorry," she whispered. "I didn't realize—"

How many times had he pitied his old friend? Yet he couldn't bear being pitied in return. Luckily, she would never suspect him of such rank hypocrisy.

Leslie was busy covering her embarrassment with talk of Billy. "—and would you believe he got a promotion at work? So, he's been feeling good about himself, and we have you to thank." She put her hand on Sam's arm. "But you *are* coming back, right? We miss you."

Sam realized he missed his patients as well. At least at work, he could *sometimes* see a path from problem to solution, even if it wasn't always clear-cut.

"I miss you all, too," Sam said, avoiding her question. Mumbling a vague goodbye, he continued onto the elevator with Zoey and made his way to Francesca's office.

"The Sandors have arrived! Come in, come in! Zoey, I am so happy to see you this afternoon. Now we are *Franny and Zooey* together again. Right?" She laughed.

"Shhhh. Secret code name," Zoey said, putting a finger to her lips.

Sam looked from Francesca to Zoey, but he didn't get it right away. Then the penny dropped. Right! Salinger.

"Yes, very good. Now your father knows our little secret, why you are the only person allowed to call me Franny. Right, *cara*?"

Zoey nodded, though Sam could tell she wasn't sure what the therapist was talking about. Still, he had to admit they had made great strides since June. What might have been lost with someone less visionary than Francesca?

"Did you bring your Memory Book with you today?" she asked Zoey.

Zoey looked to either side of her in the wheelchair and shook her head. Sam handed over the book. At least he had done something right today.

"Oh, look, your father has brought it! Can you open the book for me?"

The binder opened right to Sam's fresh entry. Zoey looked down at the page with her head tilted to one side. Thank goodness she could still read. Her head swiveled back and forth between the book and Sam and Francesca, as if she were trying to connect the dots.

"What do you have there?" Francesca asked.

"A story."

"Did someone write a new entry in your Memory Book?"

"I don't know!"

"Let's read the story, shall we? Then we'll talk about it. Will you read for us?"

Zoey began to read in her silvery lilt. "*Even when you were little ...*"

Sam held his breath: How would she react? But after a few words, she faltered.

"I'm tired. I need a break."

"Wouldn't you like to hear the rest?"

Zoey nodded. "I want my dad to read it."

Sam blushed at the thought of reading his own tender words out loud, but he cleared his throat and picked up where she'd left off. As soon as he reached the line *You used to love climbing our old apple trees and shaking the blossoms down to the ground*, Zoey started looking back and forth between him and Francesca.

"What are you remembering, Zoey?" Francesca asked.

Silence as she swiveled her head. Sam shifted impatiently in his chair and almost missed her answer.

"Blossoms," she whispered.

Francesca nodded. "You remember the blossoms from the apple trees?"

Zoey shook her head. "Blossoms in my Memory Book."

"Very good! We wrote about blossoms another time. What were we writing?"

"I don't know." She stared off into the distance.

"Try for another minute, Zoey. I know you can do it!" Francesca patted her leg to get her attention. "Where did we write about blossoms?"

Zoey stared at Francesca and started to fidget in her seat.

Sam sighed. What was the point of all this?

"Stream stories?" Zoey said, still whispering.

"You've almost got it! Not streams, but d—"

"Dreams! Dream stories!" Zoey crowed, leaning forward in her chair and tilting herself sideways to smile at Francesca.

"That's right! You told me about the blossoms in your dream! Who else was in that dream? Can you remember?"

"My dad," said Zoey, turning to beam at Sam.

"Yes. Beautiful! Your dad."

Sam's vision blurred. Zoey had dreamed about him?

Francesca was leafing through the Memory Book, and when she found what she was looking for, she handed it to Sam.

... Why are you crying Daddy I ask him but he doesn't answer me. I want to hug him my arms and legs so heavy I can't move Daddy holds on to my hand he is quiet ...

Francesca waited as he pressed the tears from his eyes with his fingertips.

"Don't cry, my Daddy," said Zoey, bringing fresh tears to Sam's eyes. He only nodded.

Francesca said, "Livie and I believe that Zoey has been trying to tell the story of her recovery through her dreams. And, from what I can gather, she still retains many of the same strong personality traits she had before the TBI: her bravery, her sense of humor, her ability to speak honestly about others, and above all, her confidence in herself—it is such an asset. She is lucky. Not all patients possess this. And I don't need to tell you how much her personality can impact her recovery."

Sam tried to pull himself together, but he didn't trust his voice.

Zoey reached up with her right hand and gave Francesca a high five.

"Good job, Zoey!" she said to herself.

Francesca laughed and turned to Sam. "You see? Confidence!" She turned back. "Yes! Good job, Zoey."

Sam joined in the laughter, but his heart felt bruised.

As luck would have it, nothing further was required of him that day. After he wheeled Zoey back to her room, she was too exhausted to say more than one word:

"Sleepy."

He transferred her from her wheelchair, kissed her forehead, and stroked her hair away from her face, but stopped when he realized this was what Mr. Reyes always did with Luisa.

"Good nap, Zoey. Mom will come soon. I'll be back in the morning."

Zoey patted his arm with her right hand, and as she drifted off to sleep, Sam began reading the Memory Book in earnest. There were at least a dozen transcribed dreams, and they contained so much of Zoey's recovery—the fear and loneliness, the hard work and frustration, the fight to retain a kernel of herself. He was amazed.

Francesca and Livie had seen everything Sam had managed to miss. Even Zoey had seen it somehow. Sam had to find a way to trust their bond again.

He needed to think. He needed Liv. There was still a piece of the Zoey equation he wasn't getting. He tried to phone Liv as he walked toward his car, but she didn't answer. He missed the days when he always knew how to reach her. What should he do now? He passed right by his car and continued walking around the massive building where so much of his life had unfolded: He had been born here, had identified his parents' mangled bodies here, had done the best work of his life here. He had witnessed the birth of his children, had seen their cuts stitched up and their sprains bandaged, and had nursed his daughter back from the brink of death.

"Semeleh!" said a familiar voice. He looked up, startled.

"Rabbi? How'd you find me?"

"Oh, it was a happy accident. I was visiting a congregant," said Rabbi Friedman, smiling at Sam, who was embarrassed once again by his own egocentricity. Of course, the rabbi was not looking for him, but here to visit the sick.

They were standing by the entrance to the Healing Garden, and Sam gestured toward a bench. "Do you want to sit down?"

"If you'd like. But I'll understand perfectly if you prefer to be alone."

"Please. I'd rather have your company than my own."

The rabbi lowered himself slowly onto the bench. He was getting old, Sam realized with a wave of love for this man who had so often stood in for his own Papa. He could use a parent right now.

The rabbi tapped Sam's knee and said, "What's the matter with your own company?"

Sam shrugged. "I'm so frustrated with myself. I've made a mess of things."

"Are you sure whatever's gone amiss is your fault?"

"Yes. No. Maybe."

Rabbi Friedman chuckled. "Well, you've pretty much covered it all there, haven't you? What feels wrong?"

"I feel like I'm failing."

"At what?"

"At … everything."

"*Everything*, Sam?"

"I've failed to meet any of the goals I set for myself when I launched this crazy Plan. I had it all figured out: I was taking this break from work so I would stop holding myself at a distance from my life. But it's not happening."

"Why is that?"

"I … I think I was secretly hoping I'd be able to devise a more complete recovery for Zoey," Sam said, blushing as he said the words out loud. "Of course, that means being the doctor all over again, not the father. Maybe the two roles *are* mutually exclusive. Anyway, I can't fix her. So, what's all my training for? I feel endlessly guilty and—stupid."

The rabbi squeezed his shoulder. "I've heard so often what a marvelous physician you are, and I've seen firsthand that you're an excellent father."

"I don't feel that way."

"Well, you might be a little … misguided. You say you want to 'fix' Zoey, and I understand what that might mean to you clinically, but what if being the best father isn't about *fixing* her? What if it's about loving her? I think that's true for all of your beautiful children."

"But I do love them."

The rabbi put his hand over Sam's. "Of course, you do, but you also expect a great deal of yourself and those around you. Don't you think they sense that?"

What was the message Zev had learned from sixteen years as Sam's son? *Not good enough.*

"But isn't it my job to ensure the best possible life for them?"

"Yes and no. We all hope to provide a strong foundation for our children, but there are no guarantees. All you can do, all any of us can do, is to apply our best efforts to the work before us. Then we must put our trust in others. And ultimately, in God."

Sam looked at the rabbi sideways and shook his head. "I can't leave it up to God anymore. He hasn't been batting on my team, in case you haven't noticed."

A look of comprehension rose in Rabbi Friedman's eyes. "You'll forgive me for saying so, but perhaps this is the reason you've been having trouble tolerating your work—not because it kept you at a remove from your family's problems, but because it made them all too real. You continue nursing the idea that God has singled you out for suffering—when there's suffering all around you, crying out for your particular gifts to alleviate it. After all, what is it you do for your patients?"

"I don't even know anymore."

"As I understand it, you show them how to accept their limitations without allowing their lives to be defined by them."

"Well, it's different with my own family. I need to make things whole again."

"It's different—but it still applies to you, doesn't it? Making them whole doesn't mean making them perfect. When you accept your human limitations and work within them, your family will begin to heal."

"But how can I do that, without giving up hope?"

"You have to find the balance. This is what I mean when I say God does the rest. Never mind about benign and malevolent entities! It's the *idea* of God I'm talking about, our acknowledgment that we're human, and not in complete control of the world. It might help if you could learn to cede some ground. God only offers you a framework for surrender."

Sam was silent, still fighting against what the rabbi was saying, what his children had been shouting, what Liv had been telling him since the beginning.

You don't have to be perfect. You just have to be mine.

Rabbi Friedman took Sam's hands in his own. "My dear boy, you're strong enough to handle this. Remember, after your parents died, how you begged me to bring them back? You said you couldn't bear the loss and asked me if there weren't some secret mystical words I knew to turn back time."

Sam's eyes filled at the memory of being that desperate boy.

"But you see, you *have* borne it, and you've made such a full life for yourself!"

Sam's tears spilled over and dripped onto his shirt.

"What I said then is still true now: We can *only* go forward, Semeleh." He let go of one hand long enough to wipe away Sam's tears, picked it up again, and squeezed. "I wish with all my heart I could give you back what you lost in June, as I wanted to be able to grant your wish thirty years ago. The difference is, unlike your parents, Zoey *did* survive, in all her imperfection. She's still with you, and from what I've seen, she's still your brave girl, with her unique humor and insight."

"She is," Sam said between sobs. "But I don't understand."

"Zoey hasn't lost the kernel of who she is. Her *neshama* is still there and is being revealed to you in new and surprising ways."

Her *neshama*—her soul. It was true—the soul of Zoey had survived. Look at her dreams! Yet he still wanted the miracle.

Anger came to his rescue. "What, are you saying Zoey got hurt so I could learn this lesson? That 'nothing's perfect'? That 'everything happens for a reason'?" He flung air quotes into the space in front of him.

"We've known each other a long time. Have you ever heard me use such expressions?"

Sam shook his head. More tears came and washed away the anger. He sighed. "The truth is, all this time, I've been sure the universe was trying to teach me something. My patients, their families, Zoey. Even my parents. It's just not coming clear. Maybe I'm too blind to see it."

"Well, you know what they say about the man who loses his sight. His other senses become sharper. He appreciates the smell of bread baking and the sound of birdsong in a whole new way. But before those blessings can come, he has to learn to live with his loss." The rabbi was quiet for a moment. "I'm so sad and sorry for all of you. But still, Semeleh, you're blessed with unique skills that you can bring to bear on your child's misfortune. You're also blessed with a devoted and loving family—in itself a bit of a miracle these days, no? You will continue to stand together, and fall together, and stand again."

"What about Zoey?" Sam asked in a small voice.

"Zoey is blessed, too, with humor and resilience and insight to help her on this difficult path. If you leave perfection out of the equation, my boy, time will work its magic, and healing will follow."

Sam bowed his head and left his hands tucked safely in the older man's grasp. He wanted to stay in the circle of the rabbi's blessings for as long as it took him to accept them as his own.

DAY 150

Mikayla has finally appeared in one of Zev's dreams, but it's too sad to even tell her about—though it might help smooth things over. And he still puts it in his sketchbook, even if it widens the cracks in his heart that much more: the tent in the living room, the little girls playing house, Mikayla standing over Zoey, reading *The Little Prince*. In his mind, he's still replaying the rest of the dream: Zoey crying in the corner; Mikayla's strange, bossy voice, saying, *You are responsible for your rose.*

At school, an unaccustomed edge in Mikayla's voice brings the dream skidding back.

"Where *were* you yesterday? You didn't show, and you didn't answer your phone! We're running out of time! If you need more help, why don't you say so, Zev? I mean, isn't that what the team is for?"

The mural project isn't going according to plan. He's exhausted all the time and distracted by the fact of Zoey down the hall. He often ends up staring into space instead of working on it. Yesterday, they'd planned to spend the afternoon on it, but Zev remembered he had other obligations he didn't want to tell Mikayla about. He had to meet with Mr. Vincent for his weekly session of lying about the progress of his art project, and with his therapist for his weekly session of lying about how fine he's feeling.

"I don't need the team for this part. I can get it done," he mumbles to the floor. He refuses to look at her, standing there with her hands on her hips. *You are responsible …*

"Well, that's great! Are you *trying* to screw us, Zev? This matters! College applications are next year! And if you don't care about your grades, what about mine?"

"Mikayla." He looks her in the eyes as his insides quail. "I'd never do anything to mess up your GPA. I'll take care of it! I'll work on it today for as long as it takes. Okay?"

The truth is he doesn't care about any of it, not the grades, not the shrink, not the artwork. Dad has never even asked him about the project, though it's practically under his nose every day. But he has more important things to do. All the proof Zev needs that none of it matters.

At lunch, he tells Mikayla he's got too much schoolwork to work on the mural today after all, and they have another fight.

"Well, I'm going out of town. I'll be back Monday. College visits, remember? And it's due what, a week after that, with Thanksgiving in between? I don't see how you can ever—"

"We've still got twelve days," he mumbles. "And I'll work on it the whole time you're gone. I promise!" But he knows he's lying, and so does she.

"I know why you're avoiding being there, Zev, but it's getting kind of ridiculous! Zoey's not, like, repulsive! She's sweet and funny. She might not be the same as before, but she's still there. You'd see what I mean if you ever bothered to go. She's your *sister*. Don't you miss her at all?"

If you only knew how much, he wants to say, but the words get stuck in his head, along with all the other things he's never said to Mikayla.

Obviously stunned by his failure to answer her simple question—a question with only one acceptable answer—she walks away.

Zev lets her go, feeling stoical. But within minutes, he's miserable that he's made her angry and swears to himself he'll fix it somehow. After school, he exits the parking lot full of purpose, then loses precious time stuck behind a school bus all the way home. He watches the flashing red lights, itchy for it to disgorge its miniature passengers. He shouldn't have let Mikayla walk away. She's the only thing he cares about these days. She makes everything better. He thinks about how she smiles at him and love for her fills up his car.

The sweetheart necklace is sitting on his desk, next to two tickets to the Winter Solstice dance. They're all collecting dust. He knows he's a coward. Who can blame her for being angry when he let her birthday pass without even a card? Just a stupid text message. He hears an invisible clock counting down. One day it'll all blow up: schoolwork, art projects, Mikayla. One day soon, she'll walk away for good.

In his neighborhood, he's still inching along behind that school bus. How many kids can that thing hold? As he stares at the bus's yawning yellow mouth, Lottie climbs down and peers all around, obviously looking for Dad, who isn't here. Has he forgotten her? It wouldn't surprise Zev. Everyone's so wrapped up in their own problems these days. Not that Lottie's a baby anymore, she could get herself home, but still, it's kind of sad.

He honks his horn, and Lottie looks up, startled. He motions her over.

"Hop in, peanut!"

She goggles at him. "But Zev, I'm not allowed to ride with you yet. Mommy and Daddy said! Not till after my birthday."

He smiles and puts a finger to his lips. "It's no big deal. Kids do it all the time, and it's only three blocks. I won't tell if you don't. Sibling Code of Silence, okay?"

Lottie only hesitates for a split second, mouthing the words to herself: *Sibling Code of Silence*. "Okay." She swings her book bag into the back seat and climbs in.

"Buckle up," Zev says. Thirty seconds later, he pulls into the driveway and carefully parks the car. As they are gathering up their things, he catches sight of Dad's car in the rearview mirror, pulling in right behind him. His heart sinks. *Busted.*

Dad jumps out of his car. Zev and Lottie exchange a look of mutual reckoning, and for a second Zev considers trying to hide her, but there's no time. Dad comes up to his car window, wild-eyed, with his hair sticking up in every direction.

"Zev, thank God you're here. Have you seen Lot—"

He catches sight of Lottie in the passenger seat, and Zev waits for the stream of recriminations to begin. He's sure he'll be grounded. There goes the Winter Solstice dance. And he'll probably lose his wheels.

But Dad stands silently next to the car, his hand resting on the frame of the open window, wearing a strange expression, like he's wrestling with something, or making some sort of calculation. Zev doesn't say a word, and Lottie, too, is still. They all stay there for about a century, till finally Dad taps the car door twice.

"Listen, guys, let's agree that we *all* blew it here. Every one of us. Right?"

The kids are too surprised to answer.

"Therefore, our misdeeds cancel each other out. In other words, this never happened—"

Zev and Lottie exhale simultaneously and start unbuckling, and Dad puts up his hand like a traffic cop: STOP. They freeze, hands on door handles.

"—this never happened, and it will *never, ever* happen again. Right, Zev?"

"Right, Dad." He looks Dad in the eye and tries to sound appropriately serious, though he's whooping it up inside his head.

"Right, Lottie?"

"Right, Daddy," Lottie says gravely, her eyes as big and round as Frisbees. They get out of the car and traipse single file into the house, scattering in all directions. Zev is ashamedly relieved that Hinda, with her X-ray gaze, is away visiting a dying friend.

What is up with Dad? Maybe the guy's finally starting to lighten up. Either that, or he's losing it altogether. Zev can't wait to get upstairs and call Mikayla. She won't believe it. Anyone who knows the Sandors knows that any traffic safety violation—no matter how small or how justifiable—is tantamount to armed robbery and punished accordingly. But he's been given an inexplicable reprieve. The Solstice dance is still within reach. If only he could work up the nerve.

Dad's break from his old routine must be doing him some good. Maybe Mom will eventually be better, too. She's been leaking misery from every pore, which is so unlike her that nobody knows how to act when she's around. Zev would love to stop feeling guilty for being the reason everything blew up the way it did.

He needs to talk to Mikayla. He feels it keenly, like a stitch in his side: The day's events aren't real until he shares them with her. He supposes this is what it means to be in love. He'll make a quick call while he's getting his books organized, then he'll get down to work.

Beep. "Hi, this is Mikayla. I'm probably covered with paint, 'cause otherwise I'd be talking to you! Leave a message, and I'll call you back after I get cleaned up. Hope it's a good day!" *Beep.*

What is he supposed to do now? He lies down on his bed and closes his eyes for a minute—which, as ever, is all it takes for sleep to claim him.

They're in school all around the square table with the sheets of rough pebbly paper and the big box of crayons. Zoey loves the colors they swirl like a rainbow and the sun is shining and she is happy drawing her picture. Zev draws a picture too and his is perfect and all the kids call out to him and they say good job Zev but nobody calls out to her because her hand won't go where she wants it to and her picture is all wrong and everyone is laughing at her. She is crying and she says help me make it right but Zev doesn't answer and she cries louder Teacher won't you help me fix it Zev doesn't want to be twins anymore. But that's not how it is. Zev is stuck he is the tall man at the front of the room he is Zoey's teacher now.

Zev lurches upright. He presses his palms to his head, trying to squeeze out the image of Zoey, though he knows it won't let him go until he pushes it out through the tip of his pencil. He takes his sketchbook out from its hiding place under the bed. Where to start? His lines are usually swift and decisive, but lately it's getting harder. If only he could get a good night's sleep!

He begins to sketch the scene but realizes something is wrong with the scale of his figures—he has made himself much bigger than Zoey, as if he's an adult and she's still a child. He knows what it means. A little at a time, he's leaving her behind. Why is she haunting his sleep this way? He can't keep taking these three-hour naps. He has schoolwork, and he's got to tackle that mural. He slaps the sketchbook shut and shoves it under the bed. He never wants to see it again.

His cell phone rings and he leaps to pick it up, not even looking at the screen.

"Hey!"

"Zev? I'm glad I caught you. This is Ted Vincent."

Zev's stomach lurches.

"Oh, umm, hi, Mr. Vincent. Sorry, I thought you were someone else. What's up?"

"I had a chance to go by the hospital to check your progress on the mural and I was disappointed to find that none of your central figures have even been sketched in yet, never mind painted. Isn't that the part of the project you assigned yourself? What have you been doing with your time? Do you understand that it's due in less than two weeks?"

Zev can't focus. *Where's Mikayla?* Oh, right. College trip.

"Yes, I do. I'm—I'm sorry. It's been hard for me to—" He stops himself. He refuses to play the Zoey card, no matter how much trouble he's in. "—to manage my time. I've got a lot of schoolwork this year."

"At this point, I'm tempted to discuss your time management issues with your parents."

"No!" Zev barks. He takes a deep breath. He has to sound calm and in control. "You don't need to do that. I've got a plan," he lies for the tenth time that day. "I'll get it done. I swear!"

"Well, you'll need to work a miracle. I'm coming back to recheck it in a week, and it will need to be close to completion. Otherwise, I'll have to take action."

"Thanks, Mr. V. I promise, you won't regret it."

Zev presses the End button with a shaky finger. He has a brief reprieve. If Mr. Vincent calls Mom and Dad, everything will unravel.

He gets up and puts together a duffel bag full of paint supplies while he comes up with a real plan. He has to find an excuse to be gone tonight. When he opens the door to his room, there's a burst of sound and fragrance: garlic and fish and spices—definitely Mom's cooking—and loud chattering and laughter. It sounds as if someone won the lottery or something. What could be going on? Famished, he drags the duffel down the stairs and leaves it in the hall, swiping Dad's key fob and parking pass from the front hall table on his way to the kitchen. When he walks through the kitchen door, Lottie grabs him by the arm.

"Zev! You'll never believe who's coming home!"

Please don't let it be Zoey. Not yet.

"It's Ethan! He's getting a fur-something."

"Furlough!" Mom and Dad shout in unison. Zev can't help smiling; they all look so happy for once.

"Yeah, furlough!" yells Lottie. "No more trips to Afganostant. He's coming home!"

"Really?" Zev looks to his parents for confirmation, and they nod together, still smiling.

"It's the end of his third six-month tour," says Mom. "Apparently, he's due for some stateside time. He says he's been working with some of the other medics on a rehab program for soldiers with TBIs. Now they want him to coordinate with the VA hospitals, so he's gotten himself stationed at the one in West Haven. Can you believe it?"

Zev is stuck on the word *TBI.* Is there no other subject that interests this family?

"Plus, guess what?" Lottie says. "We're picking him up at the airport *tonight*, and I get to stay up late and everything!"

"Where's Nana?"

"Nana's still with her sick friend in Hartford. She'll be back before the holiday," Mom says.

"Yeah, so we're all going! Isn't that awesome?"

"Awesome. Only, I can't go," he says without thinking it through.

"Why not?" Mom asks.

"What's going on? Are you in some sort of trouble?" Dad asks.

Poor Dad. The watchdog, as Mikayla says, always poised for disaster.

Zev shakes his head. Deny, deny, deny. Isn't that what they teach in the military? He starts in on his cover story. "I already told Ramie I'd stay over tonight."

Mom looks at him like he's insane. "What do you mean? You're going to *sleep over* at Ramie's?"

Too late, Zev realizes his mistake. The embarrassing truth is that he has never slept over anywhere. He always found the idea too confining, wanting to reserve the right to retreat from human company if need be. Mom and Zoey spent years trying to persuade him and they've long since given up. He should've found a more plausible excuse.

He shrugs. "I know. It's not my usual. We've gotten close while we're working on the mural. And last night his girlfriend dumped him. He's seriously bummed." He's banking on the fact that his parents will be too busy to check on his lies. "I'm just trying to be a good friend," he adds. *Nice touch*—he can hear Zoey the master schemer saying.

Mom is beginning to buy it, and he thinks Dad might go along, too—not because Family Time isn't a level-one priority, but because Fostering Zev's Independence is an even bigger one.

Lottie, on the other hand, sees right through him. She can barely suppress her smile and Zev tries not to look at her, but he can imagine what his little sister's thinking: Since when did *Zev* become so good at fast talk? But as Zoey would say: *Parents have a constant need to think well of their kids. If you speak sincerely and tell them what they want to hear, they'll believe you.*

She's right, as usual. Zev will have to invoke the Sibling Code of Silence with Lottie for the second time that day.

"Okay, Zev, just this once," says Mom, after glancing at Dad. "It'll be a late night for us anyway. But I don't want you to make a habit of it on school nights. Have you packed a bag? Do you have everything you need for tomorrow?"

Zev nods. "Yup. All set. Duffel's in the hallway." Inside are charcoal pencils, paints, and fixative instead of pajamas and a toothbrush, but they'll never know. "So, I'm gonna eat dinner over there," he says, sacrificing Mom's delicious-smelling meal for the cause. He needs to get out before they change their minds. "Good night, guys. Tell Ethan I said welcome home and I'll see him tomorrow."

"Good night, Zev. Don't forget your jacket—"

"Yup!" He's taken the thicker one. And he's even grabbed some fingerless gloves. It'll be cold outside at night. "Speaking of jackets, isn't yours in my car, Lottie? You should come and take it now."

He gives her a meaningful look, and she gets it immediately and follows him out.

"Why would Lottie's jacket be in your car?" he hears Mom ask, but they're already out the door. Dad'll have to come up with an answer to that one.

In the driveway, he turns to Lottie. "Okay, peanut, you know what I'm going to say, right?"

"You're gonna say, don't tell Mom and Dad where you're really going. Sibling Code of Silence. Right?"

"Right. You're a smart kid, and you're growing up fast."

Her secret smile reminds him intensely of Zoey.

"I know. But where *are* you going?"

"It's school stuff. I'm late with my mural and I don't want to get in trouble. I need to spend the night at the hospital working on it."

Lottie nods sagely. "You can count on me, Zev. I won't tell. What did Zoey used to say? *The Sibling Code is always in effect.*"

Zev hugs Lottie hard. "Thanks, Lottie. You're the best."

He figures at this hour, he won't even have to duck for cover from all the nosy staff. He can lose himself in the flow.

But when he's standing in front of the mural, his mind goes blank. As usual. Why is he having so much trouble with this? It's all planned out already; the germ of the idea came from the Ball of Fire, and it's grown from there. There are two central figures, a guy and a girl, who each appear twice: In the first panel they're ordinary-looking people, standing separately. In the second, their hands are clasped, they're all pumped up, and there's a big *H* emblazoned on their superhero costumes as they send rays of energy into the crowd.

Mikayla has written a little summary that she's printed on a plaque to the left of the mural:

> *The Power of Healing! This girl and guy are ordinary citizens on their own, but when they join forces, they have great powers to heal even the sickest people with their touch. Together they become unstoppable superheroes—The Healing Force. That is the message of this mural: We all need each other for hope and healing.*

He likes what she wrote. And the mural's elaborate background is all but done. Now it's up to him, but he can't conjure up the main figures. If he's honest with himself, he never even tried. He's still using up all his creative juice on those stupid dream drawings nobody will ever see. This project, on the other hand, will be totally public once the tarp comes down. He's out of excuses and out of time. He unzips his duffel and grabs a fat charcoal pencil, inhales deeply, and puts it to the wall.

Six hours later, he takes a step back and surveys his work, stunned that it's already 2:00 a.m. Once he's in the flow, he doesn't feel the passage of time at all. But still, he isn't nearly finished.

He cocks his head to the side and rubs his sore neck. Both the male figures look pretty good now. The best thing about them is no one can say they're self-portraits: Zev has given them straight black hair and green eyes. They're tall like him but they're not string beans; they have broad, strong shoulders. In the superhero version, the black hair is longer and streaming behind the guy like a mane. His chest muscles and biceps are exaggerated, and Zev has added a sort of glow around him; he looks powerful.

He has sketched a pencil outline of the female figures, too, and has tried to draw their faces, but they keep coming out looking like Zoey, so he keeps erasing them. After this last draft, he's exhausted and his hand's cramping. He needs inspiration. He slumps onto the bench facing the wall and lets his eyes go soft for a second like Mr. V taught him.

Suddenly, all the background noises of the hospital recede, and Zev is surrounded by a quiet so thick he can almost see it. In fact, something's moving—there, on the edge of his vision. He sits up and turns his head. There it is again, a whisper of motion at the side of the mural. He looks up and down the walkway, but it's empty. He walks right up to the wall and squints at his drawing, and it happens again: The picture moves.

The pencil outline of the superhero girl turns her head in his direction. Her eyes meet his.

He squeezes his eyes shut, opens them, and looks at her again. She's taking on color and mass, and her features are filling in: long, muscular legs, amber eyes ringed with brown, auburn hair rippling, skin tanned from running outdoors.

Zoey.

Again, he looks up and down the walkway for someone to confirm he's awake, but there's no one to ask. He stares as the girl steps off the wall.

"Zev."

She walks right up to him and says it again. "Zev!"

"Z-Zoey?"

She smiles at him, her teeth bright white under the harsh fluorescent. A true Zoey smile.

"How'd you get here? Is this—am I dreaming?"

Zoey shakes her head and her hair glistens. "No, you're not dreaming."

"Are we dead?"

"Nope," she laughs, "nobody's dead."

"But—what happened? Are you better?"

"No. I'm still hurt. I just missed you. Where've you *been*?"

She stands before him, breathing evenly and slowly, her skin glowing with health, her eyes warm. There's a phosphorescence in the air around her.

"I've been ..." What can he say? Nothing sounds right. "I'm sorry. It was just too hard."

She puts her hand on his arm, her warm touch radiating through him. "I know. Trust me, I get it. It's been hard for me, too. Lonely. But we used to lean on each other. I counted on it."

Tears gather in the back of Zev's throat. He tries to swallow, but his words come out choked. "I didn't think you knew the difference! And well, I've been doing okay. I mean, not really okay. But better lately, I guess."

"I know, Zev. You're killing it! And you and Mikayla? That's great. For both of you."

"Is it?"

"Why wouldn't it be?"

"Well, what if she's right, and I just want her to be the new—the new you?"

She is quiet for a beat. "Maybe it started out like that. But now?" She arches her eyebrow.

"Now ... she's something else."

They both smile at the play on words.

"She really is." Zoey pauses. "But what about me? How could you think I wouldn't know the difference without you? I always knew. Maybe you just needed to tell yourself that. Anyway, I don't want to argue about it."

"Okay." It doesn't matter what she says, as long as she keeps talking in her strong, ringing, before-times Zoey voice.

"It was such a relief when you came to see me. You know, right after," she says.

Zev is silent.

"Everything was still so scary back then. I thought I might die. But I didn't. No matter how scared I was, I held onto the idea that I wanted to live, and I got my wish."

"I didn't know people could do that."

"Neither did I." She smiles at him again, her secret smile: They know something nobody else knows. "So now, well, I'm getting used to things. It's just, I wanted to do this sooner"—she makes a circle to include them both—"but you stopped coming."

"I'm really sorry, Zo."

"I know."

"How did you even *get* here?" he says again.

Zoey shakes her head, and the room shimmers and moves. "No clue. I figure maybe this was what *you* wished for—to see me again the way I used to be."

"You can't even imagine how hard I wished."

"See? It makes sense—if I get my wish, you get yours, too. If you want it bad enough, there's always a way. Didn't I used to say that?"

"Yeah, you did."

None of it computes, but he can't waste time worrying about it.

Zoey says, "I wouldn't tell Mom and Dad about this little visit, if I were you. Better file it under the Sibling Code."

"What about Mikayla?"

Zoey shakes her head. "Better not. It'll be our last secret. Deal?"

How many secrets have come before this one? How could those days be over? But she's right. Who would ever believe him? He nods. "Deal."

All that matters is she's here, standing in front of him, her whole perfect self. He has so many things to say to her, it's hard to figure out where to start.

"That accident was so freaky and intense," he says. "You of *all* people. I still can't believe it happened. Aren't you mad? You were the strongest person I knew."

"Hey! I'm *still* the strongest person! How many coma survivors do you know?"

Zev checks her expression, but she's teasing.

"Sometimes I do get mad," she says. "It's hard to move so slowly. But most of the time I don't remember what it was like before. That helps. It's a lot more peaceful that way. I used to be on high alert all the time, sort of like Dad, you know? All those plates I had to keep spinning in the air. Most of it I don't really miss. Like, I don't miss running, or playing the cello. But I do miss you."

Tears pool in his throat again. "I miss you, too." He stops. "Wait. Is that true? You're glad you don't remember?"

Zoey nods. "I am. I mean, when something gets taken away from you before you're ready, don't you always want it back?"

"I guess," he says.

"But scc, not everything's a loss. Look at what's happened in your life since I got hurt! Like how you don't let Dad get away with shit, or how you got your license even though I couldn't be there. Or saving Rosie Kramer? That was awesome! And this thing with Mikayla—you can do that, too, Zev. You're already most of the way there. Or even deciding to come here tonight. I'm betting you had to sneak out, or make up some stupid story, right?"

Zev nods.

"See? You never used to do things like that without me!"

"But Zoey. I would trade it all in a second, if I could have you back the way you were."

"I know, Zev, but you *can't*. That's why I came. To tell you to stop wishing for what you can't have. Things can't go back to the way they were. But that's okay. I'm still in here. It's still me! Can't you see that?"

He doesn't want to make things worse, but he's only got one chance to say this.

"But what happens if—"

"If what?"

"What if I let go of the idea of, of the you from—from the before-times, like you said, and then, and then, I don't need you so much anymore?" He can't stand to look at her eyes, at the mirror of him, so he looks down at the floor.

"Finally!" she says. "I was waiting for that. Was it so hard to say?"

"Yes. You should know that."

He looks up again as Zoey wipes a tear from her cheek.

"See?" Zev cries. "This is why I've stayed away! I'm hurting you!"

"No, Zev, don't *you* see? It's the truth. Change is hard. Things were changing anyway. Even before all of this happened, we were growing up. You were getting stronger—"

"No, I was never strong. I needed you so much."

She shakes her head and the air shimmers around her. "You were always stronger than you thought. What you never got, though, was that I needed *you*, too. As if it was a one-way thing. Honestly, it was kind of lonely for me sometimes."

Zev is startled. He has never seen it that way.

When she starts talking again, her voice is gentle. "What I'm saying is, I'm still Zoey. I believe in me, but I need help keeping it up. It's not easy, you know? So, here's your chance to return the favor."

"What can I do?"

"Just be here. If you love me at all, Zev, please don't leave me alone."

"Of course I love you. I don't want you to be alone." It's true, but it's not the whole truth. Since the accident, he has never once thought about how it feels to be Zoey. "But I can't do it. I don't know how." He sits down on the bench.

Zoey sits next to him and lays her head on his shoulder. "You're the one who taught *me* how," she says.

"What do you mean? What did I ever teach you?"

"Silly! You taught me lots of things. Do I really need to remind you? You taught me the best way to climb trees, though you refused to climb them yourself. On my own, I was always getting stuck at the top, but you could see the best route down. Right?"

"I guess." Is *that* how it happened? Even after what Mikayla said, all he ever remembered was that Zoey was brave enough to climb, and he wasn't.

"Or remember how I cried for weeks—months!—'cause I wanted a puppy for our tenth birthday, and Mom and Dad said no for the hundredth time? But you said, *I know how you can have a puppy anytime you want, even in school.* You showed me how to draw those twelve simple lines. A cute dog with floppy ears and big eyes. I drew them all over my book covers for, like, years."

"I forgot all about that. But what does it matter, anyway? That's kids' stuff."

"Yeah, but almost all the important things happen when you're little."

Zoey's head is warm and familiar on his shoulder, her voice in his ear like the ten thousand times they whispered together when they were small, in a language no one else knew.

"And what about Magda's? Did you forget about that, too?"

"What about it?"

"The broken chocolate. That store is where you gave me my first lesson in letting go. Remember how I used to believe every little thing I touched had to be perfect? I couldn't stand it when things were wrinkled or dented, and I used to cry about why we couldn't get a whole, new chocolate bar instead of the defective ones Magda was always trying to give us. There you'd be, all happy eating that chocolate, and I'd refuse because it was broken! Until one day you talked me into tasting it. Remember what you said?"

Zev shakes his head, though now, he thinks he does. He just wants to hear her talk.

"You said, *If you close your eyes, you don't see the broken parts. All you see is how good it tastes.* You were so funny, the way you talked! So, I did, I closed my eyes and put a piece of chocolate on my tongue. And you were right. It tasted like heaven."

Zev closes his eyes now. How could he have forgotten that? He opens them and turns to Zoey.

"I won't forget again—" he starts to say.

But she's already gone. His words echo down the empty corridor and bounce right back to him.

DAY 158

Though she could've slept in for once, Liv rose before dawn again and padded downstairs in the cold house. She had been yearning for her old, relaxed mornings, and since it was the day after Thanksgiving, she'd promised herself a holiday as well. She found the coffeemaker hidden behind a pile of platters; yesterday's labors had felt a lot more purposeful with Ethan back—and even with Mother here, though she'd missed Zoey all day until their visit. She tried not to notice the piles of unpaid bills buried under the Thanksgiving detritus. It gave her no satisfaction to see that Sam's attempt to step into her shoes wasn't going as planned.

Liv heard footsteps and held her breath, praying her mother wasn't up already. But it was Ethan who shuffled into the room. He had been rising at daybreak ever since he returned—a military habit he was hoping to retain, since it "increased his productive time exponentially," as he'd said over dinner the other day.

Sometimes he sounded exactly like Sam. Zev had looked at Ethan across the table as if he was insane, and Liv had to admit it wasn't typical behavior for a twenty-year-old. She suspected he wasn't sleeping well and hoped he would learn to let go again over time, as the ethos of the military world faded from his day-to-day reality.

"How'd you sleep, E?"

Ethan shrugged, his dark eyes troubled. "Fair. I've been thinking a lot about the guys at the VA hospital. They're so much like Dad's patients." He paused. "I can't even imagine him without his work. Is he, like, okay?"

"I think he is, honey. This has been good for him!" she said, though looking around, she wasn't at all sure she believed it. But she pressed on. "Before, he was so exhausted and … divided, you know? Now he's got a chance to focus on what matters most—all of you. And it's not forever. We just need to get Zoey home."

In truth, Sam had still said nothing about when or if he would return to work, though Liv couldn't imagine him turning his back on his patients forever.

"But what about money, Mom? Do we have enough savings to make it through this?"

"Oh, you don't need to worry about that. We're doing fine."

Liv took care to keep her voice light, but she had asked Sam the same question only yesterday. He'd said something elliptical, like, "As long as we're careful, we'll be okay."

She had much less confidence in Sam's reassurances nowadays, but it bothered her that Ethan was thinking about these issues. Had he somehow overheard them? She was about to question him more closely when she heard Sam's tread on the stairs.

She stood up and put a loaf of fresh bread in the warming drawer and began to take things out of the fridge: eggs and chives and cream cheese and smoked salmon, the ingredients of her favorite omelet. If she couldn't have peace and quiet, she might as well cook.

"Morning, Livie. Hey, E, you're up early."

"Hi, Dad." Ethan straightened up as always in his father's presence. "I've got a program at the VA today. But I'm glad I caught you. I've been wanting to tell you about this approach they're using with the amputees over there. It's called mirror therapy. Ever heard of it?"

"What? Oh, yeah, phantom limb pain, right? But I've only got about"—Sam looked at his watch—"five minutes. I want to get to the hospital before Zoey starts PT."

"Oh, umm, okay. Maybe another time then. It's kind of an involved thing."

Liv watched Ethan hide his disappointed face in the refrigerator. *Sam! Look at him! Ask him what he means!* It could've been a good thing for Ethan to have Sam around more, what with his blossoming interest in clinical science. But how were things any different from before, if Sam was always rushing off to the hospital?

Out loud she only said, "Breakfast?"

By the time Sam and Ethan left the house together—at least Sam was giving the boy a ride to the VA, though even that had been her idea—Liv hoped she could still fit in a proper conversation with Shula before Lottie woke up.

"Livie! It's good to hear your voice. What's the news?"

"Oh, you, too, Shula! Well, Ethan's home safe and sound, thank the goddesses. And we survived Thanksgiving with Mother—even brought a feast to Zoey."

"That's wonderful! So, how's our conquering hero, and what does he have to say about the business of war?"

"He's—okay, I think. He did say it got to the point where he had trouble remembering what he was doing there. And that war is a form of human madness."

"This is true."

Liv often forgot her sister had served two years in the Israeli Army.

"But that's a sophisticated perspective for a twenty-year-old. I'm impressed," Shula went on. "Please tell him we're so glad he's returned unharmed."

"Thanks, I will. I was impressed, too. He says he realizes he was raised in an atmosphere of privilege and security, unlike most of his fellow soldiers, never mind the people of Afghanistan. So, get this. Now my studious boy wants to become a trauma surgeon! He says he can't keep his head buried in books forever. But can you imagine him stitching up human bodies?"

"It's not so startling. Professionally, Sam's a wonderful role model, no matter how confused he is personally. Are you so surprised that one of the children wants to follow him into medicine?"

"With all the trouble Sam's had lately? It's hard for me to fathom anyone wanting to go down that road, and I certainly never saw it coming—though I'm sure Zoey's injury played a big part, for better or worse. Sometimes I feel like I don't know my children at all, you know? I mean, look how Zev has practically stepped into Zoey's old shoes in the past five months."

"Yes, no one could've seen *that* coming."

"I know. I think it's the best and worst part of being a parent—the endless mystery. We're forever letting go of who they're supposed to be, to make room for who they are."

"That's not such a stretch for you, Livie. You always manage to keep an open mind. Sam, now, he's a different story."

"Hey! No casting aspersions on my husband!"

Shula laughed. "Why? Am I wrong?"

"No, you're right. He's a stubborn one ... but hey, speaking of stubborn"—Liv laughed at her own clumsy redirect—"I wanted to ask you about Mother. I don't know what's gotten into her, but she's been downright approachable lately! I would almost venture to say *kind.* Have you noticed anything different?"

Shula chuckled, too. "I agree, she has been a little less impossible on the last few calls."

"Why, do you think?"

"To tell you the truth, though she would never admit it, I think Sam scared the hell out of her before, inviting her to leave like that. You know, she's alone in Chicago, and she's getting old. Maybe she realized how much she was risking by going on in her usual way."

"Huh. That does put things in a different light." Liv was silent for a moment. Mother made it nearly impossible for Liv to empathize with her. How had Shula managed it?

"And you know, she's a good one for getting things done, if you're stuck."

"True. Heaven knows, the house would be a disaster right now if it weren't for her. But it's not just housekeeping—I'm struggling with Sam's whole crazy Plan, and I don't want to invite Mother into the middle of that mess. Sam and I need to find our way back to each other. I hate that we've grown so distant."

"So tell him that! Sam might act like he's got everything under control, but it sounds to me like you're both a little lost. You need to talk to your husband, Livie. Say, *I promise.*"

"Okay! You're right. I *promise.*"

A kernel of hopefulness—or at least purpose—stayed with Liv after she ended the call. She and Sam couldn't go on this way.

"Why are you shaking your head, Mommy?"

"Oh, nothing. Good morning, Lottie love, you're up early. I was hoping you'd sleep in a bit, since there's no school."

Lottie nodded. "Couldn't sleep." She climbed onto Liv's lap, and Liv wrapped herself around her baby like a blanket. "Mommy, what happens to all the medals when the person who won them doesn't care about them anymore?"

"Well, maybe a clever little jewelry-maker finds a way to make a necklace out of them."

"But then, how will the person who won them remember what to be proud of?"

Liv looked down at her lively face, still creased with sleep, and saw how hard she was working to be brave. Her two girls had shared much more than a room: Zoey had embraced the adventurer in Lottie and together, they'd reveled in a spirit of dauntlessness.

"She'll find new things to be proud of. People change over time, you know? And the things they want change with them. And that's okay, as long as they know they're loved."

Lottie was quiet for a time. "I miss Zoey. Can you take me to see her? I want to tell her to come home for my birthday."

Lottie was right: It was time for Zoey to come back and fill in the empty spaces she'd left behind—whatever that might mean.

"Okay, love. Let's go tell her."

After a short visit to the hospital, where they saw no sign of Sam, Liv and Lottie returned home to find Zev still asleep. Lottie went off down the street to play with a friend, and Liv gave herself two hours in the bakery before starting on Shabbat dinner.

"You know, you wouldn't be quite so overstretched if you didn't feel the need to fuss over the food," Mother said. "It's just dinner."

"It gives me pleasure to cook, especially for Shabbat with my family. It's a fundamental part of who I am, even if that's hard for you to understand. But Mother," Liv hurried on, before Hinda could respond, "it occurs to me, there is something else you could help me with today. We need to make the house ready for Zoey, and Sam is being sort of impossible about it."

"Oh? In what way?"

Liv pushed on through the twinge of disloyalty that made her stomach clench and explained the problem as succinctly as possible before making her impulsive request:

"Could you find a couple of good, experienced contractors to call, explain that it's a hundred-year-old house and maybe gather some information about what's involved? And if they need to come here, which they will—maybe have them come when Sam's out? I'm hoping if I present him with a fully fleshed-out plan, he won't keep arguing with me until we're forced to carry Zoey up and down all those stairs to get her in and out of the house."

"Goodness! I thought Samuel was more practical than that. To be sure, a wheelchair ramp is unsightly, but there must be a solution. I am certain we are not the first people with aesthetic concerns. And Olivia—if it would help you to keep the peace, you may tell him it was my idea, that in fact, I insisted. Would that make any difference?"

Liv was silent with amazement. Mother had never explicitly taken her side before. Beyond that, she was offering to throw herself under the bus for Liv's sake! But Liv couldn't agree to such a thing, however tempting it was—not only because it implied a greater breach with Sam than she could bear to contemplate, but because she didn't want to give Mother carte blanche to make decisions. She only needed to move the needle a bit.

"That is such a kind offer, Mother. Thank you. But I wouldn't want to do that when you and Sam have just reached détente again. If you could gather some strong intelligence for me, I can take it from there."

DAY 159

"Can I look now?" Mikayla asks.

"Wait. Wait. Now!" He lifts his hands away and watches her face as she takes in the mural. As he hoped, she gives a gasp of surprise and grabs his arm.

"Well? What do you think? I mean, I left some of the most important paintwork for you," he starts babbling, "because, like, I don't have your gift with colors. Gideon and Rami are coming too, tomorrow, so we can get it all finished and neatened up, but I did everything I—"

"Oh my God! I was only gone for a couple of days. How did you do all this? You must've been here all day and night!"

"I was."

She turns to him. "Really?"

"Yeah. Well, one whole night. It was—intense."

"Was someone else helping?"

He is glad for the note of jealousy in her voice. "Not exactly."

"Zev! What does that mean?"

"It means …" He realizes he's going to tell her the Last Secret. It's true he promised he wouldn't, but telling Mikayla is the single biggest thing he can do to prove his love. He takes a deep breath, blows it out, and looks right at her. "It means I need to tell you something."

He grabs her hand and pulls her onto the bench. He starts at the beginning and leaves nothing out, even when Mikayla's eyebrows have practically disappeared into her hair, and he can't tell whether it's from surprise or outright disbelief.

When he's finished, he waits for her to laugh at him or maybe get up and walk away. She looks at him for a long time, and he forces himself to sit still and look back. She stares at the mural some more, and he tries to breathe into the quiet.

When she turns back to him, she's crying and smiling at the same time. She puts her hands on his arms and makes a tiny sound at the back of her throat. Then she leans forward and kisses him on the lips.

He recoils as if he has received an electric shock, but she grasps his arms tighter and holds him there until he knows. *This is happening.* He softens his lips on her mouth, inhales her sweet, lemony taste, and cradles her soft hair with the palm of his hand. Tears spill from his eyes and mingle with hers.

DAY 162

Liv took extra care setting the table and made the tagine her centerpiece: a golden bed of Israeli couscous laced with dried fruit and almonds and piled high with the chicken and its oniony sauce, fragrant with cumin and cinnamon. It was a lot of effort for a weeknight, but she imagined her family would be soothed by the heady scent of the food and would be brought closer together by having to reach toward the center of the table for their meal.

The reality was that Lottie made a face as she picked around the dried fruit on her plate, and Zev sat in enigmatic silence, eating less than usual. Liv nudged him with her foot under the table.

"Why so glum? Wasn't your mural due today? I'd have thought you'd want to celebrate! When can we have a look?"

Zev shook his head. "Not until Mr. V sees it. And he says he won't be able to do our review for almost a week! It's torture."

Liv chuckled. "I know it's hard to wait, but *torture*? Really? I bet you already know how good it is. I have confidence in you."

But Zev didn't respond. He just sat there, brooding. And as if that weren't enough to dampen Liv's optimism, she watched as Ethan tried again to engage Sam.

"So, Dad, I've been wanting to talk with you about this mirror therapy thing."

"Hmmm?" said Sam as he shoveled forkfuls of food into his mouth. "Oh, right, the VA. What about it?"

"What if it has, well, other applications? Though as you said, they've been mostly using it for phantom limb pain."

"What's that?" asked Lottie, her eyes enormous. "It sounds like a hospital ghost story."

Ethan hesitated and looked at Sam, as though waiting for him to answer—or at least, to ask Ethan what he meant by "other applications." Could he be talking about Zoey? Liv wondered. But Sam barely looked up from his plate. Liv wished she could tap *him* with her foot, but they were sitting at opposite ends of the table.

"Well," said Ethan, "phantom limb pain is when someone's arm or leg, let's say his arm, gets hurt so badly it has to be amputated—that means cut off, peanut—so it won't make the rest of him sick. And after, he feels like his arm is still there, and still hurting, even though it's not."

"But that's so unfair! His arm's gone and it's *still* hurting?" said Lottie.

"Yep, I know, it's awful," he said, sounding almost apologetic. "But see, there are these things called nerves under our skin, they send messages to our brain. That's how we feel things, and our nerves memorize the path those signals are supposed to take. Sometimes those signals keep going back and forth, kind of automatically, even when the thing is gone. Like ... like a game that's still flashing on the computer even when no one's playing."

"That was well put, Ethan," said Hinda. "You will make an excellent physician."

"Agreed!" said Liv, delighted that Mother had said it first. Sometime during this ambitious lesson, Sam finally took notice, too. She wished he'd been the one to praise Ethan's articulateness and instinctive empathy, but at least he was showing an interest.

"Aw, thanks for the vote of confidence, everyone. Such a nice thing to say, Nana." Ethan turned to Sam. "So, Dad, the OT at the VA was explaining that although phantom limb pain is real nerve pain, it's also conceptual. Like, the patient perceives the missing arm as a fresh wound, so it continues to hurt. He's stuck in a closed loop, wishing for the return of perfect symmetry. Right?"

"I hadn't thought of it quite that way, but go on," Sam said.

"So, that's where the mirrors come in—for symmetry. If you seat the patient at an angle in front of a mirror, and make sure he can only see his good side, when he moves that side, it looks whole again. As if both sides are working the way they're supposed to. So, it turns out patients who spend a half hour a day on this are showing across-the-board improvements."

"Have there been studies?"

"Yes. Several. I'll get them for you. Also, I've been taking notes in sessions, if you want to see them."

There was a pause. "Sure, son, I'd be glad to take a look," Sam said quietly.

Liv let out a breath. He hadn't exactly thrown the boy a parade, but at least he'd taken the proffered gift. Ethan looked pleased, if a little winded. It was only when Liv rose and began to clear the table that she realized she hadn't eaten a thing.

•

"Sam, can we talk for a minute?" Liv turned to face him in bed, chagrined at being the one to initiate their pillow talk. She knew he was exhausted, but when wasn't he? She had to at least try.

Sam sighed and opened his eyes. "What's up?"

"Zoey's discharge is coming up fast, and I feel like we don't have a plan of action."

"For what?"

"For getting her in and out of the house."

"I've already said, I've got it covered."

"How?"

"What do you mean?" He was getting angry. It happened so quickly these days.

"*How* have you got it covered? Because unless you know something I don't, Zoey can't get into the house right now without being carried."

"So, I'll carry her if I have to. It won't be for long."

"What? But that's not even safe ..." Why was he being deliberately obtuse?

He sighed again. "I'm working on it, Livie."

"I know, but why put yourself under that pressure? Or her, for that matter? She's making great strides, you've said so yourself. A wheelchair ramp would take the—"

"I told you, I don't want it!"

"Well, you're not making sense." She took a deep breath. "Anyway, the clock is running out, so I asked Mother to go ahead and call around. She found—"

Sam sat up in bed. "You had no right to do that!"

"No *right*? If you'd just listen—"

"It's completely out of the question! I don't want to hear any more about it!"

"*What?*"

"It's the only thing I have left of them," he shouted even louder, "and I *won't* tear it up."

"Sam! Let me speak. What I was *trying* to say is that Mother found a couple of contractors who specialize in accessibility for historic homes. As you know, she's not exactly easy to please, but she says they know what they're doing. They've given us estimates and they have a plan for the *back* entrance, where it will be much less obtrusive. They're ready to start work whenever we—"

"This is my house!" he shouted. "It's not yours to alter as you see fit."

"Do you even hear yourself?" Liv whispered. "I never forget this is your parents' legacy. But I *love* this house. I cherish it. Because it's where we all live. Together."

She couldn't stop her tears, but he made no move to comfort her, and she gave him a hard look as she wiped her eyes.

"It's time for Zoey to come home." She felt more angry than wounded. "You were the one who told me we've got to advocate for her. We can't get ready for her here if we pretend it isn't happening. And it *is*, Sam. It's happening, no matter what."

"Are you saying *I'm* not advocating for her?" He was shouting again. "I'm watching the therapists like a hawk! I'm killing myself trying to fix that left neglect! I just need more time!"

"But don't you see? You've traded one obsession for another! Zoey's not a problem you can solve. She's our daughter!" Liv was yelling now, too. As strange as it felt, it also felt good to release some of the pressure. "You've got me out there trying to sell *cakes* instead of attending to things here at home. And where are you? You're *still* at the hospital all day!"

Sam flung back the covers and got up to pace the floor. "I'm trying to do the right thing! Anyway, you *wanted* to sell your cakes!"

"No. That's what *you* wanted. To—I don't know—justify this misbegotten Plan of yours! But we can't leave Zoey in the hospital until you satisfy your need to save her! You're not a one-man army, and there *is* no perfect answer! If you need to be a superhero, you should go back to seeing patients. God knows, you're not focusing around here!"

Sam stopped pacing. "What's *that* supposed to mean?"

Liv lowered her voice again. "It means things are falling apart in your precious house."

"What's falling apart? Maybe things are a little disorganized, but what else is new?"

"Not a little, Sam. The place is a mess. And Mother can't do everything." She paused. "The storm windows aren't up yet. The bills are overdue. There's a crack clear across the front steps at the third stair." She paused, adding in an even quieter voice, "Also, Lottie told me you've forgotten her at the bus stop more than once."

She got out of bed, too, and stood in front of him, but Sam resumed his pacing, talking to the carpet instead.

"She's not a baby! She can walk home."

"For God's sake, you're the one who decreed the kids couldn't walk alone through the park until they were ten. She's just trying to obey your never-ending safety rules."

"*Never-ending?* Those rules are for her own good! If it were up to you, the kids would wander around unsupervised, jumping on trampolines and getting into all sorts of trouble!"

"Sam. You're being ridiculous, and unfair."

She reached out to him, but he strode by. "Please, will you stop pacing and listen to me? You said you were taking this leave of absence to spend more time with the children, but you don't have any idea what's going on! The fact that Zev is failing three of his classes—"

This stopped Sam in mid-stride. "What are you *talking* about?"

"His guidance counselor called to say a progress report had been sent home, as well as a note asking us to call about his schoolwork."

"I honestly had no idea."

"Of course not. It's all sitting in that pile of unopened mail on the counter."

"Well, I'm doing my best! You haven't exactly been a picnic yourself, you know!"

"How could I be?" Liv started crying again, tears of frustration and loneliness. "I mean, this thing I love, my baking, of all things, is turning into a misery!"

"A *misery*? We spent thousands of dollars on that misery last year!"

"Oh, Sam. I'm so grateful for that beautiful space, but don't you see? This is not the *time* for growing my business. Things would have to be so much less insane than they are, for your Plan to make any sense. The kids need me here. *You* need me! I *love* cooking for all of you, but that's all I should be doing! That, and taking care of Zoey. Isn't that enough?"

"Well, Francesca might've decided your baking is the answer to all of Zoey's problems, but it won't get her up the stairs, will it?"

"What does that even have to do with what I was saying? You're being so irrational, I can't talk to you like this." Liv's throat hurt. "I'm going to sleep."

Without waiting for him to answer, she turned off the light.

DAY 163

Never, in the history of their marriage, had Sam deliberately made Liv cry. It had been a point of pride, once he understood how much bullying Liv had endured from Hinda. But now he couldn't stop himself. Nor had they ever gone to bed angry before—not in almost thirty years as a couple! The sound of her shouting at him was so bizarre that it was physically painful for him to hear. His stomach clenched every time he thought about it. He couldn't believe she'd fallen asleep.

He spent the whole night churning over their argument, trying to make sense of her words, his actions. He could still hear her yelling, *this misbegotten Plan of yours*. Had he considered her needs at all before launching into his grand scheme? Had he asked her what she wanted? He couldn't remember doing so. What was he thinking? Where was he running to?

In the morning, he got up before Liv and took inventory of the house. When he looked at it through her eyes, he was doubly ashamed of what he'd said. Even when all the children were little, she had never once let it get this bad. He was the one being careless with his parents' legacy. He would come home early from the hospital today and spend some time dealing with the bills and getting the house ready for winter. Surely, he could allow himself that.

He went back upstairs with a cup of coffee for Liv and found her staring up at the ceiling.

"I'm sorry, love. I didn't want to start another day without telling you that."

"I know, honey." Her voice was hoarse, her curls springing into a golden nimbus around her face as she sat up and smiled faintly at him, reaching for the cup.

"Are you okay, Livie?"

"I want us to be able to *talk* to each other again," she said softly.

Sam nodded. "It's my fault. I've been a ... a fucking mess. The house. The kids. Us."

"It's *all* been a fucking mess. But I have to say, you've made more than your share." She chuckled quietly. "You know what I've been thinking about?" She set down her coffee cup and reached out absently to rub his knuckle.

"What?" He leaned into her touch.

"The reason Mother was always so hard to live with is because she's terrified to admit that she's *human*. Why, I can't imagine, but that's her MO. I only started to see it clearly because she's been a little more human lately." She smiled at him, all the way up to her lion eyes.

Smiling back with relief, Sam nodded. He'd seen it, too, an unaccountable softening in Hinda after all these years.

"Well, I don't want us to fall into the same trap," she said, squeezing the hand she'd been rubbing. "It's got to be better to admit our vulnerabilities and face them together, than to run screaming away from them all alone."

"Is that what you think I'm doing?"

"Well, aren't you?" Liv looked up at him, not accusing, but sure.

Rabbi Friedman had said the same thing. For most of his life, Sam had been dogged by fear, which he'd tried to control either by playing it safe or by playing the hero.

"Old habits, I guess," he said. "I know I need to work on it. But honestly"—he took both of her hands in his—"I don't know where to start."

"Why don't we start by calling the contractors and telling them okay?"

Sam sighed. "Okay."

"Good. You'll see. It's the right thing." She paused, held on to his hands. "And Sam—I know I'm pushing my luck but—will you consider going back to work, once Zoey is home?"

"I'm already considering it."

Liv gave a nearly comical sigh of relief. "That's wonderful."

"Is it?"

She nodded. "I know you'll feel better. And I'm positive I will!" She smiled again teasingly.

"Well, then, I'm sure you're right. I trust you, Livie."

"I am damn glad to hear it."

•

Sam continued to go to the hospital every day that week, even on the weekend, but he could feel himself straining toward another change—a reversion? A reclamation? He wasn't sure. He only knew he had to hold off until he saw some real progress with Zoey. He always found her sitting on the front of her bed, staring into the mirror.

The next week began the same way, until finally, he sat behind her and put his hands gently on her shoulders.

"Hey, cookie. Whatcha looking at?"

"I'm not a cookie, silly Daddy! I'm a girl. See, in the mirror?"

"Yep, I see. My beautiful girl."

"But … how come, in the mirror, it's my *other* hand that works?"

"It's not, Zoey," he said. How many repetitions would it take to stick? "It's still the same hand. It just looks opposite because that's how mirrors work." He bent over her shoulder and picked up her left hand. "See? Here's your other hand …"

Then, as if a blindfold dropped from his eyes, Sam saw the connection between what Ethan had said about mirror therapy and what Zoey had been saying about her hand every day. Instead of feeling the arm was still there when in fact it was gone, *Zoey felt as if her arm was gone although it was still there*. Either way, the result was an asymmetry her brain didn't know how to decode. The same "closed loop" effect Ethan had been talking about with phantom limb pain might apply in cases of neglect, only inversely. A mirror, Sam thought as he looked at Zoey watching herself, a mirror could instantly restore symmetry.

He changed the angle of the closet door so Zoey could see her working arm. "Which hand is working now?"

She moved her hand up and down, cocking her head to the side. "I don't know!" she said, but she was trying to figure it out. He worked with her until she got antsy, and by the end, he thought he saw a subtle change in the speed with which she recruited her left hand. When he delivered her to the PT gym, he explained the idea to Derek and Em, pointing out that this had potential for her balance issues, too, and they both gave him a look he recognized as professional excitement. Sam felt it, too. Afterward, he sat down to read through Ethan's notebook, now crumpled under a dozen medical journals and forgotten since Sam had put it in his briefcase. Ethan's notes were meticulous and possessed a nascent voice of authority.

Here's the most elegant part of the concept: The reason it works is that the patient's brain is convinced that the bad side is functioning correctly again, and this causes a change in the neural pathways. In other words, the patient's own belief paves the way for healing. It's magic!

Magic. Sam sat back and shook his head. The great Dr. Samuel Sandor, post-catastrophic cartographer, had forgotten the first rule of mapmaking: You must know your starting point. He had started with the assumption that he alone held all the answers, and now he saw how far off the mark he was. Mirror therapy might be the answer for Zoey, coming from the most unlikely of places—and as a direct result of the risks Ethan had taken, of his desire to do work that *meant something*. A desire he'd expected his father, of all people, to understand.

Sam remembered Ethan's anxious, wide-eyed look when he handed over his notebook, and this image brought more distant memories in its wake: Ethan in his new uniform before his deployment, saying, "I should've known you would never give me your blessing." Zev outside the synagogue, yelling, "You have kids so you can point to them and say, look what a perfect thing I made." Ethan standing in front of Sam year after year with that same anxious look as he handed over his perfect report card and awaited his father's stingy words of praise. Sam felt a stab of grief for his sons. Why in the world had he made them work so hard for his approval?

He left the hospital early, eager to tell Ethan that he'd inspired what felt like a breakthrough, and most of all, to tell Liv about the day's insights. In the before-times, events had never felt real until he shared them with her. Now he knew he had to get that connection back.

He was crestfallen to see there were no cars in the driveway.

"Hello? Anybody home?"

The house was silent.

Sam went upstairs to look for Zev and, finding his door ajar, entered without knocking. The room was empty, a perfect opportunity to see what was going on with his inscrutable son. He drifted aimlessly through the hodgepodge: textbooks, notebooks, sketchbooks, balled-up socks, dirty jeans, charcoal pencils, crumpled dollar bills, tickets to a school dance. So maybe Liv was right about Mikayla, too. He found it all reassuring—evidence of a normal sixteen-year-old boy's life.

As he was leaving, he spotted another of Zev's drawing pads, all but obscured by the quilt trailing on the floor. He reached under the bed to pull it out and sat down to leaf through the thick pages. They were extraordinarily good illustrations, but there was something eerie about them, and they were strangely familiar, as if Sam had seen them all before, though he knew that was impossible.

He focused more carefully on the figures, turning the pages back and forth, and his stomach did a little flip. They were all of Zoey, every one of them, and all marked with a date, starting from the day of her injury. Poor Zev. He had lost so much this year. Here she was inside an igloo, in the figure of a snow angel like she used to make after the first snowfall of the year; here she was surrounded by stars in an impenetrable black sky, a look of fear on her perfectly rendered face, reaching out for Zev, who looked as marooned as his twin in the inky pool. And here she was as a little girl, surrounded by other children who were clearly taunting her. The teacher at the blackboard also looked like Zev.

Why did he have this unshakeable feeling of déjà vu?

"Sam?" Liv called from below.

"Up here! I'm in Zev's room. Come and see this!"

"See what?" She poked her head around the door.

"Look at these amazing sketches. They're all of Zoey—and Zev's in a lot of them, too."

Liv took the drawing pad and sat down next to Sam. "I'm glad you're home. I have something to tell you."

"What's that, love?" Maybe it was just sleep deprivation, but Sam had never been happier to see her.

"I was at a meeting with Dafna, and I told her I'm going to hold things steady where they are for now." She'd started turning the pages as she was speaking. "I'm barely handling the new business, and I don't want to expand it any further, at least not—" She stopped with a gasp. "But Sam!"

"I know. Aren't they so strange and beautiful? What I can't understand is why I feel like I remember all these drawings, when I know I've never seen them before."

"Honey." She turned to him, her face alight with amazement. "That's because—" She laughed and took his hand. "I can't believe I'm saying this! But Sam, that's because *these are Zoey's dreams*."

"What are you talking about?"

"Don't you see? These images that Zev drew. They're familiar because you've *read* them in Zoey's Memory Book, where Francesca's been transcribing them for months! The outer space scene, the classroom where Zev is the teacher, you with the blossoms …"

It all tumbled into place for him. He clutched at her, his heart galloping. "Livie! Wait. That's crazy!"

"I know!" She laughed again. "But it's also true!"

Sam laughed too, with delight and astonishment. They held each other silently for a while. Then, in a whisper, never letting go of her, Sam told Liv all that he'd realized at the hospital, about the mirror therapy, and Ethan's role, and his relationship with the boys.

When he finished, Liv whispered, "That's incredible, Sam. It's all so, so good." Her arms were still around him and she held him tight. "Are you that surprised, by any of it?"

"I am. But I guess I'm not surprised that you're not." He smiled sheepishly and realized he was utterly exhausted.

Liv didn't look tired at all. She looked energized. "These drawings are making me miss Zoey. I think … I think I need to see her right now! Would you mind if I went to the hospital for a little while? Ethan is already picking up Lottie, since Mother is away again. Okay?"

"Of course," Sam said. "Thanks, Liv. That'd be great." He kissed her. "Go. I'll just sit here a little while longer."

DAY 168

When school lets out, Mikayla rides with Zev and they meet up with Gideon and Ramie in the hospital courtyard, exchanging fist bumps and anxious looks and mutters of "*finally!*" as they wait for Mr. V to come and do their review. Was the delay some sort of punishment? Zev can't help wondering as he fidgets with the little jewelry box in his jacket pocket. When the teacher arrives, he treats them to several excruciating moments of silence as he stares at the mural, and Zev is bouncing up and down on the balls of his feet.

"Well, I'm flummoxed!" Mr. Vincent says at last. "After your race to the finish," he eyes Zev meaningfully, "I thought I'd find all sorts of slipshod work here. But no. I'm equal parts surprised, moved, and impressed."

Zev exhales and doesn't really hear anything else. Mr. V talks for a while, asks some questions—which Zev mostly lets the others answer—and as he's leaving, says, "That was cutting it damned close, Team Zev, but this is fine work. You're all getting an A."

The guys whoop for a minute and then they leave, too, with knowing looks that Zev just smiles at. And then, he takes Mikayla's hand and sits her down on the bench again and asks her to the Winter Solstice dance and finally, *finally* gives her the necklace. She looks truly happy after he's clasped it around her neck.

And the kissing … the kissing is …

Zev is still in a fugue state when he walks into his bedroom an hour later. He's ready to fling his jubilant self onto his bed and replay the whole thing a hundred times—until he freezes at the sight of Dad, lying there at a weird angle, face slack, eyes closed, a sketchbook in his hand.

Panic drops over his skin like a shroud.

"Dad? Dad!" Zev shakes him by the shoulder, hard. "Dad! Wake up! I *mean* it, Da—"

Dad's eyes fly open. He sucks in a huge breath, sits up, and mumbles something that sounds like "memory book."

Zev doesn't care what he's saying, as long as he's breathing. He slumps down next to his father, hand to his chest. "Holy shit. Dad. What are you *doing* in here? You freaked me nearly out of my skin! When I saw you lying across my bed like that, I thought …"

What did he think? Obviously, Dad isn't the only one poised for disaster.

"I'm fine. Just tired. Sorry I scared you, son." Dad's voice comes out thick and he clears his throat. "How long have I been asleep?"

"Sheesh. I don't know. I just got home. It's dark out, and Lottie's in the kitchen with Ethan. No idea about Mom."

Zev's breathing slows. He hears pots rattling in the sink and the distant cadence of conversation, and the sounds bring a memory: When he was little, Dad would sit on his bed and read stories to him and Zoey while Mom washed the dinner dishes and hung out with Ethan. He remembers the intense pleasure of listening to their faraway murmuring and Dad's deep voice next to him in the drowsy moments right before sleep. The luxury of knowing he was totally safe.

"Seriously, Dad, what are you doing in here?"

Dad looks at him blankly.

"How'd you find my sketchpad? Were you, like, checking up on me?"

"Too many questions, Zev. Let me get my bearings."

He has to admit Dad looks harmless enough. Maybe he should give the guy a break. Dad looks around the room slowly, then sits up ramrod straight.

"Listen. Forget about all that stuff," he says, rubbing his face. "Your sketches—they're *beautiful*, by the way—I need to tell you something about them. No, wait. First, I need to ask you something."

"What is it?"

"Don't look so worried. It's nothing terrible. I need to make sure—you've never seen Zoey's Memory Book, have you?"

"Zoey's what-book?"

"Her Memory Book."

Zev shakes his head. "I don't even know what that is."

"Right." Dad looks like he's trying to decide something. "Would you do me a favor?"

"What kind of favor?"

"Would you come with me to the hospital, to Zoey's room? Mom's already there, and—there's something about that book you should see."

"Why? What is it, like some kind of journal?"

"We usually use it to help patients keep track of—I can try to explain, but it'll make so much more sense if you see for yourself. It's not a trick to get you there. I swear."

Zev is quiet, thinking.

"If you want to wait until Zoey comes home, you can. She'll be bringing the book with her. She takes it everywhere." Dad takes a breath. "I won't drag you to the hospital. But if I were you, I wouldn't wait. This is kind of mind-blowing."

What could he mean? What could possibly blow his mind after the last few months?

"Okay."

"*Okay?*"

"Yeah, I just said, didn't I?"

"Okay! Let's go!" He starts out the door, turns back. "Oh! And bring that sketchbook with you."

This makes even less sense, but Zev decides to go with it. He picks up the drawing pad and follows as Dad practically flies down the stairs, grabs his coat, takes his hospital badges off the hall table, runs into the kitchen to tell Ethan something, and they're out the door. Zev fiddles with the radio while Dad drives too fast. He usually drives like an old man. As they pull into the staff parking lot, Zev's arms cramp: He's been clutching the drawing pad to his chest like a life vest.

Dad steers him through the hospital without a word. In the hallway outside Zoey's room, Zev hangs back but Dad pokes his head in the door.

"Hi, Livie. Hiya, Zoey! I brought you a visitor."

"Hi, Sam," says Mom. "Zev. It's good you're here." Her voice carries a smile, and she is calm, quiet. "We've been having such a nice visit."

As if this sort of thing happens every day. Which it does, only Zev's been missing it. He steps into the room behind Dad. Zoey is sitting on the bed wearing her heart pajamas, turning the pages of a big binder with Mom's help.

He exhales slowly. She looks okay, but what was he expecting? Blood and guts? Even his own guts are fine so far, besides a few butterflies.

Zoey gives Dad a wavy sort of smile. "Hi, Daddy." She spots Zev in the doorway. "Zev!" Her smile gets huge, and she drops her book onto the bedcovers.

"Hi, Zoey." He feels unaccountably shy here—in front of the only people he's never been shy with. But also, there's a sudden inner stillness, like an out-of-kilter piece of the universe has slipped into place.

Zoey tilts her head. "Did you bring me a present?"

Zev looks down at his sketchbook. "Oh! Umm. Did you want me to … Is Zoey supposed to see these?"

"Oh! Zoey, why don't you and Zev trade books for a minute?" Mom says. "He's never seen your Memory Book, and you'll like his new drawings. Okay?"

Zoey nods with that puzzled smile, looks down, and sees that she's not holding her binder anymore. It's as if her brain is moving in slow motion.

Zev holds the sketchbook out for her to take, but she's still busy trying to extricate her binder from the jumble of blankets. Mom passes it to Dad, and they exchange a Look. What now? Some new Parental Plan? But they don't look upset. They look happy.

Dad hands the binder to Zev as he tries to pass the sketch pad to Zoey, but Mom intercepts it and opens it like a picture book in her lap, holding it so Zoey can see.

Zev stares at the cover of the binder: *Memory Book of Zoey Sandor*. But he's too distracted to open it. He jackknifes himself into one of the reliably uncomfortable chairs.

"Zoey, do you see how Zev drew you as a snow angel? Does that look familiar?"

Zev arches his eyebrows in a silent question. Dad smiles at him but says nothing, so Zev starts leafing through the Memory Book. There are all sorts of entries in here from hospital people, plus pictures Zoey has drawn, all of which are missing their left half. It's like a history of her life since …

"Hey, that's me!" Zoey keeps saying over and over, in that silvery little voice, pointing awkwardly with her right hand though she's always been a lefty. Is that what they mean about *left neglect*? Weird.

"Zev drew all these pictures of you while you've been here in the hospital. Aren't they great?" Mom says.

Dad says, "Zev, you might want to look for entries that are transcribed by Francesca."

He feels Dad watching him as he turns the pages, until he finds an entry marked with the words *Transcribed by Francesca Garibaldi, SLP*, at the bottom.

I am standing in the middle of a circle and everybody is clapping and laughing I wear a fancy dress, long and shimmery and silver. I have done something wonderful some good magic and everyone is proud of me but I don't know what it is.

"What the—"

Zev shoots straight up out of his chair. His cry and sudden movement startle Zoey, who begins rocking back and forth, but Mom talks to her quietly and soon she calms down. Meanwhile, Zev's brain is careening around as he sits back down, trying to understand what's going on. He remembers this scene, because *he's dreamed it*—this is the bat mitzvah one. He turns the pages of the binder and sees that there are lots of other scenes Francesca has transcribed, and the thing is, all of them are *his dreams*.

... there is a whooshing sound coming from my body it is a big hole where my heart was and cold air rushes through the hole. I see the stars on the other side of me and I am afraid I will disappear and I look for help and there is Zev floating in the distance and I call Look I have a hole in me.

"Oh my God. Mom. Dad." He speaks quietly so he won't startle Zoey again. "Are these—?"

Mom nods. "Zoey's dreams. Well, she calls them 'dream stories.'"

Zev keeps turning the pages and reading, his body flooded with adrenaline and his mind singing a mantra of amazement.

I lie on the hammock and look out the front porch I hear crickets I see stars wink at me from the dark blue sky. In the yard there are white blossoms our apple trees glow in the dark ...

"That's me! And look, there's you, Daddy!" Zoey is saying.

Zev tears his eyes away from the binder to see Zoey pointing at the sketch of her and Dad on the front porch of the house, surrounded by apple blossoms. Zev's been reading the same dream she's looking at.

"Yes, that's us, together on the porch. Do you remember this dream?"

"Franny writes down my dream stories," says Zoey.

"Yes, she does," says Dad. "You know, Zoey, if you keep working on that left hand, maybe one day you can write down your own dream stories."

Zoey looks down at her hand lying in her lap as if it doesn't belong to her.

Zev swipes absently at his eyes.

"How's it going there, Zev?" Dad's voice is soft. "Learn anything new from that Memory Book?"

"I don't know, guys. I've got a lot of questions."

"Ask them."

"Well, how come her drawings look so shaky after all this rehab, and how come the left half of each one of her pictures is missing?" He thumbs quickly through the book to find the pages. "Is that the *left neglect*? Like here, there's only half a flower, and here, there's a wobbly part of a clock with just the numbers from twelve to six. Or here, she's trying to draw a dog the way I taught her in, like fifth grade, but the left side of it's not there?" He glances at Zoey to make sure he isn't upsetting her, but she's calm, staring at his sketches.

"Yes. It's because of the location of her brain injury, on the right side of her brain. So, she's not aware she's leaving out half of every picture."

"Huh." He's silent for a minute. "I thought maybe she was drawing that way because ... well, because *I've* been missing, and I'm kind of like the other half." He blushes because it sounds so stupid.

Dad's eyebrows shoot up.

Mom says, "What an amazing insight!"

"It is," says Dad. "Absolutely amazing. You know, in all my puzzling over the problem of her neglect, that emotional aspect never occurred to me."

Zev blushes again at the unexpected praise.

"Now that I think about it," Dad says, sounding jazzed, "other aspects of Zoey's recovery are telling us the same thing. We've started using mirrors to help her see her right side—the side that's working better—as if it were her left, so her mind can integrate the two halves into one working whole. Like the work Ethan has been doing at the VA, right?"

Ethan's mirror thing only ever made marginal sense to Zev, and now he's sidetracked by guilt about being the only one who has done nothing to help Zoey.

Zoey looks at him then. "Daddy's fixing my mirror dream!"

Zev knows that dream. "You mean the one where you're holding your schoolbooks?"

She nods slowly. "I don't like that one."

"I get that." He pauses. "What do you mean, *fixing*?"

Zoey doesn't answer him, but Dad looks excited. "Maybe Zoey thinks the mirror therapy will unite the disparate dream-images of herself. See? Everything is pointing us in the same direction! The missing half!"

Zev shakes his head. "I still don't really get how ..."

"Well, she may not perceive it as conventional memory, the way you and I would, but make no mistake. Zoey is deeply affected by what happened, and she's been trying to tell us that in her own ways."

"You mean like—the dream stories?"

"Exactly."

"I'm still trying to wrap my mind around that part."

"Which part exactly?"

Dad's being so calm and easy, for once it's no problem to talk to him. "It seems like Zoey and I have been, well, sharing dreams, I guess? And sometimes, they're not even on the same *night*. But it's been going on for the whole time, since she got hurt." There. He's said it out loud, and Dad isn't even looking at him like he's lost his mind. "I mean, could that be right?"

"Yep! I dream you and you dream me!" Zoey says suddenly.

"It sure looks that way to us." Dad smiles around at all of them and Mom smiles back.

"But Dad! How is that even *possible*?"

"What do you mean by 'possible'?"

"You're the brain expert. Tell me how Zoey and I could've been sharing dreams! It sounds like science fiction!"

Before Dad can answer, there's a quiet knock on the door, and Ethan and Lottie appear. The small room starts to feel pretty crowded with everyone there—but also, somehow, just right.

He waits for Mom or Dad to say that Lottie shouldn't be out this late, but they exchange one of their Looks and smile at each other.

"Hey, hey!" says Dad.

Lottie goes straight to Zoey and softly takes her hand. "Hi, Zo! I can't *wait* till you come home. Mom says you might even be in time for my birthday!"

"Good job remembering to be gentle, Lottie," says Mom.

Zoey looks only a little more confused than she already did as she nods at Lottie. "Will there be cake?"

"Hi, guys," Ethan says over Lottie's answer. "Hope it's okay that we're here—and that we borrowed your car, Zev. After you all left, Lottie and I felt funny ... like we needed to be here, too."

"Good thinking, E," says Mom. "It's about time we were all together again."

When was the last time? Zev can't remember.

"What were you talking about?" asks Ethan. "Did I hear you right when I came in?" he says to Zev.

"Yeah, it's the weirdest thing ever. Zoey and I—well, here, look at these," Zev says, passing his sketchbook and the Memory Book to Ethan. The room falls silent for a moment as they wait for Ethan to see for himself what they've seen.

"What? What is it?" asks Lottie. "I want to see, too!"

"You'll get your turn next, peanut," says Zev. "It's my drawings of dreams I've been having, and it turns out Zoey's been having the same dreams while she's been here—"

Lottie nods. "Right. Twin stuff."

"—and I was asking Dad how that's even possible," Zev finishes, smiling at Lottie and the way she always gets it. He turns to Dad again. "What were you going to say?"

"Lottie's got the right idea," Dad says, smiling at her, too. "If you're looking for a scientific explanation, as far as I know there isn't one. Though there's plenty of anecdotal evidence that twins who are separated still share intense experiences."

"But don't you think there's got to be some *logical* reason?"

"No, honestly, I don't. This is one of those things science can't explain."

"It doesn't sound so far-fetched, really," Mom says.

"I think it sounds totally crazy!" Zev hears the slight edge of hysteria in his own voice.

Zoey drops into the conversation again. "Don't worry, Zev. Mom and Dad can fix you, too."

Zev tries to relax his face enough to smile at her. "Thanks, Zo."

Ethan looks up from the books in his lap, shaking his head. "This is wild!" he says in a hushed voice. "So, what *do* you make of it, Dad?"

"Think of it this way," Dad says. "Zev and Zoey have been super-connected ever since birth. Since *before* birth."

"Okay, that's true," Zev says, fighting for control of his voice, "but this—this goes beyond connected. This is like … ESP or something." He pauses, glancing at Ethan. "I feel idiotic even saying that."

His conversation with Zoey-from-before—was that ESP, too? He's not even tempted to bring it up. Things already feel supercharged.

"No, I think you're right," Dad says. "There does appear to be a kind of extrasensory perception at work here. And also, a type of survival mechanism."

"What do you mean, *survival*?" Ethan and Zev say at the same time, and Zev adds, "I'm not in danger, and neither is Zoey. Not since the coma, which was months ago."

Zoey looks up again. "Am I in trouble, Daddy? Everybody sounds worried."

"No, you're not in trouble, sweetheart. Parents just worry about their kids—and since you got hurt, we've been worrying extra. But maybe we don't need to worry about you quite so much," Dad says, smiling at Zoey, who smiles crookedly back.

Everybody sounds worried? Zev mouths a question at Mom, but he doesn't want to say it in front of his twin: Is this sort of emotional insight normal for the new Zoey? Maybe there is no "normal" anymore. It's just what it is.

"Look, there are all kinds of things human beings need to survive," Dad says, turning back to Zev. "I don't necessarily mean *physical* survival. But the unconscious mind is extremely powerful. You two have always relied on each other at an elemental level, and when Zoey got injured, there was an interruption in the way that you've been existing since your time in the womb. Your minds couldn't accept that interruption, so they found another way to connect. As much as things have changed since June, your connection to each other is still so strong. Only, the bridge is being rebuilt while you sleep."

This is the most amazing thing Zev has ever heard. He looks at Ethan, who sighs and shakes his head again.

"That is not at all what I thought you'd say, Dad," Ethan says.

Dad shoots him a wry smile. "Well, I'm glad I can still surprise you. And hey, E? You surprised me too, in the best possible way. I'll tell you all about it when we get home."

"Sure, Dad. I'd like that," Ethan says, looking a little dazed as he passes the notebooks to Lottie, who immediately opens them up on Zoey's bed.

After watching his sisters for a couple of minutes, Zev goes to stand by the bed, too. Now that he's beginning to get it, he wants his twin to get it, too. "Hey Zoey, did you see how my drawings are like your dream stories?"

She looks up. "I like your drawings, Zev. Good job!"

"Yeah, I like your stories too," he says slowly, stuck on the fact that she hadn't answered his question until something else occurs to him.

"Hey, Zo, you know what? Between your stories and my drawings, we almost have a complete illustrated record of your time in the hospital. Like, we could put them together and, I don't know, maybe make some kind of book out of it."

"I love that idea!" Mom says.

"My God, that's brilliant!" Dad says at the same time. He grabs Zev by the shoulder, all excited, and Zev knows this isn't empty praise.

Then, without warning, Zoey begins to wilt. She starts listing to one side and just stays there. Dad says it's their cue to leave, and they all tell her good night. She's asleep before they've left the room.

As they're walking in a clump down the corridor toward the exit doors, Zev says impulsively, "Wait, guys! Now *I* want to show *you* something." He grabs his parents, one under each arm, and steers them out the side entrance. "Ethan, Lottie. This way!"

Once outside, he walks ahead quickly, before he can talk himself out of it, and they follow. When they come to the familiar bench in the courtyard at the end of the walkway, Zev turns and points at the wall, draped with a large, paint-spattered sheet and a sign that says *Work in Progress. Do Not Touch.*

"You want to see?" he asks, unable to hide the tremor in his voice.

"Ooh, what is it?" Lottie asks, practically vibrating.

"Is this—" Mom says.

"Umm, yeah. This is my mural project. You've probably walked past it a million times, but it's been under this tarp." He lets Dad process this information for a minute. "You'd be the first ones to see it, besides my art team and Mr. V, who just signed off on it."

He can't help smiling at the memory of kissing a member of his art team in this spot earlier today.

"Honey, we're honored," says Mom.

"We'd love to see it," says Dad.

Zev notices that his parents are talking like a unit again, and it gives him courage. He nods, takes a shaky breath, and pulls away the drop cloth. They stare at the giant mural, and Zev sees it through their eyes as if for the first time. It's fantastic. Mikayla's colors are dazzling, his lines are confident, and the backgrounds are equally strong. He has made authentic art here on the walls of his father's hospital.

Dad turns to Zev with a stunned look. "This is yours? *You* made this?"

Zev nods.

"But it's—it's astounding."

Zev breaks out in a huge smile. "You really like it?"

"Like it? I'm blown away! It's glorious! And what a boon for the hospital!"

"It is. You've done something extraordinary here," Mom says quietly.

"Whoa!" says Lottie, gazing upward.

"Man, I had no *idea* you were at this level," Ethan says.

"Well, it wasn't only me," Zev says. He's trying for modesty, but he can't stop smiling. "Gideon and Ramie and Mikayla worked on it too.

A lot. And that's Mikayla's awesome narrative." He gestures proudly. "But it was my idea and my design, and I feel pretty good about it, even if it was, well, down to the wire." He pauses. "Did you notice the girl figures?"

"I've been trying to take in the whole scene: the crowd, the buildings," Mom says. "So much detail!"

"Mommy, look, it's Zoey!" Lottie shouts. Then she practically whispers, "She's so … so … *Zoey*," and her voice gets all trembly.

Zev takes her little hand in his and watches as the rest of them scan the huge tableau until, one after the other, their eyes come to rest on the superhero girl. Their little gasps make his pulse jump.

"Oh, it *is* Zoey," Mom whispers.

Zev nods, bouncing a little on the balls of his feet. "*Both* girls are Zoey."

The "ordinary" Zoey has softer features and an air of stillness. He hopes he got that right; he guesses only time will tell. He knows he took the biggest risk with the "super" Zoey. In living color, ten feet tall, he has recreated the joy and power and radiance of Zoey-from-before, the version that belonged to them for almost sixteen years. Now she'll belong to everyone. He feels a shiver of importance.

"And wait! Is that *you*, Zev?" Mom says, turning to him with an amazed smile.

He stops bouncing as he gets a little shock of his own. The boy figures look more like him than not. How could that be? He leans in and sees Mikayla's handiwork. She's added some curl to the hair. Found a way to change the eye color without it getting muddy. And he can see now that she didn't even have to alter the shape of the face. It was always Zev's. How has he not noticed any of this before? And how could he have thought it should be any other way?

He feels around inside himself for a flare of anger or a squeeze of mortification. But it's all okay in there.

He takes a deep breath and nods. "Yep. That's me."

"What a beautiful tribute," Mom says in a choked voice.

Ethan comes to stand on the other side of Zev, hugging him sideways without ever taking his eyes off the mural.

Dad is staring, too, totally silent, until finally Zev can't help asking: "What do you think, Dad?"

Dad turns and grasps his shoulder, tears glinting in his eyes.

"Zev. I don't know how you did it without your heart breaking into a million pieces," he says, "but I know this much: I thought I was bringing you here tonight to teach you something. And instead, you've taught me a lesson I'll never forget. It took more courage to paint this picture than I've been able to show all year."

EPILOGUE
DAY 747

The day that I died, my old self met my new self in the doorway of my house. Or at least I dreamed it that way, which I know cause Zev drew a picture of it and Franny wrote it down in my Memory Book. In the dream I stand in front of a mirror and there's bright light everywhere and I hold up my hands to shield my eyes, but my left hand in the mirror never moves and I reach out to touch it and the other me vanishes. Now it's a door I'm standing in front of and I'm carrying a lot of books, my eyes send out golden sparks, I am powerful, I am going places, I open the door and try to come out but there is the other me coming in and my left hand is curled up and my eyes are staring. I can't get past but I want to more than anything and the other Zoey says, It's okay, Zoey. You can have your Heart's Desire.

I don't know where those words come from—your Heart's Desire—but that probably got lost with a lot of other things when I died, which happened when I went running in the park which I know cause I've read it a hundred times where Dad wrote about it in my Memory Book. He says everything I need to know goes into that book so it has to be with me ALL THE TIME. I can't remember dying but Zev says that when you die it changes things forever.

I always wake up slowly from my mirror dream because it makes my head feel fuzzy. We tried to fix that when I was still living in Dad's hospital, Franny tried and Dad tried and even Ethan, and it's lots better but we couldn't get it fixed all the way and Mom says maybe it's perfect the way it is, but I don't know. Sometimes when it's raining outside I get all stiff and I have to use the wheelchair to go out. I have to go down the ramp in the back and we bump around to the front and use the lift to get into the van and everybody's voice gets a little higher and I don't like that.

I don't get out of bed right away, instead I rub my toes over Willow's soft fur and look all around my room. There's the shelf where I put my schoolbooks and the table where I keep my Memory Book and there's the book I made with Dad and Zev that's called "Sharing Dreams" and on the cover is a picture of Zev's giant mural. A reporter wrote all about it in the newspaper which I know cause that page is hanging on my wall in a frame with glass that Rabbi Friedman gave us as a present for our last birthday and Zev said I could keep it. I take care of my stuff. A Place for Everything and Everything in Its Place that's what Franny always says so I can remember where to find things but I still lose things a lot.

I get up and walk over to look in the mirror to check if the dream is true but it isn't and I'm happy the two Zoeys look the same here in my room. I don't like the mirror dream cause I like being just ONE Zoey. Someone's knocking on my door. It's Dad hey Zoey are you up sweetheart cause everyone's waiting he says and I say COMING. I know there's something good about today and that's why everyone's waiting but I can't remember what it is. Willow stares at me like I better get down there anyway. Watch the eighth step it's got a loud creak and it startles me but that's okay, mom says those are good sounds cause they remind us that this is our house and we love our house.

Zev comes out of the kitchen and says Happy Birthday Zoey and I remember it's our birthday and I say Happy Birthday Zev and he gives me a hug and we go in together. Mom and Dad are here and Lottie and Ethan and me and Zev. That makes six people in our family but also Mikayla hugs me hard cause she's my best friend and Zev loves her too so she's like family. Also my Aunt Shula and Uncle Oren and my three cousins are here though they live in Israel and my Nana is here so that's thirteen people in all which I know cause I'm still good at math. I think thirteen might be bad luck but Willow is here meowing for her breakfast so that makes fourteen creatures in the kitchen. That's better luck but it's LOUD and I get nervous so I look at Mom and she smiles at me and her eyes say it's okay Zoey and we BREATHE like she says to do whenever it's too loud.

The big birthday cake is on the table. Mom said we could have it for birthday breakfast and that makes me happy cause we made it together—plus, it's cake! I picked the flavor myself chocolate with coconut frosting and Mom and I mixed it and baked it then Zev made the number 18 cause he's good at drawing. Mom says "Zoey you've been such a good apprentice, how would you like a job in the bakery when you graduate from high school like Zev?" I nod yes I want to work in Mom's bakery where it's warm and she's always there and it smells good all the time but WAIT what did she say about Zev?

She says "you remember Zev is going away to college" and I say DON'T GO AWAY ZEV and even though it's really really loud he hears me and says "I have to go, Zo, but I'll come home a lot" and Dad says "that's okay it'll be just the lovely Sandor women and me, and won't we have fun?" A feeling comes up inside me like a giant wave, it smashes over me and maybe it will fill the whole kitchen but then everyone sings happy birthday and the wave washes away and it's time to blow out the candles. Nineteen candles is a lot, Lottie says that's one for every year of my life and one for good luck. Everyone says close your eyes and make a wish and Zev closes his eyes so I close mine too and I wish for cake.

Zev and I blow out all the candles and Mom cuts the cake and there are three layers that's enough cake for everybody in the room and maybe even leftovers. Mom gives me the first slice and mine has part of Zev's number eighteen on it that's made all out of pieces of broken chocolate. I try to remember why that's important but it's in the foggy part of my mind where the mirror dream is and that's not where I want to be. I just want to be here in the kitchen where Zev is smiling right at me and I can't wait anymore so I take a piece of chocolate off the top of our cake and close my eyes and put it on my tongue.

It tastes like heaven.

ACKNOWLEDGEMENTS

This book took a long time to appear in the world—in part because I was so shocked to be writing a novel that it was three years before I admitted it to anyone. I wrote mostly at Starbucks in our suburban Connecticut town, in the time I could steal between dropping my kids off at school and going to work.

But it all started years before that, when my then-husband, David Feingold, and I took a mighty chance so he could realize his dream of a private medical practice dedicated to neurological injuries and illnesses—and I, with no medical or administrative background, could be his first practice manager. That venture, which grew (itself and us) in ways we could not have imagined, spanned the second half of our twenty-five-year marriage. We strove to create an empathetic, person-first atmosphere in the office, as a counterweight to the many truly terrible medical encounters his patients had already endured. Working with David, seeing him care so deeply for this population, was life-changing for me, and it became a tremendous resource and a wellspring of inspiration for this book; he is still doing his good work every day at Physical Medicine and Rehabilitation of Hartford, LLC. The staff that were with us during that time—notably, Karen Logan, Susan Smith, Karen Velleman, and always, Cindi Manliguis Celani—provided me with a bounty of clinical insight and personal wisdom that I've woven into this story.

While the remarkable courage and resilience of David's patients and their families inspired many of the characters and situations in

Broken Chocolate, they are all fictional amalgamations, inventions of my imagination. Likewise, while some details about the Sandors' lives come from my own experience as the mother of four creative kids, a passionate home cook, and the spouse of a brain injury rehab expert, the characters in the novel are not meant to represent any of us—they are purely my creation, as is the TBI Rehab wing at Yale.

The visionary, smart, and hardworking folks at Vine Leaves Press have made my novel debut a reality with grace and ease—despite the mid-stride hiccup of my lung transplant! From the early, spot-on insights of editor Ann S. Epstein and the unfailingly-positive-but-diligent developmental edits of Ashley Crantas, to the impressively thorough and thoughtful copy edits of Timothy Repasky; and, of course, the grand shepherding of publishing director Amie McCracken and publisher Jessica Bell, with their clear communication, careful editing, brilliant cover design, and not to forget, the mad optimism required to launch a new book into the world—I've known all along that I'm in the best hands.

My immense gratitude goes to all the people who took the time to read and respond thoughtfully to this story in one (or many) of its iterations over the years: my kids, Gabriella, Serena, Jake, and Raisa Feingold, who morphed into spectacular adults while this book was still waiting to be born; David Feingold; Myron and Carole Gubitz; Sonia Gubitz; and Llewellyn Berk, Elissa and Aaron Tessler, Ahna Tessler, Marcia Jacoby, Noah Wilson, Lynn Nevins, Alise Panitch, Miranda Volpe, Rabbi Tamara Miller, Jeremy Warner, Swarnavo Sarkar, Marcia Bernstein, Keith Cohen, Lauren Johnson, Shira Klapper, Jen Ludwig, Therese Doucet, Leah Chatinover, Dode Levenson, Denton Loving, June Gervais, Brian Morton, Alice Mattison, Emily Mohn-Slate, and Joshua Henkin.

A whole cast of talented writers in my MFA program at the Bennington Writing Seminars helped to shape this book into what it has become, in workshops and lectures, readings and revisions, late-night conversations and Lambic-fueled dance sessions. My brilliant teachers there included Jill McCorkle, Rachel Pastan, David Gates,

Lynne Sharon Schwartz, Bret Anthony Johnston, Amy Hempel, the inspiring and ever-responsive Brian Morton, and my dear Alice Mattison, without whose lightning strike of a statement, "I think you belong at Bennington," I might never have found my place in that community. For an immigrant like me, who is always searching for a sense of belonging, that is no small thing.

Finally, deepest thanks to my parents, Carole and Myron Gubitz—may their memories be for a blessing. Their belief in the power of the arts to lift us up never wavered, and their love of books—of stories in all forms—surely fed mine. I know they would have been thrilled to see this one come to life at last.

VINE LEAVES PRESS

Enjoyed this book?
Go to *vineleavespress.com* to find more.
Subscribe to our newsletter:

www.ingramcontent.com/pod-product-compliance
Lightning Source LLC
LaVergne TN
LVHW030915080826
845145LV00013B/2912

* 9 7 8 3 9 8 8 3 2 2 1 8 0 *